MW01138098

Published by:
Grand Mal Press
Forestdale, MA
www.grandmalpress.com

copyright 2014, Ben Johnson

Library of Congress Cataloging-in-Publication Data
Grand Mal Press/Johnson, Ben

p. cm

Cover art by Grand Mal Press
www.grandmalpress.com

FIRST EDITION

A SHADOW
CAST IN DUST

by
Ben Johnson

GRAND MAL
P R E S S

Ackowledgements

To Claire Caraska for copyediting, and to Arabella Harrison for being the first reader. Valuable feedback from both.

To Mom, for making me love books at an early age.

Special thanks to Dick Dutton for showing me a different way to see.

For Monique, who helped me turn it all around.

A SHADOW
CAST IN DUST

1

The boy's hands began to bleed as he ripped through the bushes into the darkened canyon. Behind him, across the dim parking lot, the warehouse door swung closed on rusty hinges.

He had to move quickly to distance himself; they'd be coming for him in a minute. Maybe less. He'd never truly run any real distance before, never having had the opportunity, but he pistoned his little legs wildly. They burned, as did his lungs, but the terror of what would happen if he got caught propelled him beyond the pain. The air felt different in the canyon. It smelled of dust and freedom. His foot caught on a rock and he tripped along the uneven ground. As he righted himself, he realized the outside world was showing its own perils.

Back in the warehouse, he never had a name, or at least none he remembered. They just called him "boy".

It was two moons past when they brought the girl. She had come from the outside already grown, unlike himself, who had been brought in as a baby. There were other people in the warehouses–young, old, men, women–but he rarely saw them. It was rarer still that he saw any a second time, except the people with the knives, and the spidery boy named Oliver. And then Ysenia.

She had told him of the world outside, something he had only read about or seen through the window of the warehouse. Thinking back, he remembered there had also been trips in one of the trucks that stopped there. He never recalled the journeys except exiting the truck and going in another building, always accompanied by the woman who had claimed to be his mother; the blonde woman named Nuala. Then nothing.

One day, with a grasp of his hand, the girl had shown him brief glimpses of his earlier life, when he was so very young. A woman held him and laughed. It was difficult to make out her features in the dreamlike trance that came over him, but she was not Nuala. This was his real mother, he could feel it in his bones. When the girl let go of him, the vision ceased, and he came face to face with the concept that Nuala was not his mother at all, something he'd suspected for years.

He wondered if the others knew the girl could do this. Awaken memories.

He never thought he'd be leaving the place he'd been confined to for so long. It was the only world he had ever remembered, until the girl had showed him how to get out. He was confused when she insisted that she would be staying behind, but assumed she had her reasons. The girl assured him she would be alright, that the captors were waiting for something that would come to pass after he was gone. She implored him to think of his own safety in the world outside.

Now, the boy's eyes adjusted to the shadowy canyon landscape. The city's lights glowed on the horizon, illuminating the huge wild area on the edge of town, just off the freeways.

She said there would be someone to help him, someone he could trust. How would he know? He pushed on, ripping his shirt on a fallen eucalyptus branch as he crawled along the drainage gulch.

A high pinging alarm tore through the air, coming from the warehouse. Now they knew he was gone, and would be coming with their two huge wolf dogs.

He ducked his head and sprinted up the dry creek bed toward the rendezvous point described to him, hoping whoever was there had an ironclad plan of escape. When he reached the pepper tree, he rounded the trunk and found the white stone that the roots had entwined, setting the tree apart from the others. This was where he needed to be. He looked around, dismayed to find no one there. The girl had been right about the rest, now where was the help? The dogs would be here soon. Very soon. He could hear their snarls and barks in the distance.

As he sank down in despair, he noticed a reflection from the bushes. It blinked. He jumped back as a medium-sized black-and-gold dog emerged, shook its head, and gave an almost silent bark.

The boy flinched, putting his arm up. The sight of the dog sent his mind reeling. The only dogs he had known were those two guards chasing him, plus the unfortunate stray he had seen thrown to them once. He fought to suppress that memory as the little dog cocked its head inquisitively. It didn't seem like it was going to attack. The boy slowly lowered his arm, keeping a wary eye on it.

Was this the ally he was waiting for? How would the dog help his situation? There were two dogs headed for them right now, trained to maim and kill. Their barking was joined by the voices of the goons from the warehouse. This would end poorly.

The dog pulled a leash from the bushes and dropped it at the boy's feet. He picked it up, but she growled when he put his hands toward her. Instead, he grabbed both ends and let the middle dangle. The dog wagged her tail, then charged into the bush and up a steep hill that became a small cliff, away from the dogs and the men's voices.

He dutifully followed. There was no time to rest.

Grabbing at roots and small branches for handholds, he climbed, scraping and slipping at first, then getting the hang of it and slowly gaining on the little dog. Sweat began to form on his skin. His lungs strained, his breath wheezed, but with a concerned look from the dog he tried to push on in silence.

They finally paused for a look high up on the cliffside path. Steadying himself against a palm tree, the boy chanced a peek at their pursuers. The two men were just letting the dogs off their leashes. He could barely make out the two sleek shadows as they bounded away from the restraints and straight up the hill toward him and the little dog, weaving quickly between the dark bushes.

As he turned to run he saw the shadow of a smaller human, one his own size but with long spindly arms, quickly scampering after the dogs like half an animal.

Oliver. Nuala's new favorite. The hopelessness of the situation just increased. Oliver was a freak, and they had given him a name. The boy had never understood why. Oliver was the one other kid he saw often, and he had seen far too much of him. He remembered the pain, most of all.

The small dog's bark made him double his time up the last few yards of the cliff's face.

At the top was a semicircle of grass with a fenced-in play structure. The park was surrounded by canyons, with one street leading up to it. Squat one-story houses lined the road, silent in the night.

From the bushes, he looked down once more. The dogs were halfway up the cliff already. Oliver was just behind, nimbly crawling over rocks and plants like a spider.

Far faster than I can go, the boy thought.

The dog trotted to the center of the grassy area and sat down. The boy picked up two rocks, then ran around behind her, leash over his shoulder like a sash.

This plan seemed horrible. If this dog was trying to get him caught it was doing a pretty bang-up job. He slowly crept away from her before she barked fiercely, freezing him.

Full of rage, the wolf dogs exploded from the bush and charged the smaller dog, who, for what seemed an eternity to the boy, stood perfectly still. Just as the huge beasts were about to tear into her, she uttered a tinny whine and cocked her head to the side.

The wolf dogs yelped in fear, shaking as their eyes glazed over and the ferocity drained from them, replaced by abject panic. The boy's bravery grew.

The little dog continued the whine, locked into the beasts' eyes. Terror swam within their minds.

One fell on its back, piss raining down and splattering its fur. The other fled down the hill simultaneously barking and whining, twisting its head back and nipping at an invisible predator. Just after it sank beneath the cusp of the hill and out of the boy's line of sight, a shriek rang out. The panicked barking stopped.

The bush rustled and bent as Oliver crept out of it, trails of steam rising off his body from the blood. He looked at them through dead eyes, his mouth a straight uncaring line.

The boy had "played" with Oliver when they were younger, in what were called preparation games in the training rooms, deep inside the warehouses. But he hadn't seen him in a while, since it was decided Oliver would be groomed for something unknown.

The boy had been thankful for that. Oliver did not play well with others. The girl had told him tales of growing ruthlessness, things he was allowed to do to some of the other captives. The stories were chilling. Nothing, however, compared to now seeing Oliver with a glint in his cold eye, covered in the blood of his own pet.

The boy thought of saying something to confuse him, like they did in the books, but couldn't find words. He simply looked at Oliver like a deer in headlights, frozen.

The little dog made the sound again, which sent Oliver into a rage. He charged. Whatever the little dog did to the wolf dogs was not working on the spidery youth. He closed with amazing speed.

The boy threw the rock, blasting Oliver full in the face. His neck snapped back from the blow, but his body still shot forward. Without registering pain or even emotion, Oliver ran, wiping the blood off and growling from the pit of his lungs. His eyes were full of crazed violence as he lunged through the air.

The boy pulled the leash from his shoulder as he ducked beneath the charge, and its loop hung in the air, intersecting Oliver's trajectory. It caught on his ankle and sent him shooting to the ground, ramming his already-injured face into the turf. Before Oliver could respond, the boy brought the other rock down onto the side of his knee with a crack. Oliver's howl pierced the night.

"Oliver!" The men's voices could be heard approaching the ridge of the cliff.

The boy wrapped the leash around Oliver's smashed leg and both wrists, slapping his hands out of the way while he tied a quick knot, then jumped back. Good enough. Oliver glared at the boy, who raised his middle finger and put it close to Oliver's face.

The small dog put her forepaws on the boy's leg, looked in his eye and bounded down the other side of the park and into another dark canyon. He understood he was to follow her, and not stop running. As they retreated, the voices of Markuz and Peik came from behind them. They'd found Oliver, and the carcass of the dog he had killed.

The dog led the boy west, over two cactus-and-brush-laden hills and out of the sprawling canyon. They stopped and turned around, having gone quite some distance. There was no movement on the cusp of the previous hill. It appeared they hadn't been followed, but the boy had no way to be sure. The final hill had a path that ended at the terminus of a quiet street. They crept quickly through the shadows and disappeared into a dark, shadowy alley.

An unfamiliar feeling washed over the boy. This was the first time he had been unsupervised out in the world, and they had lost the predators on their tail. At this very moment, for the first time, he was truly free after a lifelong captivity. It was exhilarating and horrifying all at once.

They crept close to the fences. The houses beyond were squat little things. He stopped to look into a little garden oasis. Fruit and nut trees grew alongside a covered patio behind a little blue-and-white house. It smelled heavenly, and the boy momentarily got lost in a feeling of comfort. The dog sniffed the gate, then prompted him with a small bark to hurry along, away from any watchers in the night.

After three blocks, they came to another canyon and descended. A sign had a telephone number to call if you wanted to report someone with their dog off a leash, as well as several other illustrations depicting rules to follow. One of them warned against smoking, a symbol he recognized on the trucks that came to the warehouse. Another thing the sign showed that he had seen before was a rifle.

Glancing from the phone number to the dog, he remembered leaving her leash wrapped around Oliver. He scoured the ground for something he could use to give the illusion he had this dog under control, the way he had seen the men do with those horrible wolves. He found a bungee cord, a small length of rope, and a plastic shopping bag then tangled them into a seven-foot-long mutant thread. The dog scampered up a hill to the end of another street and sat, waiting for the boy to catch up.

Once on the leash, the dog broke into a good trot, testing the boy's underdeveloped and weary legs. When she saw he could still run, she picked up the pace until both were at a dead sprint. The sky behind them was getting lighter, and she had little time to get the boy where they would not be found.

They saw the first car on the one semi-busy street they needed to cross. The woman driving thought nothing of a boy in filthy jeans and sweatshirt, sprinting with his dog tethered on a leash made of trash at 5:30 in the morning. She waved them through the stop sign, smiling, and they darted on.

A few people were stirring in their windows and some were beginning to leave their houses for early shifts at work. The first rays from the sun shot over the mountains to the east. They were late by the dog's reckoning.

She barked, surprising the boy, but not half as much as what followed; a ring of translucent smoke shot from her mouth, defying logic as it stayed in form, flying through the air in front of them, impervious to the wind. The boy's vision distorted in its wake, like rings on a murky pond, stretching out and away from them. As they followed in its draft, they went unnoticed by the wakening denizens of the street. Trails of colorless distortion wrapped around their bodies as they skirted the trees lining a golf course and hugged an alley that ended atop sandy desert cliffs. They crossed one last street, and disappeared into the bushes. The next hill steepened until they were completely hidden inside a copse of live oak and palm trees in the wild southeastern reaches of Balboa Park, the giant canyon system in the middle of San Diego.

The dog guided the boy to a tent nestled beneath the roots of an upended tree, fallen down the hill years before, completely hidden from public view.

The sun rose over the hills as the boy crawled into the tent and sat down, panting with exhilaration. He wrapped the sleeping bag around himself and looked at the little dog, who stood sentry at the mouth of the tent, and waited.

He'd made it out.

2

After listening intently for sounds of pursuit, fighting against exhaustion, the boy had finally drifted off to sleep with the dog curled at his feet. Long shadows crept across the camp by the time she set out to get something for him to eat, the day having passed them by while he slumbered. She'd waited patiently, not venturing far into the light of day, but he would need food when he awoke, and there was none here now.

There wasn't much in the way of food in the canyons, at least of the sustainable and filling variety. Many plants are edible, the dog knew, but trial and error in the wild was a gamble with death by poisoning with every bite. The little dog didn't have a taste for the plants anyway.

There were plenty of discarded scraps from picnickers, however, and there were always the cottontails. She didn't dare chase rabbits too far from the boy, lest he be recaptured on her watch, but she had to feed him. She trotted in a tight perimeter, staying close.

After only seconds, a cottontail shot from a nearby bush and she instantly gave chase. The rabbit darted in zigs and zags through the desert shrubs with the dog hot on its heels. The frightened creature could begin to feel hot canine breath on its tail and hind legs as the dog readied for the fatal lunge. Cutting hard and disappearing into the roots of a willow just as the dog shot forward for the kill, the rabbit instead gave the little hunter a mouthful of dirt to chew. The dog's plan stymied, she trotted back toward the tent and boy, dirty and dejected.

Her nostrils quivered as she caught a smell on the wind near the campsite. Nose in the air, she followed the scent to the edge of the lawn in the park. When she had convinced herself no one was watching, she burst from the bushes and darted to a large concrete cube, one of several in the park used as barbecue pits. The smell was coming from inside. She put her forepaws up and was just tall enough to peer over the rim. The pit was cold, but on the grill lay a full chicken breast and two strips of carne asada, left there by picnickers too full to care about it. The little dog deftly leapt up onto the rim and snatched the chicken breast, then turned tail and sprinted back to the boy.

The boy shrieked in fear when his eyes opened, but calmed down upon realizing he was out here with the dog and not in his former place of imprisonment. He smiled when he saw her standing in front of him and wagging her tail, a large cold chicken breast in her mouth. Famished, he reached out and was relieved when she allowed him to grab and bite into it. The dog watched him eat for a second, then ran off again into the park.

As he ate, he thought of the warehouse and those in it. His memories were spotty. He recalled the girl's arrival, and what she had shown him, but before she had come there were long gaps. Some as long as months, he guessed, but he could never be sure.

Each time the gaps occurred, the last thing he would remember seeing was what the grown people called a "snare", a slick black cone with carvings on it. When he thought of it, his back and sides hurt. He lifted his shirt between bites of chicken and felt the welts, like circular scars, that dotted his skin. They burned slightly under his touch.

The dog returned with a strip of beef, thin and spiced. She dropped it near his lap and sat down. He handed her a bite of the chicken, which she quickly devoured, then he pointed to his throat. She barked and nodded her head at the foot of his bed. Following her eyes, he reached for a canteen with the name "Max" written on it.

The water it held was crisp and refreshing, and invigorated his tired mind. When he had had enough, he began to poke around the camp. There was a duffel bag at the foot of the bed. Next to it lay a little kitchen set up with silverware and a black-and-white clay bowl; further away was a pot and stove and a few old paperback books. As the boy read the titles the dog turned around and shook her tail so hard her entire torso heaved back and forth.

The surrounding shrubs rustled, then a thin man with dark skin and closely-shaved black hair emerged. He wore work pants and a denim jacket with old hiking boots on his feet. As he took off the backpack he was wearing, the man and boy locked eyes. The boy readied himself to run and escape, but the little dog whined with glee, putting her paws up on the man's thighs. The man bent down and kissed the dog on the forehead, pulled off his jacket and hung it from a hooked stick positioned inside the root shelter.

Witnessing the dog's actions, the boy lost his suspicions. Once he saw there was no danger, there was no more fear. He felt surprisingly calm. It was a new feeling, one he had only felt with the girl, and of course very recently with the dog. Now this guy. Was there someone else? He didn't remember.

The man smiled as he crouched down, put out his hand and asked, "How you doin', little man?"

The boy looked at the proffered hand with confusion, then remembered other adults doing this, and slowly put his hand into the man's.

"Good, I think," the boy said as they shook.

"Haha! Right on, my friend. Maximilian is my name. You can call me Max if you like."

"Um, okay, ah . . . Max."

"That's right. This girl's name is Luna," Max said as he scratched Luna's head. She shoved her head up into his hand. "So what's your name, buddy?"

The boy searched his memory, so full of holes. He was frustrated and embarrassed by the result. Luna approached him and licked his cheek, and the frustration melted like butter. He didn't know his name, and had several problems besides that, but there would be solutions, eventually. This was a new day.

"I don't know my name, but you can call me Buddy, I guess."

"Haha! Alright, Buddy. That's what we'll do." Max leaned forward. "She has that effect on a lot of people, the whole feeling thing."

Buddy believed it.

"You sleep well?" asked Max. "Nobody followed you?"

"I don't think so. I mean I don't think anyone followed us. I do think I slept okay." said Buddy, trying to answer both questions.

"Good. Alright then, first things first. We're going to make sure nobody's creeping around here looking for you. Secure the perimeter, as it were. I've been around here checking all day, and it looked cool, but I'll show you how to do it."

"Okay."

"Then we'll teach you some other stuff. So let's get going," Max began gathering things into a small backpack that lay against the side of the tent.

Buddy was willing to follow Max pretty much anywhere at this point. He had a grown-up person talking to him like an equal outside of the prison they called a warehouse. He never in his life imagined this would be a reality, yet here he stood. However, he felt he really needed some sort of explanation.

"Max?" he said, "Wait a second, please. Who are you? And what, or who, are the people I was with? And why did they want me? Do we have time to tell me that?"

Max looked confused. "What don't you know?"

"Um, a lot?"

"Alright," Max sighed. "Keep an open mind, these things are weird to get a hold of. There are webs, running in and around and through everything, that connect the world, and beyond. That is the first step. Okay?"

Buddy nodded, having no idea what he was agreeing with.

"You don't have to pretend to get it right now, you will."

"Good."

"Okay, now, there is a group of people who monitor, and in a way, protect the webs of the world. Make sure things run properly, on a different level. Don't worry about what that all means, just yet. They're called Keepers.

"They live a long time, and pick people to take over for them when they get old, if they get old. Usually they try to pick people for certain qualities. Someone just and gentle, for instance.

"Now, some of these Keepers are more powerful than others, and can give these gifts away without their own abilities getting weaker, or disappearing altogether. They also live a lot longer. They are called Makers. Those people that kept you imprisoned, with their knives and other weird shit, are what happens when they choose the wrong people for this sort of thing. They're power hungry."

"So are you one of those other ones? The gentle ones?"

"Me? No, I'm a little more complicated than that," said Max, smiling. "The webs and their ways are hard to fully explain. Helen's better at this anyway."

"Who is Helen?"

"My friend. And more. We had to learn of this world all by ourselves. It was a very difficult road, but we survived, and eventually flourished, while watching these people. That's how we found out about the usurped spirit. Stolen, that is."

Buddy crooked his neck. "Wow. So you know about them, but they don't know about you?"

"That's right, Buddy," said Max. "For now. But I've got a feeling that might have changed."

"And then you get people out of places before they know what's going on? And you use Luna so they can't find out who you are?"

"Yep," answered Max. "Pretty sharp, kid."

"Sweet. How many times have you done this?"

"You, my boy," said Max, "have the distinct honor of being the very first."

Buddy was speechless.

"Shall we get going?"

"Yes please," said Buddy.

Sticking to thin trails along the sides of the canyon cliffs that surrounded the park, Max showed him around. Beneath a live oak, he reached down and picked up a bottle thrown from the picnic area above, grumbling about people that leave their trash.

"Do me a favor, Buddy. Don't throw garbage around like these people. It's disrespectful."

"Okay."

The sun had fully set, and dusk shrouded the park as they neared a modified shopping cart, the front cut off to form a seat, tucked behind a thicket of live oak shrubs. Max had Buddy sit in it, then put a thin sheet over the top. He could see out, as if through a film, but no one could see in.

"You okay in there?" Max asked.

"Yeah."

He pushed Buddy up and down the alleys, sifting through containers. For what, Buddy was unsure. Max checked the surroundings constantly while he spoke, careful not to move his lips too much. Something caught his eye, and from beneath a dumpster he pulled a sharp black cone.

When Max showed Buddy, the boy's eyes grew wide with panic, and didn't relax even when he saw it was nothing more than a black candle, barely melted at the top. Seeing it affect the kid, Max threw it in the dumpster.

"Why do I have to be in here?" Buddy said, feeling claustrophobic. "Can't I just wrap the sheet around my head or something?"

"No way. They even see your hands, or even your size, and people are gonna get very suspicious. Even if it's not the people trying to get you back. They don't know who I am, yet, but there's other things we have to be concerned about. Plus, you've only been out here one day. Everything is a risk right now. Just hold on, little man, alright?"

"But it's dark out."

"Not dark enough."

Max explained that onlookers would be curious enough to question why an eleven-year-old white kid was recycling cans with a forty-something black man. This led to an explanation of race and people's perceptions of it, something entirely too much energy was burnt thinking about, Max said. Of course there could be several explanations for such a teaming; adoption, an uncle by marriage, or godparent for instance. However, if they had to explain themselves to anyone it would already be too late.

"Anything that draws attention to you is bad," said Max. "Don't increase the number of people already looking for you. But you're right, let's get somewhere you can stretch."

They walked beneath an arch of plants to a hidden clearing. The lights of downtown shone bright in the distance, as did the naval hospital on the other side of Florida Canyon. Max took the sheet off the top and let Buddy out, then sat on the ground while Buddy stretched his limbs and looked out at the city.

Max explained things he should know of the world in general, both as a boy and as a canyon dweller. The former included what schools were, how stores worked, who the police were. The latter included the edible plants in the canyons, how to steal fruit from surrounding yards without getting noticed, and of course, how to escape into the canyons from anyone after him.

Buddy was an apt pupil, Max found. His gift of retention was beyond anything Max had expected, and he thought Buddy was going to be alright as long as they stayed out of sight. One thing the kid couldn't do, no matter how much they talked, was remember much about his past. Max thought that might not be such a bad thing right now.

Max stashed the cart under another thicket of branches, and they walked down a hill along the border of the park, beside a chain-link and razor wire fence. Pointing around, he warned Buddy about some of the other residents of the canyons, and made sure he avoided all but Helen. Max didn't trust them. Especially the man called Garth.

"Garth is a major alcoholic, and a pervert," Max said, explaining about Garth eyeballing children in the park in his drunken stupors.

"Seriously, avoid him at all costs." They looked down the cliff that cut into a small forest of live oak. Max pointed toward the entrance to the city mechanic's yard that stretched along the park to the west. Just beside the entrance to the yard, through the trees, they could barely make out an area littered with garbage.

"That's where Garth lives. Never go down there."

Buddy looked down the hill. A pit of trash was strewn at the bottom, among the dark shadows. Scraps of garbage hung from the trees and shrubs. He could almost smell it in the distance. Garth must be disgusting. They kept to the shadows as they walked over a few hills, back to their own camp beneath the roots.

"So who is Helen?" Buddy asked.

"She lives out here, also. An amazing woman. Sometimes you'll be with me, sometimes her, sometimes both. And on rare occasions, like last night, you might have to be with just you and Luna, which is why I'm gonna prep you on some defense. Tomorrow, though, not tonight. It takes a clear mind."

"Right on," said Buddy.

"Right on, indeed."

Max was the only the second adult Buddy had ever felt safe with, and now there would be a third. He was excited to meet her.

Buddy got a faraway look. He remembered the first; a man named Jeb, who used to visit the warehouse so very long ago. What happened to Jeb? How could he remember him? He wanted to tell Max. Not now though. His brain was overloaded, and he needed to lie down.

When they got back to their camp, Max stretched a hammock over the entrance to the tent, and shooed the boy and dog inside.

"Tomorrow we kick it up a notch," he said, then laid down in the hammock and fell asleep instantly as the eastern sky grew rosy from the dawn.

Buddy stared at the ceiling of the tent while snuggled up to Luna. He thought of his place at a crossroads of the world. His old life, his new one, and whatever was to come. Eventually he drifted off to sleep.

• • •

The man with the blazing blue eyes looked up from the tantō he was polishing. The small Japanese sword made to perform seppuku was so shiny he could see his reflection in it. He gazed at himself, still unable to believe the Korean had been able to locate it, truly a talented procurer of goods who would be used again. He slowly swished it through the air between himself and the team sent to capture the boy. They did not appear victorious, he noted.

"We were unsuccessful in trying to recapture him, Frank. I'm sorry. He got the best of Oliver," said the pale man in the blue tracksuit. "Before we caught up."

Oliver crept out from behind the giant who stood slightly apart from the pale man.

"It wasn't my fault," said the spidery boy. "He had some dog that could do weird things."

Frank held the tantō still, looking at his reflection. "So do we. Two of them, if I'm not mistaken."

He put the sword down on the desk and flicked the handle with a finger. Like a nefarious game of spin the bottle, it twirled around in perfect balance. Beams of light reflected off the polished metal and whipped around the walls. They illuminated books on shelves, crude pottery, and a glass trophy case with various steel balls and a knife of polished grey stone hanging in the rear. Empty spaces lay above and beneath the knife.

The sword slowly came to a halt, pointing at the boy. Only then did Frank notice in the dimly lit room that Oliver was covered in blood.

"What happened to you?" he asked.

The giant, Markuz, was silent, but the pale man tried to answer for the boy. "The dog got between the two boys and was a casualty of the situation."

Peik was sure that this youth's twisted life had left him a psychopath, and the pale man took pity on the boy, in his way.

"I did not ask you, Peik," said Frank. "I asked Oliver, and I will ask him again. Why are you covered in blood?"

"I killed the dog. I lost control. I'm sorry." He didn't dare make eye contact.

"Which dog?"

"Genghis."

Genghis was the smaller but smarter of the two wolfen dogs Frank had trained. His favorite.

"It's funny you should use that word. Control. Look at me, Oliver. Put your hand on the desk."

Markuz took a step forward. "What?" he said, holding him back. "Stay, Oliver."

"This is my business, Markuz. Peik, get a hold of your goon." Frank didn't like Markuz, but Peik had hired him for security, and the man-mountain was an unparalleled physical specimen who could fight anything. His loyalties seemed lacking, however, and Frank had decided that Markuz would need to be handled eventually.

Markuz gave a low growl when the pale man nodded to him, but lowered his hand. The boy didn't move.

Frank leaned close to Oliver, and in a very low whisper, so that no one else could hear, said into his ear, "Aash Xashuol."

A milky glaze rose from the bottom of the boy's eyes and slowly overtook them.

"Come to me," said the hook-nosed man, backing away and beckoning with his finger.

The boy obeyed, shuffling toward the desk.

"Put your hand on the desk. Palm down." He did as he was told. "Now," continued Frank, "that dog, that animal, took me quite some time to train exactly the way that I wanted it."

As he spoke, he curled the boy's thumb under the palm of his planted hand. "And as you know, I have a saying. Do you remember what that is?" He tucked the index finger and middle finger to meet the thumb. "Hmm?"

The boy, lost in a trance, said, "Blood for blood."

"That is correct!" Frank curled the pinky finger underneath while picking up the tantō. "Good job!"

The boy's ring finger stuck out from his fist, alone on the surface of the desk.

From behind the two men, a woman with long blonde hair entered the room. Seeing the scene in front of her, she said, "Frank? What the fuck are you doing? Put the sword down!"

"No. He killed my dog. It's just one finger. He must learn a lesson."

She stepped forward. "Frank! I absolutely forbid you to—"

Her sentence was cut off by the thunk of the sharp blade on the desk followed by Oliver's screaming.

The finger twitched its final nerve, rolled along the desk, and came to a stop in a puddle of its own blood.

3

Stewart Zanderson snapped awake to the sound of his alarm clock screeching beside his ear. He hit the snooze button, which didn't work, then tried the power, but it was set to "off" already. When he pulled the cord from the wall, the alarm died. Apparently the clock's time had come, old and used as it was. The curious thing about it was that Stewart never worked before six o'clock at night, and hadn't set the alarm since Mother's Day over a month ago.

Stupid clock. He rubbed his eyes and stared at the unplugged cord. From there, his focus shifted up to his bedroom window, following a fluttering movement outside the glass.

A lone mockingbird peered at him from just inches beyond the window. It clicked its tongue. Deep within Stewart's mind, the voice of the bird birthed an indescribable emotion, and with it a foggy memory, hard to place.

Birds were plenty off his second story balcony, but none had ever stood staring into his eyes and clicking at him that he could remember. He shook his head, but the uneasy feeling remained.

He threw the clock on the floor. its plastic face clattered into the corner.

"Fucking figures," he said.

Stewart had many good qualities. One that was not so good, however, was his inability to properly manage his anger. It had caused him more than a few problems in life.

He waved his arm in the air and yelled at the bird. It kept one eye on him and pecked at a bug.

Stewart was at a loss. "What the fuck is your problem?" he shouted, flapping his arms.

Pictures flipped through his brain, options of how to handle the bird problem. None plausible. He breathed deeply, like he'd been told by amateur anger experts, and realized how absurd the situation was. Who cares about some weird bird? He'd brush his teeth and ignore it until it went away bored. The little bird squawked and pecked hard upon the window as Stewart shuffled into the bathroom.

The old faucet creaked as he turned on the water and started brushing. He looked at himself in the mirror. His fortieth birthday was in three days, so there was finally hope this wretched year would pass. In the past twelve months he had seen his girlfriend of three years leave him for someone in his own band, then the subsequent breakup of that same band, a project Stewart had single-handedly held together for seven years.

This was followed very closely by the forming of a band much like the previous one, with Stewart's former girlfriend and bandmates in it, and Stewart, not surprisingly, absent.

Stewart was still pissed off nine months later. He'd already been incredibly bitter, but as the new band's popularity had eclipsed the old one, he was inconsolable. Actually eclipsed may not be altogether the right word, more like pulverized.

At least he still had his job at Auntie Frieda's, barely.

Auntie Frieda was a very large black woman who didn't take shit from anyone, evidenced by her being one of the first female bar owners in San Diego that had been able to stay open beyond their first year. She'd been given the bar by her father in the late seventies, an era when rival owners would show up with baseball bats and smash all your inventory while corrupt policemen stood watch outside. San Diego had still been the Wild West then, and in some ways Auntie Frieda thought it still was, but she was hardcore, and she wasn't going anywhere.

The bar's name was her own: Auntie Frieda's. It had been, and still was, Stewart's favorite live music spot in town. Frieda had hired him several years ago, and she was a great boss, if you worked hard. Stewart did, and she'd been pleased with him for a good many years. However, since Stewart's double breakup, she'd had several complaints about his attitude behind the bar. He'd always been a bit hard-nosed, but it was getting out of hand. She'd let him slide for a couple months, but here it was nine months later. Recently, she had told Stewart they "needed to talk," a terrible phrase to hear from anyone, let alone your boss.

In her small office, Auntie Frieda had told Stewart that if she got another complaint about him, he'd have to go look for a job somewhere else, and that it had been over nine months, and maybe it was time to move on if he couldn't rein in his emotions.

"Take a few days off," she'd said. "You can come back on the twenty-first, but that's your old band's first gig. You might want to skip it."

"It's also my fortieth birthday," he'd said.

"Well, happy birthday. But . . ." She'd looked to Stewart with tender eyes. "If you do work that show, I need you to behave yourself. I really don't want to fire you, Stewart, but you're becoming bad for business."

He splashed water on his face, trying to clear his head. It didn't work. More memories snaked into his head.

Last September hadn't been the first time he had had a band break up from under him. Once before, a long time ago when he was just barely what people refer to as an adult, his bandmates had disappeared on him. Only that time he had never seen them again. It was still strange. They cleared out their stuff from the room they had practiced in without a goodbye, and no apology. That was it. In the relatively small music scene of San Diego at the time it was odd to never really hear of someone's comings and goings, even if you were trying not to. They simply had vanished. Ditched him, basically. Being in a band was a little like being married to the people in it, and he had gotten divorced without anyone so much as talking to him about it.

It took him years to get over that one.

The ring of his kitchen phone snapped him out the past. A beige plastic artifact hanging from the wall, it was something he never used except to give the number to bill collectors. It rang five times and Stewart's voice answered.

"This is Stewart, leave a message. I'll, uh, try to get back to you later. Thanks."

A dial tone droned for two seconds, then silence.

He shrugged and kept brushing. Score one for me, he thought.

It rang again. He ignored it. And again. Five rings and a dial tone, pause, repeat. He had to reset that stupid thing to one ring or perhaps get rid of it entirely, maybe today.

He rinsed his mouth out, grumbled into the kitchen, and picked up the receiver. No dial tone, no sound at all. He stared at the phone in disbelief, hung it up with his finger a couple times, got a tone, and replaced it on the cradle. Shaking his head, he returned to his bedroom.

He had almost completely forgotten about the mockingbird. The mockingbird, however, remembered him. When it saw him it cocked its head and clicked its tongue.

A deep clear note resounded through the pane of glass, as loud inside as outside, like something was in the room with him. He looked around in a circle, then back to the bird, who repeated it. The tone and feel of the bird's clocking tongue was like a stone dropping into water. It made Stewart almost have a memory of a river, a rock, and another bird. Older. Different. So long ago.

He paused, fixated on the bird. What was that memory? Was it even his? Perhaps a remembered story. What had happened? The thought serpentined just beyond his mind's reach.

"Go on! Get!"

He thrust out his arms at it. No reaction. Next, he began walking slowly towards the window, yelling as primally as he could, but the bird calmly stared. Putting his hand on the window, he poised himself to pull it open. Rather than retreat, the bird fanned out its grey wings and pecked hard on the other side of the glass, millimeters from his hand, making him pause. The bird was outside, he was inside—why tempt fate? Stewart narrowed his eyes. The mockingbird razzed at him.

Within the sound, his mind wandered again into the past. An unseen agreement through a haze.

The realization reared its head that the mockingbird, with its weird clicks and chirps, may be waking memories within his brain, unlocking little worms of thought. Memories he had worked hard to block out since the day they occurred, when a bunch of assholes left him in the lurch.

"Aaaaarrgh!" He shook his head and yelled, trying to drown out more triggers from the bird. Life had tired of untrustworthy humans to throw at him, now it was giving him crazy wildlife as well.

He walked away holding his ears and shouting, trying to ignore it. Before he rounded the corner, he looked back once and raised his middle finger.

Fuck you, stupid bird.

He needed some food. In the kitchen there was only one bowl, an old black and white glazed clay thing that looked as if it was someone's first ceramics project five hundred years ago. He got it at a swap meet some time past, and couldn't ever remember why he bought it, ugly as it was. But it still held liquid, and that was as good a reason as any to keep it around. Plus it went with his one plate, one spoon, and one fork, which was all he had left when his former girlfriend and bandmate moved out.

Stewart held the bowl and box of cereal when the phone rang again right next to his ear. The bowl dropped to the floor and erupted into countless black-and-white glazed clay shards. He'd never seen a dish explode quite like that before.

"Shit!" he grumbled. He had grown to love the thing.

When the machine picked up, his voice sounded distant, and echoed around the room. Expecting a dial tone afterward, he was surprised to hear a voice from his past.

"Stewart. It's Craig James. Long time . . . anyway I was wondering what you've been up to lately, if you had talked to anyone from back in the day recently or anything. Lemme know if you want to get a drink anytime. My number is—"

"Nickel," Stewart interrupted, picking up the phone and calling Craig by his old nickname. "What's up, man? I haven't heard from you in eons." His senses returned to normal a little.

"Yeah, how's everything?" asked Nickel.

"Alright, y'know, same old same old," answered Stewart, trying to believe it. "Just livin'. Workin'."

"I hear you. Hey man, what's your schedule like? You wanna get together sometime?"

"Yeah, I could do that. Actually, how's breakfast sound? I just turned my house into a disaster area and—shit!"

Pain shot up Stewart's leg. He looked down at his left foot. A large shard stuck out of the webbing next to his big toe. Blood started to ooze around it and down his foot, then drip onto the floor. The spatter of blood over the shards of clay formed a strange pattern, dizzying his mind. He stepped sideways, near his kitchen window.

With the receiver cradled in the crook of his neck, he noticed rivulets of blood flowing down the sole, then pooling and dripping off his heel. He grabbed a towel off the stove handle, and propped his foot on a chair. In one motion, he pulled the shard out and clenched the towel over the wound, stemming the blood flow.

"You okay, Stewart?" asked Nickel, hearing the disaster through the line.

"Yeah, I'm–aiiagh!" Stewart screamed.

The mockingbird appeared from around the corner and flew at the window, aiming for Stewart's face. It shrieked and fanned its wings out, pulling parallel to the window and flapping inches from his eye.

Stewart threw his left arm up to protect himself from the charge of the bird. It couldn't actually reach him through the glass, but he freaked out nonetheless. He jerked away, and his body teetered backwards, crashing on top of the shattered bowl and piercing his flesh in dozens of places. His head slammed backwards onto the floor. Pain stabbed everywhere while he stared sideways out the window at the bird. It landed, a glint in its little grey eye. A shudder crept over Stewart. His eyelids grew heavy. The world spiraled. His vision blackened, starting at the top right corner and closing in scope until he could see only the bird, so still. Then nothing at all.

The bird's clicking tongue echoed in his mind one last time before he lost consciousness. Like a stone dropping into water . . .

"Stewart!" Nickel's distant voice trailed from the receiver, now laying on the floor. "Stewart! What's going on?"

A hard rap on the door pulled Stewart back. His eyes stretched open to the long sideways view of the kitchen floor, tiles littered with bits of blood and clay. Beyond the debris was the kitchen door, which framed a short, round-featured man with tattoos in its glass, knocking. His eyes were large and panicked, but they relaxed when he saw Stewart move.

Stewart got up, pulling little bits of bowl out of his leg and arm. Small pools of blood welled up from the wounds. His head screamed, and he swooned when he stood up to let in Nickel.

"Hey, Stewart. What the hell happened, man? I got over as quick as I could. I'm glad you still live here. Jeez, that's a mess," he said as he walked into the kitchen. He made to give Stewart a hug, settled back for a handshake, then opted for a soft tap on Stewart's shoulder, which had nothing sticking out of it.

There was blood on the floor, but the small cuts had stopped bleeding as quickly as they began, only the one on his toe felt truly painful.

"Ugh. Luckily for me I still do, I guess. I just had a very unlucky morning," he said.

"I'll say. Why don't I sweep this up, you clean yourself off, and we'll go get some food?"

"Sounds good. It's good to see you, Nickel." Stewart turned for the shower, groaning.

"You too, bud. Where's a broom and mop and shit?"

Stewart pointed to a closet, then limped off to the shower. "Thanks," he said.

● ● ●

Stewart and Nickel walked down a small street with brown sandstone canyons dropping off to one side, the golf course on the other. Imported eucalyptus and pepper trees shaded the native laurel sumac and live oak. And always palms. San Diego's plant life, like its human population, is a little mix of everything from everywhere. Beyond the canyon, to the west, was the huge naval hospital and farther on were the museums and zoo housed within Balboa Park.

"You still playing with that band?" Nickel asked, referring to Stewart's now former group, The Skeez.

"No. We broke up a couple months ago. Long, stupid story." Nine whole months sounded so bitter. He didn't want to seem like he cared too much.

"That sucks. I like that band."

"Fucking tell me about it." It was still hard to talk about, every day he got pissed off about it at some point. There was a hole in his life where music used to live. In the ultimate irony, working at Auntie Frieda's was almost like having his nose rubbed in it. He didn't care if he never heard another band again, yet a couple nights a week he heard three or more. At work he just tried to concentrate on the working part, and not getting fired.

"How you been doin' lately?" Stewart asked, changing the subject.

"Not bad. I do a work from home thing three days a week and go in two for an ad company. Mostly graphics." Stewart believed it, Nickel had some faults, like everyone, but had a pretty decent knowledge of layout and graphics. Back in the day he'd made everyone's posters. They were never that great, but they got the information out there.

"Pays the bills," said Nickel.

"Gotta pay them bills," Stewart replied as they neared the cafe. He never remembered Nickel paying for anything.

They entered Irene's, a little breakfast joint near a golf course sports complex inside the park. The smells of sausage and eggs hit them as they opened the swinging door to the cafe, making them salivate instantly.

A local culinary breakfast hangout for years in San Diego, Irene's had recently become very popular, along with its surrounding neighborhoods. On weekends there would be a wait for at least an hour to eat, but on this bright Tuesday morning it was merely at three-quarters capacity. Stewart walked to a booth in the corner nearest the kitchen and slid in, waving at a couple people he knew from around. Nickel mirrored him on the other side, minus the waving.

The server, May, whom Stewart knew well and liked much, skipped up and said hello to them, though she didn't know Nickel. May liked Stewart, she saw through his angry facade, and thought he was sweet and awkward. She scrawled down their orders, consisting mainly of egg, potato, meat products and coffee. Stewart also ordered an orange juice.

She skipped back to the kitchen, returned with the coffee and OJ, then half-danced off to another table whose two occupants she thought were a bit unhappy, but she couldn't help everyone's attitude. Stewart's eyes unwittingly followed May, and rested on the older, paler one of the men at the booth. He was of good build and wearing a blue track suit. The other man was a massive fatigue-clad and chiseled mountain of flesh who looked like he could take on a tank with his bare hands and win.

Stewart noticed the pale man staring back at him. His gaze made Stewart feel briefly nauseous, and he redirected his line of sight. He felt the pale man's eyes drift off him. Nickel aimlessly pushed around the salt and pepper shakers on the table.

"So let's cut to the chase. What's this all about, Nickel? I gotta say I was a little surprised to hear your voice after so long." Stewart draped his arm over the back of the booth, very comfortable in Irene's. He ate here at least twice a week.

"Yeah, I know. It's been a while." Nickel took a deep breath, leaned close to Stewart, and said, "Okay. The real reason I called is I'm kind of looking for Jeb Rawls."

"What?" The shock was all over Stewart's face. Jeb Rawls was a name he had stopped thinking of long ago, and one of the three he had never seen again from his first band, The Beneathers.

"Why would you ask me how to find him? I haven't seen him in like twenty years or something," said Stewart.

"Well, you were tighter with him and his brother and Nuala than I was, and you're the only person from back then who still lives in the same place."

These were true. He was a little closer to that group; Jeb and Frank Rawls, along with Nuala McCafferty and Maria Kaminski, who had not only been his bandmates but also his core group of friends before the first three stopped hanging out. Stewart had been hurt, and pissed off. His nerves still rankled when he heard Jeb's name.

"I might have been closer, but those guys totally fucked me way back when. Why would I wanna find them?"

Nickel looked at him honestly. "Well, I was hoping you would do it as a favor to me, I guess. If for nothing else than for helping you out today."

Well, Stewart thought, that was very convenient. How had Craig even known he would need help? And if he hadn't, what other angle would he work?

"Man, I can't think of anyone I'd rather not hang out with than any of those three, but I'm a sucker for my friends, even if I haven't seen you in years. Okay, you got me. I'll help," he said, feeling like he may be getting himself in a sticky situation.

Stewart was a bitter man, true, but that did not dissuade him from helping people out. He had a very strong idea of what was right, and what was wrong. He also had no reservations about voicing or acting upon them. Nickel had helped him, suspicions be damned, so he would help Nickel in return. Period.

It was also true what Nickel said about where he lived. Stewart loved his apartment. He'd moved in sixteen years ago and wasn't going anywhere anytime soon. Casa De Oro was a giant Spanish Colonial apartment complex with twisting staircases and small balconies everywhere. It had been built in the 1860s and was a landmark of the area.

It didn't hurt matters that his landlady, Mrs. Myers, loved him. When Vivian, his former girlfriend and guitarist for the band that recently reformed without him, had in a sly move convinced Stewart a real man would move out even if a girl cheated on him, Mrs. Meyers had told Vivian very simply and directly that no matter what sort of warped reverse chivalry she was trying to enact upon Stewart, she'd still be moving out. Vivian had been furious, and had launched into a litany of verbal assaults against the landlady. It wasn't until Vivian was threatened with bodily harm by three of the female residents that she shut up and left. Vivian had not been very popular with the other tenants.

"So, why do you want to find Jeb Rawls?" asked Stewart, getting his brains back on topic.

"Somebody delivered a box to my job, addressed to him, care of me," Nickel said, folding the corner of his napkin.

"Wow. That's pretty off the mark, eh?" Stewart's eyebrows furrowed.

"That's what I thought."

The food arrived. Stewart was famished, and ate three large bites before speaking again. "Well, I wouldn't have the first clue of how to locate Jeb; he could live anywhere by now. It's literally been forever." He swallowed, sipped his coffee.

"No. They're in town," Nickel said, staring into space and chewing his food. "This food is really good, man . . . nice neighborhood diner."

"Hmm? Oh, yeah . . . wait. How the hell do you know they're in town? Don't you mean 'he' anyway?" Stewart asked. "What's going on here, dude?"

"What? Well, I just assume so," Nickel said, not convincingly. Stewart thought Nickel's eye twitched, and his suspicions continued to rise. Nickel was either sure or assuming, but one cannot be both.

Before he could question this, the giant man from the surly booth got up and walked by them, bumping their table on his way. The jolt made the coffee cups slosh over their rims.

The man was a mountain in his black military clothing. He made no acknowledgment he had touched anything, and continued walking uninterrupted toward the restroom. Stewart steadied his coffee cup as he gazed at the man's swinging hands. They were massive, nearly the same size as his own head. Stewart decided against bringing the table nudge to the giant's attention.

"Whatever," Stewart said. He tore his sight from the man's hands. "Have you opened the package at all?"

Nickel was watching the giant. He looked back and said, "No. It's not mine."

"But your name's on it," said Stewart, mopping up the spillage into a napkin.

"Yeah, I was hoping we could do it together."

"Yay. When did it get to your work?"

"Over the weekend sometime."

"Hmm. Who sent it?" Stewart pointed at Nickel with his fork.

"It didn't have a return address, and no receipt from a shipping company or post office. Just my name and Jeb's."

"So you don't know how it got in there? Where is it now?" Stewart soaked up the last bits of egg and potato up with his bread, shot the last gulp of coffee.

"Still at my desk. I didn't want to bring it home, my house is kind of a wreck most of the time."

Having also finished eating, Nickel looked at May and made a pen-writing-on-paper signal for the check. "It's much safer at my job. Plus almost the whole staff is on some team-building retreat all week. Nobody will notice it for at least a couple days."

"You're not building with the team?"

"Not so much."

"I guess you want me to go check it out?"

"I was hoping . . . "

"Yeah, I know, Nickel. You were hoping we could do it together." Stewart smiled sideways, trying not to feel victimized.

The cheery May skipped the check over. Stewart said he'd pay the bill and Nickel could get the tip. The bill came to $19.97. Nickel threw two dollars on top of Stewart's twenty.

"Still a nickel and dimer, eh, Nickel?" said Stewart, shaking his head and throwing another five dollars on top. "Jesus," he sighed.

Thanking May, he slid from the booth. Nickel shrugged and followed suit, sliding around the giant man returning to his table. The giant's pale partner trailed them with his eyes, making Stewart shiver like someone had driven ice beneath his fingernails. They hurried out the door, not looking back, into the warm and cloudless day.

• • •

After walking back to Stewart's, Nickel drove them in his little rusty bucket to his workplace on the east side of downtown, near the 5. He punched a code into the panel on the front door and the lock clicked open. Then he looked up and down the street before they slipped through the door and into the hushed brick building.

The air inside was cool and still. Nickel's office was housed in a reclaimed and refurbished stable house built in the 1880s, when San Diego was the Wild West in the truer sense of the phrase. The company had kept the brick interior and added steel and glass partitions to connect the old oaken beams holding up the roof. All in all a pretty good looking renovation, it seemed to Stewart.

The place was almost deserted, save for an aging janitor replacing a trash bag in the lunchroom as they walked by. The old man made no move to signify he had even seen them, fluidly going about his memorized duties, his gnarled hands deftly maneuvering over the building and his tools by rote.

The offices themselves were spacious yet minimal, with all the thought of flowing inspiration they were deemed to have needed.

They looked expensive. Nickel's was toward the rear, not quite a corner, but nearing one. He unlocked the door and entered, Stewart right behind him. Like the rest of the offices, heavy curtains draped the room in darkness. The whole place was also far quieter than Stewart expected.

"Jeez," said Stewart, then was mystified at the sound of the word dying as it left his mouth.

Nickel's office was sparsely furnished with a large desk taking up most of the space. Dark wooden bookshelves lined the walls, but few books were displayed. There was a desktop computer and a fist-sized stone holding down a few sheets of paper on top of the desk, and very little else; no pictures, plants, action figures. In fact not much had been done to personalize the room at all. It seemed a dark and curious place for someone to find the artistic inspiration Stewart thought would be needed for graphic design.

Nickel rounded his desk, unlocked a drawer, and pulled out the package. It was wrapped in plain brown paper, and had Nickel and Jeb's names and the office's address on it, with no ZIP code, stamp, or return address. Hand-delivered. It was the size of a wide shoe box.

"Are you sure it's not a bomb?" Stewart asked.

"Who's gonna leave a bomb for someone care of somebody else?" said Craig.

"Who's gonna leave a bomb period? Somebody crazy! So how should I know?"

"I don't think it's a bomb, Stewart, alright?"

"OK, you're probably right. You gonna open it?"

"I guess. I feel kind of weird, though."

"You don't know the half of it."

Nickel's eyebrows perked up. "What do you mean?" he asked, stopping short of breaking the seal on the clear tape.

"Well, shit," said Stewart. He hadn't considered telling Nickel about the mockingbird, but his mouth had betrayed him. Again.

"First thing this morning a bird attacked me from outside my window, that's how I broke my bowl. It freaked me out so bad I fell on top of all the broken pieces. That's why that crap happened at my house. Some maniac bird. So it's been a pretty weird day already."

The timing was horrible, but it started gushing out. He felt embarrassed, but relieved he had told someone.

"That is weird, what kind of bird?" asked Nickel, not missing a beat.

"A mockingbird, I think," Stewart said, a bit concerned at Nickel's lack of interest.

"Well, they're kind of kooky anyway, I wouldn't worry about it." Nickel was gripping the package tightly. "Anyway I don't see what that has to do with the package, so let's just go ahead and focus on this, OK?"

Nickel carefully removed the brown paper wrap. When the first corner was peeled back, a slice of silver light radiated from inside. He peeled the paper all the way off to reveal an ancient-looking silver and oak box with gilt leaves covering it in spirals. Even the hinges were made to resemble oak on carved stone. The silver caught any spare light in the room and illuminated it further, sending shards of light bouncing off the walls. Silver leaves seemed to breathe and grow, spirals to turn. The entire room glowed brightly, then began to dim and settle.

"Jeez. That's pretty intense," said Stewart.

"Yeah," answered Nickel dreamily. "Crazy."

He set the box down on the desk, pushing over the stone paperweight. It rocked back and forth on the desk before Stewart quieted it with his hand.

When he lifted the hasp and the box's lid was cracked, the silver light was almost unbearable, and a low hum filled the office. Almost imperceptible at first, the hum rose in intensity the more the lid hinged back. When it was completely open, the hum was almost as loud as human speech, and inside the box lay a dagger. The light emanated from the silver gilt oak with a bright and steady glow.

The dagger had leaves on the far end of the handle stretching into spirals on the guard and continuing down the blade. Silver with white oak laid into it, the knife was a masterpiece. As the glow leveled off, they noticed the blade was more of an elliptical cone than a solid piece.

Nickel put his hand on it. The hum stopped as soon as he touched it and his arm hairs stood on end. His body felt the hum inside of him now. He saw in his mind green fields, rolling waves, grey mist, and finally a pine forest. He smelled the dust of the forest, pine needles ground into mulch and still finer. A part of the air itself. He felt the filtered sun on his face mixed with the scent of loamy soil from the shade. Thoughts within his head snaked together with those he never had.

Stewart looked into Nickel's face and saw it go slack. No one was home. "Nickel!" he shouted. "Snap out of it, man! You're freaking me out!"

The sound of smashing glass came from down the hall, near the entrance. It didn't sound like the janitor. Stewart slapped Nickel hard in the face.

"Uhh . . . " Nickel groaned, still clutching the knife. "What's going on?" A red handprint was emblazoned on his cheek.

"There's someone coming, I think! What are we gonna do?" Stewart was beginning to really freak out now. "I think they kicked down the front door."

Nickel was not freaking out, even a little. "We're not gonna do anything yet," he said, smiling. The shock of the slap had worn off. Nickel's leering smile did absolutely nothing to calm Stewart's nerves.

Footsteps came tromping in their direction, finally slowing on the other side of the door. Stewart looked toward the covered window first, then surveyed the room looking for a weapon. Anything would do.

The handle turned slightly, making a click as the lock stopped its motion. Silence followed, then a deafening crack as the office door was kicked in. The ham-fisted giant from the cafe stepped into the room.

A plume of dust swirled around the huge brute as he stared down Stewart and Nickel. They heard a zippering sound, and the pale man glided in around him, his polyblend track suit swishing with each step.

Stewart edged backwards toward the desk, hoping to get between the pale freak and the silver box. The man's cold eyes pierced Stewart's spirit, then drifted over to Nickel. Stewart's trembling hand slowly crept nearer to the box and the stone paperweight. The pale man looked to his massive partner, then to the knife clutched in Nickel's hand. The bigger man grinned, extending his hand to Nickel.

Nickel grinned back at him. "Come and get it, fuckface," he said. His knuckles were white against the knife's glowing hilt. He chuckled.

Stewart was shocked. The big man stood over six-and-a-half-feet tall and hopelessly overshadowed Nickel, who was maybe five-foot-seven on a tall day with cushiony sneakers. He didn't remember Nickel being nearly this ballsy.

"Nickel! What the fuck are you doing? Just give it to them, man!"

"Fuck that. They're gonna have to take it. Heh."

Stewart was reaching the conclusion that Nickel had gone completely psychotic.

The pale man spoke. "I assure you, Craig, this will not end in the manner you envision. Surrender the blade and everyone leaves happily, hmm?" He inched closer to Nickel all the while, his voice a harmonic lull. "Please just hand it to Markuz, everything will be just fine."

"How the fuck do they know your name?" Stewart asked. His fingers at last brushed on the stone paperweight, and his hand curled around it until he held it tightly in his palm, out of sight of both of the invaders.

"I don't fucking know or care." Nickel was shaking, or maybe humming. Then his grip and vision slackened, and his body drooped. The bravado seemed to have left him. "Here you go." He took a deep breath and offered the knife up to the giant, who closed in.

Just as Markuz was about to take the blade, Nickel slashed at his arm, leaving a bloody scratch. Nickel laughed, and tried to bring the blade back around, but Markuz slammed his huge fist into Nickel's face, demolishing his nose completely. As his head snapped back from the blow, blood arced in long trails from his mouth and nose. A red mist hung in the air.

The spray slowly rained down on Stewart, coating his skin. Nickel tried to scream through the blood, but instead made a choking high-pitched gurgle. He still held the knife.

For a man of such size, Markuz moved like a thought. Nickel howled in pain, his eyes pooled with blood and his nose gushed bloody mucus all over his chest. He brought the blade around again in a wide blind arc.

Markuz grabbed Nickel's wrist in mid-swing and twisted it, sending the blade clattering to the ground. Like a shot, the giant also caught Stewart's neck in a vicelike squeeze, cutting off his breath.

Markuz held each man off the ground, arms horizontal, while they flailed around, trying to wriggle free. Stewart concealed the rock behind his body, grappling at Markuz's wrist. Markuz slammed them together. As his body collided into Nickel's, Stewart could barely manage to hold the stone. His body was twisted in such a way that hitting the giant with the rock was impossible, it was all he could do to hide it in the small crease between his buttock and thigh.

A spark of amusement shone in the pale man's eyes as he walked over to them.

"Very nice," he said. "No one gets the drop on Markuz like that. What do you have in here that would slow him so? Undoubtedly the same thing you've done to the door to keep us from opening the lock and making us kick it down. Not very hospitable." He bent and picked up the blade, turning and inspecting it closely. As he did so, his manner seemed to stiffen.

Stewart had no idea what the man was talking about. What does who have in here? What the hell is this place and who the hell are these people? And if that was considered slow, how fast is Markuz usually?

Nickel was a different man without the knife in his hand, terrified, gurgling blood up and spitting it down his shirt. His bloody nose throbbed on as he began to shake and weep.

"Get a hold of yourself, Craig," the pale man said as he passed the blade from his left hand to his right and back. "Don't be pathetic." He looked in Nickel's eyes, which were flowing tears of pain and fear. The pale man stared somewhere into the center of his brain.

His gaze turned to Stewart, and the accompanying feeling was like an invisible tendril sloshing around, probing. In short time the man's brow creased with wonder. He said nothing, shifting his stare back to Nickel.

The pale man pulled away slightly and steadied his grip, staring at Nickel's quivering body, then savagely plunged the blade into Nickel's right side between the ribs.

Streams of scarlet trickled up the blade as Nickel screamed out, a shrill sound that ended with a gurgle as the blood flowed up through his lungs and windpipe, then flooded his voicebox. Markuz's grip stayed strong on Nickel's wrist, as well as Stewart's neck.

The blade emitted a guttural rumble, and the scarlet strands of blood slowly filled each spiral embedded in the blade, moving like sap made of ruby light. Nickel could no longer catch his breath. Coughing and retching, his own fluids seemed to be drowning him.

Staring into Nickel's pleading eyes, a slight smile curled over the pale man's colorless lips. As the blade drank of the blood, its roar quieted to a hum once more. The thing shone like fire and diamonds.

When the pale man had plunged the blade into Nickel, Markuz's body pivoted from the force. Stewart, though still gripped tightly in the giant's clutches, now found himself in perfect striking position.

He swung the stone hard into the giant's face, connecting right between the temple and eye. It made a wet and pulpy thud. The giant let go of the men and held his crushed orbital bone. Blood flooded into his eyes, seeping quickly between his fingers and dripping onto the floor. As Stewart and Nickel's bodies were released they dropped to the ground with Markuz. The floor shook mightily when the giant jammed his already battered face into the ground.

Stewart writhed, pinned down beneath Markuz's unconscious body. Fortunately the pale man was more interested in Nickel and the blade.

The pale man's eyes widened in shock as Nickel's body fell forward and tore the blade from his grip. He grabbed it again and tried to rip it from Nickel's side, but the blade, which had turned sideways in the fall, snagged on Nickel's rib and lodged tight. Nickel howled.

Stewart strained while the pale man's attention was diverted. The pale man grunted and pulled as Stewart managed to finally extract himself.

Preoccupied with the blade, the pale man didn't see Stewart

drive the rock straight down on the top of his skull. His chalky hands shot to his bleeding head, leaving the knife sticking out of Nickel's body. The blade was now shining brightly. Stewart swung the rock down again in the same spot, and the blue track suit made a final swish as the pale man's body crumpled onto the carpet.

Crouching down next to Nickel, who was barely breathing, Stewart whispered, "Hang in there, man! I'll get us outta here!"

Nickel spat blood from his mouth and said, "No. Just leave! Pull this fucking knife out of me and take it the fuck out of here. Somebody screwed me!" He coughed up a sinewy clump, then said, "Find Jeb."

Stewart felt dizzy and nauseated as Nickel's eyes filled with a milky substance, and he lay motionless on the floor.

He felt horrible about it, but Stewart couldn't argue with him; it wouldn't be helpful to wait here. He'd have to explain to everyone what had happened, plus very likely lose the knife to someone's evidence shelf. He hadn't the first idea of how to explain all this.

He bent over Nickel and grabbed the handle of the blade. Visions of battle flooded his mind. Men in horned hats and armor, a battle stag standing bloodied on a field, saddled with no rider. A snake poised to strike.

He pulled upon the handle of the blade, found it still wedged in the bone, and had to push it back into Nickel's body slightly before he could free it. Nickel's milky eyes widened as the blade squished. It shook frantically, then stilled itself.

Blood poured onto the rug. Remarkably little was left, Stewart thought.

Nickel's body twitched. Breath rushed out. His eyes found Stewart's, but no recognition was there. Stewart watched while his friend writhed, helpless. A shudder ran through his vocal cords and out of his mouth. Stewart had never seen anyone act this way before, assuming Nickel was in the throes of death, but was not as affected as he thought he would be. He thought of the brave members of his—

"What the hell?" he said aloud, and wrenched his mind from the ancient battlefield overlapping it "Get it together, man!" He felt Nickel's neck, found a pulse.

Stewart hated to leave him here, but saw no other options. He stood over the bodies of Nickel, the pale man, and Markuz. What to do with the goon squad? He knew full well that even influenced by this crazed knife he couldn't just take the life of someone, especially just lying there like that. He had a problem killing certain bugs. Pulling his cell phone from his pocket to call 911, he found it had been crushed in the melee, and he wasn't going to touch the office phone or anything else in here.

His best and most realistic option was just to get the hell out of there as quickly as possible, like Nickel said. It was time to go.

As he made to wipe off the blade, he found it silvery and polished already. His mind bounced from the battlefield to the office, blurring the distinctions. Forcing himself to return the blade to the box, he closed the lid and effectively stopped the visions. Then he wrapped the paper around the box, put it in the trash can, and put the stone paperweight inside, it being the only thing he'd touched other than the blade. He'd watched enough cop shows to know not to leave fingerprints and DNA all over the place, even on a rock. Slick with sweat, he tried his best to keep it from dripping. Who knew what they could do these days? Certainly more than he knew about. Best to just get out of there and hope he got lucky. He felt shitty leaving Nickel, but what could he do?

He wiped his face with his shirt, then took the black trash bag with the blade and stone out of the canister, tied it in a knot, and quickly and quietly walked out of the room.

The hallway was thankfully empty, no one having responded to the men kicking down the door in the middle of the day, not even the janitor. The air smelled different, as if it were electrically charged. He hurried towards the shattered and broken front door.

When he got outside, he looked at Nickel's car. He hadn't grabbed the keys. Shit. There was no way he was going back for them.

He glanced down the street, curiously empty for a city at midday. A woman walking the other way and the huddled rags of someone sleeping in a doorway were the only signs of life he could see.

Sirens sounded from blocks away. Maybe for Nickel, but he didn't see how that was possible. They echoed off the buildings, seemingly nearing, but difficult to tell. Stewart tucked the bag beneath his arm and walked as nonchalantly down the sidewalk as possible for a man whose world had just been turned upside down. He made it a little more than one block before dizziness overtook him, and he had to sit down.

Scooting back behind a large concrete tree planter, he tried to make sense of the reappearance and sudden demise of someone who had come back into his life after so long. To no avail.

From across the street on a ledge three stories high, a mockingbird clicked five little clicks in rapid succession, a signal almost completely lost amidst the siren's wail. It jumped to the wind and flew east. Two others dropped from an adjacent building and followed in its wake.

4

The heat accompanied the dawn, snaking in with the rays of sunlight. Luna stood up under the edge of Buddy's sleeping bag and peeled the cover off him with her teeth so he wouldn't wake in a sweat. She stuck her nose out and sniffed the air.

Max slept outside the tent in a hammock strung between two exposed roots poking skyward. His eyes opened automatically and he nodded to Luna, who set off in a tight circle around the camp to see if any of their signals were disturbed.

She sniffed at an upturned pinecone. Usually it sat in the center of the small overgrown path, but was now laying to the side, underneath a leafy shrub. A partial footprint lay in the dust and pine needles. It smelled of human, mixed with something she didn't recognize. Not her boy or man. Even if it was a random human, they would still have to move their camp. And now.

Max and Luna were prepared for this, and had a second area scoped out. The glaring problem was that it was much closer to Garth's camp. Another were the park rangers and police who drove through the park.

Luna ran back and put her paws up onto the hammock where Max lay staring through the leaves and pine needles up at the sky. He looked in her eyes and knew; this spot had been compromised.

Max started packing everything up quickly yet methodically. He never panicked.

When Buddy yawned and opened his eyes, everything besides his sleeping bag had been rolled up and stacked, ready to go.

"Here, Bud." Max gave him a granola bar and the canteen. "We gotta roll."

Buddy was a little confused by the activity, but if Luna was with it, so was he. Trust. It was a strange feeling, hard to wrap his mind around.

He had dreamt of Jeb. Jeb was a scientist, in his way. The man who had tried to make the others stop shoving the black snares into him. In a dark room, Buddy witnessed a stalemate. Jeb against another man. Buddy understood it to be Jeb's brother, but his face was always hazy. The standoff ended with a terrible fight between the brothers. The blonde woman who called herself Buddy's mother, Nuala, stood and watched from afar as the dream vision swirled into an illuminated web. When it cleared, Jeb was gone, the tendrils of dream snaking off with him.

It was the first dream he had ever remembered. The feeling was awful and scary.

A sharp bark jerked him from his haze. Luna was staring at him with her head cocked. It was time to go.

Max had a backpack with carabiners attaching all the cooking and eating utensils, fastened so that none of the metal clanged together. He looked like a well-laden mule. Luna had little saddlebags on. Max handed Buddy the small daypack and they set off.

Above them was the manicured lawn of the park, below was the street that separated the live oak grove from the golf course. They stuck to a thin trail halfway up the shady hill that sloped to the park, weaving among the shrubs and trees, beneath the palms on the ridge. Max scouted the landscape constantly, but there was no movement. If they were to see someone on this secret trail, it would not be a coincidence.

Along the way Max quietly pointed out more edible plants, many more than Buddy would have thought, as well as tricks for separating out the poisonous ones. Mainly there were plants that would complement a rabbit dinner, if Luna could ever catch one, Max said. Having seen rabbits from the window of the warehouse, one of the few things that had given him any joy, Buddy stayed silent about how unhappy he would be to see any of the rabbits killed, even if they ate it.

They skirted the side of the hill until it dropped through the center of a small canyon separating two wooded hillsides. Crossing over a main pathway, they went straight up the next hill, climbing into a tunnel of plants that obscured another game trail. When they ascended and leveled out amidst a small round of pines, Buddy found they were at the same peninsula as the night before. The point looked down toward the filth of Garth's area. They couldn't actually see his campsite, just shades of a blue tent through the bushes near it. And the glut of trash.

In the opposite direction, concealed by the cusp of a hill, stood a rusty chain-link fence topped with razor wire, impossible to scale without shredding one's hands. Beyond it was a triangular patch of earth twenty feet across, which then dropped off a forty-foot cliff to the city's mechanic yard. This dusty plateau would be their camp.

Max held his hand up. Buddy and Luna waited until he dropped it, then the three scampered down the embankment and along the fence, out of view from anyone in the park. A downed willow branch clump was stuffed inside a big gap beneath the gate. Max pulled it out, shooed the boy and dog through, then hopped through himself and pulled it back inside, watching to make sure they hadn't been seen.

Three willow trees made a dense knot on the peninsula under the fence, and Luna leapt into a break in their branches. Buddy followed, and was astonished to find the trees open up into a perfect little dome that filtered light in, but hid them from the mechanic's spread and the park. It was a little living house, hidden up the cliffside.

Inside were two pallets with one piece of plywood on top, holding them together. When Max had squeezed through the branches, he deposited his large load onto these and started arranging the camp. After he had everything secure, Max said, "You okay?"

"Yeah. Fine," said Buddy.

"Cool. Since time is precious, I'm gonna cut right to it. I've tried to teach you a little bit about the world, and surviving in it. I hope I've done a pretty good job considering we've only had a little time, and we haven't even gotten to the defense yet."

"I think so," Buddy answered.

"Good." Max smiled. "I'm afraid it gets rougher, though. We

need to talk about a couple things. Like how much you know of the web tricks, and what was going on where you were, in the warehouse. We've been tracked by someone, obviously. It happened pretty fast, too, so the odds are somebody's looking for you from that group. We really have to hit that topic now. Sorry. But I think you're man enough to hear a little bit more about what's going on, so get ready."

Buddy put on a brave face and nodded. "I appreciate that, Max."

"Heh," Max looked at him with pride. The kid was tough. "Maybe you will, and maybe you won't. But the truth is, we've both gotta know some things. Sit down, OK?"

Buddy sat cross-legged, and Luna came and plopped herself into his lap, which made him feel brave.

"We're going to start with some tricks," said Max. "I want to know if you've seen anything like this before, if you can remember, alright?"

"OK," said Buddy. "Is this the defensive stuff?"

"Kind of. Look at my hand," Max said. He also sat cross-legged, facing the boy. Luna got up from Buddy's lap, and lay between the two on the dirt floor of the willow dome.

Max hummed, and the center of his palm shimmered and distorted, then grew a bright green filament from the center, like an illuminated hair. The boy watched as it danced and swayed, separating in two lengthwise tendrils. Swirling and twisting, the two became four and continued their dance. The ends stretched themselves out and lightly touched the lowest lying branches of the willow, snaking through and weaving themselves into patterns within the branches and filtered sunlight. All the while the threads of light kept growing from Max's palm until he pursed his lips and made a pop, which sent them wriggling into the branches.

The threads glowed, moving like snakes through the canopy. They slithered over Buddy's head, stopping as if to observe or smell, it seemed. Max held up his hand again, and all but one burrowed back into his palm. He looked at Buddy. The boy was intrigued, but not blown away.

"You seen anything like that before, Buddy?" Max asked. The lone filament wrapped through the branches above his head.

"Yeah, with Jeb, and um . . . " He trailed off, his battered memory unable to recall the other personalities of his imprisonment.

"Wait. You remember Jeb?" asked Max. "You didn't mention him."

"I dreamed about him," said Buddy. "This morning."

Max's eyes narrowed. "Interesting. You remember Jeb's brother's name, or the lady's?"

"Jeb's brother? No. But he was in it. The lady is Nuala," Buddy said, a taste of bile trickling into the back of his throat. "I couldn't see Jeb's brother though. Who is it?"

What's with this kid? Max wondered. Buddy was getting the dreamtime to reveal his memories. And fast.

"His brother's name is Frank," Max said. "That name doesn't mean anything to you? He has really light blue eyes and a hook nose like a bird."

From the stories Max had picked up over the years, Frank did the experiments. Nuala procured the victims. They would then psychologically and physically torture them. When the spirit was broken, the feelings of terror and confusion culminated in a dizzying effect which made the transformations so much more electrifying. Frank had seen that fear heightened the true effects of the snares.

The more Max knew about Frank, the less he liked.

"No. I'm sorry, Max," Buddy said.

"Me too, kid. Maybe it's best if you don't remember Frank for right now. But suffice to say, he's a fucking monster." He leaned close, peering into Buddy's eyes. "You even hear the name Frank, you run the other way, alright? That's another lesson for today."

"OK, I understand." Talking about Frank made Buddy feel sick.

"Good. So what did they teach you about the webs?" asked Max. "Try to remember."

"Mostly they tried to make Oliver and me fight using them." He reached up and rubbed his throat, remembering the throttlings the older boy put on him. "I'm not good at it. He isn't either, though, so he would just beat the hell out of me with his fists while they watched. It wasn't fair."

Max held up his index finger. "Hold on, Bud. Fair is what you make it sometimes. I know being in that warehouse was a heavy burden for you to bear, but if they didn't pit you against him, you wouldn't know as much as you do about them, or the webs. At this point in time, it's probably a good thing you got trained a little bit. Now, I can't imagine why they'd train you at all, but the fact that they did means that you have the recipe for victory"

"Yeah, but I don't remember," Buddy protested.

"You will. Just hold on. Training is hard in these things. I wasn't too much older than you when my world was rocked. Now, I wasn't imprisoned for my youth or anything, but when my cousin and I stumbled upon the web it was horrifying and we had no one to teach us anything, and it almost killed us. We dealt with that as kids, before we figured out how to control the strands. If we didn't meet up with Helen, I don't know what would have happened. She's gonna help you, too."

Buddy couldn't wait to meet Helen.

The new location seemed to be secure, and the hours slid by as Max tried to help Buddy with the threads of light. Buddy was right; he didn't seem that talented with it. It didn't concern Max, as different people had different ways of manifesting the webs. Obviously the kid had something going on, or Frank and his asshole friends wouldn't have kept him for so long. He peeked at dream control already. Maybe that was his best defense.

"We're gonna try something now," said Max.

"I want you to clear your mind, and shut your eyes. When you feel a bad thought come from me to you, I want you to slap it away with your mind and throw it back at me."

"What? That's insane," said Buddy.

"It is with that attitude. Trust me. Just try it."

Buddy did as Max instructed, breathing deep. He felt a cold coil creep into his brain, tasting of steel, and curled into a ball on the floor. Fear saturated him. The feeling receded when he heard Max's voice.

"It's okay, Buddy," he said, shaking the boy's shoulder. "But I think you can do better. "

Buddy had to learn some of this if he was to survive. He knew that. "Let's go," he said.

This time, when the cold tendrils entered into his head, he

deflected them and lashed out, traveling along the tendril with his own strike to its source.

He heard Max cough, and opened his eyes. Max spit and hacked, doubled over. When he straightened out again, he had tears welled up in his eyes.

"Damn, Buddy," he said between hacks, "I'd say you got some skills already."

Buddy was as shocked as Max. "Sorry! Oh man, I'm so sorry, Max."

Max grinned, then tousled Buddy's hair. "Not at all, my man. I'm happy. You should be, too."

And Buddy was.

"Do you remember what Jeb was working on for his brother?" Max asked after catching his breath.

"There was a silver knife. Like a tube with carvings on it. It could do really crazy things to people, like take part of them inside it. Then they'd be kind of like puppets." The more Buddy spoke, the more details came to him. "Jeb was working on making other ones, like black cones, but he had some trouble at first. I think eventually he got it, but then he didn't want someone to have them, maybe that guy you were talking about. That's when he left, I think."

He looked off in the distance. "He was working on something else, also. Something he never told his brother about . . ." His voice trailed off as he stared blankly.

"Well, what was it?" Max asked eventually.

"I can't remember exactly, but it has to do with the control of the web things you were talking about," Buddy said. "Like how to make more people see them, maybe. Revealers, is what he called them."

"Hmm. Where did Jeb go, do you know?"

"He's in the canyon."

"Which one?" asked Max. "There's tons around here, you know."

"I don't know."

It was time to give the little guy a break. Or himself. Max looked down to the road at the bottom of the hill. Close to his face, one tendril still slithered in the willow canopy.

A hummingbird landed on a willow branch, twitted something,

and flew off again. The filament shook, made a sound like air escaping a balloon and widened out, then shot from the branches back into Max's hand. His eyes perked.

He grabbed the empty daypack. "Shit. There's something I have to go get, Buddy. You stay here with Luna. I'll be right back." He threw a towel in the bag, and nothing else. "If you run into trouble, try to do that thing you did to me."

"What?!" Buddy couldn't believe it. "Does it have to be now?"

"Sorry, man," Max said. "But it does."

Buddy and Luna watched Max plug the hole with the knot of branches and disappear down the hill, and a pit of terror opened up deep within the boy. What would he possibly do if Max didn't return?

The minutes dragged by. Every sound made him jump.

Max was only gone a half hour, but it seemed like a week to Buddy. He felt like crying tears of relief when Max returned with the daypack full and heavy.

"How was it, little man?" He pulled out several curved pieces of broken black-and-white lined pottery.

"Long. And horrible." He watched Max line the shards up next to each other, then pull three unbroken bowls from inside the burlap bag.

"Long, eh? Seemed like only a couple minutes to me. Weird, that."

Buddy looked at the bowls. "That's what you had to leave me out here for?"

"Yup," said Max.

Buddy sighed and moved over to help. When he touched the first shard, a vision birthed. A cave. Ancient Earth. Talons and hands. He let the pottery fragment drop to the ground.

Max chuckled. "Powerful shit."

"Wow," said Buddy. "Where'd you get them?"

"Found 'em. Somebody threw 'em out. I think I've got the whole set, now."

Max assembled the shards with superglue, but the bowl was still missing some pieces.

In Max's set, the smallest bowl was the size of Buddy's fist, the largest twice that of his head. Of the three complete ones, the grooves did their best to line up, but small pieces had been lost to dust. Still, they were bowls.

"Well, I'll just have to show you what I've got already," said Max.

He reached into the pack and pulled out a car battery, some wires, and an old record player/speaker combo briefcase. Buddy recognized the car parts, having seen stripped-down trucks and cars occasionally in the warehouse. The record player was new to him.

While he worked, Max spoke about music, and Buddy remembered a song from long ago. What was it?

"Alright, Buddy, here's a record."

The needle dropped upon the spinning vinyl, and through the crackle came a song sung by a woman. A beautiful yet sinister melody came from the band backing her. Buddy's hairs stood up on his arms. He was enchanted. Haunted. He forgot about his memory, and let this song wash over his mind. When it ended, Buddy had tears rolling down his cheeks. He turned away from Max to hide them.

"Don't worry about that, little man. That's the power of music, that's what I was telling you about. Shit, I feel like that sometimes, too."

Buddy wiped the rest away.

"You ready? Alright. So, all these bowls, they're like records. People's hands act like that needle and record the sounds into this clay when they make 'em."

He brought out a flashlight set on a customized stand with a metal guard on it. When he turned the light on, a pinpoint beam shone through the tiny hole in the guard. He replaced the record with a bowl, positioned the light, and turned up the volume.

The light ran across the grooves on the bowl, and the sounds of children playing and women laughing in an unknown language came from the speakers. He felt himself transported to the room they were made in, long ago, and could feel the sense of peace.

After a minute, Max replaced the bowl. The next one had sounds of wailing and screaming, a chorus of mayhem. A voice frantically whispered in the same language as the other bowl, but not a woman's voice. A man's. Buddy inched away from the speakers. Max took it off.

The third was the new one. It had blood caked on several of its corners. When Max played it they heard another voice. This one was chilling; a cool, methodical drone in an ancient tongue. Joining it was a voice pleading in English. "Get away! Stay away from me! No!"

A blood-curdling scream rang from the speakers, then stopped suddenly when the light hit a hole in the clay. Max repositioned the light, farther down toward the base of the bowl.

A voice said, "That is how one creates the legendary—" The light hit another hole, then, "—you see?"

Luna growled, but the voice had stopped. Max turned off the flashlight.

"That sucked," Buddy said.

"Yeah," agreed Max.

He was putting the bowls in the bag when the hummingbird came back. It clicked with its tongue, and Max's body stiffened, eyes wide. Buddy hadn't seen Max rankled like that, and it scared him. When the hummingbird shot away, Luna growled.

"Listen to me," said Max, his eyes deadly serious. "Someone is coming for you right now. And I have to go become a diversion so they don't find you. In order to do that I have to leave right away. I don't know how long it will take."

"Can I go with you?" asked Buddy, desperate.

"No. Sorry," said Max. "We can't let anything happen to you. What I'm gonna do is too dangerous."

"More dangerous than staying here alone?"

"You may not believe me, but yes. Very. I need to go do this by myself. I'll be back before it gets dark, if I can. But if I'm not, Helen's coming back. She'll know what to do. Okay? Meanwhile, stay on this side of the fence. You got this," he said, reaching into one of the bags and handing Buddy a short club with a leather strap connected to the handle.

"If anyone comes in here, you wallop them with this, okay?" Max set off under the fence and through the high bushes.

Luna whined to Buddy and brushed her head on his knee.

"I know, girl," said Buddy. "I've got a bad feeling, too."

5

Buddy peered beyond the fence into the bushes. He shivered, though he wasn't cold. Luna sat next to him, her muscles rigid.

The sun was setting. It would be dark soon, and Max had said he'd be back before that. As the shadows grew, Buddy walked over and rechecked the willow branches that plugged up the entrance.

A sharp crack of two colliding rocks sounded just beyond the wire, in a thicket of plants. Buddy froze.

Luna jumped up. Buddy picked up the club and stood behind her, a few feet from the cliffs. He looked down. It was a long drop.

A twig cracked, and he saw a rock the size of a grapefruit sailing down from high above the fence, arcing for Luna's head. Buddy reacted instantly, batting the rock with the club before it hit her.

The smack of wood on stone so close to her ears startled the dog, and she leaped backward. She shot too far, and disappeared over the cliff, pistoning her muscular legs in midair.

"Luna!" Buddy screamed, then lost her in the shadows.

His wrist throbbed. As he tried to rub some feeling into it, he smelled an acrid stench. He recoiled from the sting of urine and vomit. The bushy area that the rock had sailed from moved, and Garth oozed out of the bushes.

"Hey, Buuuddy," he said, a drunken slur stretching his words out. His crust-caked hands pushed and pulled at the willow bundle.

Buddy swung the club and smacked the area of chain-link fence directly in front of Garth's face. Garth flinched, then began jerking the willow plug back and forth manically, breaking it apart after a few seconds. Handfuls of twigs and branches flew into the air.

Buddy tried to hold the remaining branches steady, which he quickly realized was a terrible plan as Garth jerked the mass toward himself and pulled Buddy's face and chest hard into the fence. A cut opened up on the boy's forehead, another on his lip. Blood trickled around the bridge of his nose and into his mouth. He sat stunned a few feet from the fence as Garth ripped the last of the willow branches from the hole.

Garth got on his knees and wriggled through the small opening until the steel cut into his flesh. His body was too big. He fought on, impervious in his drunken state, hands splaying along the ground, clawing for purchase. The pointed ends of the steel wires peeled swirls of flesh off his back as he gained ground.

Buddy brought the club down hard on Garth's hand. His wrist sparked again with pain as he hit. He switched hands. Garth had his body up to the waist through the hole, his clothes and flesh on his back shredded and bloody.

Buddy swung again with his left, but the delivery was weak. The fat man took advantage and backhanded the club off the edge of the cliff.

Buddy stepped back and threw a stone at Garth's face. It smacked squarely on his cheek, and a hollow thunk filled the air. Garth's face grew beet red. He shredded his back and ass on the fence, bursting the rest of the way into the camp. Buddy barely avoided Garth's flailing arms as the drunk stood up.

"C'mere, you li'l mother fugger!" Garth slurred.

Buddy tried to jump around him to get through the fence, but Garth's body was still too close to it. The man's meaty fingers swooshed through the air as he just missed grabbing Buddy's shirt. He'd have to lure Garth out toward the cliffs to be able to shoot through.

He inched backward and stood a foot from the cliff's edge, his left foot planted behind him on a small willow stump whose roots still anchored into the shifty red sandstone, making it one of the few stable sites on the lip. He looked at Garth and said as clearly as he could, "Come over here if you want me, you fucking shithead."

Garth was fueled by drunken indignation, and was not going to be insulted by some little kid. He crouched down and prepared to pounce. When the horizon straightened itself out he was gonna do this.

"Any day now, you fucking idiot," said Buddy. He could smell the filth rolling off the man.

The quickness of Garth's reaction surprised Buddy. Garth used all his energy to propel himself, and Buddy's duck was too slow. As Garth sailed over Buddy's head, heading off the edge of the cliff, he snatched onto the boy's shirt collar and pulled Buddy backward into the abyss with him.

Buddy lurched forward with all his might, barely staying on the cliff. He had nowhere to slide. His shirt was choking him, and he teetered on the precipice with Garth hanging off, both of them about to fall down the cliff onto the pile of discarded metal on the asphalt below.

Buddy kicked his legs out behind him and dropped onto the stump, holding it with both hands just below his chin. His hands felt as if they'd rip off his arms as Garth hung off his body.

Every joint strained, elongating. Buddy twisted and writhed, trying to shake loose, but made himself slip and start to fall further in the process. Garth found purchase. Slowly but surely, he climbed up the boy. Buddy's strength was about to fail. Garth had both hands on Buddy's shoulders now, and still was ascending.

They heard a growl. Luna burst from the darkness, sprinting toward them. Buddy ducked his head hard to the earth, and she sailed closely over him, chomping down on Garth's face when she landed. All three swayed backward with the force of the dog. About to careen off, Buddy weaved his arm into the willow roots up to his armpit and folded his arms together, gaining a grip on the small rooted stump.

Garth tried to keep a hold of Buddy and simultaneously hit the dog off his face. Growling filled the air as Luna twisted her body and avoided the blow, keeping her jaws locked on Garth's lip and cheek. Blood flowed and gurgled while Garth attempted a scream. The fluid bubbled into Luna's mouth, and the acrid taste burned her senses. She almost had to let go, but bit down harder, thrashing her head back and forth. A gout of blood shot out from his shredded face.

The roots of the small stump exposed themselves as the

shifting weight started to rip it from the cliff. Buddy was powerless to do anything but hang on.

Luna chomped down again, hard. Finally both of Garth's bloated hands released the boy to bat the dog off of him. Luna kicked hard off his chest, propelling herself onto the edge of the cliff. She began to slide down. Buddy grabbed her scruff with his free arm, then pulled her safely to his chest.

Garth reached for Buddy as he fell backwards, but the boy was just out of his range. He fell head first into the dark, screaming, then landed with a loud crash atop the tangle of steel in the repair yard below.

Luna hopped up onto the dusty cliff from Buddy's arms. He grabbed her collar, then dislodged his other arm from the roots. Luna pulled hard while he scrambled up. They lay on the ground exhausted before chancing a look down.

The area below was cloaked in shadow. There was no way to tell what happened to Garth from here, but either way it was time to go.

They had to find Helen.

Buddy stuffed the bags while Luna patrolled the cliff's edge. A cold wind blew up the cliff's face. He made sure to pack the camping equipment into the first duffel bag he'd take, like the small stove and the sleeping bag.

Luna brushed up against his leg. The boy reached down and scratched her head. "Yeah, I've got you girl. Thankfully," he said.

Precipitation had crept inland from the ocean air, making the trek down and back up the canyon slippery with mud. The cold and warm weather fronts collided, and storm clouds shot upward into the sky, illuminated from the lights of the city. Soon fat raindrops began to fall, making the canyon sound alive in the dark. Buddy's shoes could not find a grip on anything, and it took him a considerable amount of time to lug the bag backwards up a wet trail that ran next to the fence. The trees helped, providing handholds up the hill. Luna assisted him as much as she could, which consisted of biting the back pocket of his jeans and pulling, something Buddy was unsure helped at all, but couldn't hurt.

Soon they were able to make out a green domed tent beneath a tangle of plants above them on the wet hillside. The rain began to fall in earnest as they scrambled up the hill near the camp. They would not be going back for the rest of the stuff tonight. He hoped it stayed dry.

There was no sound from inside when they reached the entrance. Buddy was scared, but they needed to get out of the rain.

Without warning, Luna disappeared into the tent through a small side flap. Buddy peeled it back and looked in at Luna sitting in the middle of the tent, tail wagging. The smell of sage trickled to his nostrils. Inside the empty tent was homey and comfortable looking.

He lugged the bag into the tent and shoved it into the corner, then pulled a towel from the bag and wiped his face, Luna's fur, and the bag. The ebb and flow of adrenaline began to catch up with him, and the warm, dry tent with its swirling aromas made Buddy sleepy. Pictures danced in his mind.

Luna had curled into a ball near the head of the bed and peeked at the child from the corner of her eye, then shut it and gave one heaving sigh. Buddy slipped off his shoes and pulled the cover over himself and the dog, listening to the raindrops on the tent as he drifted off.

6

Stewart stood up. The street was still deserted. Good. None of the windows showed anyone inside the surrounding buildings, either. The sirens were blaring as they came closer. He walked away from them.

He'd been sweating steadily since the office. Looking down at his shirt, he saw Nickel's blood sprayed all over it, mixed with his own perspiration in a gruesome swirl. He looked into a window beside him, and jerked back in shock at the blood-smeared face looking back. Ducking into a doorway, he pulled the shirt off, rubbing his face vigorously with it. He put it back on inside out and walked away, looking at his reflection again to see if he'd made a difference. Thankfully, he had.

Nickel's office building was in an industrial area just east of downtown, where tent cities flourished beneath the freeways and the more ragged citizens drew scarcely a sidelong glance. He walked on, unnoticed, heading for his house and his car. Checking his pockets, he had his keys, wallet with thirty-seven dollars in it, broken phone, and a lighter.

He was pissed about the phone until he wondered who he would call anyway. Someone to come pick him up while he waited, covered in blood? Too many variables. He'd have to explain his situation, and he really didn't want to do that. Walking was the only option. It was only a couple miles anyway. He stuck to whatever shadows he could find, not plentiful on a sunny midday.

It was about a half-mile to his neighborhood of Golden Hill, which he reached without incident. He climbed a steep hill and took the first left, along the razor-wire perimeter of the city mechanic's garage.

The driveway he walked down was filled with empty police vehicles awaiting their turns to be fixed. To the immediate west stretched the concrete expanse of the maintenance area; a long stretching group of garages and offices that trailed up beside the southern reach of Florida Canyon. On the eastern side of the driveway were eucalyptus trees and palms in a narrow strip, and beyond them a hill sloped down and back up into wooded canyons among the southeastern reaches of the park.

Slipping through the small canyon and up into the trees, Stewart could just make out his apartment building through the branches, still quite far away. The huge stucco Spanish Colonial masterpiece, with stairways and balconies covered in bougainvillea, shone against the blue sky, cotton clouds floated above.

He plunged into the trail covered over with sagebrush and scrub willow, instantly relieved to be out of sight in a familiar area. He trudged through the plants until he was under the burly twisted limbs of a coastal live oak, centered in the mouth of the dusty ravine. The tree's bark was grey and cracked with age.

Crouching in the shade, he looked for leaves rustling or anything that would signify his being followed. Seeing nothing save a few small brown birds flitting around, he relaxed a little, and sat with his back to the trunk of the oak, panting. He crabwalked around the trunk until he could see his apartment building in the distance. The big stucco building looked peaceful. Everything was looking entirely too calm since Nickel's office. Not that he was complaining. It was just weird.

His balcony was on the top floor, and something was moving on it. It unexpectedly jumped off, fanning out its large wings as it took to the air. Some sort of bird. Shit. The mockingbird?

As it neared, Stewart realized it was a massive raven. It pulled its wings in toward its body, shooting out of the sky directly for Stewart's tree, then straightened them out and dove beneath the outlying branches before swooping up and silently alighting near the trunk. The bird looked old as it eyeballed Stewart and flapped its ragged wings, wide as the tree branches.

It croaked out a syllable which echoed upon itself, and calmed Stewart's rankled nerves with its tone, beyond any rational explanation. Surely the bird had not actually spoken, yet its voice had the effect of a parent assuring a child that everything would work out fine, however unlikely that may be. Its glinting eye stared at him between the old leathery cracks of its face.

"Seriously?" Stewart asked. "It's clear? It's okay?"

The raven clicked a deeper tone, making Stewart's body sway as if a wave had pushed against him. It dropped under the wide branches of the oak, catching a thermal current and gliding away down the canyon.

Stewart stared in disbelief as it faded into the distance. There was apparently a whole new set of rules in this life he was completely unaware of. Things were just getting more and more strange.

He recalled Nickel's eyes as he lay on the floor. The milkiness. This whole day was ridiculous. The mockingbird. Nickel. Jeb. The two goons. The knife. Now another bird communicating with him. Or whatever that may have been. It made him wonder what that little mockingbird was trying to say that morning.

He started the uphill creep to his building, easily navigating the paths through the desert brush, making it to an old grown-over staircase. Its steps were reinforced by roots running along them, some twisting and also serving as handholds. Stairs over a hundred years old with a history lost ages ago. He stopped at the very top, next to an old fountain. After scanning the area he walked quickly across the street to his building, toting the bagged-up knife tucked under his arm.

Cora Vasquez, the girl in number 16, greeted him on her way down. Stewart smiled and waved without stopping.

Mrs. Myers, the manager in 3, whom Stewart had known for close to twenty-three years now, called his name as he jumped past her. Mrs. Myers was Stewart's landlord as well as a close friend of his mom. Inevitably this had led to his being the de facto handyman around the place, which would have been unfortunate had it not been for the greatly reduced rent.

He answered that he really had to use the bathroom, and he'd talk to her in just a bit.

Once inside his place, he swung the door shut quickly, locking both his locks.

As he walked through his house, he was a little surprised to find everything the way he had left it, assuming the big bird had been with someone. He grabbed a small duffel and placed the silver knife in its box in the center, surrounded and protected by a towel. Then he put the stone paperweight in a planter box on his balcony.

From just beyond his front door, barely audible, a raspy wheeze sounded. The doorknob rattled as two feet cast shadows through the crack at the bottom.

Stewart froze. He expected to be followed, but this was too quick.

The doorknob rattled again, louder.

Grabbing the bag, he glided backwards onto his balcony, slid the glass door shut, and crept up onto the thick rail. There was one other balcony on his upper level, even and parallel to his own: number 16. Just a few feet away. Stewart leaped across the divide, rolling when he landed, then scooted back toward his own balcony. A pounding, followed by a loud crack, then sounds of splintering wood came from his apartment.

Stewart thought of trying to make it up onto the roof. Too late, he thought, and tucked his back against the wall even tighter, hoping he was shielded completely from whoever followed him. His stomach fought with itself.

He could hear guttural snarls mixed with the sounds of his possessions being strewn around, then the glass door to his apartment sliding open. The snarls turned to a giggle that sounded so wrong and twisted Stewart's toes curled in his shoes. A high squealing peal of laughter, facing Stewart's hiding place.

He wrapped the handle of his tote bag around his hand tightly, ready to smash it into the thing's face. It was flush to the floor, poised to strike. Hopefully the old box would withstand the force of a face bash.

The laugher's breath panted and giggled, inches from the balcony, hanging almost above Stewart. Whatever it was, it was probably seeing the end of the bag, possibly even his clenched fist. Stewart waited, ready. As soon as he saw anything peek over the balcony it was going to have the bag launched into its face hard and fast.

He stared straight up at the handrail, shaking and sweating, hearing the laughing close in. The frantic moment lingered, tense.

Screeching ripped through the air, and out of the sky three dark streaks sliced through Stewart's vision. Cacophonous chirps and shrieks rang out after the blur, and feathers flew in a cloud from Stewart's balcony.

The warped voice squealed.

"AACK! What?!" It sounded familiar. A thud shook the building, and he heard his little bench clatter along his balcony, then gurgling noises from the laugher. High-pitched squawks rang from the birds.

"Fakkoffme!" the voice spat.

The gurgling retreated into Stewart's apartment. The birds continued screeching and squawking until he heard the glass door slam shut. His racing heart began to calm as the voice faded back inside. He could hear it now grumble, now shout from room to room.

The destruction continued as the laugher ransacked his apartment. Eventually the thrashing stopped. Footsteps faded, then silence.

Still staring up at the sky, daring not move, Stewart jumped when the little mockingbird from that morning hopped onto the railing. He froze, wondering if it was going to attack him now that it had him in the open, but it gave a little click of its tongue and flew over to the locked glass door instead.

The other two mockingbirds landed. He realized any of them could actually be that morning's terror. This is what it feels like to lose your shit, he thought. A shell game. With birds.

The first bird hopped up near the door and flapped its wings, hovering in front of the lock. Its voice made a soft *clock clock* sound, then a swishing chirp, and the lock sprung open. It flitted back to Stewart, razzing.

Stewart's eyes were wide as he scooted on his belly over to the door. He reached up and pulled it open. Looking back in wonder to the birds, he crawled inside and slowly slid it shut.

Everything was hushed inside Cora's apartment, as if the sound had been sucked out through a vacuum. Making a hiss through his teeth to make sure he hadn't gone deaf, he was relieved to hear a sound, though it died immediately, with no echo. The room was darkened by thick curtains and smelled of herbs. Books lined bookshelves everywhere. Trinkets and pictures hung from the walls.

Stewart crept through, stopping at the door. He pulled it open, just a crack at first. Sound rushed through the gap. No wheezing laugh, no thrashing around, just a breeze whistling, distant voices, cars. Sounds he was used to.

He walked into the hallway, looking at his splintered door and resisting the urge to check out his apartment. At the staircase, he looked down into the courtyard. Nothing stirred. Slipping down the stairs to the arched entryway, he looked back, making sure for the billionth time today that he wasn't being followed, and ran straight into Cora, spilling the iced tea she was drinking all over her shirt.

"Stewart! Watch it!" she said, swiping at the spill with her hand. "Damn!"

"Oh! I'm so sorry, Cora. I didn't see you." He tried to help her, but most of the spill was confined to her general breast area, so his hand hovered between them.

She stared at the hand until he put it down. "Apparently. Where are you sneaking off to so soon?"

"Sneaking? I'm not sneaking off anywhere, uh . . . nowhere. Um . . ."

"It's OK, Stewart, it's just a word I use. Did your friend Nickel find you?"

"What? Oh, this morning? Yeah, I saw him earlier."

"No. Like five minutes after you went upstairs, he ran past me. He was all grumbling and sick-looking. He asked if you were upstairs. I said I thought so. Does he do drugs? He wouldn't look in my eyes, and he kept laughing and stuff. His eyes looked really cloudy, plus I could hardly tell what he was talking about when he wasn't laughing. I just pointed up the stairs to get rid of him."

Stewart looked blank. He felt sick again.

"Drugs? Probably. And I can't understand him at all, to be quite honest with you. Well, he came and went, I guess."

"You guess? You were home, dude," Cora looked puzzled. She shrugged and walked toward the stairs.

Stewart watched her go, baffled. He had to get going. It wouldn't be long until Cora saw the door to his apartment laying all over the hallway. He didn't want to deal with that just yet.

Stewart owned a rusty Japanese beater from a bygone era. He rarely drove it, and it was pretty unpredictable when he did. But he needed to find Jeb. He had no idea where to start, but he had to try.

He assumed he was being watched, and tried to stay behind cover, looking underneath his car to see if there was a bomb or tracking device. Not that he would even know what one looked like.

His driver's side door didn't work. It had jammed a year ago. He slid into the car from the passenger side and moved over. It started on the first try. Stewart was marveling at this good fortune when the car gave a mighty backfire, like a blast from a shotgun. It stopped the engine dead.

"Shitass," he whispered.

A small dog looked at Stewart from across the intersection by the liquor store.

He tried the engine again. Nothing. Not a click. He stared through the windshield, anger boiling, forcing himself not to punch the car. His knuckles gleamed white as he strangled the steering wheel.

As his hope waned, the three mockingbirds landed on the hood of the car and clicked their tongues at him. One flew to a big brown sunburned Buick, hovering by the lock on the door. Cora's car. The bird made a whirring sound, and Stewart saw the lock on the Buick pop up.

The sliding glass door was one thing, and Stewart was too frantic then to even think about it, but now the bird had unlocked a car door with nothing but sound. His world felt like it was tilting. Did the bird want him to steal Cora's car?

He got out of his busted ride and slid into her's. The bird hopped in after him, sat on his right knee, and made a click with its tongue, which started the motor.

" I bet that doesn't get old," Stewart said.

The bird whistled as they pulled from the curb.

On the balcony, Cora Vasquez burned sage and willow bark in a silver bowl as she whispered a forgotten chant and watched her car being stolen. Her dark, thin hands made symbols dance in smoke and shadow.

• • •

The office was dark. Frank's hand trembled with exhilaration as he set down the metal orb. It rocked back and forth on the desk, teetering on the lip of the words inscribed along its face.

It was an ancient tongue, one lost to man. His brother had deciphered their meaning, trying several times before finding exactly the proper intonation to unlock the power of the orbs, but Jeb had taken them when he left.

In his haste he left one behind that was of a very curious nature; when the words etched into it were spoken just so, it allowed the speaker to gain control of someone whose spirit was ensnared. Distance didn't seem to matter, nor did who held the vessel. Only this orb was necessary. It was an exquisite bit of knowledge. Total control. Bound by the black orb.

Sitting back in his chair, Frank let the excitement wash over him. The first time inside someone else's skin had been a partial success, so the takeover wasn't the problem. On the contrary, it had gone without a hitch.

The problem was that even in the commandeered body, he hadn't been able to locate and retrieve the blade. Damned birds.

He would get better at it.

"Thanks to you," Frank said to the milky-eyed Craig James, who sat in the corner staring at nothing.

7

Birdsong awoke Buddy and Luna. The sun shone on the last raindrops dripping from leaves when Buddy opened the flap. There was still no sign of Helen. He hoped it was her tent.

Max was supposed to have brought back food. They were nearly out. A granola bar and some rice from a Mexican food joint was all, and it didn't look like this tent was very well-stocked, either. Buddy found a nearly-empty bag of cashews near the pillow and offered one to Luna, who gingerly took it and ate it. She refused a second one, trotting out of the tent and down the hill.

Buddy pushed his duffel into the corner, then put some of their host's clothing on top of it and hoped it would be safe. The granola bar and some water served as a quick breakfast. Then he set off after Luna to the willow camp. She bounced ahead, barking.

He rounded a tangled shrub, and saw Luna with her forepaws on a frightened cottontail. As he approached the animal, the rabbit gave a horrified squeal. Brilliant filaments of golden light shot from its mouth. Like the ribbons of web that Max had shown him, but wilder. The tails of light spasmed and jerked, thin and precise. They stilled, then shot beneath Buddy's skin.

When they made contact with him, his mind was set ablaze with the pain and fear of the rabbit. A few also touched on Luna, who recoiled from shock, confused that this meal had just communicated with her Her appetite waned instantly.

The rabbit's tendrils loosed themselves from Luna, connecting to Buddy and burrowing into his skin. He twitched and spasmed, the ribbons filling his mind with the wind of the chase, the blessed escape, hiding in broad daylight. The rabbit's spirit, not of his particular animal alone but of all rabbitkind. Stealth. Speed. Treachery. The tricks of one of the tricksters.

Luna barked repeatedly at the rabbit, but whenever she inched closer to it a solitary tendril would shock her backward. Eventually she kept her distance. It seemed the boy was alright, but she growled anyway.

Visions of desert landscapes flew through Buddy's mind. In his inner sight he witnessed a clearing with all manner of webs stretching as far as he could see, even up into the sky. He stood breathless as the thousands of different colored threads weaved themselves into a pattern. The longer he beheld the pattern, the more it familiarized itself, until he finally found himself looking into the face of a giant rabbit made of light.

Deep undertones vibrated as the massive rabbit's mind melded with Buddy's. The tendrils pulsated, sending ripples down its fur, forming systems of nerves and muscle. Buddy found himself blinded. Inwardly, the rabbit spoke, and Buddy found his mind expanding with the creature's words. He understood.

The rabbit unwound itself, tendrils flowing off into the canyon air. Then it was gone. All at once Buddy was looking at the tiny rabbit. It jumped and disappeared into the brush. Buddy stood still.

When he felt he could move again, Buddy and Luna continued on the path to willow camp and their belongings. The ground was still muddy, and he slipped, but quickly righted himself. Luna looked surprised at his grace. Step by step, he found a new agility he'd never felt.

Things had changed.

They cautiously made their way back to willow camp, not wanting to rush into an ambush by Garth again. Luna crept ahead and barked when the coast was clear. The rain had washed the blood from the fence where Buddy's face had rammed into it. He ran his tongue over his lips and tasted the scabs.

They ducked under the fence and Buddy began bundling everything up. Max had been steadfast about making sure they didn't leave anything behind. They strapped everything to themselves, then looked at the car battery. It wasn't going to make it. Buddy wrapped it in a plastic shopping bag and stuffed it under the bushes.

When they were set to depart, Buddy looked down the cliff. At the bottom was a pile of wreckage, steel ducts and vents that had been ripped from one of the old garages, thrown into a pile. Red streaks were the only sign anything had happened down there. Garth was gone.

Voices sounded from below, and Buddy ducked back. When he looked again, no one was there. Out of the corner of his eye he saw two men conversing all the way across the yard. He could not only read the lips, but hear their conversation, so far away. He looked around in disbelief, but it was true. Every word.

"Where?"

"Behind barn two," came the reply. "There's shit scattered around and a bunch of blood, kind of washed around in the rain, but it's definitely blood."

"Maybe a coyote fell off the cliff in the rain." said the first man.

"I've never heard of that, but maybe."

They made their way across the yard, walking quickly. Buddy didn't need to know what they thought of the whole thing. If what Max had told him of the police were true, there were going to be people all over the area soon. He stuffed himself through the hole in the fence, avoiding the bits of flesh hanging from the steel.

The first voice rang out when the men had reached the bottom of the cliff. To Buddy's heightened awareness it sounded as if they were right next to him. His muscles, before he knew what was happening, released themselves, making him buck and run.

The bushes raced by in a blur as he covered the length of the canyon in seconds. Luna whined as he stopped far away from her. She ran to catch up, trotting at first, but when Buddy shot away from her it was much quicker. She ran. Buddy ran faster. Luna dropped into a dead sprint, charging as hard as she could, and only then could she match his speed. In wonder, they sprinted around and through the trees and bushes along the hidden pathways of the park, forgetting for a moment the danger they were in and reveling in the gift that the rabbit had bestowed upon the boy.

Buddy let out a laugh that grew and grew. It sounded strange to his ears, and tears of happiness ran down his cheeks as he cavorted with Luna. Sheer joy, never before felt.

From up a hill, several cottontails observed the scene. When it came to pass that Luna espied the little rabbits, rather than giving chase as before, she dipped her head.

The pair ran off into the park, staying out of sight, running until they were both out of breath. The duffel was still outside of the fence when they returned for it.

The sun beat down, drying the earth rapidly as they lugged the last of the gear up the hill to the green tent. Though easier than the night before, there were still slick spots that the sun hadn't touched. It was already very hot, though still early. The green tent lay in the shade of a palm tree and several oaks and shrubs, considerably cooler than most of the park.

As they neared the tent, Buddy thought he heard noises from inside. The soft rustling and breath of someone asleep. He could sense a presence, and crept closer to the opening, then reached out to open the flap.

As soon as he made a slight gap in the fabric, Luna charged into the tent. Buddy watched through the flap as the dog scooted over to a large snoring woman and began to lick her face.

Helen awoke and broke into a deep and earnest laugh. Her body shook as she laughed with delight at the sight of the dog.

She scratched Luna behind her ears, and said, "Ooh baby, Luna! How are you girl? Good to see you! Where's that beautiful man Max at, Luna? Huh?"

Luna's tail went crazy again when the lady said her name, and she let out a soft whine. "And who's that little boy outside my tent? Huh, girl?"

Buddy couldn't help but smile at the lady when she peeked at him, spreading joy naturally. He peeled back the flap and came inside the tent a bit further. The warmth and comfort inside was intoxicating. Even more so with the woman inside. As the smells perked parts of his memory, his head swooned a little bit.

"Are you Helen?" He knew, but he thought he should ask.

"Yes, I am, sugar," she said, nodding. "And I already know who you are. That is, I think I do. You are the boy from the warehouse?"

"Yes. My name is Buddy."

"Well, hello, Buddy." She scratched the dog's ear. "That's a cool name, Sugar."

"Max gave it to me."

"He did, did he? And where is Max, Sugar?"

"Someone followed us," said Buddy, "He had to go lose them, I think."

"Jesus. When? How long has he been gone?"

"Since yesterday."

Helen's eyes and nostrils flared, her skin flushed red. "Are you joking with me, Sugar? Were you okay?" she asked, noticing his split lip. Her hand moved toward his face slowly. The boy flinched, but she brought her hand down on his shoulder. The smell of dried herbs filled his nostrils with her touch, and his cuts and wounds felt better instantly.

"We were, after the whole Garth deal," he said. "That was scary. Not as bad as when we left the warehouses, though."

"What? Who? What do you know about Garth, Sugar?" Helen was astonished.

Buddy told her of their battle with Garth, and Helen fell silent. When she next spoke, there was no more humor in her voice. "Did Max say who he was trying to protect you from?"

"No."

"Goddamn that man."

Buddy hung his head. "Did I upset you?"

"You? Oh, baby, come here. I'm not upset at you. Max is just a maverick sometimes is all. He's still a hell of a man. He left to keep you safe, and I'm sure he's fine. The main thing is that you, my little man, are okay." She ruffled his hair playfully. "You'll overcome this and a lot more when I'm finished with you. Am I right?"

"I guess so," replied Buddy, sheepishly.

"Wait, you guess so? I know so. Everybody has it rough at some point. Look at me! There's some people who pity me and say how I got it bad because I don't have a house, but the truth is I used to have a house, and in that house was a horrible man who beat me up every single day. Those were some problems! Now I got my own little corner of the world I live in, and I get by. And, my young friend, I don't feel I have it rough now, but that's because I took control and made it easier on myself."

She patted the bed and waved Buddy over. He dragged the bags inside and took his shoes off, placing them next to hers, then got under the flap of cover she held up for him. Luna adjusted herself between the two humans and gave a sigh as she snuggled up to Buddy's side.

Helen noticed something. "Did you have an experience with an animal besides Luna?"

Buddy was surprised. "Yes. A rabbit that Luna caught."

"You feel different?"

"A lot."

"You, my boy, are way ahead of the curve." Helen laughed. "Now, I don't know what's taking Max so long, and I'm not sure where he is, but until he comes back I'll take care of you, I promise. Okay?"

"Okay."

"How 'bout that dog? You all good with her?" She winked.

"Yeah, she's the best." He pushed his face into her fur. Luna opened her eyes, licked his face, then curled up and fell back asleep. Soon Buddy felt himself getting tired.

Before he drifted off, he asked, "Helen, what happened to the bad man in your house?"

She opened her eye a crack and said, "He's not around anymore, Sugar."

Falling asleep, Buddy licked his lips. The dried blood was gone already.

8

Clementine Figgins had never wanted to be a police officer. This had abruptly changed with the disappearance of her son ten years ago.

At the time, her small resale shop had gone belly up, and she'd been forced to re-enter the workplace. As a young single mother, she was in a bind. She hated to leave her darling boy, he was only a year and a half old. She needed to get paid, though.

After an exhaustive interview and background check process, she had left Rupert at home with a babysitter. The young blonde lady was sweet and courteous, and seemed quite professional. Clementine felt she had gotten to know her quite well given the abbreviated circumstances.

It was really only a one hour trial run to the store. She returned to an empty house. Her precious son and new babysitter were missing. A bag had been taken with diapers, a sippy cup, and other necessary items for Rupert's care, making everything appear quite deliberate.

Clementine's ears rang like locusts. She collapsed in tears, her worst fears being realized. Screaming through the house, she called his name, but she knew. He was gone.

The sitter was not to have gone anywhere, that had been talked about extensively. Apparently Clem had not known her quite so well as she had imagined.

When she called the police, the operator tried to assure her the babysitter was probably just on a walk. It was only when she had frantically started crying and hyperventilating that the dispatcher grudgingly relented to send an officer to her house.

In the ensuing weeks, the police searched exclusively for the child's father, believing that the sitter must have worked for him in an effort to grab his own son. The investigation stalled when the father was located months later, lying comatose in a hospital bed. He'd suffered a stroke a year earlier. Though the timeline cleared him, the detectives still tried to question the man who drooled and stared directly up at the ceiling, but they got no answer.

When they finally realized it had been the babysitter all along, she had walked off the face of the Earth.

Each day Clementine would call the police station and ask to speak to one of the detectives. She'd tell them something she remembered about the woman, a detail she had maybe neglected to mention about Rupert; his interest in his blue stuffed bear, his favorite cereal, anything to feel involved and active. Her guilt ate at her.

She felt like the investigating detectives were a pair of dipshits who couldn't find their own assholes in a hall of mirrors, and wasn't exactly shy about who knew it.

Two months deep, one of the detectives had raised doubt within the department about the existence of the babysitter, setting off a string of events that culminated with the bleach-brained news anchor of a local station running an exposé. In it she'd accused Clementine of "disappearing" her own son.

Clementine's new employer, a small but growing ad company, had turned around and fired her as a result of the terrible publicity. Her only course of action available had been to sue the television station, her now former employer, and the police department for slander, and wrongful termination. She did, forcing each to settle for decent sums, as well as relieving the accusing detective of his post. This, of course, did nothing to ease the pain of loss, but it had enabled her to cope together with other parents who were enduring similar trials.

They had actually laughed at her when, after four months passed with no progress, she had walked to the central police station and asked what she had to do to become a detective. When she graduated at the top of her class with a special recommendation from the mayor of San Diego for her work with FoundNation, they weren't laughing anymore.

Clementine had been pouring her settlement money into the

new network comprised of mainly mothers and fathers working to locate and retrieve missing children, and it was showing. Twenty kids had been located since her infusions of cash. While this gave Clementine joy, none of them were Rupert, and there remained a hole in her spirit.

While working to find Rupert through FoundNation, she also began her meteoric rise to detective, achieving the rank two weeks faster than Hap Grinwald, the legendary special investigator from the '70s. People were taking notice, but all Clementine cared about was her baby boy.

Months turned to years.

The years turned to a decade.

What did he look like now, she would wonder. Had his hair darkened? Was he tall? Would she recognize him if she saw him? She had to believe, but how? She'd been running on maternal instinct for ten years straight. A mother knows, or does a mother only suspect? It ate at her.

Her partner Jim Garrett always said that very few victims make it past the first forty-eight hours. Of course she knew that, but she wouldn't let that deter her. Not until she found Rupert, living or not. Plus, Jim was an insufferable idiot.

Like now, on their call to downtown's East Village, Garrett babbled on about the beneficial use of steroids in weight training, shutting up only when Clementine had pointed out that they increase muscle size, yet decrease the size of the brain and penis, and you'd really have to be pretty stupid to think that was a good trade-off.

This particular call was to check out a possible robbery in progress, a job not usually reserved for detectives. The property, however, was on the mayor's "hot list"; a catalog of the largest campaign contributors' ownings to be investigated fully if there was any crime versus their property. The name at the top of this list was a Mr. Stillwater, a very wealthy, very reclusive landholder in San Diego.

Clementine and Jim were two of four Special Investigators for the police; a team that undertook those responsibilities that were not covered by the larger groups such as Vice and Homicide. Missing persons and crimes against certain properties were theirs, among other things.

This building had never had a call. It was owned by Stillwater Enterprises.

They stopped in front of the brick warehouse that had been transformed into offices. The shattered glass and wood door hung off its hinges. Shards and splinters littered the ground.

"This looks like the place, 'Roid Ranger," Clementine said to Garrett.

"Good one," he said.

"Thanks," said Clementine, undaunted. She hopped out of the car, slowly drew her gun, and crept up to the door. There was no movement inside. The air hung still and heavy.

"Who called this in, Jim? Where's the squad car?"

"I don't know, and late, AKA I don't know."

"Very informative."

"Yes," He lurched through the door. Jim had a good foot of height and a hundred pounds on her. If nothing else, he was perfect for a human shield.

"You're not gonna wait for backup?" Clementine asked. His body was already fading into the darkened building. She followed her partner, like it or not.

The air was different than outside. It tasted of chalk. Sounds died immediately. As her eyes grew accustomed to the dark, she saw Jim at the smashed open door.

"One . . . two . . . three!" he mouthed, and they popped into the room, Jim aiming high and right, Clementine low and left. At least Jim worked well from a tactical viewpoint.

The room didn't appear to have been robbed or even ransacked, if there was anything in the room to begin with. A smashed door, so something went down. And scratches on the desk. Something dragged on it? She walked to the window, pulled open the heavy drapes. Sunlight filled the room, and Clem saw a dark, wet spot on the rug.

"We got blood, Jim,"

She pulled on her gloves and stuck a swab into the bloody spot which became a puddle when the rug was pushed down. As it regained its form, the puddle reverted to a spot. She lifted the corner to reveal much more blood. It started to ooze after a few seconds. Long, thin streams dropped onto the floor. Sending Jim to the car for tape to secure the room, she called the crime techs.

Outside, a police car pulled up, swerving around Jim and lurching to a halt, two wheels on the curb. One officer rushed out and opened the rear door for a small but fit man in a grey suit. He walked toward Jim, slick grey hair pulled into a ponytail.

"Detective James Garrett?" He stared at Jim, dizzying him, then sniffed the air.

"Yeah, who wants to know?" Jim looked at the man's hand before shaking it, surprised by the short man's grip.

"My name is Myron Fox. Chief of Security for this building, as well as all the holdings for Mr. Stillwater."

Jim was shaken. This case just became a career-maker.

Or breaker.

"Please," said Myron Fox, "enlighten us as to the nature of this vandalism." He waved his arm at the door as he spoke.

"Well, someone kicked in this door, judging from the partial bootprint right here." Jim motioned to the broken door, which had a massive waffle-sole indenting the grains. "And then they made it into someone's office. There's more inside with my partner, c'mon." Jim walked into the building with Mr. Fox and one uniformed officer, the other cop remaining by the cars.

Clementine was surprised to see someone she didn't recognize in a grey suit come in with Jim and some rookie officer she'd seen once or twice, Gary something or other. She nodded at Gary, asked Jim who the little fellow was. The short man extended his hand and announced himself.

"Myron Fox. Chief of Security for Stillwater Enterprises. You must be Detective Clementine Figgins."

"I must," she said, "and you must stay out of this room for the time being, Mr. Fox. At least until it's cleared by the techs. That goes for you too, Gary. Back it up, guys." She shooed her hands, shepherding them away. Mr. Fox seemed unpleased, but Clementine long ago had stopped trying to please people. Jim shook his head.

The techs walked down the hall, toolboxes in tow. When they had entered the room, the young officer pulled Clem aside.

"Um, Detective Figgins?"

"Yeah, Gary?"

"Um, well, my name's Gray, not Gary. Gray Lowehaus. No biggie."

"I'm sorry, Gray. I'll remember, I promise."

"It's okay. That's not what I was gonna ask you." He combed his hair out of his eyes, a well-built but awkward teenager in Clementine's eyes. Jesus, they took 'em young these days.

"What were you going to ask me, Gray?"

"I need to meet with you privately about something I heard concerning your research and missing children, alone somewhere. Without your partner or mine. You don't know or trust me, but name a time and place and I'll meet you there. This is something that'll be hard to believe, so please bear with me."

This was the last thing Clementine expected this fresh-out-of-the-academy kid to say to her. She looked back at Mr. Fox and Jim, who were watching the technicians work.

"Cedar Ridge Park. Tonight at eight. Do you know where it is?" she whispered.

"I do. Okay." He turned and walked away.

Clementine stared after him, filled with hope and confusion.

9

After they had driven a couple blocks, the mockingbird tapped at the window with its beak. Stewart opened it, and the bird leaped out into the headwind, in front of the big car's chrome grille. He thought he might hit it until it tucked its wings and increased speed. After that, he was more concerned about losing it, or losing control of the vehicle barreling down the quiet residential streets. Two mockingbirds joined it, flying impossibly fast.

They wound through the streets east of his neighborhood into the knot of canyons and peninsular communities near Balboa Park.

The road narrowed and curved into a dusty cul-de-sac. Landing in front of the car, the birds twitted amongst themselves. Stewart parked and got out.

The end of the lane disappeared into a copse of live oak trees. Two small houses, one on either side of the lane, peeked from beneath the branches. Both were made of wood, and identical in structure. The house to the north was light-colored, almost white. The southern cottage was much darker, as the wood had not been blanched by the sun. Both homes had figurines on their porches. The lighter had what appeared to be small humans clad in animal suits, made of ceramic or clay, while the darker house had crude misshapen figures made of bundled fibers, wire, and string.

It was hard to tell if anyone was inside through the dust covered windows. In the center of the cul-de-sac sat the old raven Stewart had seen at the oak tree. It stood and cawed a laughing sound. At least he thought it was the same bird. It was certainly big enough. And the cracks along its face looked familiar.

Mist wisped along the ground as the three mockingbirds joined the raven. One by one they touched beaks with the old bird, then all four flew farther down the canyon, just out of sight.

The temperature dropped suddenly when he followed them into the oak grove. It opened up into a clearing, revealing a large man wrapped in filthy blankets sitting in the center upon a chair fashioned from a gnarled oak stump. His face was caked with mud, hair jutting out in dirty clumps. Shadows from the canopy fell in a broken pattern over him, and streaks of sunlight illuminated the dust that hung in the grotto.

The man coughed, shooting out a cloud of smoke. Heavy and blue, it drifted down and hung close to the earth, mixing with the red dust. The visual effect was mesmerizing. Several smaller coughs followed, which sounded like laughter. His eyes were fixed on Stewart.

"Excuse me, have you seen some birds fly down here?" Stewart asked.

The man looked amused. "Birds? Oh, yes. Several." He had a voice of leather. "All day long." He shuffled his foot, blending the smoke and dust, which danced together into a red and blue swirl, then a spiral. Stewart somehow wrenched his eyes from the sight.

"I mean, of course, just now? Um . . . a few mockingbirds and a crow or something."

"Mockingbirds chasing a crow? No, I haven't seen that today."

"Well, they weren't exactly chasing it, per se. They were more like hanging out."

"Hanging out? That doesn't seem very realistic. They don't quite get along. Where are my manners? Would you care for some?" The ancient man held the burning end of a joint or cigarette toward Stewart. It was covered with dark oily patches and stank horribly, and looked to be wrapped in an old brown paper towel, or part of a bag. Stewart backed up.

"Ah . . . no. Thanks. So . . . no mockingbirds and crow hanging out? I should keep looking. Thanks anyway." He started walking.

"Is that them?" The man pointed behind Stewart.

Stewart wheeled around, but there was nothing there. He turned back, anger rising, but the man was gone. A cloud of smoke hung over his chair, shimmering. Stewart's hair bristled as he turned in a circle. When complete, the old man was in the chair again, without any smoke. He chuckled.

Stewart was over this already. "What the hell's going on, man? I know you know!" he said, trying to be menacing.

The old man laughed and peeled back his dirty blanket, bundling it so it looked like a bag hanging from his fist.

Stewart stopped. The blanket started to shake and rustle, then the man opened his hand, unfurling the fabric. The raven and mockingbirds shot out of it, squawking wildly. Stewart screamed, threw his hands in front of him, and ducked down into a crouch as the birds flew harmlessly over him and landed further down in the clearing.

The old man laughed uncontrollably, a sound that was both annoying and disconcerting to Stewart. The laughter increased and reverberated in the little wooded clearing, taking on a life of its own. The birds chirped and squawked in response.

Stewart lost it. He clenched his fists and ground his teeth. A vein in his temple throbbed.

"What in the fucking hell is going on here?!" he screamed. "Who the fuck are you and why the fuck am I balls deep in your fucking bullshit?!" Spit flew everywhere.

He tried to grab the old man's blanket, but the old man spryly tapped his wrists to the side, and Stewart's inertia sent him sprawling to the ground. Another round of crackly laughter erupted from the man, louder this time.

"Ha ha ha! They said you'd be pissed! Oh! I just can't help myself sometimes!"

"What did you say?" asked Stewart, from the dirt. "About 'them'? Who the hell are 'they'?"

"They are those who are not you," said the man, smiling at Stewart.

"Are you even talking to me?" He seriously could not take much more of this guy. "Is Jeb part of 'they'? Where is Jeb? I need to find him," he said, slowly enunciating as if he were talking to a deaf person.

"Jeb? Who said anything about Jeb? Does he have a home? He's probably at home, Stewart," said the man, mimicking Stewart's demeaning tone.

Stewart cocked his head, put out that the old man knew his

name already. He wasn't going to take the bait.

"OK, I guess I'll just go there," He wheeled around, walking away from the confounding old freak. The four birds made clicking sounds to each other.

"Atta boy! A real self-starter that one!" the old man said to the birds. "Look at him go! He's gonna find Jeb Rawls' house and save the day!" He pursed his lips and imitated a trumpet's charge.

"So you do know him?" Stewart turned around.

"Of course I do."

"And me, apparently." Stewart glared. "I'm trying to help Jeb. I don't know why. You might be his friend, and you might be his enemy. Hell, you may be using me to get to him, and have the birds brainwashed, or they're enemies too. And you offer me something you faked to be smoking, luring me to hit it for some reason. I assume to glean information you believe I have. So, I'll just leave your annoying ass with the fucking birds and go find Jeb by my damn self, thanks a lot for nothing!" Stewart was pretty impressed with himself. He tried to march away, but found he couldn't. His legs wouldn't move.

The old man rose from his chair, cutting a much more imposing figure than Stewart had prepared for.

"Fake smoking?!" His eyes were bugged out, exaggerating. He made a "boosh" sound with his cheeks, then parted his hands, flattening the palms parallel to the Earth. His cracked hands looked for a moment like two old birds flying away from each other over the sea. When Stewart tried to pull himself from this thought he found himself frozen, muscles not responding to his brain. The man continued grumbling inaudibles and backing away. Stewart felt his body sway toward the man.

What he thought to be multiple blankets over the man's large frame turned out to be only one as he threw the end of the poncho around his neck like a cape. He was thick and strong, his arms wrinkled yet defined, his belly a proud and wonderful thing. His eyes bored into Stewart's electrically, a stern look on his face. He made slow strides toward Stewart, never breaking eye contact, still grumbling. He closed the distance with large steps, his legs huge and powerful like oaken trunks. The earthen floor of the grove shook with each footfall.

Stewart had never actually wet himself from fear. This would be the first time.

The man was almost upon him. His foul, smoky breath hit Stewart's nose. Then the old man's eyes softened and he broke into a smile. It was not the condescending trickster smile of before, though; rather it was a smile of pride.

He wrapped his arms around Stewart's rigid body, and Stewart smelled the sweet sagebrush and desert dust waft into his nostrils. Warmth and feeling returned to his body, and he found his muscles once again listened to their owner. As soon as they did, he tried to wriggle out of the embrace.

"Easy, easy," the old man said. "Relax." He held Stewart. The anger and tension drained from him.

He led Stewart to the wooden chair and sat him in it. His hand disappeared into the folds of his poncho, and came back with a brown wineskin. Stewart looked into the man's eyes skeptically at first, unsure whether to trust him. The birdman shrugged, took a sip himself, then re-offered it.

"Fuck this." Thirsty as hell and with a swooning head, he grabbed the bottle, drank a sip and felt flooded with an energizing light from within. It tasted like water, thankfully. Like silver water.

He sat back and listened to the old man.

"I am Abraham Blackwing. Those are my homes," the man said, pointing up the path to the two houses, but from the implication he may have meant the clearing as well, perhaps even more so.

"Jeb is here," he said, tapping Stewart on the forehead between his eyes.

A vision came to him, and Stewart saw in his mind a small cabin in a wooded area with myriad construction supplies strewn about. Solar panels, unassembled wind turbines, indeterminate scrap. He saw a figure inside the cottage but couldn't make out who it was.

His vantage point seemed to be from a tree, and without warning his sight flew. It blurred and sped away from the scene within his mind above the rooftops of what Stewart recognized as one of the neighborhoods just to the east.

The cottage disappeared as his vision sped. Houses and streets whizzed by faster and faster until Stewart saw Cora's Buick at the end of the street, then this path and himself standing with

Abraham. His inner sight landed in a tree, and looked at himself, who was in turn looking back at a hummingbird. The little bird gave a whirring click and ruffled its tiny feathers. In stillness, Stewart was left staring at the bird, regaining his own perspective.

"Stewart, this bird will take you back to Jeb. If that is where you want to go."

"What was that?" Stewart asked, rubbing his eyes. When he opened them again the bird and he were still locked together. "The streaking vision thing, and the hummingbird?"

"That? Oh, that is the birdsight," he laughed again.

"Of course," Stewart said, blinking repeatedly. "What about the 'if' part of your statement. 'If that's where I want to go?' What's that about?"

"This may not be your battle, Stewart Zanderson." He took a drag from the filthy joint, exhaled it. "But that is your choice, not mine."

"I don't know what you're on about with the battle and choice stuff. Here's my deal: Jeb was at one point my friend. Whether he's still my friend is a moot point. The reason I need to find him is because it is the dying request of another friend that I do so. At least I think he was dying. Anyway, that's what I'm doing. Period. No matter how insane that sounds. Then I'm done with you people."

Filled with bravado, Stewart grabbed the paper towel joint and took a mighty draw off it, then immediately regretted it while he hacked his throat apart coughing up what tasted like smoke from marijuana, tobacco, herbs, and maybe an old shoe or tire.

"Well, be careful, you poor idiot," replied Abraham as he turned and shuffled back towards his two homes, chuckling. Stewart walked behind him coughing, unsure if he would ever catch his breath again. His throat on fire, he tossed the burning cone on the ground and crushed the butt underfoot. He stared at the unidentifiable glut of herbs in the road, silently cursing the old asshole.

Contented chirps rang from the ground as the mockingbirds were greeting the hummingbird and preening him. When Abraham turned, they flew up the path and back near the Buick. The raven hopped after the old man.

Abraham said nothing, did not turn back as he entered the light-colored house on the north side, just let the bird hop in, then shut the door, giggling. Stewart rasped out three breathless coughs and flipped Abe off behind his back. Condescending laughter was one of Stewart's great many pet peeves.

The shadows were growing long as the hummingbird zipped along the maze of streets to the east, weaving around canyons. Even after being guided by the birdsight, Stewart didn't think he'd ever recall this twisting route again.

Two of the mockingbirds had stayed near Abraham's area, and the female he had now grown accustomed to was pecking around on the seat. The streets bent and curved, and Stewart sank further into the idea that he did not truly know this town. There were whole little neighborhoods where he recognized nothing.

The hummingbird stopped on a branch. Black sage bushes and laurel sumac grew as tall as trees. They mixed with scrub willow and made a knot of branches twenty feet high. At the base were cholla cacti intertwining and locking together with the shrubs in wild, impassable patterns. It was a living wall that reached off into live oak trees.

Stewart parked close to the trees, grabbed the backpack, and got out. The mockingbird hopped around him. He walked alongside the green wall, and in changing his viewpoint the seemingly solid wall of plants revealed an opening. Inside was a pathway lined with a wall of branches on either side. It turned upon itself twice and stopped. Stewart felt around inside the tight scrub for a latch or opening but couldn't find one. It got hard to see anything, as the branches formed a tunnel so thick the fading sunlight had trouble shining through.

Flitting up above Stewart and landing in the thicket, the mockingbird poked its head deep into the plants. Stewart heard a peck, then a scrape, and stepped backward as the branches dislodged and the dead end burst open. Beyond the opening in the green wall, a path wound through the dense trees.

"Nice job, bird," he said.

"Chik-wheet!" the mockingbird replied.

The hummingbird blasted past them into the trees, then hovered, waiting.

As he followed the birds, the trees gradually thinned, opening up into a small clearing that housed a tiny one-story cottage surrounded by wooden decks.

Not seeing anyone, Stewart began to walk around the house, stopping at some piles of construction materials. Some, such as solar panels and large fans, Stewart recognized from the birdsight. Others he hadn't noticed. Among the debris was a pile of small disc-shaped mirrors, three generators in various states of disrepair, ducts, tubes, wire, and a kiln.

When he reached the rear of the house, he saw a tall, tousle-headed man in jeans and a brown flannel crouched over, facing away from him.

Stewart tensed. When the man turned around, Stewart looked into the eyes of a person he had not seen in many long years; his former friend and bandmate, Jeb Rawls.

"Hey, Stewart, how's it going?" Jeb smiled as he walked closer. "How you been?"

Stewart was in disbelief that Jeb could be speaking to him like they hadn't seen each other in a couple weeks, rather than the twenty years that had actually passed. They shook hands.

Jeb pulled the handshake into a hug. The sage of the canyon smelled strongly on his shirt. The hug was awkward. Stewart didn't like hugging people, but he was so tired. He swooned.

"Whoa, buddy! You're falling asleep on your feet! C'mere." Jeb picked up Stewart's limp body and sat him down on a log chair. "Now lemme get you some water."

Stewart saw concern in Jeb's eyes. Jeb patted his hand on Stewart's shoulder, sighed and walked to the cottage, glancing into the surrounding trees.

Stewart noticed the birds. A few at first, but the longer he looked the more little eyes and heads appeared in the foliage. Soon there were hundreds of small birds peering at him, unsettling him more than he was already. He didn't want to do this. To see Jeb, pretend like they were friends. This was as far as he said he would go. Why was he staying?

Then he thought of Nickel.

From the cabin, Jeb returned with a large glass of water. "Good to see you, Stewart," he said. "I'm really glad, but how did you find me?"

He handed Stewart the water. Stewart was skeptical, but was so thirsty he slurped it up within seconds. Its silvery taste was exactly like the water given to him by Abraham.

He couldn't believe that Jeb didn't know the story, but was a little relieved that everyone wasn't omnipotent. Either that, or Jeb was role-playing and seeing how much Stewart knew.

"Well, it started this morning, with that bird." The mockingbird razzed. "And Craig James, or Nickel, as we used to call him." He unslung the bag from his shoulder. "And that."

He tossed the bag to Jeb, who opened it and pulled out the box.

"Shit," Jeb said, frowning. Instead of picking it up and observing it more closely, he set it down and put his hand to his temple.

Stewart was crushed. "Really? You don't want it? You gotta be kidding me."

The mystery he thought would be clear when he found Jeb had only compounded itself. Jeb actually looked scared, and if Jeb was scared, what should Stewart be?

"Jeb, Nickel got stabbed in front of me with this thing and he told me to get it to you. As you can see, both your name and his name are on the wrapping. Are you telling me that you don't recognize this box?"

"I recognize the box, and I know what's inside of it. It's bad news, is what it is. Why don't you fill me in all the way? I need to know exactly what happened with the snare."

"The what?"

"That." Jeb pointed to the box.

Stewart told him about his day.

"What color was the bowl?" Jeb asked.

"What?"

"Your bowl that broke. What color was it?"

"Um, black and white? I don't see what that has to do with anything."

"Everything means something," said Jeb.

The light was fading quickly, and Stewart was getting tired. He leaned his head back and stared up at the branches stretching out like a net, filtering the approaching night. He felt his eyes closing, and soon fell fast asleep in the log chair.

Jeb scooped up Stewart's prone body, threw it over his shoulder, and walked into his house carrying the bag.

The mockingbird clicked her tongue. It reverberated throughout the trees, sending many of the birds off into the darkening sky above Jeb's canyon. Then she flew behind the men, entering the house as Jeb slid the glass door shut.

• • •

Morning came. The smell of eggs, bacon, toast, and the enticing aroma of strong coffee pulled Stewart from his sleep. Dreams of people from his past and others he had never met broke apart in the face of the alluring smells. He opened his eyes slowly as the dream's last vapors vanished. His head was swimming and pounding simultaneously. The small bed Jeb had put him in was sunk beneath a false floor with the lid latched open. The top had a rug stapled to it.

He climbed out of the cubby in the far corner of the room and looked around groggily. Jeb's home was cluttered with junk old enough to be considered antique; a spent pomade can, an archaic soda bottle, yellowed newspaper headlines pasted on the wall. Apparently everything told a story to Jeb.

The clink of dishes sounded from the kitchen, but Stewart made no sound. He didn't know how to deal with it yet.

Jeb hadn't seemed too concerned when told of Nickel's possible murder by thugs, or his uncanny reappearance at Stewart's house, laughing and thrashing.

He knew about the knife, though, and wasn't happy about it. Stewart felt around for the box, but it wasn't with him. He was slightly indignant that Jeb would take it, before he realized it was really Jeb's blade and not his own. He didn't want the thing anyway.

The sunlight filtered through the oak canopy and into the room through the windows. One ray of light landed on a small glass cone that sat on a table beside Jeb's well-worn mattress in the center of the room. It refracted the light around in small ovals of rainbow. These ovals in turn hit on the metal discs that were placed around the room. When the light hit them they chimed. The sounds and light grew in intensity until Jeb entered and chuckled. Stewart flinched at Jeb's voice.

"My alarm clock," said Jeb. "One of the things I've been working on."

"Pretty out of control, man." Stewart wiped the remaining night's sleep from his eyes. "Crazy."

The beams of rotating light hit his eyes, and left trails in his vision.

"Get dressed and let me show you around the house, and we'll eat some food," Jeb said, walking out.

"Uhhh . . . sure?" Stewart responded to the empty doorway.

He pulled on his clothes slowly. He was drained from yesterday's physical and mental beatings. The sleep had helped, but not enough. The coffee beckoned.

He shuffled out to the small dining table, set with the steaming food and coffee and took a sip. Instantly his mind shone with a phenomenal clarity, shoving the weariness from it. His eyelids raised and his skin warmed. He took a bite of the egg on toast, then the bacon. The pain drained from his body, replaced with vigor and energy. Taking another sip, he noticed his hands pulsing with an electric glow.

"Jeb, what's in this food?" His voice sounded rich to his own ears. Soothing. He rotated his hand in the air.

"Just TLC, Stewart, and some pepper. What's up? You feel alright?" Jeb's rangy frame seemed to have taken on an opaque quality. His voice echoed, though the room was small.

"No. I feel fantastic. Really. But I felt horrible until I ate it, you know?" he said.

"TLC is a powerful thing." Jeb returned to his food.

Stewart wondered what that meant. Some new drug called TLC? If he had just been drugged, it seemed like a pretty okay concoction. He felt great. Confident.

"So . . . did you look at the knife?" Stewart asked.

"A little. Eat a bit more, dude."

Stewart was getting a little frustrated with Jeb's nonchalance. He was seeing things clearly, thanks to the TLC, and one thing he saw was Jeb not taking him seriously. Anger bubbled within him.

"I'm ready for this, man. I'd really like to know what happened to Nickel so I can bounce out of here being sure you've got this," he said.

"Bounce? Alright, man. Later," said Jeb.

"What?"

"Like I said, if you wanna hit it, there's the door. In fact, you should. They're going to find me eventually, and you probably won't want to be around when they do."

Stewart was indignant. "So, you think I'm like you? I leave my friends in the lurch and take care of myself? That's your shit, not mine, Jeb. I can handle whatever. Plus those goons already know who I am, so I'm fucked if I leave here. But you already know that, don't you? I put my shit on the line to get this box to you. The knife. That stabbed your friend." His fists were clenching. "You fucking need me for something.

"So are you going to give me any answers? Did you check out the knife? Do you have any idea what the fuck we are dealing with at all? I'm losing my mind over here and you and that fucking crow-training motherfucker don't tell me shit! I'm fucking over it and I want some answers right goddamn now!"

Jeb looked at him sternly, and said, "Do not talk about Abraham that way, someone might hear you."

"Whatever," Stewart rolled his eyes.

Jeb cocked his head. "Okay, you'll get some answers. It's almost noon right now. I've been up since six working on what's going on. Like I said; try to eat and drink a little first." Jeb stuffed a wad of food into his mouth and swallowed. "Because you're gonna need it. Shit's gonna be heavy."

Stewart stared at Jeb. "You're fucking impossible, dude.".

"That's exactly what I am."

They finished breakfast in silence.

After the food was gone, Jeb carried the plates to the sink.

"Grab some more coffee and meet me outside," he said as he washed off the dishes. "It's time to get started."

Stewart obeyed without argument, feeling trapped. They walked out to the small clearing, baking in the sun. Sweat beaded on his skin until it ran down in rivulets. He could see so many more colors than he was used to; one bush had so many shades of green it didn't look real. The overwhelming scent of sage filled the air.

TLC my ass, he thought.

Jeb was holding the conical knife beneath a ray of sunlight. The grooved patterns on the knife glowed, trickling along like silver and ruby liquid, sending a hum from the blade. He peered into the oval opening, looking down the barrel, turned it this way and that. He didn't appear overwhelmed with the same battlefield memories that Nickel and Stewart saw the day before.

"Nickel's in this," he said.

Stewart had had enough. "What in the fuck are you talking about?"

"This," He turned to Stewart, knife aloft. "is a spirit snare. When you saw Nickel being murdered, he was actually being drained of his life force. Trapped inside this, leaving his body an unthinking husk." Jeb looked at the knife, his brow furrowing. "They are very rare, and usually very old, as this one is."

Stewart's mouth hung agape. He didn't notice it until he tried to speak. "Sooo . . . Nickel is inside of that knife?" His own voice sounded foreign to his ears, he shook his head to clear it.

Jeb turned the blade in his hands and said, "That thing in your house was the physical Nickel. A spiritless husk that clings to control words and suggestions. These means of control are not known by many. The people using this have access to very specialized knowledge.

"Stewart, we have to get you up to speed quickly," Jeb said, putting the knife back into its case. "Before something terrible happens."

"Worse than what's already happened?"

"Much."

"Shit. So who are the people responsible? That pale guy and the huge dude?"

"No," said Jeb. "Those are henchmen for the real psycho masterminds, who are people you know well: Nuala McCafferty, and my brother, Frank."

Stewart should have known it was coming. He felt a sickness crawl along his innards.

10

"I'm ready," Stewart said, sitting on the log.

"Okay. Watch me."

Jeb turned around and walked away from Stewart, into the trees. A lattice of light filtered through the canopy of live oak, and waves of wind rolled through the branches. Shadows rippled along the ground.

Stewart became unable to focus on Jeb, who was surrounded by a mist, making his body less substantial. He rubbed his eyes. When he opened them he could no longer see Jeb at all.

"Jeb! What the fuck, man? Where are you?!" His panic was evident in his voice. "Jeb!—"

"Right here." Jeb spoke from just behind Stewart's ear.

"AAAGH!" Stewart flew off the seat. The birds in the trees jumped and flew from their perches. Reacting instantly, Stewart clenched his fist and swung it hard at Jeb's opaque form, landing a solid blow on the scraggly man's jaw and dropping him to the ground. The milky mist steamed away, fully revealing him.

"I am over this shit!" Stewart yelled, standing over Jeb's body.

Jeb scissored his legs around Stewart's and snapped them shut, hurling Stewart on the ground while shooting himself back upright.

"Ha ha! Good show, Stewart!" he said, rubbing his jaw. "Ow, okay. I'll tell you a few things. You do deserve an explanation."

He held his hand out. Stewart entertained the idea of punching Jeb a second time, but let it go.

Jeb pulled him up. "That was the first lesson. What you just witnessed was not me necessarily disappearing, but rather manipulating my environment. Illusions. Reflecting and refracting light."

Stewart breathed in the desert air, its heat filling his lungs. "Wow. Big surprise. You lost me."

"Hmm. Okay. We'll start from . . . well, we'll just start," Jeb said. "The first tenets of this whole . . . thing, are that everything is alive, whether it breathes, or has blood, or not. And that everything is connected. People, trees, animals. But also rocks, rivers, even a car or tractor. Things are the sum total of their experiences. Sights, smells, memories. Things that happen on a mountain are just as much a part of its existence as the tectonic plates shifting and pushing it skyward, or the rain and wind wearing down its jagged peaks. Likewise a house takes on some of the characteristics of the residents and events over the years, and so on.

"How we doin' so far?" Jeb asked.

"Uh, good? I don't know." Stewart couldn't see how that had to do with anything, but was trying to wait patiently.

"Sorry, just bear with me," Jeb said. "There are strands, or webs, that connect everything. Some join breathing things, some connect physical, non-breathing things, and some connect ideas. There are more, but we will start with those.

"Everyone can feel these webs or strands, but few can actually see them. Of those, there are far fewer who can manipulate them, even with training. That is what I just did; change the strands that surround me, as well as the frequency at which they are transmitted.

"It's the art of being lost in a crowd. Manipulating strands of webbing to mirror the world around you, inside a frame.

"Say you hold a strand of spider web, then rotate it. At different points of the rotation there are glimmers along the web. This is the art of manipulating those webs, those glimmers. There are many other tricks, but this is the first one I ever learned. It helped immensely."

"So this is an initiation into something?"

"This is the initiation into not getting trapped in one of these." He motioned to the blade. "Or killed by Frank and Nuala's goon squad."

"They have more knives?"

"They do. Very few of the snares exist that were made over a thousand years ago, cropping up around the globe at the same time, like pyramids. That is one of the secrets of the web; simultaneous global realizations.

"Of the remaining knives from that period, I think Frank has three, maybe four now. But there are new snares, black cones. I know because I was the one making them, before I realized what they were for." Jeb looked off into the distance. "Frank and Nuala have fallen very far into an abyss, and it has taken their minds. We'll get into the how and why later. Right now it's incredibly important that we get you learning the basics."

"So, by helping you guys I've made myself a target for either getting murdered or having my soul trapped in a knife you made?" Stewart's head was splitting. "Wow. Thanks, bud."

"Spirit, really, but in a nutshell, yes," answered Jeb.

"That totally sucks."

"Yeah, I'm sorry." Jeb's eyes were wistful. "I'm also sorry about how we left you so many years ago, for what it's worth."

"Honestly," Stewart replied, "it's not worth that much."

Stewart tried to compose himself. It was a heavy load of information, and who could tell if it were real? He argued with himself in silence, and finally accepted Jeb's way. "Okay, I'm ready to learn. Do I clear my mind of all voices?"

"No. I can't even do that," Jeb said. "Envision the web. See its strands glimmer."

Stewart peered ahead, searching off in the distance. Jeb tossed a rock about five feet in front of them, which sent a little kick of dust into the air, between two oaks. It swirled in the sunlight.

"Shift your gaze to just above that rock, into the dust, and unfocus your eyes slightly. Concentrate on one strand." Jeb spoke in an even monotone. His chanting voice sent Stewart's mind into a place of comfort.

"See how the light falls on the dust," he said.

"There's nothing there." Even through the hypnotic lull of Jeb's voice, Stewart was growing impatient with this new age stuff.

"Then stay there until there is, and when you see it, try to split the strand lengthwise. When you have done that, step into the split strand, and you will have mastered the first task." Jeb's voice returned to normal. He walked back to the house, leaving Stewart alone.

Stewart stared into the dust cloud. Nothing. He relaxed. Still nothing. He tried for hours with no result. Changing viewpoint, intention, anything. It had to be possible. That, or Jeb put something in his food. He became increasingly paranoid he'd been drugged, psychedelics if memory served. It had been a while.

Whatever else happened today is just some elaborate hoax by two blast-from-the-past assholes who had no place in his current life, anyway. A big joke. Was that it? He quit trying the web trick. "Fuck this shit."

He stood up to leave. Jeb was still in the house, and probably wouldn't notice Stewart's absence until it was too late. Then the joke's on him.

The mockingbird, who had sat so patiently, ruffled her feathers and chirped, trying to get his attention, but was ignored. Taking wing, she rounded the trees, then shot directly for Stewart's face. As she sped by, inches from him, Stewart flinched. His heels hit the chair, and he fell back into it. When he looked up, he saw a faint line glowing in front of him, hanging between the trees. A shimmer ran up and down the ghostly wire like a spark.

Emotions washed over Stewart; the first was relief that he had done it, the second was thankfulness for the mockingbird. But they were both eclipsed by the growing horror that this was an extremely dangerous world that floated silently alongside the one he knew. Not a joke. Or a hoax. Or a drug fantasy.

It was real.

"Well, thanks, little bird, I think." He kept eye contact with the web. The spots of light gained momentum, running up and down the strand. "I guess that's the hard part."

The mockingbird mimicked laughter, then flew to a branch.

Stewart was now resolved to tackle the problem no matter what. Time passed, and he could make the strand appear and vanish at will, but was no nearer to splitting it along its length like Jeb had said. He sat back, rubbing his weary eyes hard and long, and heard the mockingbird make a dual-toned razz.

When he reopened them, the view in front of him was breathtaking. Tendrils of light criss-crossed, spilling from the first strand. Wires of different colored light stretched out, connecting everything he could see. Thousands of hues. Some were clear, or nearly so, some greying or blackening.

The first thread glowed in the center, its brilliance seeming to make its the others dim by comparison. A nexus of web hung like a huge nerve bundle. A cocoon of lights. He stared, breathless with awe.

If the brilliance of the one could dim the light of the accompanying strands, he wondered, why could it not dim its own core? He concentrated his intention on pushing the luminosity toward the edges, making the middle appear void of web.

It worked. The edges opened, revealing a center rife with millions of tiny glowing microfibers, almost invisible. Small bands of light ran down the filaments, into a yawning and living abyss. At its mouth, thicker tendrils formed a gate, shooting strands off in every direction. Inside was a hive of writhing filaments.

Stewart sat, mesmerized. Inside of him, a voice spoke, but not in words. He listened, and rose with a sigh, plucking up his courage. He could barely breathe as he walked toward the shimmering mass. A low hum sounded from the glowing knot, and the ribbons streaked around the entrance, beckoning.

The cocoon pulsed with colored light. Stewart cautiously entered the webbing, the sounds from the outside muffling as he left them behind. The silk hung thick, obscuring the view as if a gelatinous coating were over his eyes, or the world. The sounds drifted from far off, wet echoes resounding.

Inside, one bright green tendril reached out. He followed it nervously with his eyes as it snaked toward his arm, brushing lightly upon the fine hairs, magnetizing.

It slithered onto his skin.

Upon contact, the strand filled Stewart's mind with fields of grass, brilliant green blades reaching for the sunlight, and down through their veiny lengths into the roots stretching below the surface of the earth. There they connected with one another and formed a subterranean web blanketing the vision. His intention fused with that of the green filament. His consciousness drifted upward and outward, into the web of roots sprawling and meeting with the grove of live oak that surrounded them. His spirit stretched with the green tendrils into the canopy of the oaken leaves, forming a lattice above the floor of the clearing, mirroring the grass web in its own way. Another web formed in the sunlight falling on the oaks, which left dancing shadows on the ground. Patterns overlaid themselves in an endless field. His consciousness flowed out along the web.

A deep blue strand then touched his skin, and Stewart's mind halved. The visions of green remained, joined by the rippling glint of sunlight upon the surface of the ocean. He perceived the light as a web upon the waves, another in the sunlight below the surface, fingering out along the ocean floor amidst the sand, coral, and kelp. The green and blue strands fused, blending into an aqua and incorporating both.

A feeling of oneness filled him. In an instant he was brimming with knowledge and understanding of the cycles of these things. The ocean peeled off into rivers and seas, frozen icecaps on glaciers. Water evaporated and was carried in clouds, then dropped back down to the Earth. The systems of water and of plants spilled arcane knowledge into Stewart's mind. He was vast.

These feelings vanished when a steel grey strand rubbed on his forearm, burning it. Visions of cogs, gears, and sludge clouded his thoughts. The grey webs were angular and menacing compared to the soft edges of the lighter-colored ones. He saw the green and blue being blackened and choked, changed. Confusion replaced the easy feelings. He adapted, breathed.

Another wire, one lacking color, rather an opalescent shimmer, brushed his neck. Stewart saw inside the soul of the new machines, webbing on the verge of sentience. Ideas floated through him of every kind. Non-verbal voices spoke in silent tongues of ones and zeroes.

Suddenly there were hundreds, then thousands of different tendrils touching him, and the sheer number of images was staggering, emotions of every sort clustered his thoughts. Strands of every color and beyond.

Stewart felt he was losing control, and had no clue how to extract himself from the cocoon. He didn't know if he was obscure or invisible, and he didn't care. More and more webs. They entered his mouth and nostrils, smaller ones began to snake into his pores. More systems. Space. Blood. Wind. Every color. Hundreds of strands. Bitterness. Hope. Loss. Fatigue. It was taxing Stewart's mind and spirit to the fullest.

He felt his consciousness slipping off into the endless maze, and he started to follow beckoning images deep into the fold. He was wholly a part of this. He no longer needed to breathe.

In a panic, he realized it was all too much. His consciousness bubbled outward, expanding as his spirit began to seep into the webbing. Something was horribly not right about this, he felt intent and control leave him, powerless to remain in his body. He felt the core of his being becoming hopelessly lost.

All at once, his ears were filled with a wet, ripping sound that demolished the silence within the cocoon. A hand thrust itself into the thickness of webs, wrapped around Stewart, and started tugging. The webs twitched violently, some snapping off. Though many were injured from the rip, the remaining tendrils held fast for a brief moment until they resonated within a low and steady note, which caused them to slacken their grip.

With the tone, which he realized now was a voice, Stewart's drifting consciousness flooded back into his mind. The filaments snaked back out of his pores. Once they were cleared, they slithered off his torso, then out of his nose, mouth, and ears, and off of his face.

The next tug pulled his head from the luminous cocoon, and he gasped a huge breath of the grotto's cool air, gulping it down. He looked into Jeb's eyes.

Inside of Jeb's tone, the tendrils continued their release of Stewart's body and spirit. With the final tug, Stewart found himself shivering on the ground in Jeb's arms, covered in sweat and viscous slime. The clearing was dark.

Jeb was looking very pale next to him, the guttural sound still vibrating from his throat. His arm was tightly wrapped around Stewart's waist.

"I'm sorry. I'm so sorry," said Jeb.

His eyes were darting around the clearing.

"Uh, ugh," Stewart tried to speak. He was puzzled, afraid. Why would Jeb be sorry if he was trying to keep him from harm's way? He felt sick. Alone.

"C'mon, let's eat," Jeb said, helping Stewart to his feet. "I'll tell you everything tomorrow."

Stewart followed him to the house, realizing he was now more scared than ever. And famished.

They ate bread and soup in silence and retired immediately after. In the cubby-hole bed, Stewart fell asleep instantly.

• • •

The house was dark and silent when Stewart awoke. He felt immediately alert. When he sat up, he rammed his head on the underside of the floorboards with a thud, making a small goose egg rise on his forehead. He'd forgotten that he was inside the cubbyhole bed. Thrusting open the door in the floor, he saw that it was morning.

Stewart was shocked. Jeb's belongings were strewn all over the house, the place having been ransacked while Stewart slept. Nothing was where it had been except the little rug nailed above his hidden bedspace.

He looked through his bedding for the blade and box. They weren't there. This was not good. Quickly and silently, he got dressed and crawled around the room, searching for the bag, the box, the knife, Jeb, anything. He crept into the dining room and was relieved to see Jeb sitting at the table, facing away from him.

"Jeb? What's going on in here?"

Jeb remained motionless. Stewart walked toward him "Jeb? Seriously, let's uh, clean up and talk about yesterday." As he spoke he gently shoved Jeb's shoulder from the rear.

Jeb's head rocked back a fraction of an inch, then rolled forward. It fell off his neck, down his chest, and landed on its ear with a milky splash into a bowl of cereal. His dead eyes stared past Stewart at the ceiling, bits of milk and grain plastering his face.

Stewart lost his balance, tangled up in a pile of strewn clothing, and fell down. He had to get out of here. Now. Screw the knife.

At the front door he paused and looked out into the clearing. A heavy mist hung in the air, obscuring the thick plant life that surrounded the cabin. Stewart couldn't tell if anyone was there or not. He looked back briefly into the house before sprinting along the path, back up toward the Buick, as fast as he could. When he was far enough away to look back at the house, he stopped to catch his breath.

A short man in a grey suit was rounding the porch. From an oak tree next to the house, the mockingbird made a shriek, swooping down at the man. He swatted at her, just missing as she flew back toward Stewart.

The grey man sniffed the air, stared straight at Stewart, and waved. Stewart began walking backwards and hesitantly returned the wave. The grey-clad man began slowly walking toward him for two or three steps, then abruptly broke into a run.

Stewart freaked out, breaking into a sprint while looking back at the man. When he spun his head around he found himself barreling toward a column of teddy bear cholla, a cactus so named because of its cuddly appearance. In actuality, the "fuzz" are minute tines, sharp and brittle, next to impossible to extract from skin once they pierce it.

The path split at the cactus clump. One fork climbed back toward the car, the other shot almost straight down for several yards, then wound into a thin canyon trail leading between two cliffs and into the dry creek bed at the bottom.

When Stewart was inches from the cactus, he recognized it, and lunged to the right, avoiding the spikes successfully. In his haste he plummeted down the steep hill. There was no time to correct his course. He was essentially falling, quickly tapping his feet and hands on the cliffs. As the path leveled, he turned and saw the man in the grey suit at the top, some thirty yards behind. What looked like a very large fox made of smoke was running just behind him; both were ghostly and translucent.

Looking too long, Stewart slipped on the sandstone incline and lost his balance as the floor of the small canyon dropped off, then leveled again. The eroded soil was brittle. He tumbled through the brush for a few feet on the floor of the side ravine until the bottom gave out completely, and he found himself flying through open space, twirling his body like an airborne cat. He grabbed at a small plant hanging out of the cliff, but it offered almost no resistance.

The canyon turned sharply. His airborne body did not. The momentum slammed him into the sandstone, his shoulder blade hitting squarely upon a round rock embedded in the wall. It made an awful cracking sound, and Stewart's left arm filled with steel fire as he dropped to the rocks on the canyon floor.

He turned around, then screamed in pain as he rolled onto his back. His left side burned from his ear to his ankle.

The grey man and fox looked down at him from the cliffs, neither entirely substantial, but both frighteningly real. The man walked to the edge, turned his back, and began to descend, using the shrubs as handholds. He stared at Stewart, not bothering to watch what he was doing. The fox quivered, then unravelled into smoke that streamed toward the grey man. When the smoke touched him, the ghostly sheen left. His shoes scraped dust and pebbles from the cliffside as he gained substance.

Stewart tried to stand but howled out and sat back down, dizzied from pain and exhaustion. He picked up a rock and threw it weakly at the man, but it fell well short of its target. He grabbed another and waited.

The mockingbird had been forced to monitor the proceedings from a distance. Now seeing Stewart helpless, she flew to him and gently brushed her beak against his ear, then flew at the grey man, pecking at his hand when the other reached out for something to hold. His balance was compromised. She chirped as she dislodged him, and he slipped and scraped down the cliff's face, trying to right himself.

In midair he swung wildly at the pestering bird, making solid contact with her body. The mockingbird was sent spinning hard into the cliff, and fell down to the ground, where she lay still.

The grey man landed, then picked himself up, unhurt, and brushed the dust from his suit. As if alive, the dust eddied around his knees, forming a shape. It swirled more tightly until the dust molded itself, and became the fox. The grey man's ghostly sheen returned, and both leered at Stewart.

"Leave my fucking bird alone! What the fuck are you?" Stewart screamed and threw his rock at him. It was a much better shot, and made the man duck to avoid it. Stewart was surprised the rock didn't just travel right through him, at the rate things were going.

The man smiled, not mirthfully.

He was very old. Lines covered his face. His suit was vintage leaning towards ancient. He stepped closer. His grey eyes were petrifying.

A low rumbling came from up the small canyon, behind Stewart, then a ferocious growl sent a chill through him, and made the frightening smile disappear from the grey man's face. A hot, viscous liquid dripped onto Stewart's cheek, leaving an oily essence.

The man stepped no closer. The fox retreated.

Stewart looked up into a gaping void filled with spit and teeth, breathing stinking breath like decayed vegetables upon him. Another drop of drool seeped down onto Stewart's face. The mouth moved on and Stewart stared down the golden-brown jaw, neck, shoulder, and chest of a giant female bear.

The huge bear stood over Stewart and spat a mighty roar at the man and fox. They shuffled backward, staring at her with wide eyes. The bear surged at them, roaring, and they scurried away.

She opened her mouth, craned down and began to close her jaws around the mockingbird.

"No! What are you doing?!" Stewart screamed.

The bear, unfazed, put the bird into its mouth. She turned, walked up to Stewart, and reopened it. Stewart, not knowing what to think, threw up his arms and shrieked. The bear stayed put, her hot breath on his arms. Eventually Stewart looked between his hands and saw the bird lying on the bear's tongue. She opened her eyes and gave a weak chirp to Stewart. A tear broke down his cheek.

The bear put the bird down gently and picked up Stewart's wrist with her teeth. Scared, but too weak to resist, he complied. She crooked her neck, guiding his hand behind her head. He grabbed on tightly, pulling and shifting until he was almost fully on her back, each movement a fiery jab of pain.

She picked up the bird again, then ambled off into the undergrowth with her two riders.

It was less excruciating than Stewart thought it would be, once he was secured. Relaxing a bit, he drifted in and out of consciousness along a trail that seemed too long.

The sound of motors grew in volume, then faded into a distant echo as the bear approached a large drainage tube beneath a freeway. Their path was blanketed by desert shrubs thirty-feet high stretching up to the large tunnel and weaving with a pepper tree near the entrance. Gnarled branches hung down from the roadside.

A breeze came from the tube, smelling of ancient desert dust.

And something more.

The bear sniffed the air in three directions before descending with Stewart and the mockingbird into the large opening and down toward the cave beneath the roads.

11

The coarse fur on the bear's neck made for a good handhold. Stewart's right leg was slung over her haunches, and his left side hung loose, foot nearly scraping the floor. With his face deep in her fur, his -nostrils were filled with the smell of bear, but also of sage and desert wind. The drainage tube was filled with him on her back, his body narrowly missing the roof in places as the huge bear plodded on into pitch blackness, the din of traffic now silenced far above them.

After several minutes, the concrete tube became a cobblestone-lined tunnel descending deep beneath the surface. The path widened out and the ceiling arched up, revealing a massive cave with fissures at the top of its domed ceiling, through which slices of glowing light pierced the center.

The rays illuminated plumes of dust dancing off the bear's fur as she walked them through the cave, away from the sunlight and into a cracked opening in the cave's interior wall.

Stewart felt a shift in the air as they entered the crack and plodded into a smaller cave. It was warmer by degrees, and dry. The bear's footsteps seemed quieted, her breath more shallow. Stewart could barely see through the fur to one wall in the little cave. On that wall were things decidedly human, including a shelf containing rows of jars with dried plants inside, labeled not with words but crude symbols. Also there were books, some clothing, and several mobiles made of roots, bones, and what appeared to be teeth, held together with string and wire.

The bear stopped, sank down to her belly, and leaned slightly to her right, then rolled all the way onto her side, maneuvering Stewart onto a mattress made of bound cloth with layers of blankets on top. He let go of her fur and lay on his unbroken right side, grunting in discomfort. The bear rolled back up, leaned her head near Stewart's, and deposited the mockingbird directly in front of his face.

He could see the bird was still ailing, and realized he would be dead a few times over if it weren't for this curious creature, which he supposed was now his greatest friend. He wondered how hurt she was.

The bear turned, and slowly walked toward the crack in the wall that led out of the caveroom. At the exit, she disappeared through the hole that seemed too small. Stewart saw, through the darkness, what had been concealed behind her.

A woman's body lay prone in a stone chair in the corner opposite him, her eyes closed. He couldn't tell if she were alive or dead, sleeping or awake. She was dressed in layers of dark rags, and looked very old.

Stewart felt the vibration of the bear's body thumping to the ground outside. Simultaneously, the woman in the corner snapped her eyes open.

Her gaze remained fixed on Stewart as she rose, slowly but intently, from the seat of stones and walked across the room. Her eyes were cloudy grey, her skin like leather. As she approached, her wiry and wrinkled arm emerged from the rags, and pointed at his face.

"Wait. Wait!" he protested. "Stop! Who are you? Who is that other guy? The bear? The fox thing? What's going on?" Every word hurt to say, but they spilled out.

A metallic taste flooded his mouth as he spoke. He turned, spitting out the disgusting fluid. When he turned back around, the woman's eye was very near his own. He jerked in fright.

"Sshh." She put her finger on his lips.

Stewart's body involuntarily relaxed with her touch. Time slowed. He saw she was very old, powerful, and beautiful. Her fierce eyes scanned his face as she picked the bird up from the mattress and held it next to her breast. From a fold in her garments she pulled a leaf, placed it in her mouth and chewed.

She looked at the mockingbird, and brought it close to her face.

From her lips came a combination humming and whistling sound that vibrated the air in the cave, followed by a greenish-grey vapor trail that snaked from the woman's pursed lips and into the beak of the injured bird.

The little bird fluttered, its eyes opening a crack. Stewart breathed a sigh of relief when he saw the bird perking up. The vapor continued pouring into her until her eyes became alert and bright. She sprang upright on the woman's hand, belting out five loud tweets, then held out her wings and slowly moved them back and forth, inspecting them.

When she was convinced she was okay, she leapt off the woman's hand and circled the small caveroom twice before landing on her shoulder and tweeting something in her ear. The woman smiled. The bird flew across the room to the stone seat.

The woman returned her attention to Stewart.

"Listen to me," she said, as if he had a choice. Her voice was like gravel, ancient and earthy. "Do not speak, Stewart." Her smile had disappeared.

Of course she knows my name, he thought.

She stood and turned. Stewart could see her long silver hair braided down to her thighs as she walked to the shelf and pulled down a jar.

"Something has been taken from you. Something important. It was taken long ago—" she paused, "—by the standard of your short life."

She pulled leaves from one jar, stopped it, shook out smaller, darker leaves from another, and put both varieties into her mouth.

"Taken by people you trust in a moment of weakness, and it has ruined them." Her voice muddied as she chewed, looking at him with a pity he didn't want.

Stewart had no idea what she could possibly be talking about, and it showed on his face.

"You poor child," she said. "You want to ask me where your bag is, your box, your knife. I am not talking about the silver knife. I do not care about that. I merely know who you are. You, however, do not. Because Jeb did not tell you what you need to know."

"And what is—"

"Silence," she cut him off, walking behind him.

He wondered if she knew about Jeb's demise, and wanted to tell her, but this didn't feel like a discussion. It would take so much energy to tell the tale, energy he did not have right now.

She pulled his shirt up. He gasped nervously. The whole shoulder blade area was already bruising. She pushed her hand into it, and Stewart squealed out in pain. Ignoring him, the woman spat the pulpy plant matter into her hand, pulled a vial from a fold in her clothing and dropped one drop onto the herbs, then mashed it together in her fingers. She knelt down and rested Stewart's head on her knee. He was too weak to resist as she spread the mixture onto his shoulder blade evenly with one deft motion of her hand.

The poultice began to work immediately, soaking into his skin and oozing down through muscle and sinew, then seeping into the broken bone like sap.

The mockingbird hopped up and down on the stone seat and chittered wildly, flapping her banded wings.

The woman leaned down and whispered into his ear. "You need to get back what they stole." Then walked out of the cave.

She returned holding a glowing stone in her hand, protected by an old, leather glove.

"You've gotta be kidding," Stewart said, not taking his eyes from the rock.

"Tricksters joke. I do not."

The rock was a perfect red-hot orb. She held Stewart down with surprising strength.

His scream of protest may as well have been silence for all the good it did. The woman did not waver, but drew the rock along the pulpy salve on his back while keeping him pinned to the ground. Steam blasted into the air as the rock began to dry the herbs rapidly, the woman's hands running it just above the skin like an iron.

The sappy fluid that had flowed into the bones' fracture solidified under the heat, forming an epoxy-like bond with the bone. The pulp she had spread on his back protected his skin from peeling off. Stewart could feel his scapula slowly fusing itself back together, which hurt exactly as much as breaking it apart, only more slowly. His high scream echoed through the cave.

"Aaargh! What the hell, lady?" He was beside himself with pain, his muscles spasming. Tears welled into his eyes as his bone tingled and itched, completely impossible to scratch. He writhed on the mattress with the woman's strong hands stilling him.

She looked right in Stewart's eye, inches away, holding steady both the rock and his helpless body.

"Silence," she said again through her gritted teeth.

Her eye was deep and vast. Old. Incredibly wise.

And it was perhaps the single most terrifying thing Stewart had ever seen. He agonized quietly.

She began a low, chanting song. Words, tones, and notes unfamiliar. Jagged yet flowing. So strange. Each sound produced a different vibration, and a different emotion within him. A separate part of his brain reacted to each respectively. He breathed deeply, impossible moments ago, and almost relaxed. Visions danced within his mind, fleeting and unreal. The ghosts of memories.

Aromas from the smoldering herbs filled the hot cave. The woman's voice grew louder, echoing. A nasally tone joined the low chant as she sang in two voices. Stewart widened his eyes in amazement.

Dust shuffled. The great bear's eyes were milky as she plodded back into the caveroom and shook her fur. Standing upright behind the woman, it let out a roar that shook the walls of the cave and rattled the glass vials on the shelf, joining her in song.

Time slowed to a crawl as the mockingbird leaped off the throne and attempted to fly to the bedside. Her body flew as if she was travelling through molasses, caught in waves of a slowly oozing turbulence. Still airborne, she sludged through the tones to Stewart, who scooped his left hand around her and plucked her from the thickened air.

Marveling at how good his shoulder felt, he cradled the bird in his hand, shielding her. Her long grey tail and smooth head poked from opposite ends of his fist.

The woman and bear's song rose, waves of sound lapping upon each other. Dust and pebbles began to dislodge and fall from the cracks in the walls. Stewart's eardrums felt like they were about to burst from the pressure.

Both the singers' eyes were milky white now.

Fissures at the top of the cave pulsated with light, brightening until snakes of web began to cascade down, tendrils drawing magnetically to the chanting pair.

"Fuck this," Stewart whispered.

He sat up, bird in fist. There was no sign the woman and bear had noticed. He felt better. Felt amazing, in fact. Stood. No reaction from them. Took a step. Nothing. The webs began to serpentine around the woman's arms, swaying in the ripples of sound. The filaments magnetized toward his presence and began to follow him.

He tried to walk quickly. Found he couldn't. He was stuck in the same turbulence that had trapped the mockingbird. Looking back at the woman and bear, he saw the tendrils moving faster than he was. They slithered their way over to the mattress, then seemed to gain purpose as they sensed his absence.

Stewart was halfway across the room, pulling his legs along while swimming with his hands through the thick air. The tendrils gained on him. He was almost at the exit when a solitary tendril landed on his calf, and sent his mind into chaos.

Stewart ripped his mind, then leg from the thing's cold embrace and made it to the exit. Behind, he could see the tendrils spasming. It made him think about the communication of a hive, of simultaneous actions and reactions.

He popped out to the larger cave, realized he could move at normal speed, and ran as fast and far away from the hole in the wall as he could. The cave was far larger than he had thought, and there were dozens of branching tunnels.

Which one?

So many choices. The chanting and roaring droned on from behind them, the ursine pair still occupied. For how long? Tiny heads of tendril were poking out of the smaller cave. He had to make a decision.

Choosing a tunnel he thought was best, he began to descend when he felt a sharp sting on his hand. The bird had pecked him.

Oh, no! I'm crushing her.

He loosened his grip. When he did, she chirped and flew from his hand, leaving the mouth of the cave Stewart had chosen, and landing on the floor of the next one over.

"You got it, bird."

A chill shot over him as he sprinted up the tunnel after her.

The dry heat from the surface warmed Stewart. Near the top of the tunnel were crude tool marks where steps had been chiseled out long ago. These stairs grew longer as the cave mouth opened up, from tiny hand-hewn things to broad platforms. The top was a wide and flat plateau about twelve-feet square with round river rocks set into it, forming a large spiral. The corners were carved with crude rounded symbols. Somewhere between runes and petroglyphs, separate and untouched by the spiral. Just beyond the entrance was a dense wall of brush and small trees, which filtered the sunlight, and beyond them lay an unfamiliar canyon. A small tunnel through the plants opened at the bottom. Stewart couldn't see any houses or buildings.

He stood on the carved stone, felt a terrible dizziness, and sat back down, realizing he hadn't eaten since Jeb's. Based on the sun's angle and his own hunger, that had been last night. His stomach growled. He felt sick.

The bird snatched a grasshopper out of a snarl of weeds and gulped it down, then flew into a small thatch of bamboo. She returned shortly with a larger grasshopper, which she deposited at Stewart's feet, pinning it to the ground. The big bug kicked its legs out repeatedly, to no avail.

"You're kidding," he said to the bird. "No burritos in there?"

He grabbed the bug. Sighing, he accepted his fate, and shoved the grasshopper into his mouth. It kicked his inner cheek twice as he bit in. The insect's guts flooded into his mouth, made him almost vomit, before he steeled his resolve and forced his way through it.

He felt better once he'd swallowed the last of the guts. They were gritty, and stuck to his face. He stood, and didn't throw up, a minor victory in itself.

He wiped sweat from his brow. *Damn it's hot.*

The pathway was grown over with the spring shoots that had mostly dried out in the early summer heat. He got low and tried to crawl, but after a couple feet had to get on his belly and commando through the bushes. Any piece of exposed skin was ripped by spikes and tines as he crawled through the knot of twigs. After fifteen feet, the trail stopped dead. He was trapped, fuming and sweating.

"Son of fucks and bitches," he said.

Every muscle tensed. He was not going to take this shit anymore.

With a massive effort he thrust his body upright, forcing the branches to give way. They broke and snapped until he was standing. Then he shoved and maneuvered his arms upward as far as they would go, grabbing handfuls of spiked twigs to pull himself up and out.

At first the meager branches simply bent down to him, but he kept going, stretching his hands up and pulling until he was a couple inches off the ground. After several of these, he got his hands out over the tops of the shrubs, then his feet. He evened his weight between all four limbs, until he lay sweaty and bleeding on top of the bush, fifteen feet off the ground, barely held aloft by the army of thin branches. He looked around and decided the only thing was to try to roll off the top and hopefully be carried free of the huge gnarled knot. From atop the bush, he could see the path he was supposed to have taken off to the left, winding away from the tunnel.

He rolled, landing on his hands, legs stretched to the sky, then twisted and somehow came to on his feet, astonished at his fortune.

The only thing that didn't hurt was his newly repaired shoulder, although whatever compound the Bear Woman had put on him was wearing off. Also, he was fantastically lost. He sat down to catch his breath. So very tired. Where was he?

The bird chirped. Another grasshopper. Stewart grabbed it. The things tasted terrible, but he couldn't deny it had sated his hunger. He tossed the twitching insect into his mouth and chewed, holding his breath. The thick guts were trickling down his throat when he heard the sound of stones clacking upon one another, then a hushed voice drifting on the breeze.

The bird twitted and flew onto a palm tree. The branches of the neighboring shrubs rustled, and a young boy rounded the trail's corner with his dog off its leash. The boy froze in his tracks. The dog began to growl and to bark furiously, inching closer to Stewart, unafraid.

The boy had Stewart's bag.

"Hey kid, that's mine," Stewart said, pointing.

The boy did not respond.

"You wanna do me a favor and get your dog the hell away from me?" Stewart asked.

The child stared, mutely, while the dog raged.

"Can you try, please?" asked Stewart, as the dog lunged at him. A successful feint, as Stewart flinched and put his arms in front of his face.

At first it seemed like the boy may not speak again, but then he whispered, "Come here, girl," provoking no reaction from the dog. "See? Nothing."

"That sure is funny, little guy. Can you perhaps try a little bit harder?"

"Little guy?" He cocked his head. "Fuck you, man." Then walked away, leaving the dog snarling and barking, pinning Stewart against the bushes.

"Okay! Big guy! Come back here and help me, big guy!" Stewart put his foot up between himself and the dog, pissing off the dog and making it go for his foot. He pulled it down and the dog missed, but landed right next to him. It was about to strike when a sharp whistle blew and the dog bounded down the trail after the boy.

"Give me back my fucking bag, you little shit! What the fuck!?" Stewart stood up. Another wave of dizziness washed over him, and he fell back down on his butt in the dirt.

The mockingbird jumped from the bush after she watched the tandem disappear, landing on Stewart's shoulder as he sat in the dust cloud. She perfectly mimicked the boy's whistle.

Stewart chuckled. He nudged his nose into her cheek, and she snuggled her head up to him in return.

They had to get that bag.

Before that, however, he was going to have to eat, and not just grasshoppers. He was a mess, physically and emotionally, and he needed somewhere to rest where he'd be left alone, somewhere to try and make sense of everything.

His house had been ransacked, so why would anyone return there? It was risky, but so was everything else at this point.

Fuck them anyway, it's my house.

The kid had also conveniently gone in the most likely direction of Stewart's apartment. He hoped he wasn't too far away.

"Two birds. One stone."

The bird tweeted a bent note.

"Sorry, girl. Figure of speech."

The path merged with a main walkway. Soon after, Stewart began to see houses on the canyon's lip. There was no sign of the boy or dog, no clue as to whether or not they had gone this way, but home would have its own rewards. Chiefly a shower, meal, and nap.

His energy was almost gone.

The sun's last rays shone on the pink clouds. Stewart smelled horribly, covered in the gore from Nickel's, mixed with his sweat and the Bear Woman's salve. He took off his shirt and balled it up.

The wide path turned from the canyon, up a hill covered in loose rocks and trash. The garbage had blown down from the end of a street. Stewart picked up a shopping bag from the ground and stuck his shirt in it. He stuffed a few handfuls of trash on top of the shirt. Maybe it would help his karma.

When he reached the top of the hill, he threw the bag in the trash. The first street sign he saw was 31st and A streets, roughly a half-mile from home. He knew his surroundings again for the first time in . . . he wasn't sure. Thinking of lost time, he realized he never got his shift covered at work.

He gave a whistle to the bird but got no response. The last place he had seen her was with the boy and dog, he realized. Well, she could fly and he couldn't, and he had to get home as quickly as possible, so he set off in that direction.

A mother and two daughters, speaking Spanish, walked by him. The two girls ceased speaking and cautiously eyed the blood splattered, shirtless man.

"Buenas tardes." Stewart said, smiling.

The mother made the sign of the cross, gathering the girls and quickening her step, not looking at Stewart.

He picked up the pace.

As he neared his house, he cut through a deserted lot with a drainage ditch slicing it in half, filled with palm and pepper trees. A trail led up the small hill and through the wispy branches heavy with peppercorns. Loamy smells wafted from the mulch below them. The mockingbird landed with a chirp on a gnarled branch and alerted Stewart to the strange sight unfolding before them.

"There you are," said Stewart.

Halfway up the hill he could see the dog. Stewart watched it through the hanging leaves and peppers, inching his body behind the trunk.

The dog stopped after a few steps, sniffed the air, and barked. Her signal brought the kid popping out of a thicket at the trailhead one block opposite Stewart, the bag containing the knife still tucked under his arm.

Screeching tires sounded, followed by a shouting voice. Stewart watched in shock as the boy and dog were confronted by a pale man in a track suit. *The* pale man. He was agitated, walking quickly toward the boy.

The boy said something. The pale man reacted violently when he heard it, lunging at the boy and dog, who separated at the last instant, making him shoot between them. He quickly turned and readied for another attack, looking pretty lively for an old dude who was brained not too long ago, Stewart thought. They regrouped, the boy retreating a few yards while the dog defiantly squared off.

The pale man stood still. His hand crept into his jacket pocket, and he brought out a slim black cone. It looked sleek and shiny; Stewart couldn't really tell what it was from where he stood.

The dog retreated, not taking her eyes off the black cone. The pale man cocked his arm and threw it, but the dog twisted just enough for it to whiz by her ear. The cone clattered into the street, and the dog scampered after it. She picked it up and bounded after the boy.

The pale man stopped trying to chase the boy and dog almost instantly, seeing their pace far exceeded anything he could match. He glared after them as they sprinted down the pathway through the ravine, directly toward the tree Stewart was hiding behind.

Stewart jumped into the pathway to block them. Instead of grabbing the boy, his hands got thin air, as both boy and dog moved like blurs around him, dodging as if he weren't even there.

Stewart didn't see the black cone fall from the dog's mouth and bounce down the hill behind him, into the mouth of a corrugated metal drainage tube.

They disappeared. Where they had been, or seemed to be going, was nothing.

Back behind the tree, Stewart saw the pale man had been joined by a tall blonde lady whose eyes drifted over Stewart's hiding place.

Stewart recognized her immediately. Nuala. The good friend of the now-murdered Jeb. And one of their bandmates back in the day.

She berated the pale man. He tried not to make eye contact with her, but she grabbed his face in her hand, forcing him. She pointed down the pathway, then shoved him back toward their car. His head hung down.

Nuala. Shit. The kid is wrapped up in this.

When they pulled off in a black sedan, Stewart set off in a dead sprint the rest of the way back to his apartment. The last block before home he was pushing himself so hard he tripped over a piece of sidewalk tilted from tree roots and tumbled until piling up next to Cora's empty parking spot.

"Fuck me," he said. He had to go get her car back. Not right now, though.

He stood and hightailed it up the stairs. His broken door swung open, revealing the mess that Nickel, or whatever, had left. After he had put the pieces together, the door clicked shut and he shoved every heavy piece of furniture in front of it. He thought of food but stumbled to his room, fell down on his mattress and blacked out completely.

12

Rustles and clanks pulled Buddy from his deep slumber. He slit one eye open and saw, in the darkness, Helen dressed to go outside. She wore several layers of clothing topped with a green puffy jacket and flowery skirt over camouflage cargo pants. Plastic bags spilled out of her pockets, all fifteen or twenty of them. She put a few items into a bag with her back to Buddy.

Luna sat watching Helen prepare. When she saw Buddy was awake, she wagged her tail, hopped over to him and licked his cheek. He scratched her head and yawned. Helen turned around with a soft smile on her lips. She chuckled when she saw the little dog nuzzling up to him.

"She sure likes you, Sugar. Like she's never liked anyone, not even Max, and that little girl loves Max."

"Maybe she just likes kids," Buddy reasoned, knowing it was more. "Is she Max's dog?"

"Lulu's her own dog. Sometimes we don't see her for days, then she stays here for a week. Don't you, Lulu?"

Luna rolled onto her back and lopped her tongue out. Helen rubbed her belly.

"She's what they refer to as an 'independent woman.' Much like myself." She pulled the bottom of her jacket for emphasis.

"Well, is she like me? Did she run away and she doesn't know what's gonna happen to her?" he asked.

"C'mere, Sugar." She wrapped her arms around him. "Now what did I tell you about making your own way and all that feeling sorry for yourself stuff? Luna's a happy dog, but that's not exactly what's troubling you, is it? You just got a friend in Max and you think maybe he left you. That ain't true, Sugar. The truth of the matter, honey, is that wherever Max went, and whatever it is he's doing, he's doing it to protect you, even if it means something really bad could be happening to him. He will go through all that to make sure you're safe. That's called sacrifice. We just have to wait. There's other stuff going on. It's all connected."

Buddy cocked his head.

"Another thing is that lady right there." Helen pointed to Luna, "She got you to safety, saving you from that horrible man Garth, leading you to Max, and to me. Lulu would do anything to protect you. There aren't many dogs like Luna out there. She has a special ability to communicate deeply and clearly with friends and enemies, as I'm sure you are aware."

Buddy nodded. Luna had slunk into his lap and closed her eyes. Of course he knew what Helen said was true.

"Furthermore," she continued, "you only just met me, but I know who you are. I've known about you for a while. It took a long time to spring you out, a lot of planning. And I'm not gonna let them get you back. I already like you too much." She halted, looking affectionately at Buddy.

"I already love you. Do you know what that means?" she asked.

He wasn't sure, but he was starting to get a pretty good idea. He shrugged.

"It means, Sugar, that I would lay my life down so you could survive. Right this second." She looked grave, letting him feel it. After a second she smiled. "So lighten the hell up, Sugar! Okay? That's three of us looking out for you right there, plus Ysenia."

Upon hearing her name he shivered. "What will happen to her?"

"She's safe for now. Soon it's gonna be her turn, but not yet. There is a time in a young lady's life when she is transformed, a time when blood comes to them. And power. Ysenia's transformation will be formidable. Those people don't know what they've gotten themselves into with her, so don't worry." Helen winked.

"There's a couple more people on our team, even if some of them don't quite know it yet. In case something happens to me, which is unlikely, or we get separated, I've gotta teach you a little bit more about the things we do, so you can stay safe. Like how to use the rabbit's gift."

"Did a rabbit give you the same kind of thing?"

"Not exactly, but speed and surprise are things I'm pretty good at. And concerning illusion, there's not many better."

"How am I gonna be able to do all that stuff?" It all seemed so overwhelming.

"Sugar, I'll teach you. That's what I do. It's all a part of the web. Bending 'em and placing 'em. It's hard to understand at first. I had a horrible time of it, and I didn't have anyone to help me. You've got me, though, honey, and I'm gonna make you incredible," Helen playfully rustled his hair, "if I do say so myself. Now get up. There's work to do."

Helen gently tossed his bag at him and exited the tent. Very lithe for such a large woman.

Outside, Buddy was surprised that the sky was getting darker, not lighter. Night had fallen during their conversation.

He followed her into the canyon, catching up at a defunct fountain made of rock, sunk into the hillside. A live oak tree spread its branches over the fountain and the circle of stones surrounding it, with what appeared to be the silhouette of an owl high in its branches.

Smoke drifted in circles in front of the large stone bowl, where Helen drew symbols in the air with a lit bundle of sage. Wisps of white smoke curled around her fingers and up her arms, slightly illuminated from the distant streetlamps.

She shook smoke from the bundle over them, catching the trails and pushing them into the boy's hair and the dog's fur. English, Spanish, and another older language ran through Helen's throat and lips as she wound smoky spirals around them, then smudged the stick out into the earth next to the fountain and smiled down on the little pair. "Sage. For purification of you guys, and to protect us here, Sugar. Okay?"

Buddy was filled with an inner peace.

"Yes," he answered.

Another scent, metallic and dim, accompanied the sage's fragrance. Buddy felt fear drain from his body. He was in his element.

His canyon.

"Remember this feeling," Helen said. "Let your muscles learn this route to fearlessness, relaxed and ready. So they may return when needed."

From his feet and hands, throughout his body and up to the crown of his skull, a tingle ran, his nervous system and musculature were charged, electric.

Helen slung two cloth bags around her shoulders and looked at her two companions. "Ready?" She could see the change in the boy.

"Yep, we are!" Buddy was infected by the lovely woman's enthusiasm, so different from the warehouse. His guard was softening.

"Then let's go teach you how to kick some ass! Haha!" She bound up the stairs, quickly and soundlessly.

Luna and Buddy caught up to her beneath the ancient fig trees in the park's center, and they walked through the mist.

In the center of the grass field, Helen faced him. "I'm going to train you to use your newfound talents, and those you were born with. Through this whole process, and very likely for the rest of your life, trust your natural instincts as your principal guide. Always go with the gut. If you got a bad feeling from someone, get away from that person as quickly as possible, and say and do whatever you can to do so. Max probably showed you how to do things without being seen. Now I'll show you what to do if you are."

"The first thing is called obfuscation," she said. "It's like hiding in plain sight. Does that make sense?"

"Not really," Buddy answered.

"Fair enough," she chuckled. "Look at me, Sugar."

She was standing in front of him, plain as day.

"Okay. What am I looking at?" he said.

"Just keep looking."

As she spoke, her body seemed to lose its clarity, as if shrouded in a milky fog. It continued until she appeared to vanish. The trees behind her were hazy, but visible.

"Helen? Where are you?" He walked toward where she had been until his hand felt the puffy jacket, and then he could see her again. "Whoa," he said.

"Yes, whoa," she chuckled, then patted Buddy's head. "I'm not actually becoming invisible, now. I'm merely manipulating the strands of the web to reflect something other than myself. You see?"

"No," the boy replied, shaking his head. He wanted to, but couldn't wrap his brain around the concept.

Helen gave another soft chuckle. Reassuring, not derisive. She pulled a compact mirror from her pocket.

"Check it," she said.

Looking into Buddy's eyes, she raised the mirror between them. It was tilted so as she held it higher, it showed the large fig tree reflected in the mirror, superimposed over her face. She moved the mirror closer to Buddy until it blocked her whole head with the reflection of the tree, then slowly moved it away.

"It's like that, only with webs as the mirror."

The lesson worked. Buddy laughed.

He practiced being able to see the webs for a good hour, with almost no luck. Helen patiently sat on the roots of the old fig. Sighing, he joined her on the roots, dejected.

"Motherfucker," he said.

Helen lit up when she heard the expletive.

"Haha. That's something that will get attention if you need it. Curse words." She smiled. "Good idea, kid."

Buddy smiled back.

"There are very few things that make people take notice like a little kid cussing his tail off, even if they've heard it all before," Helen said. "Which you may already have found out, I think, when you baited Garth."

Buddy nodded as Helen leaned close.

"Now, these are in an emergency only. If you're trying to stay out of sight, don't even think of them. But if there's nothing else you can do, I want you to shout something like this."

She whispered a stream of profanities that shocked him. Some he'd heard, others were new, but sounded gross. He found himself backing up from her subconsciously, intimidated by the filth.

"I, uh, see what you mean," he said when she had finished. "Should I practice?"

"Oh good gracious, no, Sugar." She waved her hands to shoo the very idea away. "The effect is too powerful. Almost anybody would check that out, even this late. You can only practice them in your mind. You seem pretty good at it anyway."

"Alright."

"Good, Sugar. Now, if you have to do it, do it loud. After the cussing there'll be a moment when the person coming after you will be frozen, because there's no way on this green Earth anyone's gonna expect a string of curse words to be slung at them by an eleven-year-old boy. That'll be the window of time you have to get away from them and disappear. They'll have to figure out whether to follow, or get out of there before anyone sees them trying to snatch you. You still with me, Sugar?"

He nodded.

"Okay, then. Just say the word 'go' at me. I'll wait a sec, then try to catch you before you reach those trees." She pointed to the Torrey Pines that spilled over the hill above Buddy's original root camp, barely visible in the darkness.

It seemed simple, especially with his new rabbit speed.

"Go!" He ran, not top speed. He wanted her to have a chance. After only three steps, he felt the ground behind him shake. When he turned his head she was in midair, arm cocked to strike. With a cuff to his shoulder, she sent him somersaulting sideways, spindly legs pistoning.

"You're not the only one with speed, cocky little bunny. Ha!" She made comical kung fu moves. "So now you see even more that not everyone is what they seem. Never underestimate your opponents, and try not to overestimate yourself. Those are both potentially deadly mistakes. Let's try it again." She lifted him off the ground.

Buddy improved each time, zigging and zagging across the grass. After the tenth attempt Helen reduced her response time to almost zero and he still made it to the trees.

"There we go! Good job, Sugar!" She hugged Buddy, whose chest heaved.

Luna jumped up and put her forepaws on them. Strands of web wrapped around the three like living smoke in the misty night.

●　　●　　●

Taking a break, they shared granola bars, beef jerky, and juice from out of Helen's pockets. Luna chewed slowly on the jerky and looked along the perimeter.

Buddy looked up into the tree branches. "Helen, who are those people who had me in the warehouse? Why did they choose me? What are they doing? Max told me some stuff, but I don't really get it."

She raised her eyebrows. "Okay. I don't know everything, but I'll tell you what I do know, because we're equals, you and I. And that means if you want to hear about those horrible people, then you, Sugar, are a man." She gazed at Buddy with pride, "No matter how old you are."

"I'm kinda scared," he admitted.

"If you weren't, there'd be something wrong with you. But you can handle it.

"First things first. That woman, Nuala, is not your mother, as you've figured. I don't know who your mom is, Sugar, but that's one thing we're gonna work hard to find out, okay? Nuala is part of a group that went wrong somewhere."

Buddy's eyes were far away. He had known, in his heart, about Nuala. His real mother was out there somewhere. Not right here. He rubbed his eyes.

"What's wrong, Sugar?"

"I was starting to think you were my real mom," he said, fighting back tears.

Helen reached for a handkerchief, and mopped up tears of her own before passing it to Buddy.

"Sorry, Sugar. I wish that too," She held him. "But I'll be your friend. I'm definitely an improvement over that last lady, though, huh?" She chuckled. "Maybe we'll find your mom, too. Nuala stole you ten years ago, and your mom really must want you back."

Buddy was overcome with emotion. He took a moment and wiped his face clean.

"Do you need some time, Sugar?"

He slowed his breathing, sighed deeply, and said, "No, Helen, I'm okay. You're an awesome lady whether you're my mom or not."

"That's sweet, baby." she kissed his forehead, stood up. "Now, to tell this story I have to use some tricks. You'll be safe, okay?"

Buddy nodded, straightening up and wiping his face again.

"So, we know about the web, that's what this whole thing is about. It stretches and permeates everything. People like us can twist it and shape it in different, individual ways. Max does Max stuff, I do Helen stuff. Which, by the way, makes teaching a little inexact. I'm assuming we are that far already."

"Yes. we are."

"Okay," She beckoned him to a fig tree and sat down. "Now breathe deeply. Take in the smells, and let them teach you. Some stories are best without words."

Buddy did. The scents triggered knowledge and memories. The bark of the tree swirled and changed, its lines forming vaguely familiar shapes. He soon could make out shadowy figures in the vision playing on the tree bark.

A circle of cloaked beings stood around a massive stone, their fingers twisting in the dark. Faintly luminous threads connected the beings to the boulder, as well as one another, then off into the sky. As his eyes adjusted, Buddy could make out certain clothing and jewelry that individualized each: a collar for one, a headband of laurel sumac for another. Their faces were obscured. Soon others emerged from the shadows, bringing trays of food and water, then departing.

The weavers of the web, he thought.

With a loud crack, the boulder split in two. With it, the group halved, encircling each stone. The split stones cracked in half, then again. The cloaked figures could not keep up as a chain reaction set off, leaving boulders strewn about the circle. When it was done, each figure had one stone beside them. They picked them up, carrying them in different directions, the webs trailing.

The scene was empty, save for shards of the stone, small as slivers, littering the circle. A figure rose from shadow, picked up several shards, and sneaked off down the hill, beneath the hanging branches of a pepper tree.

Buddy's vision followed.

The thief had blazing blue eyes, and handed the stone, now a black conical knife, to the blonde woman. She took it and departed.

The sight shifted.

The blonde woman is running through the canyons, a young

child in her arms. The child cries. Buddy beholds his young self.

The vision stopped. With a sigh of relief Buddy looked at the fig tree, solid and unmoving.

"That was me."

"Yes," Helen answered.

He rubbed over the scars on his back, silent for a time. "Okay, what else?" he said.

"You ready? Okay. Those people are trying to steal control of the tools that shape the webs. And now they're making their own. These tools are called looms and snares. Looms reroute threads, which alters their meanings somewhat. Snares kink strands and take certain things: ideas, even people, wholly out of the web. Got it?"

"I'm lost," he said.

"Hold on." She sang one note, another, then a song.

"Cuando el niño se
convierte en un hombre,
Es como ver el conejo
a la deriva en el filamento."

Buddy's mind raced sideways. His electric nerves melded the webs from the rabbit within. He understood in his very cells the meanings and powers of the all-encompassing web, uniting and binding all things. He soared as the rabbit over myriad colors of threads, stretching into the infinite, leaving the park behind, yet fastened to it.

His spirit raced over the webs until he came to a thread that circled upon itself, and a squat-looking pudgy man looked back at him with pleading eyes. Colorful pictures covered the man's arms. He looked hopeless. Only a few sickly looking tendrils connected the man to the web The rest swirled around him like a school of wild fish, not touching him.

Snare, the thought came.

Buddy sped away down braided lights, streaming like a blur. He'd seen that man before.

The shimmering landscape changed, dropping in temperature. Before him lay threads that changed color dramatically. When he passed from the pearlescent blue section of thread to a discernibly different grey hue, his insides grew cold. The very meaning of the threads was being altered; the strands of water and sky were changed as to resemble themselves, but in his core Buddy saw them as false visions, transformed.

Loom. The information blipped in his core.

Buddy saw Max creeping in the dark bushes surrounding a small cottage in a grove of live oak trees, dark and silent.

Another vision. He saw Max, only he was in a warehouse. No. *The* warehouse. Bound to a chair. A trickle of blood shone from the corner of his mouth.

Which of these was real?

Buddy focused on one of the two visions.

In the oak grove, Max crept closer to the house, then on the porch. He made pops and clicks with his mouth, each time pulling on the door. It remained locked.

The vision re-entered the darkened room, and Buddy beheld the scene of his long imprisonment. The warehouse. He wasn't sure if this was happening now, had happened, or was yet to occur as he drifted closer to the Max who was tied to a chair, face bleeding. The pale man and the giant walked from the shadows and stood over the beaten man. Blood dripped from the giant's gloved fists. The man in the chair bore a striking resemblance to Max, but something was off. This couldn't be him.

"Where's the child, Max?" asked the pale man, pacing in front of the prisoner, his track suit swishing as his thighs rubbed together.

"I keep fucking telling you, my name is Raymond, and I don't know what kid you guys are talking about!" the man shouted through the rising blood in his throat. He spit a crimson trail onto the ground.

Small freckles dotted the man's dark skin. He also had the corners of tattooed wings peeking out from beneath the collar of his shirt. Max had neither freckles or any tattoos. These men didn't know who Max was.

Peik produced a slim black cone, small markings etched upon its length. Buddy recoiled, and a ripple in the vision occurred.

The giant looked in Buddy's direction, sniffing the air.

Buddy's heart thudded in his chest as he watched Peik stab the cone into the bound man's left lung, just below the heart.

The man screamed. Blood and webs of light streamed and scrambled from him into the blade as his terrified voice echoed through the warehouse. The cone glowed with an amber fire.

Raymond's head slumped over. The cone twitched and shook in Peik's hand. He held it aloft, eyes wild, and gestured to the rear of the room.

Buddy froze upon seeing the hooknosed man with Oliver and the dog beside him.

Frank walked from the shadows straight for Buddy. He could see the rabbit adrift on the web.

As Buddy turned and ran, he heard a shout.

His legs churned, but something was slowing him. He looked back to see his hindquarters stretching off, trapped in the warehouse. Webs flowed from the hooknosed man's hands and intertwined with the rabbit hairs, weaving together and holding him fast. He looked at Buddy hungrily.

Buddy kicked hard, shouting, and exploded away with a pop, racing down the pathway of light. He whizzed past the tattooed man in the snare . . .

Helen's jacket. Her intoxicating essence. She held him, but he couldn't keep his eyes open . . .

Max circled the house, frustrated.

Something was different.

This is the dreamtime, a voice, attached to nothing. *There are different rules.*

His vision shifted.

Frank approached Raymond. Buddy bucked and tried to escape at first, but found he wasn't being detected.

Look at your hands.

They were translucent. He watched his life force pump through the nerves and veins, arteries, muscle and bone, and an understanding came to him. He was undetectable.

Different rules.

"Get up, Max," Frank said to the limp body. Peik and Markuz watched from behind.

The man did not move.

Frank whispered something into Raymond's ear.

"Get up, Max."

Still nothing. "Get up, Raymond."

The corpse opened his eyes, straightened his neck, and tried to rise from the chair, but the ropes forced him back. He tried again, then gave up and waited for instruction.

Frank's left eye twitched. "Well, gentlemen, it seems you have heroically captured the wrong person. This is a disaster, to say the least." He pulled a hooked blade from inside his jacket. "Who would like to take the credit for this catastrophe?" His eyes darted between them, eyebrows raised.

Eventually Markuz said, "I will," and raised his hand slightly.

"Wrong," said Frank. At once he was upon the pale man, the curved blade breaking the skin underneath his eye. Blood trickled down his white cheek.

Frank's skin grew red and splotchy with anger as he whispered, "There will be no more mistakes tolerated, Peik. Do you grasp that concept?" The trickle ran down the blade.

"Yes, sir. I do." Peik's voice trembled.

"Good. Now go find the actual person named Max, and the boy, immediately." He returned the knife to his jacket after wiping it on Peik's shirt, a bloody smear in its wake.

Peik scrambled out of the room. The giant looked at Frank.

"Yes, Markuz, you go as well."

Markuz nodded, then followed in Peik's footsteps, taking Oliver with him before Frank had any more ideas.

The man named Raymond groaned, expressionless. Frank picked up the black cone from the table. He bent his head and peered into it.

"Just you and me now. How did you get mixed up in all this, Raymond?"

Frank placed the cone on Raymond's lap, then cut his ropes with the curved knife. The man sat still on the chair, staring lifelessly through milky eyes.

"Aash Xashoul," said Frank, making a slicing motion with his hand as he did so.

The man in the chair picked up the conical blade from his lap, then, with a sudden burst, plunged it deep into his own neck. His body convulsed, falling onto the floor. It twitched, then lay still. A puddle of blood spread slowly across the tiles as Frank's chuckling laugh echoed throughout the chamber.

Buddy gasped, but Frank couldn't hear. He walked backwards through the wall.

The cabin in the oaks.

Max threw the rock at the largest window. It held firm, but sent a loud crack through the grove. The rock had broken to pieces. Shards lay next to the house.

Rustles and a muttering voice from the trees. Max distanced himself, keeping the house between him and it.

As he retreated, a glint of metal caught his eye, high up in the interwoven branches of two trees. He paused, as if considering further inspection, but the approaching sounds from the trees made that impossible for now.

"Stop!" The shrill whisper of a second voice.

Max froze. It took him a moment to realize the voice was talking to the mutterer, not him. Monitoring one person out here was risky. Two was stupid.

The bright moon, almost full, shone in small rays through the canopy, lighting Max in small frames as he disappeared from the oak grove.

Buddy awoke in Helen's arms. "Max will be back today."

She looked intrigued. "That's good, but how do you know that?"

"I saw it in a dream, but it's really happening I think. It was just more real than they usually are, plus the dream was like picking up where I left off with the webs, except I wasn't the rabbit. I was more like a ghost." He rubbed his head and yawned.

"Well, Sugar, if it was so real, how did you know it was a dream?"

"It sounds weird, but I knew because I looked at my hands." He didn't mention the voice.

Helen's eyebrows arched in surprise. He'd discovered one of the most powerful and difficult things in the gateway to all this; the ability to control dreams. The hands. That's the first step.

"Actually, baby, the weird part is that it doesn't sound weird at all. Where was Max when you saw him?"

"In a grove of trees, trying to get into a little house. He was looking for something. I don't think he got it, though. Some people came and he ran away."

"Who was it?"

"I don't know."

"But he got away? You're sure?"

"Yes."

Buddy could see the relief wash over Helen's face. He hesitated before asking, "Helen, do you know someone named Raymond?"

"No, Sugar. I don't think I do. Why?"

"Well, I think the people who used to keep me locked up were trying to get Max but they got this Raymond guy instead. The guy looked almost exactly like Max. I even thought it was before I saw he had little freckles and a tattoo. Then they stabbed him with one of those cones and he went to sleep. After that Frank made the guy try to stand up like a puppet, even though he was tied down, like Frank was toying with him."

Helen was shocked. "Damn."

"Then Frank made him kill himself."

Helen's mouth hung open. When she came around, she said, "So Frank knows that Max exists, and has a relatively decent description of his appearance. And he's started stabbing people who look like him.

"However, they don't have him, and, if your dream vision is correct, then he's coming to us right now. Also, they don't know about me, or where we are. And we haven't even counted the most important thing."

"What's that?"

"You can already control the dreamtime. You don't have anything to compare it to, but trust me, not even Frank is very good at that."

Buddy was surprised. The dreamtime was a strength that Frank didn't have. But, if there were things that he could do and Frank could not, the reverse must be true. Converging paths along the web. While fearful, Buddy accepted his fate.

Buddy pulled on her sleeve. "There's one other thing."

"What's that, Sugar?"

"Peik and Markuz are coming for Max. And for me. Frank said so."

"Well," she said, " I hope they're ready to get their asses kicked."

13

Helen snored in her sleep, lying next to a short stack of books in the corner. Buddy sat leafing through a book of folktales, trying to be silent. The tales were simple, but he grasped a deeper meaning and pattern to the stories. The ones about tricksters, in particular.

After a while he yawned and put the book down. He looked over at Helen. She and Max weren't part of the ancient order they had told him about, but they certainly did know quite a bit about them. Tricksters. Connections.

He reached for the book, but instead picked up a black journal. Inside were jagged symbols and pronunciation keys. Spellings were written and scribbled out next to the symbols, some as many as seven times.

He read down the list, saw one he recognized, and froze. A symbol that had been etched into the black cones. Then another.

A chill overcame him. He put down the book, stacking the others on top.

Luna whined, then hopped up, tail wagging. She ran to the tent's flap as it opened. Buddy looked into the smiling face of Max.

"Hey, Buddy! Glad to see you're alright." He pulled Buddy close and hugged him. Buddy held on tight, trying to keep the tears of relief from falling.

"You were in a little house," Buddy said. "I saw you."

Max looked surprised. "You've been practicing."

Helen made a very audible yawn from her spot nestled in the

covers of the bed. "Actually the kid's doing pretty good on his own, aren't you, Sugar? After you stranded him here." She looked disapprovingly at Max.

"Sorry. But it had to be done. It was Peik and Markuz. Why? What happened? Did someone find you?"

"That drunk pervert Garth did. Fortunately the boy had Luna or he might not have made it," said Helen.

"Shit. But he did, he did," said Max, smiling. "You okay, little man?"

Buddy shrugged.

Helen pulled Max into the nest of blankets. They kissed lightly three or four times before Max rolled over on his back and sighed. "That was a close one. Frank definitely knows about me now." He pulled a can of iced coffee from his jacket, cracked it open and drank a swig.

"Those two goons got the wrong guy though. Some fucking asshat that robbed some old lady off the trolley. I had to screw him to make the switch. And concerning the goon squad, it didn't take a whole lot." He chuckled and sat back. "That dude did look a whole lot like me."

"Raymond. They know. They'll be looking," said Helen.

"How do you know that?" Max eyed Buddy. "Shit, really?"

"Yes." Helen cracked her knuckles. "Really."

"Well, they were here already, and there's a whole city to search before they double back. We're good for a while. Enough to get you acclimated, my man."

Buddy smiled, sensing a shift in the air.

"So . . . What'd you see?" Max asked.

"Well, Raymond is dead," said Helen, bluntly.

His smile dimmed. "Son of a bitch. Poor guy." He truly did feel terrible for him, purse snatcher or no. "It was Frank?"

"Yes." said Buddy.

"Man. Shitty. You actually saw that?"

Buddy nodded.

The tent shifted as Helen sat up. "Yes. He did. There's another thing that happened when you were away. Buddy had a meeting with a rabbit. It gave him some things."

Max smiled wider than Buddy had seen yet. "Alright, my man!

Not wasting any time!" He held up his hand. Buddy just stared at it. Max resolved to teach him some stuff about actually being a kid. "Hit me on my hand."

Buddy did, marveling at the satisfaction the high five gave him.

"Sooo," Max said, giving Luna a piece of jerky. "What happened to Garth?"

Buddy told the story as best he could, and admitted that he'd stopped worrying about Garth after he met the rabbit.

"Well, he is something to worry about," said Max. "Like a wrench in the gears. We've gotta take care of him."

Buddy had heard this phrase before. "Do you mean you're gonna kill him, Max?"

Helen and Max looked at him in disbelief.

"We don't kill people, Sugar, unless it's the very last option. Even then, murder warps the web. Makes it dark times for the murderer." Helen spoke slowly and deliberately, not breaking eye contact. "Fortunately we have other means at our disposal, and can solve this problem without further violence."

"Like what?"

"Well, Sugar." Her eyes were cold fire. "We're gonna scramble him."

"What's that?"

"Soon, Sugar. I want to know about that house, first."

"Yeah, what were you trying to find in that house, Max?" Buddy asked. "And why didn't you come back after the switch?"

"There's a silver thing. It called to me when I thought you were safe. It's a snare, but older. It's the reason anybody knew how to make the black ones."

"I can find it," said Buddy, like a matter of fact.

"You will do no such thing!" Helen wrung her hands. "What are you trying to do to this boy, Max?"

"Yeah, Buddy. It's too sketchy to even consider right now," said Max, stealing a wink at Buddy. "Let's teach him the scramble."

● ● ●

Garth's lip oozed pus into his mouth. He spat it out and rubbed his aching head, trying to make sense of his situation. His ankle and back ached horribly after his fall down the cliff. Fucking stupid little kid. Why didn't he just relax?

The big drunk sifted around with his hands in the trashy area next to the drainage ditch. He couldn't go back to his camp. He wouldn't make it. Pulling the little bottles of vodka from his pockets one by one, he looked for a solitary drop of booze in the bottom of any of them, throwing them into the bushes with the other trash when he saw they were empty. This had been his camp once, but it had gotten too dirty even for his slovenly ways. That was his pattern; live somewhere until he had trashed it, then move on. Somebody would either clean it up or they wouldn't, he didn't care.

Like a miracle, the last little one-ounce airplane bottle was full. He drank down the piddling amount of alcohol. It warmed him, giving him the energy needed to make it to the vending machine in the mechanic's yard. Chips. Then he could make it to the liquor store up the hill.

He thought he heard a song from high on the cliff as he made it to his feet. An eerie melody cascading over the expanse. Ignoring it, he made his way to the torn fence, wobbling on his gimpy ankle. His infected flesh burned and dripped, scraping on the steel. He grunted like a massive pig.

Through the fence, he saw a young boy. Not the one with the fucking shitty little dog. This boy wanted him, he could tell. He opened his arms and hobbled toward the child, and was surprised when the child spoke to him in a man's voice.

"You're trespassing, sir. The exit is that way. Please leave." The child pointed to the big northern gate.

"Shit. Just want to have a little fun, with you." He grabbed the air, hands squeezing.

"Man, I will place you under arrest right now if you don't turn the fuck around and get out of here," the boy said.

This kid was a hard ass! "C'mon, baby." Garth swayed back and forth, beckoning with his sausage fingers, then catapulted toward the boy. He was confused to find himself upended and restrained in a matter of seconds by such a small adversary.

From high on the cliff, Buddy clicked two rocks together in a slow rhythm, like Helen had told him, while Max played the one-stringed ektar and Helen softly cooed into the wind. They watched as the melody worked its magic, and Garth's scrambled mind had him trying to molest the off-duty police officer whose weekend it was to guard the mechanic's yard.

After a couple minutes, a squad car came and carted Garth away to jail.

Buddy felt positively ecstatic. Victorious, even. He knew the larger concern still loomed with Frank and the other warehouse people looking for him, but they had come and gone. He allowed himself to feel good and confident after taking part in eliminating Garth from their lives. For the second time, he thought..

They walked along the fence, down into the canyon, and sat beneath the biggest live oak in the park. The thick and gnarled branches cast a wide net of shade.

Helen and Max told Buddy some of the mysteries they had struggled so hard throughout their lives to understand. Preparedness was key. Learn fast and get ready.

Helen said that while nothing made up for the years of abuse, they hoped this knowledge would even things out just a little. They spent hours doing defensive drills.

After the lesson period, Buddy's mind was brimming. Max suggested that Buddy walk along the pathways by himself. Helen protested, but Max had reasoned that Buddy would have to get used to being alone This was the safest time Buddy might ever see.

"Only if Lulu goes," said Helen.

The boy and dog walked until they heard voices from behind some trees. Hiding in a small knot of brush, they watched while several older kids came down, drank beer and smoked cigarettes and weed and threw their trash everywhere, then left it all there.

Buddy remembered how upset Max had been by the trash in the canyon, and felt the same ire bubbling.

Tricksters.

A plan worked within, fueled by bravado.

When the group of kids left, Buddy and Luna trailed them back up a hill to their neighborhood, where some broke off to return to their homes. The thickset boy who obviously thought of himself as the leader, and was by far the most heinous litterer, walked farthest. From behind a car Buddy made note, then went back to the trash pile in the canyon. He filled twelve plastic shopping bags with trash. Threading his fingers through the handles, they crept back to the kid's house. The day had turned to evening, and the lights in the house were dim. Whoever was in the home seemed to be off toward the rear. Perfect.

Buddy opened a small penknife and sliced off all the knots from the bags, then poured the contents onto the porch. Candy wrappers, empty canisters and bags of weed, beer bottles and cans. The second-to-last bag was full of dog shit. He hadn't seen a dog with the kids, but he was trying to make a point, here. He snickered to himself, dumping the turds throughout the mess. Luna's tail twitched back and forth.

The coup-de-grace was the final bag he sprinkled on top of the now heavily littered porch; the one that contained the shredded and half-burnt homework they'd left in the clearing with their names on it and everything.

Finished, he sat back with Luna, and surveyed his work. The porch was a stinking wreck. Mission accomplished. Buddy picked up a stick that would reach over the porch, rang the doorbell with it, and ran across the street, crouching behind a bush to watch the proceedings.

A squat, pattern-balding man opened the door, his expression irate as he noticed the chaos on his porch. Something caught his eye. He bent down and picked up a piece of paper before wrinkling his nose and dropping it. He smelled his hand, now with a smear of dog feces on it.

"Eddie!" he bellowed, walking back into the house. "Get the fuck out here right now!"

Buddy laughed silently and Luna wagged her tail.

Eddie came out holding trash bag, pissed. "It fucking stinks."

"If you complain again you'll be smelling your own blood pouring out of your nose. Now to get to work," said his dad.

Helen was worried when Buddy told them, but Max laughed and laughed. He was delighted at the very idea, let alone the awesome execution of the prank. "You were born to be a trickster, Buddy!"

"Don't you encourage him, Baby!" Helen said. The act reeked of hubris, and she didn't like it, but he needed to be prepared to think for himself.

• • •

The next day, Buddy and Luna set out again, scampering down a hill into a copse of eucalyptus. Buddy stopped short when he heard voices, and metal balls ping in canisters accompanied by high-pitched blasts of air. When he peeked from behind a rock, he saw new kids spraying paint cans onto the tree bark.

When they left, the crew got into a sparkly new blue compact with the spoiler, rims, and all the trimmings. Another plan brewed in Buddy's mind.

The painted tags boasted the name of their crew, also the name of their street.

Later Buddy found the sparkling blue racer parked in a yard. Noise boomed from inside the house as music played. Voices yelled and laughed. Perfect cover for the sounds he would need to make.

Piece of cake.

Buddy pulled out the spray cans, spraying the kids own tags onto the car until it was covered.

Luna whined at approaching lights. They retreated as a black and white police car rolled around the corner, but the searchlight lit them up. As they ran the door to the house opened. Still in the beams of the police car, Buddy looked back at the older boy in the doorway, one of the kids from the canyon. Their eyes met.

Shit.

As they fled, Buddy heard the music stop, then yelling when they saw the car. That had not gone as well as he had hoped.

At the camp, he was too embarrassed to tell them how badly he'd screwed up. He left out the police, and being seen, and downplayed the amount of damage he had done to the car.

This could be swept under the rug. He'd just have to avoid those kids, which shouldn't be that difficult considering his talents versus theirs. He already knew how to avoid police.

Max seemed okay, but Helen did not seem pleased. However, she remained silent for now.

Max had told him there are good cops and bad cops, and that they weren't sure who was who just yet. If they went to the wrong person, Buddy would just be given back to Frank, he'd said. Maybe the law said that Frank and he belonged together. Buddy visibly recoiled when he heard that, and realized that the police option was too risky. He hoped the cop who had shined the light on him was one of the good ones.

Buddy stayed close, until Max asked why he wasn't exploring any longer. He felt he'd better go out, at least to decrease suspicion that anything was amiss.

They set off to the northeast. Buddy hadn't been this way, but it wasn't toward the party house, the dog-shit house, the warehouse, or the cop. And it didn't lead back into the areas of Balboa Park that housed the zoo and museums, and therefore crowds of people. This was the only option left.

They cut through the golf course, behind the diner. In between two rows of hedges, trying to stay out of sight, they were spotted by May. The waitress seemed to know Luna as she appeared from the kitchen with a couple strips of bacon.

"Is that your dog?" she asked, giving Luna one of the strips. "Because she comes up here without a leash a lot. Like now." She looked at the rope in his hand.

He awkwardly tried to attach it for a few attempts before getting it, not having used it much. "Uh, yeah. Thanks." Buddy jerked the leash and tried to drag her away while she begged for another piece of bacon. The dog won the struggle.

The waitress giggled, gave her the second piece, and watched them disappear down the hill.

When they were out of sight, Buddy said, "Dang, you're good at this stuff." He scratched Luna's ears. She gave a playful bark and stood on her hind legs.

"Showoff."

They walked beside the golf course, then up a rocky wash. Entering a tunnel, their footsteps and breathing echoed in long sprawling tones as they jogged through. Buddy had to hunch over to avoid hitting his head. There was a crack the size of his body in the middle. Cold air blew from it, casting a chill over his skin. Their footsteps rang out as they doubled their pace.

At the exit, the path ran through a wide clearing, which eventually forked off into three different canyons. Following one through brambles of Encinitas trees, they came out at the top of a hill. A man across the street looked familiar. Buddy dropped behind a car and peeked over the hood, and saw the tattooed man who had been trapped in the web walking aimlessly down the street. His eyes were blank discs, and he was muttering to himself. They sped away.

Hearing footsteps, the man's milky eyes tried unsuccessfully to follow the blur.

Buddy didn't want to backtrack after seeing him. Having cut to the north and east this far, Buddy reasoned that they only had to cut south and west the same amount to get back to Golden Hill Park. They made it three blocks before another of the canyon pathways opened up to the right. He felt better when they entered it. He was becoming at home in the canyons.

From nowhere and everywhere, a hum sounded, saturating Buddy's entire being with a silver tone. With it, he felt a call. Luna's ears were perked as she looked toward an eroded canyon that stopped at gnarled branches. They followed the silver hum, Luna growling low. When they reached the wall of plants, she disappeared into it. Buddy followed her down a thin zig-zagging pathway through the bushes into a grove of live oak. Through the thick strand of trees, Buddy could see the small cottage from the dream.

The sliding glass door was locked. Luna made a squealing sound. Buddy, nodding, made the same sounds he had heard Max make in the vision. On the first two, nothing happened, then on the third try the lock popped and he slid the door open.

"Cool," he said to Luna.

When they entered, they heard the hum coming from the kitchen. They got as far as the dining room table. Jeb's dead eyes stared from his severed head out of a bowl of granola. His bloody body sat in a chair next to it.

Following Jeb's line of sight, Luna barked at the oven. Buddy jumped away, about to get out of the house, when he felt a tug on his pant leg. Luna was straining to keep him there. She whined, imploring. He tried his hardest not to look at Jeb.

Luna walked to the oven and barked again. Buddy opened one steel door, saw nothing but a metal grill in the middle. He opened the other side. Nothing.

Luna whined and stepped forward, putting her paw inside the

oven, on a detached piece of metal at the bottom. He pulled it up and reached down into the hole. A black bag lay beneath.

He opened it and pulled a wooden and silver box out, cracking the lid. The hum became unbearably loud. Silver light shot everywhere.

This is what Max had been looking for.

Buddy reached for the knife, but Luna stood up on her hind legs, coming down with her forepaws on the lid. As the box slammed shut, he shook the chimes from his brain and wrapped the box back up in the bag, then tucked it under his arm.

On their way out, Buddy stopped at the table, looking at Jeb. "I just wanted to say thanks for everything. I know you worked hard trying to save me, and I appreciate it." After a moment of respectful silence they ran from the house and out of the grove.

When they were far away from the cottage, the view was wilderness, reaching all the way to the horizon. They followed the path as it wound down and joined another canyon, then stopped at a housing tract built in the bottom. Passing them, they came to the other end of the wash.

Buddy was feeling lost and sad since Jeb's. It had begun an awakening. On a path halfway up a small cliff face, Luna trotted beside him, ever vigilant. The plants were high in this part of the canyon, hiding them. They smelled flowering trees and desert shrubs on the hot wind blowing through. At a bend in the path, Luna froze. She turned around and snapped at Buddy, blocking the way. He tried to go past her, but she lunged at his leg.

"What the hell? What is it?"

She turned around and put her paws on a willow branch that bent earthward under her weight. As it sagged, the warehouse came into view, standing in the distance. This was where he had escaped.

A flood of memories poured over Buddy, who began to hyperventilate. Luna tried to pull him away, but he was frozen. The bag vibrated beneath his arm.

Within the vibration, another thought came to him; the girl was still there. Why haven't we tried to save her? he asked himself. I could do it now. Bravado built, then began to overtake him. He was being pulled toward the warehouse, A pain from his leg stopped him. Luna had bitten him on the calf.

"Ow!" he yelped, rubbing his leg. He looked at her, and his

expression mellowed.

"You're right, girl. What was I thinking?" he said, "Let's get out of here."

He had to tell Helen and Max everything: the kids, the cop, and Jeb. Just as soon as he and Luna made it back safely. What was he thinking, trying to do it alone?

They walked off quickly, cutting down a hill. They hadn't gone far before they rounded a stand of willow brush and came upon a curious scene.

Luna ran ahead of Buddy, erupting into barks just beyond a thick bush. As he came around, he saw her barking at a very disheveled looking man lying on the ground.

A grasshopper leg hung from his mouth. He was bloody all over from little scratches, his shirt smeared with gore. Buddy recoiled in disgust. From a perch in a tree, a mockingbird chirped wildly at them. Luna stood between Buddy and the strange man, snarling furiously. The grasshopper man asked Buddy to restrain her. Buddy said she never listened to him anyway.

When the man recognized the bag, he'd gotten angry, saying it was his. After a brief exchange of harsh words, Buddy disappeared into the canyons with the bag and leash draped over his shoulder. He whistled, and a few growls later, Luna joined him.

Buddy wondered how stupid that man must have thought he was. Your bag? Someone out lurking near the warehouse? Fuck that.

Buddy found it. It was his bag.

Luna guided them where Buddy had never been. They skirted the unused areas beside the freeway, where overgrown yards melded into the loose landscaping of the roadside, and provided cover.

Buddy knew he could move quickly, but had learned that the speed gifts only lasted for short bursts, and afterward his energy was drained, so they crept instead.

Separating from the freeway, they came to a small one-block-wide canyon that had a tree-lined path running through the center, and a three-story apartment building on one side. Buddy and Luna made it through the canyon to the top, and were about to dash across the street when they heard a screech. A black sedan slammed into the curb.

The doors opened, and out stepped the blonde woman, Nuala,

and her henchman, Peik. The pale man's blue track suit gleamed in the sunlight.

Nuala's pleasant face felt forced.

"Hello, my son," she said. Her hands were extended, palms up.

"You're not my mom, you shitbag ass bitch," replied Buddy.

Peik and Nuala were taken aback by the new language. "Watch your mouth, kid," said Peik.

"Be quiet, Peik." Nuala touched his shoulder.

"What's that?" said Peik, eying the bag. Without waiting for an answer, he leaped toward Buddy. The boy and dog separated faster than he was expecting, regrouping farther away.

"Yes, darling, what is in the bag?" asked Nuala. "Come let us look."

"That's none of your fucking business, I'm never going anywhere with your ass, and fuck you," Buddy said. "In that order."

His fingers gripped the leash. A woman looked over her balcony railing from across the street to see what little kid was so foul-mouthed. Luna barked, lunging toward Peik.

Peik had had enough. He pulled the thin black cone from his jacket pocket and flung it at the dog, who easily avoided the projectile. Nuala glared at Peik while the cone clattered into the street.

Luna picked the cone up in her mouth, and ran after the retreating figure of Buddy.

"What the fuck are you doing?" they heard Nuala scream over their shoulders, with Peik stammering in response.

As they raced back down the path, Buddy could make out the man who had been eating the grasshopper, shirtless and hiding behind a pepper tree. Everybody wants this thing.

With Nuala and Peik at the top, he had precious little time to make a decision, Buddy picked up Luna in one smooth motion and reached deep into his rabbit spirit.

While running, he looked down. Dread hit him when he saw the black cone in Luna's mouth. Feeling his emotion, she dropped the cone. It rolled to the bottom of the ravine, stopping at the corrugated metal drainage tube at the bottom.

The grasshopper man's head did not even come close to registering where the boy and dog had gone to. They'd seemingly disappeared into thin air. His fingers still clutched where he thought the bagged knife would be.

The woman standing on her balcony called the police.

Like a blur, Buddy and Luna ripped through the alleys until at last they cut by the gymnasium and into a small, unused canyon with a lone Torrey Pine tree growing from the bottom. With the last bits of his waning energy, Buddy pulled branches and needles over himself and put the bag under his head like a pillow. Luna dragged a tumbleweed clump over him, then climbed underneath it and curled up next to her boy.

Buddy's eyes were so heavy, he'd used everything. Their own canyon was only across a street and then through the park, but he couldn't make it, his energy completely sapped. And Luna was not about to leave him alone for a second, not now.

● ● ●

At the bottom of the gully sat an oriole, its vibrant yellow and deep black cut a dramatic figure on top of the corrugated metal tube sticking out of the hill. Emiliano Flynn, the middle-aged photographer, snapped several pictures of the beautiful bird, sitting on the pepper tree branches, before it flew away to the south. While reviewing the photos on the screen, he noticed a shiny black cone beneath the bird and the tube, and walked down the grassy hill to retrieve the strange item. His dark, leathery hands plucked it from the weeds.

When he picked it up, a minute hum, like a chill, prickled his skin. He marveled at the etchings upon its smooth surface. Like a language, but none he had ever seen before. He wondered what the characters would sound like if spoken.

The hum stopped when he put the cone and camera into his bag and headed for home.

14

Cedar Ridge Park stood high on a hill, above canyons that carved a peninsula at the end of Commonwealth Street. It was a large circle of grass with a small fenced-in sandbox and play structure to the west side. Beyond the canyons was a nexus of freeways bordered by a creek bed that eventually drained to San Diego Bay.

Clementine had parked half a block down Commonwealth, the only street that led to the hidden park. She cased the cars along the way. All empty. Avoiding the one streetlamp, she entered the park at its darkest edge.

She'd been here many times before. It was at one time an area of interest in the investigation of her missing son. One of the neighbors on this street, just a few months after the abduction, had seen a woman matching the description of the nanny, walking quickly through the park and into the canyon with a thin young boy in tow. The boy with her was walking, however, and was therefore too old to be Rupert, so the tip was ignored pretty quickly by the original investigators. Another log on the bonfire of complaints Clementine had about the police at the time. Just because it wasn't her son didn't mean it hadn't been the same nanny. No one had registered a boy of the same description as missing, though, and focal points shifted.

She skirted the bush-lined perimeter of the park, staying under the shadow of eucalyptus trees. A trail ran down the spine of cliffs on the opposite end. A lone willow halfway down was where she would meet Gray.

Always get to a questionable meeting early. This had served

Clementine as well as any advice she had ever been given. She had modified it, though, as nefarious people often had the same plan. At this point in her career, she was never less than an hour early to a suspicious meet. She posted up in the surrounding chaparral and waited, her flashlight and gun at the ready. Ordinarily, this was something she'd do with backup, but it was too outlandish to ask anyone.

Sure enough, twenty minutes later, a figure appeared from behind the gated play set, hunched down and waited. Someone was setting her up. Or Gray. Or both. She had chosen the spot, and hadn't told anyone.

For several long minutes she waited, watching the person. She lost sight of him briefly before a faint glow illuminated a face she did not recognize. A white male around forty, she could see that even from inside the bush. He had a nose that hooked down like a beak, proud on a chiseled face, and frigid blue eyes. The light went out as quickly as it came on.

What kind of idiot smokes when they're ambushing someone? she thought.

Gray wasn't set to arrive for another half-hour. She had to get an advantage on the smoker. Silently, she began the long creep around the park, through the bushes. The freeways would drown out the sound of broken twigs along the path, or so she hoped. The guy looked creepy. She covered five yards at a time, then waited, making sure she wasn't seen.

She pulled out her pistol, took the safety off. She hadn't used her gun in going on three years other than target practice, but she would if needed. She gripped her flashlight, its hefty weight snug in her hand. The man was on the other side of a last thick knot of bushes, or was when she started this slow trek.

She rounded the final bush quickly and switched on the light, pistol aimed. The man was exactly where he had been, except he was facing Clementine, expecting her.

Fuck. Of course the lighter was bait.

His fingers were splayed, palms out. A ring of smoke spilled from his lips and spun upon itself, trapped in midair, transfixing Clementine.

From his throat came a low hum, growling. Clementine's

muscles froze. Her voice rasped in her throat quietly as she tried to speak. Her eyes grew wide, locked with his, as strange threads of light spilled from the man's palms. Like illuminated ribbons that moved with a living energy, the curious light webs shot toward her. She couldn't will her muscles to pull the trigger, or to break from the man's gaze, as the threads came in contact with her skin.

Clementine screamed as they burned her with white hot tips and burrowed beneath her skin. Two, seven, then countless threads pierced her with their blazing needles. The world spun out of control.

Her vision blurred, and a light grew, shining from everywhere. It cast a misty glow, and a voice in her head screamed of impending danger.

She concentrated on simply moving her knees, feeling her control return as the hook-nosed man's attention was diverted to the source of the light. She lurched her body backward and snapped free as the glow focused itself into the headlights of a small car barrelling toward her and the man.

The little subcompact car shot through the park and vaporized a bush behind the man, then slammed into him. He rocketed over Clementine and into the thick bushes behind her. The remnants of luminous thread ripped from her body and trailed after him. She felt sick.

The car lurched to a stop, inches from her. She stared through the windshield at young officer Gray's astonished face.

"Holy shit! Are you okay?" he said, jumping out of the car. He stopped short when he realized he was staring down the barrel of Clementine's pistol.

"Who the fuck was that?" she asked. "And who the hell are you?"

"It's a really long story, and we have got to find that guy." He pointed in the direction the man's body had flown.

"Wrong, buddy." In a fluid motion she handcuffed his wrist and maneuvered him until she had him restrained. "You're not the only one who knows tricks. I'll find the guy."

She pulled out a zip-tie and tripped him, making him fall on his ass, then zipped his ankles together. Her heart was racing. She picked up her flashlight and followed the man's trajectory, the voice of Gray protesting from the car.

Shutting him out, she walked toward the bush where the man landed. Besides some broken branches, there was nothing.

Gray's car started, then reversed through the park. Clementine sprinted back to find the cut zip-tie and open cuffs on the ground. She ran to her car, started it up, and floored it into a tight U-turn. Gray had a good head start. There were, however, only a few ways in and out of here due to the boundaries of the freeways and canyons. If she could make it to Juniper Street she had a good chance of catching him. Or whoever was driving.

She flew down the small street, hoping nobody had witnessed anything, as it would be very difficult to explain. Turning left, she saw taillights disappear around the next corner, on the other side of a deep canyon.

Gunning the motor down the valley between them, her car started to fishtail. She eased off the gas, and let it correct itself, then revved up the other side. The street was clear as she came over the hill. They all were. Too many options. They'd lost her. She hit her fist on the steering wheel.

"You fucking dicks."

At home, she was starving, but the light from the fridge would provide a target if someone was watching her. Best not to risk anything. If he could shoot iridescent filaments out of his hands, there's really no telling the hooknose guy was capable of.

Who were these people? A young cop. The man in the bushes.

Mr. Fox. Something did not fit with him. Working for Mr. Stillwater? And who was Stillwater, really? No one even knew what he looked like. The public face of his empire was his daughter, Marie.

Clementine couldn't trust anyone. Except maybe her crime tech Amy. She grabbed some bread on the way to her bedroom and fell asleep with the drama still playing in her mind.

• • •

In the morning, a crack from the patio woke her. Gun in hand, she pulled back the corner of her curtain. A mockingbird picked up a pecan and flew into the air, then dropped the nut onto the stones again. Clementine chuckled.

She spent a lot of time at home on her deck, why wouldn't she? Clementine's Oasis, her friends called it. And it was. In San Diego, a deck or patio is as good as another room, particularly one with shade. Her trees gave her that. Fruits and nuts hung from them, ripening in the sun.

She checked around the house. There were stepping stones around her little blue bungalow, which she kept spotless. Around each stone were little furrows of earth, so if one were nudged by an errant step it would be obvious. Seeing them clean, she relaxed a bit.

At the back, the pecan narrowly missed her and cracked on the ground. She jerked, and pointed her pistol at the bird, which stood by the nut. It clicked its tongue as Clem stepped on the pecan, cracking the shell, then sang a razzing song as she scooted it with her foot.

The bird kept a wary eye on her as it picked up the nut and flew into a bush.

Tuesday was her day off, traditionally, but today would be active. She called in to the station and asked for Gray Lowehaus' extension. Gray was away from his desk, she was told. She left a simple message for him to contact her.

The morning sun was heating up. Clem sat in a chair in the shade and set her laptop up next to a mug of coffee and a bagel. When everything was just so, she entered the city database and began to investigate.

The office. The crime lab was on the blood evidence, and should be getting the DNA results to her later today. It was the workspace of Craig James, a graphic designer who had been with the company for several years, though his hours were not substantial, and his portfolio was very slim.

Clem hadn't found Craig yet. A missing person, alive or not. However, the amount of blood in the office could have been caused by a nasty nosebleed. If it weren't for the busted door it probably wouldn't be investigated anyway. Except it was a Stillwater Property.

As she trudged through deeds and title insurance claims on her computer, she saw patterns emerge, but it wasn't until she began a list of the architects that something reared its head. Almost all of the Stillwater holdings had been designed by one of three men. A further look into their identities revealed an organization to which all three belonged, and only identified by the acronym HOME. Try as she might, Clementine could find no mention of the organization anywhere other than on their business licenses, way back in 1912. Nowhere was the acronym spelled out. The blueprints and documents she perused didn't explain the mystery, either. She did find mention of the men from time to time, mainly real estate news in the early 1900s, but nothing shocking or even very informative.

The mockingbird chittered wildly and jumped out of the tree, screeching as she flew to the front of the house. Clementine drew her weapon and skirted the cottage, only to find herself pointing her gun at the frightened mailman.

"Don't shoot!" He dropped her mail and held his hands in the air.

She profusely apologized while the mailman picked up her mail. He handed it to her, then made his way as quickly as possible down the street.

The bird twittered from the glass table when Clem came back, then flew off into the trees. When she looked at her computer, the page was different. A blueprint of one of the buildings she had been investigating. She'd looked at it already. An hour ago.

She looked closer. The walls between rooms made a pattern. Cornucopia. Ram's horn. But more. What purpose could twisting hallways serve? She got a sickly knot in her stomach, looking too long.

She went back over the other properties one by one. Each building had its own signature shapes inside, and relatively nondescript exteriors. All of them unique. Expensive. Any curve was extra money spent, even over one hundred years ago. Why were these men of HOME spending so much extra money to make these buildings just so, and who had been financing the affair? She ran out of properties quickly. Most had never been scanned to a computer. She'd have to go downtown for the rest. The buildings were connected to something larger.

Her cellphone rang. Amy Munoz, the crime tech.

"Hi, Clem, how's things going today?"

"Kinda weird, Amy. How are you?"

Amy was a good friend, they had lunch together whenever possible.

"Alright, except for all the macho pricks down here at the cop shop. But I know you're just being nice. I appreciate the manners, but you probably want to know about the blood evidence. Am I warm?"

"Getting there. What do we got?"

"Quite a bit, actually." When Amy got excited she got louder. Clem held the phone a little farther from her ear and hoped Amy was alone.

"Of the seven samples you sent me, we have three different DNA signatures. Two, unfortunately, are John Does. Both male. Further testing may be able to get race or eye color likelihoods, but takes time. Let me know on that." Amy told Clem what she already knew, just like she told everyone else. That was a reason Clementine favored her work; Amy left no stone unturned.

"And the other?" asked Clem.

"Whoo," Amy said. "The other is named Markuz Vasilly Banikoff. He was a suspect in a double murder here in '99, but all three eyewitnesses turned up dead while in protective custody, in three different houses. The case against him dissolved, though it's technically still open. The thing is, he kind of disappeared off the radar six years ago, no one's been able to get a tab on him."

"I remember that case. I saw him going into the courtroom once. Huge guy, right?"

"A monster," agreed Amy.

"Shit. This just got a little beefier. What time are you doing lunch?"

"Aw, man! That's the thing. That new hot cop asked me out to lunch today! I've been vibing him for like two weeks now. You don't want me to blow that off, do you?"

Clementine got a bad feeling in her gut. "Amy, what's this dreamboat's name?"

"You have to have seen him! He's like, flawless. His name is–get this–Gray."

"Amy. Listen to me. Break it off gently, then meet me at the coffee shop on the community college campus in twenty minutes. This is serious. Do it now."

"What the hell, Clem? You like him too?" Amy half joked.

"I'm sorry. Please. You need to listen to me. I don't know exactly what's going on but there's something off about Gray. I can't say more until I see you in person but trust me right now."

Silence.

"Fuck, Clem. Okay. I'll be there." Amy finally responded, then hung up the phone.

Clementine's hands shook as she put her phone in her pocket. She grabbed her keys, looked around the house, then went to go meet Amy.

15

Amy Munoz sat on a large cement block in the middle of the courtyard, waving at Clementine. She came up to Clem's chin as they hugged. Usually she wore her black hair tied up in a tight bun, but today it hung below her deeply bronzed shoulders.

They ordered some coffee from a little snack kiosk and found a spot away from the people milling around. A breeze rustled the jacaranda trees.

Amy was concerned, and a little annoyed. "So what's the big deal about Gray?" she asked.

Clementine relayed the story, at least as much as she could without sounding out of her mind. The supposed setup by Gray, though Clementine had picked the place. The way that no one else could have known of the meeting unless she or Gray told them. She didn't, which left him. When she got to the part where she cuffed him after he'd hit the man with his car, Amy looked confused. Clem finished with Gray's abduction, or escape. The filaments of light did not make their way into the tale.

When she finished, Amy stared in shock.

"That sounds awful! I'm so relieved you're alright!" She hugged her. "But I'm missing something, I think. You're suspicious of a guy who says he has information you desperately want, and saves you from an attacker, then you handcuffed him and left him in the dirt with this psycho on the loose? Clem, it sounds to me like he should be suspicious of you, no offense." Amy shot straight, one of the reasons Clementine respected her.

"It reeked of a setup," Clem returned.

"To do what, though? I'm not trying to minimize, but just take one thing out. Say the hook-nosed guy did find out about the meet some other way. Then Gray does look pretty helpful. It's a pretty risky con game to let someone barrel into you with a car," she said. "The things that are bothering me with it are: how did he know where you were, and how did he drive into the guy and not you?" Amy's eyes were unblinking and inquisitive.

"Damn. And I thought I was the detective," Clem said. "I don't have answers."

An impasse emerged in Clementine's tale: She couldn't tell Amy about the webs of light the man controlled, as it would make her appear less than mentally capable. On the other hand, it was getting difficult to withhold the information, as the story had a glaring hole without it. Gray must have zeroed in on their luminescence. She decided to test the water.

"I'm going to need you to be open-minded about this," Clementine began, "This blue-eyed fellow with the hooknose. He, uh . . . well, he . . . "

"What, Clem? What's going on?" Amy was starting to worry a little. Maybe she was taking this too lightly. Clem could have PTSD or something from being attacked.

"It's like he could, shoot. I don't know, it's like he could control my emotions or something. I had my pistol pointed at his chest, but he blew smoke and said this strange word, or words, I'm not sure. And my muscles froze up. I swear, I had this guy dead to rights and I couldn't move an inch." She breathed deeply.

"It's true. If Gray hadn't come I'd be dead, or something. But after the guy did that I couldn't trust anyone. That's why I cuffed Gray. The freaky guy messed with my head, made me see like webs of light coming from inside him. It's like I was on hallucinogens or something," Clem spilled it out.

"Damn. You poor thing." She put her arm around Clem, wondering how much to believe.

Clementine had made it for so long with the faint hope of finding her kid, Amy thought. Maybe this ray of hope from the young cop pushed her brains over the edge.

Amy wanted Gray to be on the level. He made her fantasize about actually having a dating life again, something she'd decided she missed after the almost year-long abstinence brought on by her last hopelessly macho boyfriend.

"Let's take a step back before all that." Amy shifted so they were facing one another. "Maybe Gray is the intended victim, right? What if the blue-eyed guy was going to grab Gray before you got there, so you didn't find anything out? That would put Gray in the very small circle of people you should talk to. The current population of that circle is two—myself, and the delicious young officer Gray."

Clem felt deflated. "Yeah, but I screwed up and handcuffed him before I thought enough about it. How, if he's not with the hooknose guy, do I get him to trust me again?"

She saw what Amy was hinting at. "Oh, you sly little thing."

"I will gladly thrust myself into the fray for my friend," said Amy, chest puffed.

"Bless you. Be careful, though, Amy. I know it sounds fantastical, but I swear there's something really strange going on."

"I know, I get it. But I've got a good feeling about Gray. You always say how you trust your gut. Well, think about how you felt when you first met him at the design building. What did your gut say then?"

"My instinct about him the first time was pretty good, but the person he was with had something very fishy about him. A Mr. Fox. Kind of threw me off."

"Mr. Fox, eh? Never heard of him," Amy said. "So we're thinking that Gray may be a victim of circumstance? I'm thinking something else. It seems to me like he's monitoring these guys for someone, only because he seems pretty young to take on a couple heavies by himself."

"Interesting. So, how do we proceed, Ms. Munoz? If you choose to accept this mission."

"Well, I haven't been involved or even attracted to anyone in years, and my libido screams when I see this guy. Not the best situation for fact-finding. Great however, for Amy. Hopefully my feminine wiles can loosen up the tongue of the young officer Gray."

Clementine smiled. "Alright. I'm going to go look at records at city hall for a while. I'm back at work tomorrow. What should I do if I see him in the station?"

Amy gave her a look. "By tomorrow he will be abreast of the situation," she said with a straight face, then she laughed out loud.

Clementine joined in, so relieved to have someone she could trust.

● ● ●

Amy's friend in the parking lot texted her when Gray came back to the station.

She was in the hall, a hibiscus flower behind her ear, standing proudly in a red dress embroidered with blooming prickly pear designs. She cut a dazzling figure. Gray's eyes were magnetically drawn to her as he came out of the elevator from the garage.

"Hello, officer," Amy said. "What are my plans for the rest of the evening?"

"Umm, ah, hi. Umm, Amy," the young officer stammered, unable to take his eyes from her, not wanting to. "Yes. I mean, no. That is, well, some dinner certainly."

Jeez. Pull it together, he thought.

"I, uh, just need to grab something from my desk and we'll get going," he said, shaking his head at himself.

"Okay, Gray." She thought to herself how easy this was going to be as she walked to her desk and straightened it up, said goodbye to her fellow crime techs and a couple police, and went out to the front to wait for Gray.

Warm wind and the smell of jasmine eddied in the courtyard. The sun was low in the late afternoon, and shined upon a hummingbird sucking pollen from a hibiscus flower. The small bird flitted between the leaves and flowers in tight little darts. When it noticed Amy, it zipped right in front of her face, making her flinch. The bird hovered, still but for its whirring wings. Amy raised her finger, and the bird hovered closer, about to land on it. Something clicked and the hummingbird zipped away.

The doors to the station swooshed open, and Gray walked out.

"You ready?" Amy rubbed her eyes.

"Yes I am. I've gotta say, though, I'm not that familiar with the restaurants around here." Two whole sentences without stuttering!

He smiled.

"Leave that to me, Gray." *He even has a nice smile.* "Because I am familiar."

"Okay. Um, Amy? You look beautiful."

Amy blushed. "Thank you, Gray. You look pretty good yourself."

The line was short at Benito's. Amy's favorite place for years, it had started to really blow up recently after a string of stellar reviews. Great for the restaurant, crappy for the regulars, she thought. She'd briefly considered writing a terrible one so she could get her food without waiting in line, but then Benito told her he had finally bought his house after running his restaurant for thirty-six years, and the idea gladly flew away.

Benito himself smiled and shook her hand when they made it to the front.

"Hola, Benito," she said. "¿Cómo estás?"

"Muy bien," answered the portly man. "¿Quién es tu amigo?" he asked, smiling at Gray and offering his hand.

"Gray. Mucho gusto," answered the young cop, taking Benito's hand.

"Ray?" asked Benito.

"No. Gray. Como 'gris' en Ingles."

Benito smiled wider. "Ah, mucho gusto, Gray."

Amy smiled.

They ordered tacos al pastor and sat outside. The sky was aflame with pink and orange as the clouds reflected the brilliant sunset.

Gray's eyes lit up as the succulent pork flooded his mouth. "Holy . . . that's delicious!"

"You got that right, my friend." Benito's did not get old, no matter how many times you ate there. "So, Gray, tell me a little about yourself." She batted her eyes, playfully.

"Haha. Okay. Where to start?"

"Start with little baby Gray, where's he from?"

"Julian. Mom still bakes a mean apple pie. I moved out to San Diego when I was eighteen, though. Julian's cool, but it gets small for a kid, especially after high school."

"So, how long have you been on the force? A month?" Amy

chuckled.

"Oh, an age joke. I get it. Actually I get it all the time, especially from the old boy cops. I'm twenty-seven, and I've been a cop for two years. Before that I was in private security. I look young for my age."

Amy felt stupid. "I'm sorry Gray. You're a year older than I am. I swear, no more age jokes." She was only a little irritated that Gray looked so much younger than she did.

"Fair enough. I can handle it though, just so you know."

"I'm sure you can," Amy chuckled. "So, private security, eh? Babysitting rich guys? I don't see you sitting in a trailer at a construction site."

"Pretty much."

"Anyone interesting?"

"Not really, just real estate dudes, mainly."

"Ew. You're right, that is profoundly uninteresting."

"Told you. Now how about you?"

Already? Gray was pretty smooth after the initial speed bumps, she gave him that. She took one of the last bites of her taco. A small trail of grease leaked out and down her chin. Before she could grab a napkin Gray was already soaking up the trail into his own, so quickly Amy didn't even see him move. Then his hand was on the table again, napkin balled up inside it.

"What the hell, man? I appreciate it, but how can you move so fast?" She nervously looked around, but no one had noticed the lightning reflexes.

"What do you mean? I just got the grease before it could get on your shirt," he said.

As she heard the words Amy quite involuntarily relaxed. It wasn't a relaxing situation, though, and now her own feelings made her suspicious. Her interest in this fellow was already reaching a crescendo, without some discretion she would be very vulnerable. She had to pull back.

"I've got to say, Gray, I've had a good time, but I think I've got to get going home." Fuck. That was too direct. Her head felt jumbled.

"Huh?" he said. "You still didn't tell me anything about you. What's the problem? That I'm too quick to wipe food off your face?"

"No. Well, yeah. Things are just pretty weird right now. I kind of feel off."

"Please," he said. "Don't you want to hear what happened in the park with your friend Clementine?"

• • •

The young clerk set the boxes on the counter. His hair was greasy and his shirt was tucked into his underwear as he walked away.

It took Clementine several minutes to find what she wanted. Spreading blueprints of Stillwater Property holdings over the table, she began looking for similarities between the styles of the three architects.

Always there were curved corners, hallways that taper to nothing, and angular panels of wood. The shapes were strange to her, but as an untrained person in the field she couldn't tell if there was some other accepted purpose. She also didn't know anyone in the field, so she called the clerk over.

Alec was twenty-three years old, but still got zits on his face. He'd been a clerk for seven months, and thought it was okay, because soon his band would blow up. Then all the dicks who talked shit his whole life would be jealous. In the meantime, he had lucked out when his aunt had got him this job. He liked architecture, and often, in the huge amounts of downtime, looked through the bowels of the older structures in San Diego.

A few months ago he had even located a basement in a building that nobody knew had been there, and he and his friends had excavated the exterior door for one three-day weekend. When they finally got through, they entered a high-ceilinged ballroom that had been sealed up for decades. It was huge, and utterly deserted. After casing it out for a week, they moved all their musical equipment in, and discovered they could get away with even having band practice there as long as it was between five and ten at night or pretty much all day on the weekends. Even then people may hear tones, but with the one entrance kept hidden, no one would know where it was coming from. His two bandmates moved all their stuff in.

Alec still lived in a house with three roommates. They were gonna have to figure out something soon, though. The hidden space had live electricity but no water, and Alec's bandmates had taken to showing up at his house whenever they pleased and taking showers, pissing off his roomies.

He was at his desk when the lady detective called him back. He thought it was a little quick for her to be done already. It wasn't a huge surprise when she asked him to look at some of the designs. People often did.

The curving molds and disappearing hallways intrigued him. They looked a little like the blueprint for the building he and his friends occupied. Sure enough, he glanced at the architect's name, and it was the designer of his building.

Maybe he could help her without narcing himself off. Alec told her that all the bafflings that seemed to have no real purpose looked like they were designed to control and capture sound. To direct it, more specifically.

"See here?" he pointed to the end of a hallway that bent and twisted like a giant ram's horn. "Sound made at the end of this would amplify itself until exiting through this much larger area. It's like a huge horn built into the building. The rest of the architecture would be to deaden the sound. So whatever the horn sounds like, it would be deafening inside the building and almost silent from outside. I can't believe I haven't seen this before. It's incredible."

"It is pretty amazing. Thanks very much, ah . . . " she looked to the nametag, "Alec. You seem to know a little bit about sound."

"Yeah, I'm into music. I play guitar in a band."

"Good for you. Do you have a CD or something?"

"Not yet. We're trying to record soon. It's kind of expensive," he answered, shocked she was interested in his life.

"I'm sure. Well, good luck, and thanks." She walked out of the office.

None of the police, or any city employee, had ever asked Alec about himself. He had been so thrown he'd almost offered the lady cop a guided tour of the studio.

He rummaged through until he found the blueprints for his secret ballroom, then buried them in an unmarked tube near the back.

• • •

Amy was shocked.

Gray tried to explain. "I didn't set Clementine up. There's a connection between some missing kids and a warehouse that I believe is somewhere down in the Home Avenue area. I came on this info by accident on duty with Mr. Fox."

Amy was skeptical but intrigued. There's Mr. Fox again.

"Sometimes I feel like he makes sure I hear certain conversations to see if that information is heard down the grapevine, as a sort of test. One concerned a girl of twelve that had just been taken to a warehouse. I distinctly heard him say someone would 'throw her in a cage with the others.' I don't know who the others are, and I have only a general idea where the warehouse is. But there are others, and they are somewhere."

"Go on," she said, her mind racing.

"I told Detective Figgins to meet me, and she picked a place that overlooks the area in question. I took that to be a good sign. When I drove up, there was a bush on the opposite end of the park, lit up strangely, and shaking. I floored it. Some guy was standing between Clem and myself. I couldn't see what he was doing, but it didn't look good. I slammed into him with the car. Clem snapped out of it and handcuffed me, zip-tied my feet, and went to look for the guy."

"Damn. How did you get out?"

She almost wondered how he could process the information so quickly from inside the car, but remembered the napkin, and pushed the question away for later.

Gray put his hand into the collar of his shirt, and pulled out a brown shoelace tied around two keys. One looked like a house key. The other was for handcuffs.

"Something Mom taught me long ago," he said.

Amy hoped he meant the house key.

Gray continued, "After that, I left Clementine there. Fortunately she's alright. I shouldn't have left her alone."

Amy agreed. "No, you shouldn't, but that does jibe with her story. Okay. I'm satisfied. What do we do now?"

"The only people I've trusted to tell have been you and

Clementine. The first time with her went a little sideways. We didn't speak much. This is going far better," he stated the obvious. "We need to meet with her and figure it out, don't you think?"

"Yes, I do. But Gray?" Her gaze flitted from one to the other of his eyes. They were grey, like his name. She looked so long he grew uncomfortable. "You swear you've got nothing to do with that hooknose guy?"

"On my life," he said.

"I'm choosing to trust you. If you break my trust I will do everything in my power to destroy you, no offense. And I'm badass when I've been scorned."

"None taken," said Gray. "Hell hath no fury."

"No. It hath not. Now, I want you to trust me, too. Do you feel that way, Gray?"

"Yes. I do," he admitted.

Amy reached across the table and grabbed his shirt in her fist.

"I really shouldn't do this." She leaned over and kissed him on the mouth. A crackling electricity filled Gray as he kissed her back.

The sky was darkening as Gray drove Amy back to her car.

"What do we do now?" he asked when they were back in the parking lot.

"You, my friend, will go take a cold shower," Amy said, "while I explain this situation to Clementine. We'll all talk tomorrow at some point."

Gray was disappointed, but pretty much expected something along those lines. "Alright then."

She pecked him on the cheek and said, "Please don't get all weird on me."

"I won't," Gray promised.

• • •

When she pulled into her driveway, Clementine's cell vibrated on the passenger seat. Amy. She turned off the car and answered without getting out.

"Hey, girl, what's going on?"

"Hey Clem. Well, I took the fine officer Gray Lowehaus down

to Benito's for some al pastor, and I've gotta say, I think he's on the level, homegirl. Hopefully he doesn't just have me blinded by his gorgeousness."

"Yeah, I've definitely considered that. Did he talk about what happened at the park?"

"Yes, he did. He gives a pretty similar account to you. Said he got pissed and bailed when you left him cuffed out there," Amy said. "Said he regretted it, too."

"Hmm. How'd he get out?"

"He's got a handcuff key on a shoestring around his neck like a little kid. Popped it right after you went looking for the creep."

"Does he know the creep?" Clem asked.

"If he does, he didn't tell me."

"You make out with him?"

"Maybe one kiss," Amy admitted. "But just on the cheek."

"Cheek? Liar." Clem straightened up. "Do you trust him?"

"Haha. I do, yeah. We need to get together tomorrow and see if you do, too."

"Alright. Let's do that."

"There's one more thing, Clem. He said he originally got the information from Mr. Fox. You know that guy from the crime scene, yeah?"

"Just met him when I met Gray."

"Well, what Gray was going to tell you at the meeting last night was that he seems to think Mr. Fox has leaked false info to him in the past, as sort of a test for something. But recently Gray overheard him talking about kids and cages with someone on the phone. A conversation he shouldn't have listened to, apparently," Amy said. "Seeing as how Mr. Fox was at the design firm where you found the blood, we should definitely be checking him out."

"And Craig James," Clem chimed in. "Jim was supposed to be on him. But he looked like he cozied up to Mr. Fox pretty quickly."

Amy paused for a second, then said, "Well, we're just gonna have to backdoor Jim's ass, then, right?"

Clem laughed a deep, honest laugh. "I guess so, girl. Well, you are the greatest, Amy. This is some serious crap though, huh?"

"Yeah. It's pretty gnarly. But I think we can handle it."

That makes one of us, Clementine thought. "I'll see you

tomorrow."

She hung up the phone and sat in the car, wondering how deep she was leading Amy into danger. Amy, however, could not be persuaded to stop now by any means, thanks to Gray. Clem made a promise to protect her young friend as best she could.

Gray was due some checking out. She'd do his background along with the growing list.

Near her doorstep, the shadows shifted in the plants. She froze, watching a branch sway. There was no wind. The branch shook and the shadows danced until a raccoon hopped out of the tree followed by her two little babies, climbing over Clementine's patio wall to get some nuts and fruit from her yard.

Clementine chuckled, and tried not to disturb them as she went in the door to her home.

• • •

That night, Amy dreamt of a huge building surrounded by smaller ones. She drifted into a door, her body light as a feather, held aloft on the winds. Her ghostly self wisped down a corridor with crude plywood and steel doors. One door was open, and she drifted into the room. A girl of perhaps twelve sat with her legs crossed on the ground, defiant. She was staring at a man whose back was to Amy's ethereal self. As Amy floated around the man, she looked at his blue eyes and oddly hooked nose. She knew him, though she'd never seen him.

His eyes broke from the girl, as if he had detected something. They darted in Amy's general direction, but could not focus on her. Amy looked to the young girl and was surprised to see the girl staring directly into her eyes.

She sees me, Amy thought. The man held a black steel cone in his hand. From the corner of her dreaming eye, Amy saw movement in the far reaches of the room. Insects crawled outside the radius of lamplight.

"Rise," the man said.

The young girl made no movement, no sound. Only stared back at the man like she were about to hurt him, which given the present circumstances did not seem possible.

"Rise!" the man shouted, "Aash Xasuol!"

The girl glared at the man. The cone in his hand turned from black to a yellow-gray, then orange. Amy could see waves of heat emanating off the strange device.

"Arrgh!" He dropped the now smoldering cone to the ground. The taste of charred flesh. Metal so hot and soft it made a thud rather than a clang as it hit the cement floor. The cone drooped, etched letters misshapen and unreadable.

"You little asshole." He blew on his blistered skin.

Amy tried to get between them as he struck out. His arm swooshed through her, slapping the girl's face.

"You aren't stopping anything, only delaying it," he said. "I'm going to find that boy, with or without with your help, and then we're going to have some real fun. Actually, I'll be having fun. You two will wish you were dead."

He hit at his pant leg, and looked to see a stream of insects on it. Beetles. Ants. Crickets. He brushed it off, stomped on the bugs and slapped her again. She stared back, red handprint on her cheek.

His shoes scraped on the stone floor as he walked out of the room, locking the door behind him.

The girl looked at Amy and said, "Go find the boy. Don't let him come back here."

As if on command, Amy's body drifted up through the roof, then back into her sleeping body. She awoke in her darkened bedroom, covered in sweat, heart pounding.

The eastern horizon was turning pink. Amy had no intention of returning to sleep, and rose to make herself some coffee and start some serious research before going to work.

16

Buddy and Luna woke beneath the pine with the sky still dark, and silently stole back to Helen's camp. The last thing Buddy wanted to do was tell Max and Helen about the previous day's activities, but this was too serious. Jeb was dead, and he and Luna had been gone all day and half the night. Helen was probably worried sick. Plus, he had the thing Max was looking for.

"Sugar!" Helen shrieked, pulling his body close. "Oh my goodness, Sugar, I was so worried!"

She felt the bag beneath his arm, and her mood shifted drastically.

"Where," she said, pointing at the bag, "did you get that thing?"

Buddy held it toward her. Helen shook her head and pointed to Max, who took it off Buddy's hands.

"Yeah, Buddy. Where did you get it?" A wry smile curled on his lips.

"From the oven in that cottage you were at. I got in," said Buddy. "It kind of called me to it. I told you."

"You got in the house?" asked Max.

Helen gave Max a ferocious look, shaking her head in disbelief.

"It was in a secret place inside. There's something else, though," said Buddy. "Jeb was there. Or his body was. He was dead. Somebody killed him."

"Oh my word!" said Helen, cradling her hands to her face. "But, how do you know that someone killed him, Sugar, and he didn't die some other way?"

"Well, uh, because his head was floating in his breakfast, and his body was sitting at his table."

Max and Helen were silent.

Now that he had started, Buddy figured he may as well go all the way. "I, uh, also saw the lady who calls herself my mom, that Nuala woman. She was with the pale guy, Peik. They tried to catch me, but we lost them."

Helen looked like her top might blow off. She shooed Max away.

It was too close. They were looking for him near here, right now. Nuala, not just Peik. And people were being killed.

Helen demanded to know why he had even gone in that direction. When Buddy stammered and looked at the ground by way of an explanation, she dug into him so severely that he had to spill the beans about being spotted.

"By whom?" she demanded.

"Someone in the house. At that kid's party."

"The guy whose car you messed up?"

"I don't know. It seemed like him."

She lifted Buddy's face so he had to look in her eyes. "Well you should know. This is serious stuff. You've gotta remember people, and where you remember them from. An enemy could be anybody."

"Now, It doesn't make sense she's near us because of a bunch of dipshit kids." She eyeballed Buddy. "Is there anyone else who could have seen you?"

Helen had seen through. Of course. "There was a cop car. It got me in the spotlight."

Disappointment lined her face. "Don't leave things like that out, anymore, Buddy."

Sadness overwhelmed him when she referred to him not as "Sugar" but as "Buddy".

"Well, then, there's someone else. I've seen him a few times. Some lanky dude who lives by the market," he said. "He was out in one of the canyons. Said the bag was his."

"You think he's from the warehouse?" Helen asked.

"I don't know. I never saw him there, I don't think. Maybe just a coincidence."

"No such thing. Avoid him, too. I want you to be confident, not stupid," Helen said as she rummaged in a bag, pulling out a steel ball with a hole through it. She threaded a long leather strap through the ball, then knotted it.

"This is your new leash," she said, and pulled it taut. Easing her hands together, the steel dropped until it hung near the ground. "This is a special metal. It's light enough so it won't slow you down, but it delivers a good wallop."

She turned toward a tree stump, long dead, and swung the weapon hard into it. The ball pounded a large and jagged divot into the old wood. Splinters flew everywhere. The boy was impressed.

"What you really want to do with this is crack someone in the knee. You're so fast it's gonna be very difficult to follow you in the first place, much more so if they can't walk. Now I don't want you to think I'm rewarding you for bad behavior, because I'm pretty upset about last night. This is for protection. Things are worse without Jeb."

"So Jeb was a part of your plan?" he asked.

"He was. Even though he didn't know the extent of it," Helen answered. "Now we shift. Due, mainly, to your actions, Sugar. Like rings on a pond, born of a single drop. That drop was when you started to think that you were invincible. So much pride in yourself, and not thinking things could go wrong. Other people are depending on you, so be be safer. It worked out this time, but you make too many rings and everyone sees it."

He'd disappointed Helen, and felt terrible. Her concern for him was an emotion he'd never seen from anyone, someone so worried for his well-being that it caused them sadness. He vowed to make her proud again.

"And Buddy?" she added. "From now on you be ready for anything in a moment's notice. You hear me?"

Buddy felt he already was, but he didn't dare tell Helen that just now.

17

After a long morning in meetings at the police station, Clementine had gotten home in the mid-afternoon. The sun was hot, but her oasis stayed nice and cool with the shade and breeze. She sat at the table with her laptop, and got to work.

A search of the young officer Gray Lowehaus showed that he was the most boring guy ever. From Julian. Quaint little mountain town to the east. Played football. Mom won apple pie contest.

Are you kidding me? Clementine thought.

A couple years in school in San Diego, then some security detail before he enrolled in the academy. She'd never searched someone so ridiculously vanilla. Satisfied for the time being, at least until she could get a feeling face to face, she moved on to the other players in the design firm case.

Mr. Fox had no criminal record. Not surprising considering he was head of security for the Stillwater organization. If he ever had gotten his hands dirty it would have been covered up.

He'd been with the security branch of Stillwater for twelve years, before which he ran his own private detective firm. M. Fox, P.I. had been around a little over six years. No cases of record, really. He had gotten his certification from a now defunct small college on the third floor of a law building downtown, when downtown was still a seedy and dangerous place, Clementine remembered, not like now.

The address of the building rang a bell. One of the Stillwater holdings with all the sound-bending architecture.

That was all. Not much. Mr. Myron Fox was quite the enigma.

Mr. Stillwater was notoriously anonymous. There wasn't even a picture that came up in any searches for him, only photos of his properties.

The higher you go, the less you know.

She moved on to the only DNA hit they currently had to go on: Markuz Vassily Banikoff.

In his file was a newspaper article from Alaska stating that several years ago a body had been pulled from the Bering Sea. In the harsh waters between Russia and Alaska, bodies shut down due to hypothermia in minutes, so the fishermen who pulled out the huge man dressed in work clothes expected to be dealing with a corpse. They all reacted with shock when the man spat up water and screamed out for alcohol. After downing half a bottle of single-malt scotch in one gulp, the man sat shivering beneath the blankets provided for the ride back to the nearest port.

Markuz. He had made the papers in Alaska for a while, but in a state with thousands of miles of coastline, sea rescues are common, and the fanfare eventually died down.

The next mention Clementine could find was on the wooded coast of Northern California, almost to Oregon, a few years later. Markuz had gotten into trouble in a bar, and beaten a man so severely the man had lost vision in one of his eyes.

The giant was charged with assault, and served two years in Pelican Bay State Penitentiary. The few witnesses who wanted to talk said the injured man had used a less than flattering epithet toward the female bartender. When the giant had asked the man to apologize, the man told Markuz to "mind his fucking business."

That would be the last complete sentence the man would utter for seven weeks as he recovered in the hospital. Broken jaw, cheekbone, and orbital bone, for starters.

Markuz had gotten out of prison on good behavior. The sentence had been for five years, but while he was incarcerated he had rarely even spoken, much less caused trouble with anyone. There had been very few people who wanted to start anything with him, either. His legend had apparently preceded him.

After his release, there was no trail until his alleged involvement in a brutal double murder in San Diego in 1999. A pair of cousins, drug and human traffickers adept at tunnel building and knowledgeable in the ways of the Border Patrol, as both of them had been fired from it for corruption a few years previous, were slaughtered. The carnage was so gruesome that none of the witnesses would talk, and the case went cold. After that, there was no trace of Markuz.

Until now. With the discovery of his and two unknown males' blood in a graphic designer's office on the east side of downtown.

The thought occurred to Clementine that he could be the victim of an attack just as easily as an assailant. He had at least one mortal enemy in the guy whose eyeball he ruined, or a family member of one of the two murdered traffickers. Someone who did things like that didn't just stop, either. There would be more victims, and revenge scenarios.

Markuz's blood in the design firm office was a castoff trail followed by passive drops, Amy had told her. One other blood signature had much the same characteristics. A hit, castoff from a blunt object, then vertical drips from the fresh wound.

The third signature had been the still-wet pool on the carpet. Probably from the victim. So, at least three people were there, all bleeding. She wondered if anyone was there who wasn't.

Ending her search of the giant, she did the final person of the day. Craig James, thirty-eight, single. Never been married. Rented the same place for three years, before that was four blocks away for six years. Had worked at the design firm almost a year. She looked at his portfolio and was nonplussed by the work, inasmuch as she knew about advertising layouts, which admittedly was almost nothing.

Craig had been freelance for a long time before that, but didn't have much income rolling in. She discovered how he could survive like that with a search of his father Alan, a fourth-generation heir to a California almond and avocado baron. With the amount of money the family had, she wondered why Craig would need to work at all. It seemed no one else in the James family did. Although, she thought, what he did couldn't be misconstrued as work. Their farming forebear must be dizzy from turning over in his grave. Whatever, at least this Craig character did something with his time.

He had no criminal record. His schooling was unremarkable, but steady. A degree in art, which if it weren't for his pedigree would be worth considerably less. Connections got him the job, as his work was nothing to write home about. Why would a firm with financial backing such as the Stillwater's hire such a decidedly average artist?

And what was a Russian ex-con doing in a Stillwater property with a slacker heir and another male, possibly more, and everyone bleeding all over everything?

Clementine stared into the screen at Craig James' address, then got ready to go pay him a visit.

● ● ●

The late day had stretched into night, and in the darkness Clementine could barely see the crime tape that sealed the windows and doors of Craig's house. With a box cutter, she removed one strip of the yellow tape from over the unlocked back door and entered the house, flashlight beaming and gun at the ready.

The place was a mess. The crime scene techs were supposed to have just grabbed a brush or toothbrush for a DNA test while being overseen by Jim. There was no reason for this shitstorm to have happened. Clothes, books, broken dishes, everything scattered. She crept through the dark house toward the bathroom, her feet crunching on debris. Inside, the sink was running. Cops didn't do this, she thought. Cleanser and toilet paper formed a layer over every surface.

She holstered her gun and reached into her back pocket for gloves, placing the flashlight on the back of the toilet. To her surprise, the toothbrush was still sitting in the medicine cabinet. Inside a drawer she found the brush and comb, and wondered exactly what the hell Detective Garrett had been doing here.

A rustle sounded from just outside the bathroom door, and Clem reached for her gun. In that moment, a spidery teenage boy sped like a blur into the cramped bathroom and quickly locked himself on to Clementine before she could get her finger on the trigger, his hands wrapping around her wrists, heels digging behind her knees.

She held the gun awkwardly, and let out a faint cry as the youth bit savagely into the flesh on her right bicep, his hands pushing the gun so it pointed at the ceiling. Through tears of pain, she noticed his ring finger was cut off and cauterized. He knocked his heels into the side of her knees again while jerking her hands back and forth, and she lost her balance.

They crashed against the toilet, sending the heavy flashlight clattering to the floor. With the butt of her hand, Clementine rammed repeatedly into his temple. He bit harder. Blood flowed down her arm, but she clung to the pistol with all her strength. She slammed him again and reached for the flashlight behind the toilet. As she stretched out to grab it, she could feel her flesh begin to slowly separate from her bicep. The pain was like fire.

Finally she wrapped her fingers around the light and swung it, a solid hit below his ear. His grip loosened with the first hit. After the second he let go, howling, and jumped for the door. Clem raised her pistol in her bloody hand, about to fire, but he was no longer there. She checked the hall, also empty.

Plop. She looked down. Her blood had run down her arm and dotted the floor beneath her. *Son of a bitch!*

She grabbed a towel and wrapped it tightly on her arm. With another she meticulously cleaned up her blood, then shoved it in her bag with the comb, brush and toothbrush.

In the living room, she saw the window open and the curtain fluttering in the wind, a trail of blood demarking the escape route of the kid. She collected a sample, then went out the back door and ran to her car.

When she got back home, she showered and cleaned the wound. A sting ran screaming through her when she poured hydrogen peroxide on it, and it foamed like lather. At least it was far enough up her arm that no one would see it once she had a shirt on. When she dressed it with ointment and gauze, it felt much better.

The trip was designed to get answers. Instead, it had made more questions. What the hell was that kid doing there? And why did he attack her? More disturbing, though, was the nagging notion that her partner was caught up in something very sinister. Why didn't he at least grab the toothbrush, even to throw it away? Fucking Jim.

All she had was Amy. She'd see about Gray.

She left the outdoor lights on, and turned off the ones inside, then retired to her bedroom.

As she drifted off to sleep, Clementine thought seriously about getting a dog.

• • •

"DNA's not a match to Craig James, according to my boy Rory," Jim said. He stood above Clementine's desk, showing her his proof.

She grabbed the paper. "Rory? Is there someone new in forensics that I should know about?"

"Yeah, some guy who was working down in Chula Vista. Just started here yesterday. Chief had me throw him his first case." Jim had a satisfied glow, like a puppy with a treat.

"Wow, he must have done well in Chula Vista to get a bona fide mystery major case on his first job, eh?" Clementine was pissed. Her cases always went to Amy. Somebody was messing with her. Well, this Rory character wouldn't be getting the young Mr. James' personal grooming items, that was for sure.

"I guess so. You mad or something, Figgins? Ha ha," Jim laughed derisively, turning his back before she could respond.

Clementine walked down to the crime lab and found Amy coming out. Amy was agitated, shaking her head and rolling her eyes.

"We needed help, I admit, but this little dude's got a stick up his ass." Amy jerked her thumb backward at the bespectacled man in the blue smock inside the lab. "Dr. Science, apparently. Condescending prick, I say. Whatever. Hi, Clem."

"Hey, Amy. I heard about Rory. No bueno, eh?"

"Nothing I can't handle. What's up?"

"Are you going to the ladies?" Clementine suggested.

"Hmm? Oh, yeah."

In the restroom, Clementine told Amy about the house, and the boy. Amy hadn't heard of Craig James' test, which as the senior tech should have gone to her.

"Fuck, this is fishy," Amy said. "What do we do?"

Clementine pulled out the bag with Craig's things, stuffed it into

Amy's purse, then handed her a vial with the end of a cotton swab broken off inside it.

"Run those whenever you can. And be careful. The grooming items should be one signature, and the swab is from the psycho kid. Kind of doubt he's in any system, but . . ."

"Got it." Amy grabbed the bag and walked out of the restroom. Clementine waited thirty seconds, then exited, walking the other way.

Back in the car with Jim, Clementine said she'd like to visit Craig James' house to see what they had done on her day off concerning the case. Jim tried to protest, but eventually folded and took her. Expecting to find a calamity and catch Jim in an uncomfortable situation, she cut the tape and pushed the door open.

To her astonishment, the house was spotless. All the rooms. Even the bathroom was clean. Her eyes came to rest where her blood had been, and she would have literally eaten off of it. Jim looked smug.

The window that had been smashed was unbroken. There was no blood trail leading up to or out of it. Since the night before, the entire scene had been immaculately cleaned. As if it never had been any other way.

"See, processed," he said. "Happy?"

She was not.

Thankfully her phone rang. She left the cottage and walked into the yard, out of earshot. It was Amy.

"Clem. Is your partner right there?" she asked.

"No. What's up?"

"I ran the DNA you got. Craig James is a match to the big pool of blood in the office. Off the toothbrush and the comb." Amy's voice was quiet and quick.

"I was expecting that. How about the stuff from last night?"

"No hit, like you thought. But the blood is different. There's something about it I've never seen before. I sent it to my girl at the university for further testing."

"Like what? What's the anomaly?" asked Clem.

"I'm not sure. One thing is there is a high metallic content, and not iron. Until we get more results, your guess is as good as mine. It's all weird, this case."

"No shit. Amy, we've gotta bring Gray in on this if we can, as soon as possible. This whole thing is screwed. Is he ready?"

"I sure fucking hope so," she answered, "and I have a few hunches concerning these warehouses."

Clementine perked at that. "Really? What's up?"

"I, ah, I'll tell you when we're all together. For several reasons." Telling Clem she saw it in a dream was something she preferred to do in person.

Once home, Clementine had prepared a platter of fruit and cheese for the meeting. And bought beer and wine. The intensity of the situation did not cancel out the need for decent snack food, in her opinion.

Gray and Amy arrived separately, minutes apart. Amy was first. She and Clementine had scarcely said hello to each other before Gray parked his dented compact out front. Clem opened the door as he came through the gate.

"Hello, Gray. I'd like to extend an olive branch to you." She held a beer. Gray grabbed the bottle and swigged it.

"That'll work, for now," he said, wiping his chin, "I shouldn't have left you out there after I got out of the cuffs, so I apologize too."

Good response. This could work. Hopefully.

Amy was relieved it was going so well. "Alright, then. Should we get started?"

They briefed Gray on the DNA developments, and the kid. He had the same concerns as Amy and Clementine about Officer Garrett, and also some questions.

"At the original crime scene, did anyone estimate the amount of blood that was pooled? Is there enough to prove a homicide even occurred?"

Amy fielded that. "No, there's not. Not even close. Unless he was murdered somewhere else, we're looking at a pretty good injury to Mr. James, and relatively minor ones to Mr. Banikoff and the John Doe."

"So there might not even be a murder, but probably at least an assault, judging from the blood evidence?" asked Gray.

"Probably," answered Amy.

"What is that?" Gray pointed at Clementine's bicep. A red circle had oozed through her bandage and into the fabric of her shirt.

She tried to cover it with her hand before showing it to them. Amy shot up to administer.

"Fucking hell, Clem! What happened?"

"That fucking kid bit me."

"Why didn't you tell me that?"

"It's just a scratch."

That's not a scratch, it's a fucking wound. Why didn't you go to a hospital?"

"And let word get back that I was lurking around a crime scene getting evidence that proves the opposite result than my partner? There's no way I could have pulled that off with any doctor around here."

Amy shook her head as she went to the bathroom and got a first aid kit, then brought out a bottle of tequila she knew Clem had in the freezer.

"Drink some," she said.

"Why?"

"Because I'm going to give you some stitches."

Clementine winced and groaned as Amy sewed the oval of loose skin back onto her arm. No one could offer any opinion on how the house would be ransacked and then painstakingly reassembled. Cops would trash the place, an inhabitant would clean something. The twain simply did not meet. Everyone was pretty sure the kid didn't do clean up, but someone did. It was agreed that they'd go by Craig's house when the stitching was done.

Clementine was of the firm opinion that the spidery boy and the hooknose man from the park were connected somehow, and quite possibly everyone else they had encountered. As Amy stitched, Clem told them about the acoustic architecture and the young clerk. Sound-altering buildings. Weird lights coming from that man's hands. Child assassins, if that's what that kid was. Something was tying all these things together, and that thing was Stillwater Enterprises.

The person foremost on everyone's mind was the hooknose man. They needed to find out who this guy was, and soon.

"What was your new information on the location of the warehouse, or houses?" Clementine asked Amy, between winces.

"Well, like Gray, I think it's around the knot of freeways and warehouses near Home Avenue," Amy replied. "To the east of Golden Hill. The base of Juniper Street Canyon."

"How . . . ugh. How did you reach that conclusion?"

Amy was finished, and tying off the knot at the top of the wound. It looked functional if not completely clinical. "Well, if you must know, I saw it in a dream."

Clementine sighed. A week ago she'd want to have Amy checked out. Now, she didn't know what sounded outlandish anymore.

"Really," she said.

Gray, silent for a long time, said, "That's how I first saw it as well."

"Damn," said Clementine. "I guess I'm late to the dream party."

There were lights on inside Craig's house when they pulled up, and no crime tape over the doors. They parked and walked up the steps, hands upon still-holstered weapons. The door opened, and they found themselves looking into the perplexed face of Mr. Craig James.

"Hello?" he said through the gap in the chained door, his voice low and tired. "Who are you people?"

"Mr. James," said Clementine, taking her hand off her pistol and showing her badge. "My name is Detective Clementine Figgins, SDPD. These are my constituents: Officer Gray Lowehaus and crime scene tech Amy Munoz. Would you mind if we came in and asked you a few questions?"

"Sure," he said, unchaining the lock. "C'mon in."

He looked haggard. Rings around the eyes and three-day stubble. He had full-sleeve tattoos on both arms, Japanese art mainly.

Clementine looked around, "Mr. James, did you have an accident at your work recently?"

"Accident? I don't think I'd call it that. I swung by there to pick something up, then I kind of had a blackout and woke up here about a half-hour ago I guess. It's dark now."

"What day is today?" Clem asked him.

"Wednesday?"

"Thursday," said Clementine. "You're missing a day."

"Hm." He looked at the ceiling. "Maybe someone drugged me."

"Really? Who would do that to you, do you think?"

"I have no idea." He turned to Gray, who held a small clay bowl in his hand. "Please don't handle that. Thank you."

Gray placed it back on the shelf. "Sorry, man."

"No worries. As I was saying, I have no idea who would do anything to me. But I'd like to get some sleep."

"Okay," said Clem. "We understand. Just a few more things and we'll leave you alone. Firstly, can you remove your shirt so Ms. Munoz can assess if you've been injured? We found a substantial amount of blood at your workplace."

"I'd rather she didn't," replied Craig.

"We're actually required by law to observe you, sir, so I must insist, I'm afraid," said Clementine.

With a sigh, he lifted up his shirt. Clementine gasped at the gory wound between his ribs. "That's nothing. I ran into a fence," he said. A viscous liquid trickled from the gap.

Amy threw on her gloves, ordering Mr. James to stay still. She noticed an outer wound that's edges were cauterized, forming a ring around a smaller fresher one. A gummy scab lined the rim. This man had been stabbed savagely, had the wound seared shut, and then was pierced again in the exact same place on his body.

"You feel okay?" Amy asked.

"No."

Amy cleaned it off and bandaged it, without stitches. The flesh was gooey and the thread would rip right through. With his head turned, she swabbed the wound and bagged it.

"I think you should go to a hospital, Mr. James," said Amy.

"No," he said. "You can't make me."

That much was true. They didn't have any authority to make him go see a doctor. Their case was dissolving. There was no body, and the only person who had spilled a substantial amount of blood was not dead, but sitting and talking to them in his own house, as alive and well as you please. As fucked up as this situation was, it was certainly not a murder investigation.

"Okay. Just try to relax then?" Amy said.

"No. Just go. Please."

"Mr. James, you just said someone drugged you, and apparently someone has also stabbed you," said Clementine. "We need to bring these people to justice."

"People?" Craig asked. "What makes you say it's more than one?"

"It's a hunch."

"Well, I'm not pressing charges, so that doesn't leave much for you."

"But we can protect you," said Clem.

"You have absolutely no way of knowing that. Now. Please go."

"Alright," Clem stood. "This is getting old. There's really only one question that can't wait till tomorrow. Is this one of the men who assaulted you at your workplace?"

She showed him the years-old mugshot of Markuz. "His blood was also found in your office."

Craig swooned when he saw the photograph. Just a ripple, but it was there. Regaining his composure almost instantly, he said, "No."

Clementine's eyes narrowed. "Mr. James, are you positive? We can't help you if you don't tell us." She thought his eyes darted for an instant to the hallway. "Is there someone else in this house, Mr. James?"

She motioned to Gray, who drew his weapon and searched the rooms down the hall.

"Clear," he said, after a minute.

"See? There's no one here, and I don't know that guy," said Craig. "Now, I'm going to have to insist that you people leave me alone." He pointed at the door.

"Go to the hospital tomorrow," said Amy as they left.

"Close the door," he said.

At Clementine's, they spoke about the connections between the players. The James family and the Stillwater Corporation seemed to be linked, but how so? Allies or rivals? Whose side are the hooknose and the spidery kid on? And Markuz? Not to mention the other contributor to the logjam of blood evidence; still a John Doe walking around the city.

Everything was shrouded.

"My brain is starting to hurt," said Gray, "I think it's time for me to hit it." He looked expectantly to Amy.

"I think I'm gonna stay here with Clem for a while, Gray. We'll see you at work tomorrow." She wanted to go with him, but Clementine needed her.

Gray understood. He kissed Amy, said goodbye to Clem, and walked out the door. A pair of mockingbirds chittered loudly in the dark as he walked through the trees and out of the gate.

"How do you feel about him?" Amy asked, barely able to contain herself.

"I feel good," Clementine said. "More importantly, how do you feel about him?"

Amy chuckled. "Pretty good. In fact, the only thing I'm worried about is liking him too much, at this point."

"Well, it's reciprocated, I think. I hate to ask, Amy, but do you think you could stay over tonight? I think I might get a guard dog tomorrow. This whole thing has got me freaked out since hooknose, doubly so with the wild kid and that Craig James guy coming back. If not I understand, of course—"

"Clem," Amy interrupted. "It's okay. Of course I'll stay here. Gimme some blankets." After some thought, she added, "Dog, huh? You have the time? How about a better alarm?"

"The problem I have with another alarm being installed is how often the people who work for the alarm companies quit, or are fired, and return to the houses to rob people."

"You're weird."

"I'm a cop."

The ladies shared a nightcap, then Clementine went to her room. Amy took the couch. Neither slept very well, each watching the shadows from the trees dance in the wind before drifting off, and awakening repeatedly throughout the night.

The next morning, Clementine got a call from the lieutenant. She was informed that with the reappearance of Craig James, who had contacted the station moments earlier, and his subsequent dropping of any pending charges, there was no longer a case. It was only after Clementine suggested that she break the news to Mr. Stillwater's representatives that one of the cases on his property would no longer have the department's lead detectives on it that he had let her stay on.

"What is it, Clem? You hate the privileged babysitter gigs."

"There's something more here, I'm positive."

"Okay, but I'm yanking Jim. I can't leave you both on this."

"I'll survive." She pumped her fist in the air.

Amy had gone to work hours earlier, and called Clementine from the lab after the lieutenant.

"The only thing I found out about Craig James' blood," she said, "is that it has the same metallic signature as the sample from that kid, even though it's a different blood type. The metal is strange. A kind of silver."

Clementine thanked her, hung up, and was left to wonder what that could mean.

• • •

Clementine's shift didn't start until ten that morning, and at nine o'clock she pulled into the animal shelter. A girl of fifteen wore a vest that said "Volunteer" on it, and walked Clementine around to the various cages to observe the dogs. Many puppies jumped at the fence, eager for love, the cutest of which had little orange tags exclaiming they had been adopted. A dopey-looking Labrador wagged its tail from a distance, far too friendly for Clementine's needs. Behind the Lab peeked the head of a forty-pound golden shorthaired mutt. It growled and adopted a defensive stance.

"What's up with that dog, Suzanne?" asked Clem.

"Grifter? He hates everyone. I wouldn't suggest adopting that one. To be quite honest he may be incurable," she admitted.

They tried everything with this dog, she explained. Pairing it with the dopey Lab in some hope the docility would rub off was the last ditch before the dog would occupy a small run behind the shelter where the ones with really bad attitudes spent the rest of their days. It was rare. He would be the first in a year. This was a kill-free shelter. If it weren't, this dog would probably be dead.

"Open the gate." said Clementine.

After a small whine of protest, the girl did. The dopey Lab bounded over and licked Clementine, who pushed it gently over to the young girl. Clementine got down on her knees and held her hand out toward the smaller dog. It snarled and barked, but she didn't flinch, didn't let the dog know how scared she was. The dog quieted, sat down, and stared into her eyes. They remained motionless for an entire minute, which seemed far longer.

"I'll take him," she finally said.

"Uh . . . okay!" replied Suzanne.

The dog was muscular but lean, its short wiry hair crinkled in the longer places around the neck and chest, like a little mane. It jumped into the passenger seat quickly, as if ready to be away from the shelter. Clementine didn't blame him. It was clean and humane, but the dogs knew what was going on in there.

On the ride back, the dog sat upright in the passenger seat and looked through the windshield, for the most part. When they switched from one freeway to the next he looked over to a row of warehouses ringed by a razor wire fence and growled. The noise started as a deep rumbling, and gradually rose in timbre before he broke into savage barking. As they sped by the building, Grifter followed it with his head, the barks morphing back into a growl, then silence as it faded from view.

The warehouse sat just down the hill from where she was attacked in the park by the hooknose. And it was the area Gray and Amy mentioned from their dreams.

At home, the dog's disposition brightened considerably. First he sniffed around the perimeter, then straightened his tail, put his head up, and barked at Clementine.

"You're welcome, Grifter."

She gave him a treat from the bag of goodies she'd bought. Grifter's tail wagged as he stood up on his hind legs and rested his paws on her thigh. She put her face down close to his, and he licked her cheek. His savior.

Clementine was overcome with emotion. The long barren road of searching for her son had shut off her feelings gradually, leaving her cold inside. It was as if all this had reached a crescendo, and all of a sudden came flowing out of her. She was racked by sobs. Her legs grew wobbly, and she slouched to the ground. Grifter lapped up the tears streaming down her face. Her arms wrapped around the dog and pulled him to her heaving chest.

When the tears had finally subsided, she stood up, and felt lighter. Her problems hadn't dissipated, but she felt like she had a firmer anchor because of this animal. She couldn't explain it, it was simply a feeling of truth. Of light.

Unsure what it was, she was convinced her choice at the shelter was one of the greatest she'd ever made.

She stayed with him until it was time to go to work. His head cocked to the side as Clementine tried to explain that this was his house now, and he needed to protect it. She would be back at lunch, she said, and filled one silver bowl with food and one with water.

Grifter curled up on his new dog bed on the back patio and watched Clementine walk down the side to the front gate. She turned around, and he bounded after her.

"No, Grifter. You stay here."

He sat down. Clementine shrugged, chuckling as she climbed in her car and drove away. As she left the curb she looked one last time to see him following her with his eyes.

•   •   •

In the darkened office, Frank's sweat-drenched hands wrung together over the desk. He could finally make the puppets talk.

Jeb was wrong. He could figure it out on his own. Anything was possible. He knew how to use the orbs.

However, he would need something to make him stronger, able to last. He had almost lost control of the puppet when he spoke through it for so long to the police.

18

Stewart's dream that night was unlike any he had ever experienced. It was a graphic retelling from his past when his world shifted, seen through branches of scrub willow and marsh reeds.

That long ago day, he had been driven down to the San Diego River. Nineteen years old, a young carefree man in the backseat of a car with a girl, one Maria Kaminski. They opted to stay liplocked rather than follow Jeb, Frank, and Nuala down to the water. Maria was way out of his league, but he wasn't about to complain.

The scene shifted through haze, from the two lovers in the car to Frank and Nuala leaving Jeb on the shore. They waded out to a small wooded island in the river's center. The smoke visions shifted to the island's interior, where they were crouched over an old gnarled raven.

The raven croaked out Stewart's name. Frank replied he would not be coming, and whatever thing he planned to give away he could just give to them. Nuala insisted that Stewart had agreed, and they wore the old bird down.

The bird dissipated into smoke and in its place rose a man Stewart recognized as Abraham Blackwing, looking not one minute younger. Though obviously not fooled, he laughed at the clever children and their initiative, and proceeded to say in a jagged language a blessing over their heads. Smoky tendrils danced around them.

A mist enveloped the scene, and the focus shifted to the pair returning, Jeb asking what had happened, and his being told next to nothing. They arrived back at the car where Stewart and Maria were still intertwined. Their few questions were met by awkward silence.

In his subconscious state, Stewart watched from above as his dream self got let out at home, just as he had been twenty years ago.

The dream's focus followed Frank and Nuala as they dropped off Jeb, then drove Maria to an old warehouse down by an intersection of freeways, at the mouth of a wide canyon. The car parked. Frank got out, walked into the warehouse, and returned with Armando, Maria's two-year-old brother, the miracle boy born sixteen years after his sister. She grabbed Armando, spit in Frank's face, and walked away.

Frank's eyes were slits as they followed her storm off.

The dream vaporized as Stewart let his eyes peel open. The room was spotless. It had been so vivid that the clean room made him think the previous few days were part of the dream also, like a drawn-out epic. For one brief moment he basked in the relief reserved for those waking to find nightmares unreal.

Then he looked at his hands.

The nicks and cuts covering them told him it was not a dream. His shoulder blade began to ache, then his wounded foot, accompanied by his heart sinking. He sat up and rubbed his eyes. Everything hurt.

The mockingbird was gone.

Someone had tidied up his things, the clean-up job haphazard at best. Things had been stuffed randomly upon shelves, filling up some while leaving others empty. It annoyed Stewart. Nothing was where it should be.

He caught the faint scent of charred dirt. He'd smelled it before. He rubbed his face, and looked at the flecks of dried blood clinging to his hands. Throwing the covers off, he sat up and marched toward his living room. The smell intensified as he rounded the corner, and saw Cora and Abraham sitting on his couch. Cora waved. Abe was thumbing through a book.

The mockingbird, sitting on the rim of Abraham's tattered hat and pecking at it, chirped and flew to Stewart's shoulder. He patted the bird's head, sighed, and slumped his shoulders.

"Cora! Uh, um, hi," he said, trying to prepare a story about the car.

"Hi, Stewart. We took the liberty of cleaning your house."

"I see that. Um, I had to steal your car."

"I know. I told Klia to do that."

"Who?"

"The mockingbird. Klia."

"Klia. Of course," he said, rubbing the bird's head. "What's this guy doing here? You guys are friends, I guess."

The raggedy man looked at Stewart and said, "Just reading," then turned his eyes back to the book.

Stewart was not going to get into it right now. The guy had a knack for pissing him off, which had already worked in two words.

"I've gotta eat," Stewart said, and without waiting for a response walked into the kitchen.

Abraham and Cora looked at each other and shrugged, listening to the clatter of dishes and stomps. Stewart cooked, frying up some eggs and bacon and toasting bread, then ate alone at the kitchen table. Klia landed on a stool between the living room and kitchen, darting glances.

"Hope you're not hungry, there's just enough for me!" he yelled.

He threw bread crumbs to Klia, who pecked them off the countertop.

After the food was gone, he emerged holding three coffee cups in one hand.

As he set them on his rickety coffee table, he said, "Here's some coffee. Not that either of you deserve it after setting me up to fail or die out there in the goddamn canyons."

He turned to Cora. "And who are you? Why are you my neighbor?" Suspicions ran wild. "What the hell is going on with you people, and how in the fuck am I involved in it? Better yet, why am I involved?" Spit began to fly off his lips as he gained steam. "How much of that dream is real, first of all?"

"How would we know about your dreams?" asked the gnarled old man, chuckling.

Stewart glared at Abe. "Give me a fucking break," he said, which made Abe double over laughing.

"I'll tell you, Stewart," Cora said, "but you've gotta relax. When you hear it you may have more questions than answers. As far as the dream, pretty much all of it is real. That day you saw was to be your awakening, the entrance to our world. But Frank and Nuala grabbed hold of your destiny and tricked, or really led, Abraham into bestowing them with talents to augment their already powerful personalities."

Realizing the betrayal, the veins on Stewart's arms pulsed.

Cora could sense he was about to explode. "I'll back it up a little," she said.

"That would be incredible."

"Well, like it or not, Stewart, you are a part of our way, where everything is connected, through the webs of the world. That is what you witnessed at Jeb's cabin," she paused, took a sip from her cup, keeping her eyes on Stewart. "A nexus of webs."

Cora saw the glimmer of recognition in his eyes. She motioned to Abe and herself. "We are preservers of that web, okay?"

"I guess so."

"Good. Now, there is a council of Keepers, certain of our kind. Over time, their posts are vacated for one reason or another, and it is up to the Makers, or Awakeners, to fill their absence.

"Abraham . . . " As she motioned to him, he began to snore. " . . . is a Maker, He has control over one thing; the Raven's Gift. At the river, he was so taken with the initiative of Frank and Nuala that he gave them the mantle meant for you."

"How did he do that to both Frank and Nuala, if it's one thing?"

"It halved itself. That surprised everyone," said Cora. "It was the first time something like that had ever happened. We are at a changing time in history."

Stewart was indignant. "How the hell could he give away something that was supposed to be mine? Don't you people have rules and stuff? Nobody else had a problem with this?"

"I understand your frustration, but it doesn't really work like that. Makers are old, and form their own decisions. The council doesn't enforce rules upon them. Plus, Abraham is the Raven, a trickster. Frank and Nuala's duping you made them better candidates in his mind, not worse."

"How's that working out for you?"

"Not well," she admitted. "Frank and Nuala pulled the wool over everyone's eyes. They shared some knowledge with Jeb, a superior scientific mind, and Jeb made them new snares."

"Excuse me?"

"Like the silver knife Craig James gave to you."

Stewart started sweating. She was going to ask him for the knife, which he no longer had. He bade her continue.

"The new snares, and the newfound powers, did not take long to completely corrupt Frank. Nuala followed him into the shaping of other lifeforms. First animals, then people. Different subjects for different experiments. We don't even know who all they have in there now, but whoever it is, they are being subjected to horrible things.

"Jeb saw what they were up to, and left. He tried to free the captives, but ended up barely escaping with his own life. He did, however, steal the silver snare, then hid from Frank in a secret cabin in the canyons, continuing his research.

"Frank flew into a frenzy, but couldn't find Jeb again. He'd have to learn on his own. That's when his power grew, and quickly. We realized we couldn't stop Frank without you, the original target for the transformation.

"You are the one who can get it back. That is why Jeb sent Nickel to you with the silver snare," she said. "To steal back the Raven's gift."

"Hold on," said Stewart

"By the way, where is it?"

"Uhhhh . . . " he stalled.

"Uh what, Stewart? Do you still have it? Does Jeb? Where is he?"

These people certainly weren't omnipotent.

"Jeb's dead," he said.

Abe opened his eyes. For the first time, there was no hint of a smile upon his face.

"What are you talking about?" the old man asked.

"Shit," said Stewart, "I thought you guys would somehow know already. When I left Jeb's cabin, his head was in a bowl of granola and his body was sitting at his table. Someone had separated the two. Then someone chased me out of there."

Cora said, "We don't already know. Tell us immediately."

Realizing she may be the only person who would or could educate him, he told her the entire saga. When he finished, Cora and Abe were aghast.

"Holy shit," said Cora. "Wow. I'm terribly sorry, Stewart, but am I to believe that child has the knife?"

He looked at the ground. "Yes," he mumbled.

The room fell silent. Abe and Cora looked confused.

"Who is he?" they asked simultaneously.

"Seriously? He's not with them, or you?" He sat back heavily, which sent the mockingbird winging off. He felt queasy.

"I've never heard of him. He could be anyone," said Cora. "They've taken so many. Maybe one finally got out."

Abe spoke up, "Looks like we all fucked up a little. Heh." Cora locked eyes with Abe, "He's the one who lost the knife to some kid. Not me," he said, pointing at Stewart.

Cora put her face close to Abraham's. "For your whole ridiculous life you've blamed other people. The council looked the other way, and you had the gall to blame it on them for entrusting you with such a decision. Things are going to change if we fail, and quite drastically. So please, take some responsibility and let's move on to fixing these monumental problems."

Abraham couldn't meet her eyes. "It's my fault," he said.

Stewart began to chew his fingernails, something he hadn't done in several years. A new terror mounted within him.

Cora's expression softened as she walked over to him and kissed his cheek. Her lips were electric.

"Poor Stewart. Drink some more coffee. I'm going to tell you a story."

He did as he was told. The brush of her lips tingling on his skin.

Stewart refilled his cup, then collapsed into the chair opposite the lumpy couch Abe and Cora sat on. He blew the steam from his coffee, and took a gulp. The heat and caffeine jolted him.

Cora's gaze was like a growing vine penetrating Stewart right between the eyebrows. A flowering overtook him, and he saw the now familiar worms elongating and swaying. pictures began to dance. Shapes. A village. People in the mist.

● ● ●

1037. Ireland. A band of Druids welcomes a fleet of boats from the sea.

Many of these Earth worshippers wish to commingle with some of the strange new people, calling themselves "priests," who come to their land, and share the knowledge to better all life on the planet. This works for a time, until it becomes clear that some of these priests have less than noble intentions. Their efforts to bring control are resisted by the natives, and a split occurs when the new priest class suggests that the sacred Solstice celebration be altered to include their Jesus figure.

A young Druidic ovate argues with an old priest. The old man says that the ovate is obviously incorrect, that Jesus is the catalyst for these holidays anyway. He explains that the Druids had it wrong all these years, and should have been waiting for the priests to arrive. The priest does his best to ridicule the old ways, rankling some of the believers of the ancient Earthen traditions.

With the priests is an alchemist, not strictly a man of the priests' Jesus god.

The alchemist, intrigued by the Druids, infiltrates the radicals that do not feel that any of their ancient knowledge should be shared with these men. They are a group of mainly younger students who have broken from the main body of Druids to prepare for just these days when their beliefs would come under attack. A philosopher/warrior elite.

The oldest priest hears of the organization and sends his own assassins to root out the Druidic resistance, not knowing his own alchemist now is entrenched within the young ovate's group.

The movement has a name: the Long Green Hand, and, through the orders of the old priest, it had been given the first casualty.

The young ovate wakes in the morning and walks to the town circle to find his cousin disemboweled at the foot of the Sacred Oak. The ovate is incensed, and soon a silent battle rages. Though new to the assassin game, the members of the Long Green Hand find they are naturally adept at it, learning through the teachings and machinations of the alchemist.

Using all of their earthen and his alchemical wisdom, through incantations in both dead and living languages, they create through the elements a means of turning the tide back to their ancient ways rather than this new cult. A weapon is forged of silver and blood. Ancient words. Wood and bone. An oaken and silver box is made to house it. With this thing they would silence the horrible lies. This is the birth of the spirit snare.

The old priest gives the orders to the other men of Jesus. It is also for him that has his underlings bring young boys for "baptisms". These boys come out changed. Not into pious followers of the white Christ, but into sad shells of their former selves. It is whispered that the priest is doing unspeakable things to them.

The alchemist and the young ovate have found their target.

On the Autumnal Equinox they set a trap for the old priest. A young boy, one he had not got his hands on yet, leads him into an ambush by the members of the Long Green Hand, who promptly stab the old priest with their new blade.

Their weapon works, and they imprison the spirit of the missionary in the knife. He goes from sermonizing about Christ to anyone who will listen to bathing naked in the river with a stag horn worn upside down as a helmet, saying not much of anything coherent. People think he has either seen the "true path" or gone stark raving mad, and soon avoid him altogether. His fellow priests pray over him, or ride back towards their holy land. The children he had victimized take to throwing rocks at him as they passed. Many hit him in the face.

Word eventually reaches the church of this attack on their chosen missionary leader. They flood the area with many more missionaries. Not a sermonizing lot, rather the sort that torture nonbelievers into submission. These priests hunt the Druids down, slaughtering them with finely honed steel.

In one standoff, another Jesus priest is stabbed, this time the Druid intends with his will a release of the snare, and consequently bleeds the first missionary's spirit into this second priest's body, where their spirits commingle. The two men inside the body are powerless to move, and become horribly aware of one another sharing a body. Both minds simultaneously crack, not able to comprehend what has taken place. The knife now houses no one. The alchemist's weapon is a huge success.

Seven Druids and seventeen priests are killed in the initial carnage. The priests, however, have an endless supply of bodies from the converted masses of the mainland to draw from, and each wave is more brutal than the last. Soon innocent townspeople are slain by hundreds. Each time the priests loudly cry over the body that if the resistors are turned over to them, the killing will cease. At the planning of the alchemist, two older Druids, not actual members of the resistance but willing decoys, turn themselves over to satisfy the edict, while the remaining members board boats and sail north, reluctantly leaving their beloved homeland forever.

The priest who houses two spirits is taken back to Rome where he is immediately canonized, then quietly retires to a tower and fades into legend.

The alchemist and the remaining young Druids of the Long Green Hand land in the north. Two of them stay in Scandinavia with the Vikings. The young ovate, who had started the breakaway order, and the alchemist who had overseen it, board a dragon boat to journey to the new world that people had been hearing of since a man named Leif had come back from there years previous.

● ● ●

"Wow," said Stewart, rubbing his eyes.

"Yes," Cora said. "That is the snare. We heard only small fractions of stories about it until it resurfaced with your friends. We thought it was lost forever."

"Jeez, So this weapon thing's just been floating around for a thousand years and now it falls in my lap? And then this kid gets it? Now this is my story? Shit."

"It's okay, Stewart," Cora felt for Stewart. It's not easy to find out the world is totally different than what one thinks. At least when it happened to her she had been young enough to accept the strange concepts. Stewart was forty. This might not be pretty.

"Somehow your old friends got a hold of the old Druid knife, and Jeb figured out how to duplicate it."

"That's not good."

"No," said Cora, "it's not. Predictably, this gets worse."

"Frank and Nuala tried the first replicant snare on someone they targeted in a club randomly. The man was exceedingly drunk and followed them into a motel room, eager for Nuala. After a quick spiked drink he was ready for some action. He got some, but not what he was looking for. Frank stabbed him with the new black cone and trapped his spirit."

Stewart shivered.

"They ordered the now spiritless husk to walk forward, which it did. Then to turn right, which it also mastered. When they commanded it to turn left it grabbed Frank by the throat and hurled him into the wall. Frank is a total hothead, as you know, so he stabbed the man repeatedly, killing him and the experiment."

"What the fuck?" Stewart said. "How did you find out all this?"

"The web is full of mystery," she said. "Anyhow, they just left the man's body there. With nothing to tie them to the crime, they vanished, and it became one of the most gruesome cold cases in San Diego history.

"It took Frank weeks to make Nuala believe she wanted this as much as he did. They had left no clue at the motel room, and burned all the clothes they wore. The bar was one they had never been to, with no cameras. Nobody was going to find them, because they were never going to be anywhere near there again.

"Jeb kept working on snares and giving them to Frank, who enticed young people from the surrounding neighborhoods, then used the blades on them. But the experiments weren't working perfectly. People came out of the snares changed. Little pieces missing. When their spirits were inside something was happening. Each snare had its own complication. Memory. Color vision. Something.

"Frank decided they needed younger volunteers. Children. He convinced Nuala, and the first experiment with a child was far more successful than the adults.

"That is where everything becomes speculation concerning Frank. He no longer trusted Jeb, Nuala, or anyone. Our spying ceased to be effective after he discovered an old language which can control the snares, and other tools.

"Jeb learned on his own how to truly see and communicate with the birds, who in turn showed him the horrific experiments of his brother. That is when he disappeared, realizing that his brother was now lost in power-lust."

"So Frank killed Jeb?"

"I doubt it. There are many people who would benefit from Jeb's demise. Frank is not one of them. He needs the knowledge to complete his transformation," she said.

"Into what?"

"Into a Maker."

Stewart spit up his coffee. "How do you know I didn't kill him?"

They broke into laughter. "There's no fucking way," said Abe.

"Fuck you guys," Stewart said. "Well, what goes on now?"

"The child knows Nuala, and most likely Frank, so he may know what the snare is. We have to snatch the kid, get Craig out of the snare, then steal back part of the mantle from Frank," she said. "How's that sound?"

"Insanely difficult." He gazed up at the ceiling, if only to avoid eye contact. He'd never noticed the cracks that ran along the white surface. They began to dance and sway, and it took a few seconds for him to realize he was looking at smoky tendrils cascading down.

"What the fuck?!" he yelled, jumping out of his chair, eyes fixed on his living and moving ceiling. Panicked, he turned for the door, but Abraham was blocking the path. He blew a puff of smoke into Stewart's face while making the same low bursting noise as before.

Stewart's senses flooded on top of one another. All the memories he'd ever had of Frank, then of Nuala, Frank's best friend in their awkward high school years and beyond, and finally of Jeb.

Inside the flood was a distinct and discernible pattern of behavior on Frank's part. High school. Band practice. Not just a manipulation of Stewart but of all the people around him; his brother, friends, family, teachers, everyone. If it so happened that Frank did not have help with this influence, he would very simply be a psychopathic genius, Stewart thought.

The memories shifted: Nuala reflected in Frank's eye as she gazed lovingly into the cold blue wasteland and said she'd do anything for him. Even help kidnap the girl, barely seventeen. Then looking on in horror as Frank stabbed the girl in an attempt to find her "spirit center." He'd told Nuala to do it next, but she couldn't force herself. She loved him more than anything. Including herself. Her family. But she could never do that! They'd buried her behind the warehouse. Frank said she had been too old.

Then came the fifteen-year-old girl he had brought home. The one who made him laugh as she commanded Nuala to do her dishes, her laundry, to wash and dry her hair for her, to leave the house so she wouldn't hear them "making love." I've got news for you, honey, when a thirty-year-old man and a fifteen-year-old girl do whatever they do, it's not called "making love."

The final straw had come when the young girl ordered Nuala to bathe her so she could smell nice for her and Frank's "lovemaking." During the bath Nuala grabbed the girl's ponytail and held her just below the surface of the water, close enough so the girl could watch as she shoved the snare between her ribs and into her young beating heart.

After she had stabbed that one, watching the life drain from her eyes, the others weren't quite so hard.

Another low bursting noise sounded, and Stewart found himself staring into Abe's cloudy eyes. Abe waved his hand. Three tendrils of web extracted themselves from Stewart and wound back into the ceiling. Stewart felt like vomiting.

"Well, that's the explanation of your friends and more about the web! Two birds with one rock, eh? Haha!" Abraham slapped his knee.

Stewart glared bloody murder at him, and swallowed the drool in the back of his throat to try not to puke.

"I hate you," said Stewart, making Abe laugh so hard he fell to the ground.

"Leave him alone, Abe," Cora said. "He's right though. There's a lesson in the web."

When their vision locked, Cora clasped her hands and made a small popping sound with her lips. Stewart felt breath rush into his lungs, filling them all the way up. A tingling spread over him as he exhaled, and his being felt charged. His nerves, muscle, bones, even ligaments and tendons felt smooth. Tranquil. He was blossoming.

Into what, he wasn't sure. Cora's touch was like silk upon his skin.

"Things are going to happen for you, Stewart," she said.

In his placated mind, she had won. But he got the feeling that he wasn't being told everything. Not just about the webs. Something else.

"Yeah," he said. "A real rising star."

They sat in silence for quite a while.

When Stewart felt ready to go on, he asked, "What about those thugs? The huge guy and the milky white guy?"

"Markuz and Peik are basically Frank's generals."

"They don't seem so hardcore."

Cora's eyebrows raised. "Don't fool yourself. You were extremely lucky, they are ruthless men. Mark my words: that will not happen again."

Cora told a gripping tale involving the two men, a screwdriver, and four sets of men's eyes. Stewart looked at the ground and hoped he never heard any part of the story ever again.

"So this is our hardcore group?" he asked.

"For now, until we can snag that kid and the dog."

"How do we do that?"

In answer, Klia mimicked the boy's whistle. Stewart smiled at the bird, then asked Cora, "Why didn't you warn me about Nickel when you saw me on the stairs?"

Cora gazed at him with her deep brown eyes, long enough to make him squirm. "Stewart, is there any chance you would have believed me?"

"None at all."

●　●　●

Amidst the last few days' activities, Stewart never had time to get his shift covered, and now of course it was far too late. He parked his bicycle and locked it to the lamppost in front of the club.

"Man, you're a glutton for punishment," said Byron, the doorman. "You didn't get someone to work for you on your birthday?"

"Something came up," said Stewart, swinging open the door and slipping inside.

Aunt Frieda's Rock Club had a backlit sign above the door, and no windows whatsoever. It sat on a noisy corner of town while trains, planes, and every manner of automobile blared by. The club had live music every night of the week, but nobody complained about the sound, not even the tenants of the small apartments upstairs. They were too used to it, and the rent was cheap. The location of the club made being open in the daytime completely impractical. It simply wasn't and would never be a daytime bar, and had existed as solely a music venue for decades.

Behind the bar, Stewart saw the large and lovely Auntie Frieda smiling at him while standing next to a pudgy kid of maybe twenty-five years. He smiled back.

"Hey, Auntie," he said. Very few people called her Frieda, with the exception of boyfriends who didn't want to refer to their lover as a family member. The only other person Stewart had ever seen do it was her cousin, Max, a gangly dude that seemed odd, but Stewart had gotten used to him over the years. Max came around and spoke to Auntie almost every week. When he came, the office door that was usually open got locked, and Stewart had no idea what they talked about. But they were family, and it wasn't his business.

Max also technically lived with Auntie Frieda, although a couple of the other employees had hinted that he permanently camped in the canyons around Golden Hill.

"Hi, Stewie. You're working tonight?" she asked, obviously confused. "Happy birthday."

"It is my shift," he answered, "and thanks."

"I just thought, with your birthday, and the show tonight . . ." She looked at the stage, then back at him.

"Shit, whatever. You ready to train somebody?" she asked. A big light-skinned black woman with freckles, Frieda was about three inches taller than Stewart. She cut an impressive figure behind the bar as she pointed at the kid, who looked to be just barely old enough to be in a bar, if that.

"Always. What's up, man? I'm Stewart," he said.

The young man gripped Stewart's hand just so. Not crushing it early like a macho freak and grabbing the knuckles, and not like a limp fish, equally annoying. Stewart approved.

It has been said not to judge a book by its cover, but never by Stewart. To him, appearances tell more truths than anyone cares to admit: the walk, the dress, the look in the eyes all combine in a unique alchemical formula, individual as a fingerprint. The job dictates judgment, as it is inherently dangerous: serving a controlled drug that makes some people violent and unpredictable.

At this point in the job Stewart could basically call out to himself who would leave exactly what percent of a tip, if they would be condescending to women, or spit in a cup on the bar, upon first sighting them. Or how ridiculously someone would act after a couple drinks. He was wrong occasionally, to be sure, but not nearly as often as he was right.

If looks were a glimpse into the soul, a handshake was a long hard look. This guy was already alright in Stewart Zanderson's book.

"Esteban," said the young man. "Mucho gusto."

"Nice to meet you too," replied Stewart, looking at the stage. His old bandmates, one his ex-girlfriend Vivian, were getting ready for soundcheck. Their "new" band; basically his old one. Without him. "Well, Esteban, let's get you started."

"Hold on," said Frieda, and spun Stewart gently around, shooing Esteban away. "No trouble, Okay?"

"No trouble."

Esteban was in school for film. He wanted to make movies. They talked movies and the job equally during the training process. As he showed Esteban the opening duties, he did his best to avoid Chase and Vivian, but after their soundcheck Chase approached the bar, waiting until Stewart was behind it.

"Hey, pal," said Chase. "Can we get our drink tickets from you?"

Stewart threw his best stink eye at him, ripped off some raffle-style tickets from a roll, and threw them down on the bar with a slap.

"There," he said, "but I am most assuredly not your fucking buddy, asshole."

When he turned back around, Frieda was fuming.

"Smooth move, dickhead," laughed Chase as he walked away.

Stewart took two steps, meaning to round the bar and pummel him.

His progress was halted by Auntie Frieda as she grabbed his collar from behind and said, "The office. Now," marching him away while Chase chortled from the stage. Esteban stood behind the bar, terribly confused.

"What's gotten into you, Stewart? I already told you if there's any more complaints I'm gonna have to fire you. Now, if you can't handle it you should have got your shift covered. You're here now and you're going to have to deal with this, or call someone to come in. It should sell out. You'll be busy," Auntie said from her plush office chair. "But no more bullshit. You got me? Because I will fire you tonight if you pull that shit again."

"Yes," he said. "I got it."

The thought of the show selling out drove another knife into him. He was the one that had worked so hard to get their name out there, and now they were using it to advertise this new thing, thereby stealing his work. Auntie was right, though, he was going to have to let it go. He needed this job now more than ever, he thought. He had to admit, being at work was better than getting killed.

"I'm sorry. I can totally deal with it. It won't happen again. I totally lost my cool and I regret it."

"I know that guy is a prick, baby. And your old girl, well, she don't know what's up if she chooses that douche over you. But the fact of the matter remains that you have to handle yourself like a pro out there, alright?" The softness in her eyes showed her concern for Stewart, an old friend as well as her best employee, but he needed to get that anger in check.

"Gotcha," he said. "I know."

"Okay then."

She bent over to get something from a drawer, and Stewart looked behind her. On a table was a record player with a couple wires taken out and spliced. Some quasi-experimental instrument or something, Stewart thought. The thing about it that captured his attention, however, was not the turntable itself. Rather it was the reconstructed black-and-white striped bowl.

"What the fuck?"

"Max just brought that stuff in here. I'm holding it for him."

"I think that bowl's from my trash."

Frieda looked at him quizzically. "Really? That's weird, but he does stay around there, and he likes to rummage."

"Yeah, what's up with that? I thought he lived with you," Stewart turned his head toward the bowl. Black spots dotted his vision. He looked away. They stopped.

Stewart had met Max several times over the years, but the guy never exactly opened up, and Frieda didn't go around offering details.

"Max is a complicated dude. And he really likes fresh air. I'll tell you more sometime, but right now you gotta finish up with little Esteban, okay? We gotta open." She looked at Stewart. "You're not gonna get in a fight with Chase, now, right?"

"No, only in my mind," he answered.

"Whatever. Get out of here."

During the early part of the shift, Chase went to the other bartender, and Vivian didn't approach him at all. The first two bands played. Stewart liked the first but couldn't stomach the second. He was glad it was busy so they served as very loud background music.

After the second band was finished, Chase and Vivian were setting up their gear. The entire crowd was trying to get a drink, as happens just before the headliner. Stewart was serving three people at a time, hands swirling like an octopus. In the midst of the chaos he looked up to take the next order. A red-haired woman ordered a vodka tonic. As he moved to make the drink he looked next to her, monitoring who he'd be serving next, bookmarking the person's features. Behind her, at a table that divided the bar from the dance floor, stood the pale man Peik and the gnarled giant Markuz. The two men glared at him from beyond the patron's heads. Stewart flinched, and dropped the woman's drink on the ground.

"Shit. One second, please," he said, bending over to clean up.

When he stood, they were no longer there. He remade the drink while looking around the club, but they had vanished.

When the band started, the crowd at the bar eventually thinned, as people jammed in front of the stage to see the band. They were pretty good. They should be, the first three songs Stewart had basically written. Break time beckoned.

"Did you see your friends?" asked Byron, at the door. Stewart had worked with Byron forever.

"Who?"

"The Russian and the Viking." He winked. "They asked for you by both names. Very cop-like."

"Yeah, they're not cops."

"What are they?"

"The kind of guys where cops are imminently a preferable option."

"Shitty. Well, they left," said Byron. "You need to throw down on those dudes, you let me know," he added, cracking his knuckles.

"You'll be the first to know." Stewart walked to the corner and looked up and down both streets. Clear.

A mockingbird whistled from a jacaranda tree. The high notes mixed with the bass filtering through the walls of the club, and made a twining melody that soothed Stewart's mind. It sounded like Klia, but they probably all did. For a shining moment of clarity he was one with the night in all its aspects, his recent memories racing.

He felt better as he went back in and finished the shift. He was a part of something bigger, and scarier.

He completely ignored the band as they loaded out, though Chase crowed over and over about how great a show it was. And it was. Asshole.

An hour later Stewart locked up, said goodbye to Frieda, Byron, and Esteban, and got on his bicycle to head home.

Klia swooped down from the jacaranda and followed him, landing on the handlebars with her face to the wind when they were safely away from everyone on the dark, deserted street.

19

Buddy spent the early part of the night pulverizing five-pound rocks into dust with the leash and steel ball at the bottom of the hill, previously Garth's domain.

After they had bagged up all the garbage he'd left behind, the hillside finally looked more like a natural habitat. It was the best area in this corner of the park to make noise after dark. A road ran between the oak grove and the golf course which bordered the northern side with a high chain-link fence. It was easy to hide behind trees if any cars lit up the grove.

All that day Helen had remained upset, and did not want him out of her sight. When dusk came, however, she had finally relented, after he swore to her he wouldn't go outside the confines of Golden Hill Park.

"Things are coming to a head," she said. "Better stay ready."

Max walked him down to the grove, then made his way halfway back up the hill to stand guard.

The stump was knee high. He swung the steel ball into another rock, and a hail of stone shards shot like shrapnel. Luna backed off toward the protection of the bushes.

A high scream in the distance shattered his concentration. Helen's voice. Up the rocky hill behind them.

Max had already started running by the time Buddy and Luna bolted back toward Helen's camp. They zipped past him on the way, and burst through the foliage to see Markuz pulling Helen out of the tent by her hair, holding her face toward the ground. She was shrieking and thrashing, and swung a punch into his wrist, then shot her fist up behind her head and landed a haymaker into his face. The effect, however, was minimal. Markuz shook it off and returned to dragging her.

Max came down the hill from Markuz's blind side. Buddy saw him, and jumped in front of the giant to create a diversion, waving the leash above his head.

Markuz looked at Buddy, nodded toward the bushes to his left, and pushed Helen's head further down. Poised like a spring, the giant timed himself perfectly as he reared back and twisted, bringing his elbow smashing into Max's face. A wet pulpy sound filled the canyon, and Max flew backward, landing awkwardly in the bushes and laying in a heap, not moving.

Buddy looked at the giant in shock.

From the area where Markuz nodded stepped Oliver, accompanied by another attack dog, wolfen, large, and snowy white. Its arched backbone protruded from its skin, making it look spiny and monstrous, peering at them with one blue and one entirely black eye. An acrid scent of animal urine carried on the breeze that rustled through the oak and palm trees.

Luna barked and snarled at the misshapen dog, then gave her characteristic whine. It leered in return, growling at her as they faced off.

Buddy let the leash hang at the ready. Oliver stood between him and the locked bodies of Markuz and Helen.

The big woman gripped one of Markuz's fingers and bent it backward. His wrist moved toward the ground as he grunted and pulled, maneuvering Helen's head downward as he tried to shake off her grip. From beneath her body, hidden from the giant's eyes, Helen picked up a fist-sized stone. Markuz flexed his hand, and his finger bent Helen's wrist back.

Even his fingers are strong, she thought. When Markuz again lifted Helen's head level with his own, she shot the stone up into Markuz's throat. These studs all fold if you get them somewhere soft.

Markuz rasped and hacked, doubling his body over. Helen swiftly pivoted her body behind him and kicked the toe of her hiking boot into Markuz's testicles. The giant dropped to his knees, a long groan escaping his throat.

Helen brought the rock over her head, ready to split his skull, but before she had time the wolfen guard dog rushed at her, snarling. She twisted down and managed to duck at the very last moment, trying to slam the rock into its side. The attack was too fast, and she missed. The weight of the rock made it slip out of her hand and into the bushes. The white beast had barely missed her with its jaws, and the force of its jump carried it over her body. It landed in a bush, then instantly turned around and came at her again. As it got close, it opened its jaws.

Helen rammed her forearm sideways into the thing's mouth and pushed it back as far as she could. The sturdy denim of her jacket protected her as she lodged it so deep the dog couldn't close its mouth. She made a cone shape with her free hand, all the tips of the fingers and thumb together, and smashed it into the dog's eye, shoving with her forearm and trapping the animal's head against her thigh.

With a howl, the animal thrashed around, quickly wriggling free, then stood between Helen and the two boys, half-blind, embarrassed, and angry.

Markuz righted himself quickly for someone who just had his throat and balls pummeled. In a flash he was on Helen again. She started to defend herself while monitoring the dog, but was soon overwhelmed.

Markuz grabbed her hair and rammed his fist into her stomach. Blood shot from her mouth into his face as she doubled over. He wiped it off standing over her, then began to drag her kicking and coughing up the hill and out of the canyon.

Buddy ran to help Helen, but Oliver appeared between them. The spider boy smiled a slow grin, then attacked.

Buddy was surprised by Oliver's quickness. The dead-eyed boy had got the drop on him. Buddy swung the leash too late and the steel ball just missed Oliver's charge, his speed getting him inside the arc before impact.

The leash hit Oliver harmlessly, but the weight of the stone fell, wrapping the leather strap behind his back and around his arm. As the leash grew taut, it pulled his body sideways, and he fell into Buddy, his force sending both boys to the ground. Oliver gained the upper hand almost immediately.

Luna yapped and jumped, trying to help Buddy but not able to grab anything in the knot of flailing arms and legs. The wolf dog charged at Luna, who was ready, and easily dodged around it, then scampered a good ways away to wait for another opportunity to help. She was still confused that she could not manipulate the white dog.

Buddy's panic reached a crescendo. In response, the same guiding voice spoke inside his core. *Song.*

From deep within his frightened spirit came a rolling tone that expanded with flourish. The sound of the crags and stones far beneath the surface of the earth. Of living rock. He began to hum, then sing. As he did, the entire world slowed down, except for him and Luna. His rapid movements eclipsed everything he'd ever thought.

He swatted Oliver's hands away, then extracted his body out from underneath him. Oliver was comparatively moving through tar. The look of confusion slowly spreading across his face was priceless to Buddy.

I am the swift water between the slow-moving stones, said the inner voice as he held Oliver immobilized.

The white dog noticed Oliver's turmoil and turned on Buddy with its jowls snapping, so slow it seemed glacial. Small flecks of the dog's saliva inched through the air to the dusty canyon floor. Staying calm, Buddy jogged to the tent.

Oliver's eyes tried to follow him, only registering a blur, which he began to run after. Luna wagged her tail. He came back from the tent with a length of rope. When he ran by Oliver, the spidery youth tried to redirect his course, and ended up tripping and sprawling along the ground.

The dog had moved only a couple feet. Buddy paced it while tying its feet together, easily avoiding the slowly gnashing teeth. Tangled, it slammed its face into the root clump of a palm tree, plowing a trough in the dusty soil, then lay squirming on the earthen floor.

Buddy felt his speed diminishing as he turned and squared off with Oliver, who dusted himself off and stood up.

Buddy's legs grew heavy. The surge was leaving him, his energy turning to exhaustion. He focused all his will on staying upright long enough to bluff Oliver, squaring off and dropping his brow, looking as deadly serious as he could. He balled his hands into tight fists and crouched as if to spring, which would now be impossible.

Luna, sensing the ploy, lunged with a yapping stream of angry noise.

Oliver burst away from them, his limbs releasing like springs. Running up the hill and off into the thicket, not looking back, as fast as he could to the east.

Buddy didn't know what to do, but he no longer had the energy to run after Oliver, and considered himself lucky he had enough to remain upright at this point. He was crashing.

The wolf creature snarled, writhing on the ground. Luna barked in return, keeping her distance.

On unsteady legs, Buddy made it to Max and put his hand under his nose. He was relieved to find him breathing. With a splash of water from the canteen, Max sputtered awake.

"Bwaa? What the fuck?" Max said, jumping up ready to fight. "Where's Helen? What's going on?" His addled brain took a second to level itself. The wolfen dog squirmed in the dirt with Luna barking and snapping back at it. Buddy looked like he might fall asleep.

Buddy tried to tell him what happened, but everything was so heavy. His tongue, his eyes. Like lead. He tried to tell Max about Helen before he yawned and lost his concentration.

Max wiped blood and mucus from his face with a towel. "C'mon, Buddy. Where's Helen? Out with it."

"They got her." He had to sit down.

"Damn," said Max. "Tell me."

Buddy told Max about the speed boost, and how he had won the fight because of it. Then he yawned, and lied down in the dirt. Luna cocked her head. So did Max. The white wolf dog growled and squirmed on the ground.

"Here, dude. Eat this." Max pulled a biscuit from his jacket, seeds and grains poking out of it.

Buddy took a bite. It tasted like dirt, but energy coursed slowly through him. He smiled.

"That should work for a while," said Max. "Which direction did they go?"

"That way." He pointed to the east. "They're taking her back to the warehouse. I'm sure."

"Shit." Max pulled the bag that held the silver snare from under the pillows, and turned to the boy.

"Take this now, Buddy. I have to go find Helen," he said. "And they can't find this. Use the skills we showed you. I'm gonna get her, and we're gonna be back, alright? I don't like this any more than you do, but their whole point of taking her is to get you back. Don't fall into their trap. You're a man now. Plus you've got her." Max pointed to Luna, who darted her eyes between them.

Buddy grabbed the daypack, already stocked with the necessary items, and pushed the box containing the silver snare to the bottom. "Okay, Max." He wiped his eye.

Max pulled his own backpack on. He'd die if anything happened to the kid now. That, or Helen would kill him, wherever she was. He pulled Buddy close and hugged him, then crouched down to eye level.

"I'm scared," Buddy said.

"I feel you, my man. But you've got this." He ruffled Buddy's hair. "Now, I know we've said to trust no one, and that's some good advice, but this is what I refer to as 'exigent circumstances' you understand?"

Buddy nodded. "An emergency."

"Yeah," said Max. "And in case of an emergency we've scoped out someone who we are now positive is trustworthy. Her name is Cora. She has a raven tattooed on her leg and she lives across the street from the corner market, in that big white building.

"We've investigated her for a while, and she's okay. There might be an old guy. He's weird, but seems alright as well. Don't say too much in front of him, though. Cora should be the only one for now, understand me?" Max's eyes locked with Buddy's.

"Yes, Max," Buddy answered. "But are you sure I can't go with you? What if this is what they wanted? I don't want you to leave me alone."

"You're never alone with Luna. And if this is a trap, then you have to surprise them. Be vigilant, and hide first, strike second. You got it?"

"Yeah, but I still don't like it."

"Shit. Me neither, my man. But sometimes you gotta do what

you gotta do."

Max leaned down to pet Luna, then grabbed the pole from beside the tent and tied a rope to it with a knot at either end. The white dog snarled at him as he slipped a noose over its head and tightened the rope around its neck. Putting his foot on the pole, he cut its legs free, then picked the leash-pole up. The contraption worked, keeping the dog's gnashing teeth away from him.

"Go home!" he commanded.

The dog bound up the hill, with Max in tow. He waved to Buddy at the crest, then disappeared.

Buddy was overcome with fatigue from the speed burst, and flooded with emotion from being deserted, though it was out of necessity. He knew he should stay awake, but the bedding was still here, and it was warm. So tired. The biscuit was already wearing off. Max had given him one more, but they tasted like crap. Now he needed sleep.

• • •

Helen regained consciousness to find herself secured in the backseat of a large sedan. Her head was screaming. The last thing she remembered was a fist to her temple.

The car stopped, and she was dragged out. She couldn't focus yet, but the man dragging her was huge. Addled as her mind was, she still formulated a pretty good guess. As she made the connection, Markuz pulled her up on her feet.

They were standing on blacktop. A parking lot surrounded by chain-link fencing. She thought it might be the mechanic's yard, but these buildings were different. And there were more of them.

Her vision rolled in waves as a cloud of twenty crows passed over in the sky. They cackled wildly and sparred with one another as they sliced through the air. Helen tried to get their attention through her groggy thoughts. She was at the warehouses where Buddy had been held.

A shuffling sounded from behind her, and before she could turn she felt a prick in her back near the shoulder blade. A trap, she thought, but aren't I already trapped?

She watched the birds disappear to the south.

Accompanying the stab came a feeling of tranquility. Look at this nice boy who has come to give me a hand. He's helping me into this building. What a nice thin young man, like a spider. Don't I know you? Oh, wait, she thought, there is someone I share things with. No, more someones. Where are they? And who is this very pale man? What a pretty suit. These men are so helpful. They are going to take this old lady home. Where is my home?

"Am I going home?" she asked.

"You sure are," replied Peik.

How wonderful! At last I'm going home. Mother will be so happy. Helen thought, as Peik put her arm into his and walked her into the warehouse.

• • •

The white dog barked and growled through the canyons with Max in tow, at times barely able to hold it steady. Fortunately for Max, the dog mostly stayed to the outlying areas, void of humans. On the occasions they had to climb out onto the streets, the thing hunkered down and pulled harder, with fewer snaps of its jaws directed at Max.

The people that saw them gave them a wide berth. Max did his best to act like there was nothing unusual about a man walking an arctic wolf through the neighborhoods of San Diego fastened to a pole with a noose. The thing led him down trails and directly into dense brush that it could barely fit through, raking Max's skin with spiny brush.

At last they came to Cedar Ridge Park. The canyons stopped, and a circle of manicured green bordered the cul-de-sac. Max walked through the park, then looked down on the darkened canyons on the other side with freeway traffic snaking in red and white veins beyond it. A spine of earth led from the park to the warehouse area at the bottom of the hill where the canyons converged. The dog chomped and bit at the rope with renewed vigor.

Max brought his knife from his belt, trying to figure out how to cut the dog loose without getting himself killed. The dog, seeing the knife from the corner of its eye, whined and rolled over onto its back in submission. Max gasped at the small round scars he saw. This dog's an experiment, like Buddy. Twisted and brainwashed. What was he going to do with the dog now? What was he going to do with it before? He just wanted the thing away from Buddy and Luna.

After a few moments, he made a decision.

Max took deep breaths. Eight of them, each one deeper than the last, until sound poured from him. He chanted in two voices; one nasal, one guttural.

The wolf dog cocked its head. Tendrils of light festooned into the air and a rumbling overtook the bodies of the man and the dog. A subterranean frequency. Lost inside the deep resonant vibration, Max entered the dog's violent and mutated mind. Terror, fear and violence had been its thoughts. Max tried to still the violent chatter of the dog's spirit. The dog heard the sound within itself.

Max took the knife, and quickly severed the rope from the pole, then pulled it from around its neck. When he was finished cutting the dog loose, he ceased the overlapping sounds, and the dog stood. Max looked in its eyes, and it returned the glance, its viciousness gone. It whined at Max, walked to him, and licked his hand.

The dog then looked down to the warehouse, a dimly lit expanse at the end of a barely visible street. It growled low, then walked away from it, up into the rocky canyon next to the freeway.

Max watched it break into a run and fade away. He wondered if he'd made a stupid decision, but he wasn't going to kill any animal if he could help it. He didn't know what would become of a hybrid wolf wandering the canyons of the city. He hoped the situation, or the dog, didn't come back to bite him in the ass.

The canyon path led to a cliff that overlooked the roofs of the warehouses, some hundred yards distant. Max nestled into a willow bush and observed.

From here, not much was visible, only three big roll-up delivery doors, all shut. On the west side was a steep, dark hill leading up to an apartment complex. With no plantlife, Max would be a sitting duck there. He'd have to skirt along the warehouses to the east across the street where a dry creekbed lay.

More of a drainage ditch, the wash came from the mesas in the north and led under the freeway's nexus just a few yards farther to the south. Large jagged rocks of granite and old sidewalks had been dumped there by the city to allow more efficient drainage. Max scrambled among these, completely hidden in the gulch from the warehouse. He pulled his body up to the grassy lip opposite the parking lot, and stayed very still, scratching two rocks together and placing them in the root structure of the bushes.

A branch rested on his head as he scanned for guards or cameras. He saw none of the former and three of the latter, and only one in position to see his current whereabouts. They would surely be watching if Helen had been taken here.

He calculated the area that each could film, and could see a jagged pathway between their range. From there it was razor wire and open asphalt. Hardly a gimme, even for somebody quick who could manipulate sound and vision.

He prepared to wait until he saw a way in without being detected. Max didn't know how much time he had to spare, but he was pretty certain it wasn't a lot. He needed a plan. A security guard walked from behind a building inside the fence.

● ● ●

Back at the campsite, Luna's growl filled Buddy's ears. He woke and looked around in the dark, cursing himself for staying there. His brain still felt groggy. The dog licked his face, bringing him further in touch with the waking world. He reached to pet her, but she moved his hand away with her head and faced the rear of the tent. The silence was broken as a twig snapped outside, up the hill. They both froze.

Luna nipped at the bag, dragging it closer to him. Buddy put it on, feeling the heft of the boxed snare against his back. Listening intently, he clenched his fists in frustration. He should have pushed on last night. Remembering the other biscuit, he stuffed the whole thing in his mouth.

Buddy grabbed the leash. Luna, at the mouth of the tent, looked back to make sure he was ready, then she burst through the tent flap into the canyon.

He wasn't as quick out of the gate as Luna, being laden with all the supplies, and he almost tripped as he followed her. From the corner of his eye something moved. He looked to his right and saw a squat man in a grey suit next to what looked like a large fox. They were close enough to touch.

Luna yelped when she saw them. Buddy blinked, trying to focus on the strange animal. It was almost impossible to do, as the thing's coat seemed to be made out of smoke.

Its fur shimmered, silver in the darkness.

The man grinned. Both he and the fox gave chase. Buddy jumped hard, putting distance between himself and the ghostly team. While he strained, his cargo shifted, nearly sending him sprawling over the uneven ground. He was moving too slowly. He couldn't find the energy.

Luna sensed his frustration, and doubled back to confront the fox, now gaining steadily on Buddy. She charged full speed, teeth bared. As she neared it, she launched. Her jaws closed with a snap as she sailed through the fox, breaking it apart. A dark grey cloud shimmered in her wake, twisting in the still night air of the canyon. It continued writhing as it descended to the canyon floor where it regained the shape of the fox. When complete, it renewed its chase.

Luna lost no time and shot after the fox, a moment before the man in the suit fanned his hand in a vain attempt to grab her fur. The wind off his fingers whistled in her ears as she darted away.

Buddy turned around and saw the smoke fox again coming after him. Luna shot through the bushes surrounding the circular path, intersecting and matching the boy's stride in front of the fox.

Luna barked and nodded her head to the left. Buddy zagged as she began snarling.

Upon hearing, or perhaps feeling, the sound, the smoky fox slowed, then stopped. It lurched forward and tried to continue, straining itself to no avail. Its face seemed to wince and draw away from Luna as it looked at its own forepaws. They turned from legs into smoke, then the whole creature, piece by piece, lost its definition, unravelling. Humming vibrations distorted it.

Her tone seemed to have trapped it in midair. Trying desperately to remake itself, the smoke swirled above the ground. Luna barked, sending the smoky cloud drifting back in the direction of the grey man, who slowed his gait and stood in wonder when he noticed what was happening. Luna seized the moment of confusion and raced off after Buddy.

When she caught up to the boy, they pushed hard, running until their lungs burned. They made it a quarter-mile before they paused, out of breath, and made sure they were no longer being followed.

Remaining vigilant, they cut through the darkened golf course, passing by the restaurant and up through the dark fairways, two shadows in the night.

They were travelling far in the opposite direction of Cora, the woman Max had told him to seek out. But the fox and its man were also in that direction.

They went east, up the rocky wash, until they got to the square tunnel. Their footfalls echoed as they walked through. Buddy sped up near the crack in the center. Luna scampered after him, letting loose a low growl when they passed it. In no time they were in the large clearing.

Sitting beneath the trees of the canyon, branches swaying in the wind, Buddy was filled with a bravery he hadn't had before. No one could catch him.

The voice he had come to recognize spoke to his inner spirit.

Don't come back here. Listen. said Ysenia.

But it was too late, he had reached a decision. He would rescue Max and Helen, as well as Ysenia, on his own.

● ● ●

The guard looked toward the gate. The man they had brought from the truck into building B–Raymond was his name–was outside of the front gate, groaning and shuffling his feet. The man's eyes stared past the guard in a trancelike state, something the security guard had grown accustomed to in his three years under the employment of Placid Pool Distribution.

It had been explained to him that occasionally the warehouses used the services of recovering addicts, and sometimes they may not be entirely recovered, but Placid was helping those in need. The guard hadn't asked nor cared, he had just needed a job. His aunt had got him hired, and his family would be very unhappy if it didn't work out.

He rarely saw his aunt when he worked. Everybody said his Tia Louisa was the head Cleaner for PPD. The guard wasn't sure what exactly she cleaned, but he had found that PPD frowned upon employees that ask too many questions.

The gate creaked when he pushed the button. As it opened, the man shuffled through, like he was drawn. The guard led him over to building B, opened the door, and let the junkie shuffle inside without peeking in. Frank got mad if he caught you peeking, even if you were helping him out. The guard shut the door quietly.

When the door latched, it was dark inside. Max couldn't see anything. He allowed himself the smallest sliver of satisfaction for duping the guard, then backed himself up, feeling for the wall so he could wait for his eyes to adjust. When his fingers finally touched on the steel, he felt a prick in his thumb. A fog enveloped his mind, and he could not recall where he was, or what he was doing.

● ● ●

Buddy and Luna navigated the trails back into Juniper Street Canyon's southernmost reaches. Nothing stirred but birds and lizards. Aromas of sage drifted on the air. The warehouse loomed at the base of the dusty path.

"We can do this," Buddy said.

Luna whined, but wagged her tail as she looked at the fenced-in buildings.

Ysenia was slightly older than Buddy. The hooknose man had said he was waiting for something with the girl. Helen told him about the gateway to womanhood. The blood.

A wave of sickening understanding overcame Buddy. Luna looked sideways at him while he battled to keep his balance. He breathed deeply and shut his eyes, feeling inward with his mind as Helen taught him. His energy was good, and he hadn't even had one of Max's biscuits. It seemed that his body was assimilating and adapting. The exhaustion he had felt yesterday was gone, but he knew that each burst held a corresponding sluggishness in its future.

They slinked into the dry wash at the base of the small mesa, hidden as they scrambled over the rocks in the gully running under the freeway.

From beneath a bush, they looked over a ridge at the rolling chain-link and razor wire gateway across the dead end street. Luna's nose went crazy sniffing around the roots. Buddy looked where she was smelling and picked up a small rock with an eyeball and line design scrawled into it: Max's symbol. So he had been here, and was still, or he would have scooped the rock up, if possible.

Buddy wondered how the hell he was going to succeed where not one but both of his teachers had failed. He began to feel hopeless when Luna got into his face and growled. She'd never done that before, and he involuntarily backed away from her.

"No, I didn't forget about you," he said, and put his hand on Luna's head. With the physical contact, Buddy's mind lost the negative feelings. He looked up into a cloud that hovered over them, illuminated by the lights of the city. It swirled and changed until it looked like a brilliant rabbit.

The Rabbit.

The voice, this time without words, relayed intention into him. Wrapped in a silver hum, the boy began to draw the energy from the cloud into himself. His lungs filled with vapory strands, and his mind crackled with energy. The cloud's mass diminished, looking as if it dissipated into thin air. Invisible tendrils trailed into his lungs until there was nothing left in the sky. He felt electric as the cloud's mass danced inside his spirit.

The rumble of a diesel engine distinguished itself from the white noise of the freeway as a large box truck approached the gate. It appeared to Buddy to be standing still, barely crawling along. Buddy felt his energy vibrate at an intensely high level. Luna looked from the corner of her eye at him, then back at the truck.

The gate creaked open, the truck crawled into the lot. Buddy seized his chance and shot through. He looked back and saw Luna far behind. Trusting that she could for the moment take care of herself, he charged to the nearest warehouse door. As he thrust it open, he heard the voices of the man in the truck and another, as they discovered Luna running loose on the lot and gave chase.

They hadn't even seen him. Buddy smiled at Luna's diversion as he opened a door and plunged into the darkness of the big bunker. He hoped she could occupy the men for a few minutes.

In the hyper-aware rabbit state, his eyes instantly adjusted to the lack of light within the large room. What he saw was startling: A dozen people sat dazed, shuffling their feet in an aimless walk, as if waiting for a signal. Adults, children, all had hollow yet expectant eyes, dull in the dark. They gave no hint of interest in Buddy, shuffling around and staring at the ceiling.

He threaded through them until he came to the far side, opening a door which looked out at the surrounding fence, and off into the desert scrub. The door hung open as he ran to the next building, the central structure.

The din of voices grew closer as Buddy rounded the building and threw open the door. Luna came barrelling around the corner at the same moment, and skidded to a halt next to him.

Standing inside the opened doorway was the giant Markuz, looking every bit as shocked as Buddy.

Beyond Markuz, blocked by the big man, stood Frank.

When he saw Buddy, Frank flew into Markuz's backside and tried to claw his way over him. Markuz shrugged him off and lunged for the boy, who easily dodged backwards and away.

Buddy swung the leash out at the men, who jumped back to avoid it. He scooped Luna up and retreated at a full sprint toward the first building. The shufflers with their dazed expressions were wandering into the light from the open door. Through a crack between the buildings he saw that the big front gate was again closed. A group of people in coveralls were running toward him.

Frank shouted words into the night. Neither English nor Spanish, it was something all tongue and throat. Upon hearing them, the shuffling horde of people perked up, gained a sense of purpose, and ran screaming at the boy. Buddy ran, cradling Luna.

He shot toward the fence, holding his body lower and lower to the ground until he stomped hard, planting his foot upon a large stone. He propelled himself upward as hard as he could. The howling people were right on his heels.

His body released like a sprung trap, but rather than easily clear the fence as he'd hoped, his trajectory carried him in a low arc headed straight for the razor wire rings on top. He hurled Luna over, and tried to contort his own body above the shredding wire. It was largely a success, as his face did not become mincemeat, but his pant-leg got snared on the razors, and the momentum slapped his body upside down on the outside of the steel fence.

Luna had landed safely on the hillside, and ran back in an attempt to help Buddy escape from the shell people trying to grab him through the fence, but he was too high up. She lunged at the shell people, who backed away, repulsed by the dog, while Buddy frantically tried to free himself

Markuz and Frank were almost there.

Buddy's fingers worked and ripped at the snagged fabric, which gave way with a tear just as the two men hit the fence. He bounced from their force, and fell to the ground in a heap, quickly righting himself a few feet beyond them.

Frank was furious. He opened his mouth and howled at Buddy, making the pressure in the boy's head build. The hollow-eyed people made the same sickening sound. Terror filled him. The puppets grasped and shook the gate violently.

In an effort to shut them up, Buddy yelled back. The noise that loosed from him was a high-pitched melding of squeals that erupted with surprising force.

Frank felt the recoil of the boy's counterstrike, and grew dizzy. Waves of dissonance splashed back into the shell people's ears, the pressure now unbearable. Beneath Frank's feet, the ground felt uneven, and before he knew it he had his hand upon the asphalt, having fallen over without realizing it. He swallowed the bile and vomit that had crept into his throat.

The shell people, as a unit, stopped moving, their eyes again growing dull. They ceased their shaking and looked back to Frank, waiting for further instruction. Markuz offered his large hand to help Frank up, but Frank slapped it away, and stood himself upright. He dusted off his clothes and stared bloody murder at Buddy and Luna as they escaped into the brush.

Buddy fully expected the small army to follow them as they made it down through the drainage ditches next to the freeway, but no one came.

Curiously, he didn't really feel too burned out, even after expending so much energy. Must be the clouds, he thought. These thoughts, however, were quickly eclipsed by the knowledge that the plan had been a complete failure, and very possibly could have cost his dear friends their lives, as well as Ysenia's.

He was going to have to find the woman that Max had said to go to in an emergency, Cora. And now.

20

When Buddy and Luna made it back to Helen's camp, they found it ripped apart. Their belongings were lying on the canyon floor next to the destroyed tent. Someone had poured everything out. Buddy touched the snare in its box through the bag. Still safe.

Luna whined, surveying the landscape for anyone posted up in the shrubs and trees spying on them. Neither saw anything. Buddy scooped up the things he may need, which wasn't much, tied the rest of the stuff back up into the ripped tent, and using a rope hoisted it into the limbs of the trees above. Nothing inside seemed essential, but he didn't want to purposefully get rid of anything. You never know. Besides, he didn't want anyone gaining any information from their castaway belongings, and didn't want to leave a mess.

Once it looked okay, they walked up the pathway to the concrete stairs near the old fountain. Then he and Luna skirted the park until they reached the root camp. They'd stayed here just days ago, yet it seemed like a distant memory.

They sat on the stumps while Buddy tried to enact a plan on how to find Cora. It seemed like an impossible task. he wished that Max had given him a little more to go on. He couldn't just go ask every woman if her name was Cora, or ask to look at their legs. He knew where she lived, but the sun was up now, and that area was out in the open. They'd be exposed.

As they ate the remainder of their food, the hopelessness returned. Luna sensed the frustration, and for the second time growled at him to snap him out of the self-pitying funk. Buddy jerked back, a little shocked, then broke into a smirk. He brought her close and hugged the dog, so very thankful for her presence in his life.

A mockingbird alit in the pine tree that hung over them, and Luna scurried backward out of Buddy's embrace. She looked up to the bird and barked loudly. The bird flew off as quickly as it had come.

Strange, Buddy thought. Luna almost never paid attention to the birds. Famished, he put a handful of granola into his mouth and chewed. It was so dry. He needed water, and reached into the bag for the canteen.

Luna continued to act strangely, and began to gather the things that they had brought out of the backpack and put them back in, one by one, before Buddy could take a drink. He was confused, and didn't let his expression hide it, but at this point knew far better than to question the instincts of the dog, no matter how odd they seemed. Chewing on the dry gruel, he stuffed the items deeper into the pack, about to zip it up, as the bird returned.

It swooped down, grabbing one of Luna's biscuits. Luna let off a stream of yaps at the bird, and lunged at it. She only beheld a streak of grey, however, as the bird disappeared into the bushes. With the dog hot on its heels, the bird wove tightly between the branches of the surrounding shrubbery, the biscuit hanging from its beak.

Buddy watched his greatest friend disappear down the hill after the bird. A rustle sounded behind him, making him whip his head around.

Crawling through the plants was the guy Buddy had seen with grasshopper guts all over his face near the warehouses. The bird who had stolen Luna's biscuit was with him then as well.

A team, Buddy thought, like us.

He knew that with a whistle, Luna would come tearing back to him.

When he tried, a shower of dry crumbs shot out instead.

21

Stewart had convinced Mrs. Meyers that his door had been broken in a freak accident. She had been a little suspicious, but it was Stewart after all, and she loved Stewart. He took it to the workshop in the basement, did a pretty good job fixing it up, then put the old thing back in his doorway.

After the incident at the bar, he wanted to tell Abe and Cora, but when he returned home early in the morning, they were gone. He assumed they were in Cora's apartment. When he realized he was finally alone, he breathed deeply and sat down in peace, though he knew it wouldn't last.

Relaxing in the sun shining on his little balcony, he sipped a cup of strong black coffee and tried to focus his mind. Just as he had gotten into a productive mental space, a recognizable grey shape shot around the corner. Stewart raised his hand up, pointing his finger so Klia could land on it. When she did, Stewart raised her to his face and she pecked his brow gently between the eyes, awakening the birdsight. He was getting the hang of this.

His mind flew over to the end of Golden Hill Park farthest from his house, where the flat expanse of grass tumbled off the hill down into the trees.

As the sight carried him over the crest, he saw the kid and the dog nestled in an upturned root system, preparing a makeshift meal. This part of the park was three blocks from his building. The bird had flown straight here, and her memory was only minutes old. Now was the time.

He knocked on Cora's door, but there was no answer. When he rushed downstairs, he saw Cora's car and his own were still in the same spots on the street.

Stewart thought about it for a fraction of a second. The park's only street was one way, and circled the grassy area. In a car, it would make any escape from what would essentially be an abduction insanely risky, and subject to being trapped, so he ditched the idea outright. He thought about his bicycle, but he'd have to leave it at the park while he . . . did what?

There had been a quasi plan the three of them had concocted. He mentally set fire to that as he ran up the street, toward the park and the enclosure of roots the pair of hooligans were hiding in. It was only a couple blocks, anyway.

As always, there were several people walking dogs, jogging, or picnicking in the park, and a few more than usual on a bright Sunday morning. Stewart kept his head down except to dart a glance at the mockingbird, not wishing to attract attention to himself as he ran down a dirt trail off the paved road most people used. The fig, palm, and pine trees along the hill's cusp shielded him from most eyes. If he was nonchalant he would melt into the background. He hoped. He wished he could do Jeb's disappearing trick, but he was a long way from that.

Only one person looked up at him as he jogged down the path. An older man with a blue baseball cap and an expensive-looking camera.

Emiliano Flynn pointed his camera at the mockingbird, which, it seemed, was waiting for the jogging man. Mockingbirds are curious creatures, but this bird seemed to be leading rather than following, as well as making noises to the man. It was more of a communication than he, in his decades of birdwatching, had seen between a wild bird and a human. He snapped a few pictures of the bird, and just for posterity shot a few of the back of the gangly man as he jogged past.

Stewart slowed to a walk as they neared the trees Klia had shown him.

She flew up in a pine tree which hung off the end of the park where it cut down to the oak grove below. She could see the boy and dog eating food, and she pointed at them with her beak so Stewart knew where to go. He nodded, then went as far as he could to the edge and waited. The dog eyed Klia in the tree.

As they finished eating, Klia swooped down, grabbed the final biscuit from beneath the dog's mouth, and flew into the bushes. The dog immediately burst after her. Klia toyed with the dog down the hill, dropping the biscuit at the bottom. The dog devoured the biscuit and looked into the trees for the bird, then bounded back toward Buddy.

With the dog out of the way, Stewart headed toward the clearing where the kid was packing his bag. When Stewart burst through the trees, the boy tried to whistle, but his mouthful of food turned into a soundless shower of crumbs that sprayed on the ground.

Stewart lunged at Buddy. With reactions so quick they blurred, he turned and whipped the weighted leash smack into Stewart's shinbone. The ball made a dull chime as it slammed just below the knee, and a jolt of intense pain crippled Stewart's leg. He felt blood seeping into his pants.

Stewart screamed. Tears welled up in his eyes and throat as the boy bounded off into the underbrush with the leash and black bag. There was no choice. He had to follow, though with every step his leg howled in pain. The taste of metal rose up his esophagus, flooding enough to pool in the back of his throat. Fire burned his mouth as he spit what he could out.

A whistle pierced the air as the kid finally managed to signal the dog, then a matching whistle screeched from the opposite direction.

This was Klia's cue to confuse the dog while Stewart nabbed the kid. There wasn't much time. He tried his best to overlook the pain, falling more than running down the steep hill just steps behind the boy. Every step sent a shock through him. The kid's sweatshirt disappeared into a bush, and Stewart, seeing his last chance, leaped hard over it, landing with an agonizing jolt in front of the kid.

Buddy froze.

Stewart jumped forward, snagging the hood of Buddy's sweatshirt in his fist before the boy could duck low enough. The boy wriggled almost out of it before it got tangled with the handle of the bag. Stewart snagged an arm, and soon had the boy wrapped up.

As he was trying to wrestle the kid through the tree line around the edge of the park, the dog reappeared, charging hard and barking to the boy from quite a way behind, but closing fast.

Stewart looked back. His eyes widened, and he tried to add some speed, but his leg made it hard to even walk with the boy in tow, let alone outrun a dog. It wasn't looking good for getting out of here with the kid. He scoured the ground for a good rock or stick, with no luck.

With Stewart's attention averted, Buddy rewarded him with a heel into the injured shin, then shook violently. Stewart couldn't keep his grip. He fell to the ground, fingers grabbing air as the kid wriggled free and regained control of the leash-weapon thing. He cocked it back and swung it straight down at Stewart's face, missing as Stewart rolled his body sideways and tumbled down the embankment while the dog closed in on him.

Buddy ran into the grassy area.

"Child molester!" he screamed, running toward all the people in the park, pointing back at Stewart, who had just come over the lip of the hill. "Kidnapper! Child molester! Call the motherfucking cops!"

People began rising from their picnic tables, some coming for the kid, some for Stewart. As many as eight made 911 calls.

Fucking hell, thought Stewart, still far away, but not for long if he didn't get going.

The dog was coming. She barked at Klia, who swooped and screeched just beyond its snapping jaws.

Stewart turned and readied himself, trying to stand up. He made it onto his one good knee before the dog sprung at his face. Stewart managed to get his forearm in between his skull and the dog's jowls. Its teeth scraped across his arm as it sailed by, leaving long scratches on his skin.

Klia landed on the dog and pecked its face, narrowly missing its eye. The strategy worked, as it turned its attention back to her. Stewart ignored the pain, and ran as quickly as he could toward home. A few people were starting to chase after him from the park.

Stewart hobbled under the last of the trees, crossed a small street, and leaped over a wooden fence. He winced when he landed, but didn't slack off the pace as he sped through the courtyard of an apartment complex, then went barrelling down the alley toward his building.

His alternate plan had been an incredible disaster.

Klia joined him one block from his house after he had sprint-limped through the abandoned alleyway. He made it to his old trusty fire escape, jumped up and was astonished that he reached the pull bar on the first try. Doubly so that he did it without being lynched. The old stairs creaked down and Stewart scrambled up, unseen.

Once inside his apartment, he sat and tried to catch his breath, cursing himself, and the kid.

22

The police station was unusually busy when Clementine arrived. Amy met her at the drinking fountain, annoyed with something.

"That Rory fuck is all up in my business. There's a record of my search in the computer. I deleted it, but it's never gone. When he gets someone from the forensic computer team in here, which he will do, he's gonna see the name he wasn't supposed to find," she said quietly, looking around to see if anyone could overhear.

Satisfied, she continued. "And then we're really gonna see what's up. Either he's by the book and it shoots upstairs, or he's pocketed and it goes to Mr. Fox or Stillwater."

"Or option three," added Clementine. "We feel it out and flip him first."

"Fuck that. I felt out Gray."

Clementine realized her leverage on this one was hovering around zero. "That was quite a chore for you, wasn't it?"

"That's not my problem. I'm not dealing with that fucking weasel." Without further comment, she pivoted on her heel and walked toward the front door of the station.

Sighing, Clementine strolled into the crime lab. The new tech Rory was hunched over, staring into a computer screen. Rory was what many refer to as nerdy, even by his fellow nerds. Some of his past hobbies included creating imaginary numbers, building scale models of the Seven Wonders of the Ancient World from Popsicle sticks and glue, and solving what he believed were some of history's greatest mysteries, hypothetically. His personal obsession with true crime had pushed him down the path to forensics, and he loved it. He had already outgrown Chula Vista's police force at his young age, and moved up to the bigger city. Hopefully his next stop would be LA. Rising to the top in one of the world's largest cities would really put him on the map.

"Hello, Rory?" Clementine said.

"Yes, hello. You're Detective Clementine Figgins, are you not? It's nice to meet you," Rory peeled off his latex glove and threw it away, offering his hand to Clementine, who shook it. He had a decent grip and looked in her eyes.

"How are you finding everything?"

"Pretty good. The science part is the same. This lab is a lot bigger and a little better though," he admitted.

"I bet," said Clementine. "Have you run anything yet?"

"Yeah, I ran the hair and saliva Officer Garrett gave me versus a couple blood samples from a crime scene. No match. I gave the results to him. He's your partner, right? He didn't tell you?"

"Ah, yes. He did mention that, now that you jog my memory. Sorry. I just got a dog this morning. Little preoccupied." She motioned to the screen with a nod. "What are you working on, there?"

"I wasn't, necessarily. I was running a diagnostic test of the computer, and noticed a set of hair and saliva results, as well as some highly metallic blood samples, that Amy ran." He looked to her. "Your case, I believe?"

Shit. Any tech with some experience would see that the profile from this search would match the contributor of the blood pool, once they viewed both simultaneously. This, of course, would directly refute Rory's results concerning a comparison with the hairs Officer Garrett had given him. Rory narrowed his eyes and brought his face closer to the monitor.

Clementine had to take a risk.

"Actually," she said, "that is my case. And Jim's. From Craig James' residence. The same signature as the blood, from the office building, that you ran, right?" she asked.

"Yeah, except for some metallic difference. Silver," said the scrawny tech, looking perplexed. "So, what were the samples Detective Garrett gave me, then? I thought those were from Craig

James, and were not a match."

"Turns out he had a roommate. Two different bathrooms, both were bagged. Jim brought you the wrong one."

"I thought the communication would be better around here."

"It usually is, I swear. It's like a well-oiled machine most of the time."

"Hmm," Rory grunted. "So what was this third blood signature from? The other one with the silver in it?" he asked, pointing at the screen.

"Unrelated case. I'm thirsty, can I buy you a soda?"

Clementine didn't wait for a response before leaving the room. She returned with two drinks from the vending machine.

"Here's my number, Rory." She handed him her business card. "I know you're new here. It's weird at first, but it'll calm down. If you need to talk to someone, give me a call." She handed him a diet cola.

"Wow. Thanks." He couldn't stand diet cola.

"Oh, and if you get new results can you go ahead and text them to me? My partner's awful busy and sometimes it slips his mind to let me in right away."

"You mean you don't trust him because he's a chauvinist pig?" he said, surprising her.

"Ha. Among other things."

"Yeah, I can backdoor your partner for you. Whatever's really going on. I suppose you want me not to say anything about the contradictory evidence? How's that going to play out?"

"Just leave that to me, I'll take full responsibility if he finds out."

"Yeah, or else it's 'hello, goodbye, Rory'."

"I've got this."

"Good," he said, with an air of suspicion.

● ● ●

Now Rory was sure of his new department's lack of professionalism. He couldn't wait to skip off to LA. In order to do that he'd have to excel here, and avoid inter-office politics, a seemingly Herculean task. His one case already had the conflicting evidence, and two partners who were not on the same page at all. New people in the middle usually get the shaft.

• • •

"So, what's the scoop, homegirl?" asked Amy. She was picking lettuce from between her teeth. Clementine stood next to her at the bathroom sink.

"Well, I don't think he's in anyone's pocket. He's young, and smart. And malleable. To the right person. I don't think he likes Jim."

"He digs cougars, though?"

"Fuck you."

"Well, that's positive. What about my search?"

"I told him the samples Jim brought him were from a roommate."

"Craig James has a roommate?"

"No."

"That's why they pay you the big bucks," said Amy, chuckling nervously. She slapped Clementine on the ass on her way out. "Hope he doesn't talk to Jim," she added, walking through the door.

• • •

On her lunch break, Clementine went to go check on Grifter. The dog barked when he heard the gate open, but upon realizing it was Clementine, his tail wagged, sending everything flying off the coffee table. As Clementine knelt down to pick up the coasters, Grifter walked into her arms, whining softly and licking her face. A warm glow spread within her, and she wondered what had taken her so long in her life to get a dog.

She fed him some turkey, scratched his ears, and thought back to driving him home from the shelter, and the warehouse that Amy had seen in a dream.

Clem searched the area on the maps on her computer. The

freeways weaved over a concrete gulch that ran from the east, and eventually made its way to the bay. Next to the gulch stood six warehouses of different size, ringed by a fence, the last buildings at the east end of C Street. Beyond a chain-link fence at the end of the road was the sprawling canyon, Juniper Street open space area.

Placid Pool Distribution. She did a quick title check.

Stillwater Enterprises.

"Shit." Cold snaked over her skin. Grifter licked her hand, now covered in goosebumps, and whined.

Clementine shook the chill off of herself, shut off the computer, and took Grifter for a short walk.

The day was warm and cloudless, and she waved to the few neighbors about. One woman bent down to let the dog sniff at her hand. Grifter put his head close to the ground, and growled ferociously. He looked ready to pounce. The woman recoiled.

"Oh, my. Not the friendliest doggie is he?"

"No ma'am," said Clementine, "he is not."

When she put him back inside the house, she overheard an Amber Alert on the radio about a possible child abduction in the park at the end of 25th Street. About a mile away.

She patted Grifter's head and hurried out. The dog shot through the newly installed dog door and watched her jump into her car and speed away. He barked once, then walked slowly back to the patio oasis.

• • •

At Golden Hill Park, at the end of 25th street, the first officer to respond to the attempted child abduction gave her the rundown.

No one had seen where either the man or boy had come from, though people recognized both from around the neighborhood. When the officer spoke to the two witnesses, big Latinos who chased to the suspected kidnapper, they described him as a slim, disheveled white male of about thirty-five to forty years of age, six-foot, slim build, brown hair, dressed in brown work pants and a faded blue T-shirt. They hadn't chased him very far before he lost them around the corner, where the park ends and the neighborhood begins. They said he was pretty fast, though he was limping.

Clementine looked over the two men from the distance. Big boys. A six-foot slim-built sloth could probably put the moves on them. She nodded to them. They dipped their heads by way of recognition.

She thanked the young officer, and approached the big men. She introduced herself, then asked where the boy had come from, what the man had done, and where everybody had gone. Basically the same questions the officer had just asked them, but there was nothing like hearing a story straight from the horse's mouth.

She didn't glean any new information. After a scuffle, the boy and the dog disappeared one way, and the alleged kidnapper the other. She thanked them. They wished her good luck in finding the kid.

The site of the attempted abduction showed no further clues, just upturned dirt. The ground was too dry and dusty for a shoeprint. As she searched, a man holding a camera with an enormous lens beckoned to her.

"Hello, investigator. I have something that may interest you." The man held up his camera. "Pictures!"

Now she got it.

"My name is Emiliano Flynn. I was in the park taking pictures of birds when all this happened. I got some shots of the boy, but . . . well, I'll just have to show you." He turned his camera so she could see the screen.

Clementine thought this could be the kidnapper coming back to influence the investigation, but quickly dismissed it due to Emiliano's dark skin. He probably wouldn't be taken for a Caucasian by two other Hispanic men. She looked into the screen on the back of the camera.

Emiliano Flynn was obviously a professional, that much she could see. Several police photographers she knew didn't take pictures with this much clarity. It was uncanny, then, that the glaring exception to the rule were the faces of the boy, man, and dog. She could close up on anything in the background of the camera's touchscreen–the big men in pursuit, a knot on a tree, the stone drinking fountain–and see minute detail, but their faces were surrounded by a blurry haze. Frame after frame it was the same.

"Is this some sort of a joke?" She wasn't smiling.

"No! I swear, that's what I was trying to show you. Wait. I have pictures that you'll appreciate more. I was shooting a mockingbird, a little female, when the man came running down the pathway. What drew me in was the fact that he was making noises to the bird when he ran, and the mockingbird made noises back."

"You sir, have been photographing birds too long." Clementine cut him off. She really had hoped this guy wasn't some wacko, but she had grown used to having her hopes dashed over the years. Why should he be any different? "If you'll excuse me, I need to 'investigate.'" She made quotation fingers to Mr. Flynn.

"You are a very rude person," Emiliano said, "but even one so rude as you will not be able to dispute what I say when you see these next two pictures."

He thrust the camera's screen towards her. The frame showed the attempted kidnapper, his line of sight on a mockingbird in a pine tree in front of him. Not at all evidence. This was getting old.

"Okay, a very clear shot of a man's back and a bird in a tree. Is that everything?"

"No, rude inspector, it is not." He flicked his fingers through the pictures until he came to the very last shot. The boy was brandishing a leash with a metal weight on the end, swinging at the hovering mockingbird while the dog crouched at the boy's feet. The bird and dog looked at each other. To the side was the man, observing, his face blurred. Wavelike patterns emanated from the mouths of the bird and dog. Within their scope was clarity.

Visible sound.

Sonic grids distorted the background, like rings on a pond. Waveforms of sound, stretching. Within the visual feedback stood a very clear image of the boy's face, between those of the animals. Clementine gasped, staring. With trembling hands she took a picture of the screen with her phone.

Years ago she had used an artificial aging program on a photograph of Rupert. She had been so impressed with it, she had bought a smartphone application when they became available. The results were the same, and she'd saved it to her phone. Each year it would update itself as to his projected appearance. She opened her photos, scrolling to the most recent and holding it next to Emiliano Flynn's very expensive camera.

The faces matched.

Clementine's hair stood on end as she looked into the camera's screen and saw the face of her child, Rupert, missing all these years.

Emiliano expected a reaction to the photo, but nothing like this. He was unsure what to do when the female detective grasped his arm and began to shake as they stared at the matching faces.

The uniformed officer at the park stopped talking to the lady with the baby in the carriage and watched Detective Clementine Figgins let out a deafening wail while running down the steep hill into the canyon to the north. He thanked the woman quickly, and ran after the detective. When he got to the lip of the hill, he could see her already at the bottom of the rocky incline, screaming out a name he couldn't quite make out, Roofer or Loofer or something. He ran after her. The shifty ground gave way beneath his heavy footfalls, sending small rocks bouncing down the trail, disturbing birds and ground squirrels. Very sure he would end up flat on his back, the young officer was surprised when he made it to the bottom without grievously injuring himself. While concentrating on not rolling headlong down the hill, however, he had lost sight of Detective Figgins.

The pudgy officer wondered what the hell she was thinking.

Wheezing for air, he paused to catch his breath. Though required to do so, he rarely exercised, and it was obvious. His body was drenched in sweat. When he regained composure, he called out for the detective, getting no response. He put his hand on his pistol, and looked in a circle; just a grove of trees with a street winding between it and the golf course, and the entrance of the city mechanics' yard. He heard voices, pulled out his weapon, and followed them to the entrance of the yard, behind a hangar-like building. Clementine was showing her phone and talking to two men dressed in coveralls.

"Officer Figgins? Is everything okay?" he wheezed. He holstered his gun when he saw the mechanics.

She eyeballed him. "Did you see the kid?"

"No. I was trying to get a bead on where he went when you took off on me. What's going on down here?"

The two mechanics shrugged and pointed at the pile of debris coated with a brownish-red fluid that had streaked, then dried. The young cop had seen plenty of blood. The rain had washed quite a bit away, but the streaky stains were unmistakable.

"Old blood? This can't be from today, of course."

"No. Certainly not," said Clementine. "Sorry to leave you like that, officer–" she looked to his nametag, "–Blum. I ran down here because I'm almost positive that boy is my own son Rupert who got kidnapped ten years ago."

Officer Steven Blum was floored. "Someone was trying to kidnap your kidnapped boy?" His voice was doubtful.

"Look, young man. I've been looking for my son for ten long years. After seeing that photograph at the park, I believe I've found him. I couldn't give one bit less of a fuck if you believe me or not. I'm gonna find him, and you're gonna help me." Her words were steel. Steven Blum nodded.

"Now," she continued, "we still need to get a sample of this blood. Would you mind?"

He patted his pockets. "My kit is in the car."

Clementine pulled a small evidence kit from her belt. "Officer Blum, you need to stay focused in the field"

"Yes ma'am." He took the kit and collected two samples of blood.

They called in for help to search the park as they made their way back to the top. Clementine looked for Emiliano Flynn, but couldn't find him anywhere. The locusts in her mind began again to buzz.

The search was fruitless. Twenty officers and a couple dozen volunteers had scoured the hillsides for hours looking for the boy. While it did turn up some items of interest, it was largely a failure. There would be doubts. Doubts that could be easily answered if she were to locate Emiliano Flynn, but how? She sat on a park bench, head in her hands. Nobody was going to believe her, except Amy and perhaps Gray. She didn't even want to think about her stupid partner.

The police were getting back in their squad cars and the civilians dispersing into the coming night. Clementine knew Rupert was out here, and she didn't care if no one helped her. She was going to find him or die trying. Not tonight, though. He was gone. That was obvious. She convinced herself to go home hours after everyone else had finished. She'd be better with some sleep.

Grifter bounded up to the gate, his tail wagging so hard it actually made him fall over. He got back up and made a long groaning whine. When she opened the gate, he nearly bowled her over with enthusiasm. She had left the lights on, and her little cottage looked nice and warm. She fed the dog and herself, took him for a short walk, then cried herself to sleep with him in her arms.

Amy called Clementine first thing in the morning. The DNA from the mechanics' yard belonged to Garth Mullen, a man with one prior conviction for inappropriate contact with a minor concerning a botched abduction twelve years ago in North San Diego County. Alarm bells screamed. Even more shocking; he was locked up at police HQ on a B&E plus drunk and disorderly.

"Sorry, boy. We're gonna spend a lot of time together soon," she said to Grifter. The dog much preferred this arrangement to the kennel, that was obvious. He wagged his tail nonchalantly as she sped off to lockup, then he chased a squirrel from the back patio.

"Hello, Mr. Mullen," she said to Garth. A uniformed jail guard poked the man with his baton, then looked for something to wipe it off on, knowing full well only steel and concrete made up these cells. He'd avoided physical contact with the stinking man so far, and passionately wanted that to continue.

Garth squinted his eyes. "Hmm," he said. His pickled mind wondered where this lady had come from, and when he could get out of here and get some more goddamn vodka.

"Hemygidaddahere." His shredded lip hurt when he talked.

"Shut up," said Clementine "Where's this kid? Now." She held the phone so he could see it. Garth put his hand out. She pulled it away from him with a jerk.

"Do not touch my fucking phone, Mr. Mullen. Now, I'll ask again. Where is this boy?"

Rusty gears clanked in Garth's mind. This was that fucker from the park. Little shit didn't know when to sit still. They think I got him. They got him.

"They got him," he said, concentrating on pronouncing his words.

"Who? Who's got him, Mr. Mullen?"

"That skinny black guy and the fat white lady from the park. They keep him tied up and make him do bad work." They did have him, anyway. They probably did do bad things to him, Garth reasoned, Why wouldn't they?

"Who are they? What are their names?" Clementine asked, trying not to betray her emotions.

"Man's Max. Lady's Helen." He pointed in different directions.

After she had written down the drunk's descriptions, she asked, "What about the skinny white guy? Forty years old or so? Six-foot?"

"Who?" asked Garth, confusion stretched across his battered face. "Lots of people look like that."

He didn't know the other guy. Shit. Clementine nodded to the guard, who let her out while Garth complained.

"I thought you were getting me out of here," he said to Clementine's retreating figure.

"You thought wrong," said Clementine. "When did I ever say that?"

Unbelievable.

When they were back at the front desk, Clementine asked how long he would still be in there. The guard informed her it would only be a couple of hours unless she wanted to order a psych evaluation. Of course she did, buying herself twenty-four more precious hours.

Her Lieutenant called her as she was leaving lockup, asking what the hell she was doing there questioning some drunk. The chain of communication seemed awfully rapid. She started the car and pulled up Broadway, replying that it was connected to the boy she believed was her son. Her Lieutenant had already spoken to Officer Blum, and wasn't sure about the story with the boy, but hoped it was true in the strict sense that he couldn't afford to lose what was far and away his best detective to a breakdown.

Detective Figgins had intangibles you couldn't teach. Incredible instincts. Rarely did she make a wrong snap decision on the fly. Also her ability to interface with people in almost all walks of life. She could talk market fluctuations with a CEO, then turn around and talk about bonsai with a gardener the same way. She was a little gruff, but that wasn't a bad quality for a detective. Most importantly, Clementine Figgins got results. Her clearance rate was through the roof.

"Did your interview turn up anything new?" he asked.

"Well, the loser in lockup said something about a couple people in the park, so I'm going to check it out right now, that is, if it's alright?"

"Clem, it's going to be hard for me to justify you keeping the Craig James case on your desk and also run down what you believe to be your son," he said. "I've gotta give the James thing to your partner."

"Wait," said Clementine, "please stall that for a day. I'm begging you."

"Why?"

"I'm getting a sharp feeling that it's all connected," she said.

His end of the line was quiet for a good while.

"That would be weird. But okay. I'd feel a little better if you didn't go alone, though. Jim's your partner. Take him."

"You're going to have to trust me when I say that I cannot bring Jim on this one."

"C'mon Clem," the lieutenant sighed. "I do not like the sound of that. At all."

"Sorry, sir. I'll try harder. Tomorrow. For today, could I have Gray Lowehaus for backup?"

"Huh? The kid from Julian? What the hell? I'm not liking this either, Clem. Do not, I repeat, do not fuck me on this."

"I won't, sir. I promise. Really."

"Alright. I'm sending him out now."

"Oh, Loo? One more thing. I may need a crime tech out there. Could you see if Amy is available?"

"Do you think I don't know your preferred tech?" He paused, then added, "Clem, do you really think this is your son after so many years, and he's right under our noses? I mean, it seems a little strange. I have to ask."

"I get that, sir. But really, does it matter? We have a kid in the park who appears homeless, and between ten and twelve years old, who was the victim of an attempted abduction. There are at least four suspects, and we haven't located the child. It's a case I'd be assigned anyway, given the circumstances. I want to help this kid. If he's not Rupert, I still want to reunite him with whoever is missing him. I have to."

"Okay. But seriously, don't make me look like a fucking asshole. I'll send those two out to you now." He hung up.

Clementine wiped her palms and pulled into Golden Hill Park to wait for Gray and Amy, who arrived ten minutes later. Together. The sun was beginning to heat up, and Clementine could smell the baking aroma of pine needles on the ground as they walked up to the picnic bench.

"Hey guys. How's it going?" Clementine asked. She pointed at her own shirt while looking at Amy, who looked down and re-buttoned her blouse, blushing.

"Pretty good." Amy said. Gray nodded.

"Wow. Good." They were both adults, and it had been only a matter of time before they hooked up. She ignored any further shirt conversation, and briefed them.

"I went to see that Garth guy in lockup. Wow. What a sleaze. Anyway, he points the finger at a thin black thirty-something male with horn-rimmed glasses named Max. Six-foot-even, apparently. And a white woman, five-foot-six, one-ninety. Maybe forty years old. Name is Helen."

"What are the chances this guy is on the level?" asked Gray.

"Completely trustworthy? Almost zero. But, we did find several encampments in the search, either active or abandoned, so we've got to concentrate on those areas. Also, we should canvass the houses along the southern perimeter of the park to see if anyone recognizes these two by way of description."

"Garth is far too unreliable to sit with a sketch artist, being how pickled that guy's mind is, but we have a very individualistic sounding pair, especially when seen together. Somebody's gotta remember that. Amy, let's you and I start on the encampments, and Gray can go ahead and start checking with the residents. How's that sound?"

"Fine with me," he said. "Start with those houses there?" He started walking toward them without waiting for a response. Before he reached the first door, he turned around and saw the two women headed down the dusty hill. He admired the sway of Amy's walk, her small lithe frame curving just so. She turned her head from the distance and caught him staring. She giggled, then winked at the young officer before they disappeared into the wooded canyon.

• • •

Every house has a story. Not just the people inside of it but the cumulative experience of the house itself. It starts with the wood. Or brick. Or steel. The memories of the natural materials infusing themselves into the pores of the building. Pores, of course, are used to breathe, like tinier and tinier mouths. Therefore, each house is a living, breathing thing. Add to that the memories and experiences of all the people and animals over the course of time that live or work or simply pass through, and you approach sentience. Personality. Your house is alive.

He knocked on the first door. A woman answered with her hair in curlers. When asked if she had seen Max and/or Helen, she replied that they didn't ring any bells, and asked if Gray had a picture. He apologized for not having one, and continued on.

The next door was opened by a fit, forty-ish woman in a nightgown, who looked Gray up and down and may or may not have drooled when she was finished. As Gray was preparing to ask the lady about his suspects, a well-dressed but disheveled man walked out, straightening his suit and tie. He tried to snake by Gray and out the door, but Gray puffed up, nearly filling the doorway.

"This will just take a second, sir, if you please. I'd just like to know if either of you have seen a six-foot-tall slim black man with glasses, who hangs out with a quite large white woman. Both in their late thirties, or thereabouts. Or a boy of around eleven years of age who has a medium-sized black and gold dog. We're pretty sure they all live in this park." Gray pointed and looked at them hopefully.

The woman looked at the ceiling deep in thought, wanting to help. She asked Gray if they had a drawing of the people. He sighed, admitted he did not, then smiled politely as the lady suggested they draw some up.

The man said he didn't know of a group, but thought he saw the black guy going through cans a couple times when leaving. When Gray asked for the man's name for the record, the man refused to give it, and insisted on getting past Gray, as he was late for work. Gray watched as he got in his car, and saw the man replace a ring on the left ring finger. Gray had noticed a band of skin several shades lighter than the rest of his hand. No wonder he wouldn't leave his name.

The woman asked if he'd like a cup of coffee, or anything else she had in her house. Anything at all. A little nervous she may sexually assault him, he still accepted the invite. Once he got the man's name, he would cut out.

She bent over to fluff a pillow on the couch, her eyes locked on Gray as her nipple, then full breast spilled from her robe. Gray pretended not to notice.

"I'd love that coffee, now, if it's not too much trouble," he said.

She looked affronted for a second before a feline smile returned to her lips. "Okay, hon. I'll follow orders." She purred, tucked her errant boob back into her gown, and turned for the kitchen.

Gray had to get out of here quick. This lady was an animal. "Hey, was that Royce Merriwether, the CEO of DynoCorp?" he asked, making up the names.

She stopped and turned back around, still repositioning her breast. "Him? Oh, no. That was David Baine, the man currently married to Marie Stillwater. But, sugar, we don't need to talk about him. You sit tight while I get that coffee," she said, wandering into the kitchen. Sexuality spilled out of her with each step.

As soon as she had rounded the corner Gray slipped out the door.

That was too easy, he thought.

He decided to restart at the houses at the east end and work his way back, hoping the lady would find the mailman or someone in the meantime. He thought of David Baine and Marie Stillwater, the heiress to the Stillwater empire, falling into the case's lap. He'd never met a Stillwater, despite being on their detail. He pondered the concepts of coincidence versus synchronicity. It was either strange or it wasn't that he'd be introduced to the family he was assigned through canvassing random houses.

Farther down the street, he knocked on the door of a small one-story maroon-and-white craftsman house. No one answered, and he walked away down the path. When he got to the sidewalk, he turned around, looking at the window. He thought the blinds had been open before, but were now closed. Unsure of that particular detail, he walked on.

• • •

The first encampment Clementine and Amy found was where Emiliano Flynn said the boy first appeared. The sprawling root structure of a fallen tree formed a dome where it once stood tall. A bare wooden pallet was crammed deep underneath. Amy ran her fingers over one of the long roots that stretched skyward. A smooth groove ran around it.

"This is where somebody hung a hammock. You can see that the tension pulls it this way," she made a curved line across the fallen tree's girth to another root with much the same markings, "to this."

"Hmm," Clementine said, "The hammock would form a sort of gate to guard whatever would be inside. There's been some cleanup, rare for transient homeless. It looks like they took this game trail." A swath cut through the grasses along the cliffside. Tracks from the camp into the bushes were still visible.

"That's what I was gonna say." said Amy.

Looking down the path, they saw one set of small and one set of larger footprints, and a small dog's, muddied but still readable after the midnight rain a few days ago.

"Good tracking, Clem. Let's go." Amy followed the thin trail, weaving through the live oak and thistle. Shoots of grass were poking through the earth. Seeds lying dormant had their long thirst quenched.

They followed the tracks under the brush and trees. Down one steep hill, across a pathway, then up another incline. A couple times the path disappeared into some undergrowth, but would continue on the other side. They were dusty and sweaty when they at last came to a razor wire fence blocking the end of the trail. An opening was scraped from beneath.

Amy and Clementine saw the small hanging bits of flesh at the same time. Disgusting bits of dried human jerky sticking off the bottom of the sharp chain-links. After collecting it all, they slid under the gap.

Footprints were everywhere. The tracks weren't disturbed, thanks to the protective canopy of willow. Amy bent down for closer inspection.

"Looks like a struggle. There's a ton of prints, dog and human. We'll get them in plaster. Some skids right here." She pointed to a root clump at the edge of the cliff.

It had been almost wrenched from the earth, and jutted out from the small peak. Scrape marks from small fingers ran to the very edge of the cliff. The ladies peered over, down into the mechanics' yard. The same bloody scene Clem had seen last night.

"Shit," she whispered under her breath.

"What's with the blood?" asked Amy.

"That's what I sent you yesterday."

Amy wrinkled her nose. "The drunk in lockup? Well, looking at this scene I'd say he's full of crap. He was after the kid, but the kid and his dog somehow got the asshole to fall off the cliff." She traced her fingers through the air. "The second adult prints look older. They're covered by the other two, or rather three sets. The fight happened after someone left."

"When we're done here, I'll be paying that fucking guy another visit." She realized Garth could not possibly be the one who has had Rupert for ten years. He lacks so many things necessary for a long-term plan, she thought, like a working brain.

Amy found a plastic shopping bag with a car battery and cables inside beneath a knot of willow branches. Behind it was a thin black-and-white shard of clay. "Wonder if this has anything to do with anything."

It glinted in the sunlight, obscuring Clementine's vision. From the small burnt circle in her retina she thought she saw tendrils slowly grow and twitch. She blinked her eyes repeatedly until they faded from view.

"Bag it," said Clementine.

Amy did, then poured plaster into all the shoeprints. She had a little left over, which she poured into a couple paw prints for good measure.

• • •

Gray made his way back down the street, hearing more or less the same story; maybe people had seen one or the other, maybe not. Perhaps even the kid was seen hanging around with his dog in tow. The problem was that none of the three were noteworthy by themselves.

He stood at the door of the maroon-and-white craftsman, knocking for the third time, to satisfy the question about the curtain. Of all the houses he'd visited, only this one gave him a nag in the gut. He jotted down the address for future evaluation, and noticed a chunky youth slowly rolling by in his little coupe, a spider tattoo crawling up his neck. When he saw Gray, the kid looked at the road and sped up. Gray wrote down the license plate number, then walked back toward the park.

David Baine's mistress watered her plants in front of her house. She faced away from Gray, bent over at the waist. Her tan and fit buttocks poked from under her daisy dukes, cropped so short the pockets were cut in half. For a shirt, she wore a white cotton wifebeater tank top, with no bra. The woman was practically naked on her front lawn. Gray silently crept behind a large juniper in front of her next door neighbor's front porch and tried to wait her out.

He snuck a peek from behind the tree. The woman's ass was an eye magnet.

"Hello, officer," a man's voice said, "getting an eyeful?"

Gray whipped around, embarrassed, and tried to act as if nothing were out of the ordinary. A man in clean, pressed jeans with a T-shirt tucked in stood with a mug of steaming coffee.

"Can I help you with anything?" the man asked.

"Yes, you can," Gray said, trying to stay behind the juniper tree. "I'm looking for a thin black man of about thirty-five years old, six-foot-tall, slim build. Also, a large white woman, same age, roughly. Five-foot-six to five-nine somewhere perhaps. It's believed they inhabit these canyons in the park behind you. And I don't have a sketch."

"Hmm. You mean Max and Helen? Why are you looking for them?"

Gray was stunned. This guy actually knew their names.

He took a second, then said, "We're looking at them concerning a child abduction."

"You mean the one in the park the other day? I heard the Amber Alert. They were looking for a white male in that. I'm home a lot, and don't miss much around here." He looked Gray up and down, sipped his coffee. "How rude of me. Do you need some coffee?"

Everybody wanted him to stick around for coffee today. "No, thank you. Let's stick with the story. How do you know about Max and Helen?"

"They kind of patrol the area, in a way. They really don't seem like the type of people who would be kidnapping children. Who said they were involved? You might want to look at that person," he said, eyes closed.

There was no way he was going to tell this guy their source had a record for attempted child abduction and was living in the same canyon.

"We're on that as well," Gray said.

"Well, who is the white guy, then?"

"There's a couple theories I have. He might have been trying to free the kid from someone else." Somehow the man was now interviewing Gray. Sneaky. He had to regain some control here.

"What is it that you do for a living? Mr. ah . . . "

"Josep Janerius," the man said. "Pleased to meet you Officer . . . ?"

"Lowehaus, Gray Lowehaus." Gray shook his hand.

"You didn't tell me your name," came a raspy purr from behind. Gray turned to see the oversexed woman from next door, her nipples clearly visible through her wet wifebeater. "I didn't think you rolled that way, Officer Gay Lowehaus."

"Roll?" said Gray. "I'm sorry?"

"She thinks you're gay like me because you didn't fuck her in her living room," Josep said, barely looking at her.

"Oh, fuck you, you pansy!" she screamed. Gray wasn't sure if she was going to attack Josep or not. He really didn't want to get caught up in some neighbor spat.

Josep lit in to her. "Get your disgusting milk bags the fuck off my porch, you white trash whore! I can see your fucking vagina in that outfit." He waved his hand dismissively, walking back toward his front door.

The woman tried to rush around Gray, who blocked the way. Josep's door slammed shut, and she found herself locked in the strong young officer's arms.

"Well isn't this a fine mess?" she said, trying to nuzzle her mouth into his neck.

Gray politely but firmly removed the woman from him.

"Go home, lady, watch TV or something." He walked around the corner and back into the park to rendezvous with Clementine and Amy.

"Faggot!" she screamed at his back. Gray didn't bother to turn around.

When Gray came down the hill, he could hear Amy's voice both in the phone and beyond a bush. He hung up.

"Hey," he said, rounding into view. The ladies were lowering a large balled-up tent from a live oak tree which made an arching canopy over a round, flat spread of earth.

"Hey yourself," Amy replied, her breath short. "How'd it go?"

"It was a pretty weird trip. Only one guy had really been able to recall Max and Helen for sure. He says they live out here. The man also offered his opinion regarding their innocence. Says they are most definitely not the type."

"And how would he know?" said Clementine. "This guy in law enforcement?"

"I don't think so, I'm just passing along what he said. The next thing was that he had the idea that maybe whoever had pointed the finger may be responsible."

"Well, you can tell that guy we're on it. Garth is still locked up for another twenty hours, so I think we can devote a little more time to this," Clementine said.

"It's totally your call, of course, but I'm just wondering if we should be building some sort of case on the drunk pervert simultaneously," said Gray.

Amy held up the bag with the strips of flesh from the fence visible inside it. They looked like bits of poorly prepared jerky after drying in the sun, then rehydrating. "We are."

Gray reared back. "Ew. What is that? Nasty."

"It's people," Amy answered. "We found them at camp number two for the man and the kid. There was a struggle, and the drunk is the primary person of interest. It was his blood down that cliff. One thing we're not getting is how the drunk keeps it together enough to track them down. These people seem far too organized to be bothered by him."

Clementine chimed in, "There is no way that drunk has held my son, or anyone else, for ten years. He hasn't been living in the park for a decade either. I'm starting to think the child has been held in a different place, and just got away recently. Maybe these people are helping Rupert escape from somewhere else."

"Rupert, eh? Careful Clem," said Amy. "But that does make an odd sort of sense. But what about the other white guy? The skinny dude that tried to nab the kid? Are we thinking he's with the drunk? Or with someone else?"

"I don't know," said Clementine, "but I am damn sure going to find out."

Sifting through the tent, Clementine came across a plastic bag filled with books, and fanned through the pages. In the middle of one was a set of small fingerprints in dried mud. A child's hands. She bagged the book.

The next one was black, covered in leather. When she opened it she swooned. On its pages were jagged, unrecognized symbols next to a handwritten pronunciation key, entry after entry scratched out and rewritten several times next to each symbol. The signs made her feel sick. She shut the book and bagged it as well.

A glint caught her eye from a coffee can. It had a guitar string strung through a two-foot shoot of bamboo, attached to the can on either side.

She handed it to Gray, who put the can in the crook of his right arm and his left hand on the bamboo stalk. He hit the string, then squeezed the bamboo together and the pitch dropped. He got lost in the sounds, blissfully unaware of his surroundings.

"Gray," Amy said. Gray had no reaction, just kept on twanging the thing with a dopey look on his face.

"Gray!" she yelled. "Gray, stop. Please."

When he snapped out of it, Amy was looking into a Torrey Pine tree, and two very large red-tailed hawks perched in it. Their unblinking eyes were focused on the ektar.

Gray silenced the can's reverberating note. The hawks opened their beaks and let out long screeches that created waves of clashing sound. The effect was deafening.

When they finally closed their beaks, they dropped from the branch and glided through the grove. The sound remained, pulsing in their ears. No one said a word for quite some time.

At last Clementine broke the silence.

"Guys, I think it's high time we faced up to one repeating theme: There is something going on that's way outside the realm of my knowledge. What we've stumbled into is way bigger than I thought."

"Well, duh," said Amy.

"My point is this," continued Clementine, "I don't blame either of you if you want to stop looking into this with me. I have to find out, for myself, no matter what. But you two are under no obligation to do this extracurricular stuff. It's going to get weirder, and if they don't want me to pursue it then I'll be doing all this in my free time."

Amy watched the hawks' flight under the branches as long as she could, then faced Clementine. "That's preposterous. You want to kick us out when it gets interesting. Unbelievable."

"Yeah. Fuck that," Gray added.

A wave of relief rolled over Clementine.

●   ●   ●

Amy found another clay shard in the tent folds. "Same deal. Southwestern."

Gray held out his hand. When Amy passed it to him he looked at it closely, inspecting the grooves.

"Did either of you hear of that anthropological experiment where a few scientists used a beam of light to listen to pottery? More specifically the sounds that were made at the time of its creation?"

They looked sideways at him. "Guess not," he said.

"Anyhow. We keep seeing these shards. I'm starting to think they're something to be looked at rather than looked past."

He put it down and ran his hand beneath the bush until he found another, slightly larger piece. Holding up both, he rotated and flipped them until they fit snugly together. One groove was thicker, its sides rougher. He ran his finger along it, and a shock shot up his arm. He recoiled, dropping both shards on the soft dirt floor.

"What the fuck?" He waved his tingling left arm until feeling flooded back into it. "Thing fucking shocked me."

At the last stop in the park, the scene of the attempted abduction, a pathway led through the trees. A solitary ray of sun passed through the branches of a pine, down through the red dust and onto the needles that covered the ground. It shone upon a brownish-red-colored spatter, flat little dried pools, except for the two nearest the edge where someone had stepped in them, presumably during the search.

"Is that blood?" asked Clementine. Evidence had not only been overlooked but partly contaminated. She remembered the timing of Emiliano Flynn. Right when she was here.

"Looks like it." Amy dipped a swab in the blood and cut off the tip, dropping it into the glass vial. "Let's get this back to the lab."

Gray plucked on the tin can instrument as he followed them to the car.

The two hawks circled high above them, invisible against the sky.

23

Buddy shot clear across the park, running north before doubling back along the whole length of the razor wire fence, a good half-mile. He ended up past all the camps at the needle of land that bordered the southeastern edge of the mechanics' yard, and hid beneath a deck.

Crows squawked on the trees and fences. Two human voices cut through the crows, one low and croaking, one soft and feminine.

Getting as close as possible while staying beneath the deck, Buddy poked his head around and saw a big dirty-looking man wearing rags. He spoke to a woman much younger than himself. Buddy felt drawn to the pair. They had an air about them. A vibration.

The roar of the birds and traffic made it difficult to understand them, even for Buddy. He crawled closer, into the roots of a pepper tree.

"We've got to tell him," the woman appeared to be saying. Her beauty was intoxicating to the young boy.

The old man turned away and croaked back at her, but Buddy couldn't make it out.

The woman answered him, "The plan is flawed. We have to quit fooling people into our care. We need to evolve."

The old man croaked, his hands gesturing wildly, then he fell silent.

She faced the same direction as the man, and the crows and ravens grew louder. A mockingbird flew from the sky, tucked her wings in, and landed on the woman's hand. The mockingbird.

A breeze rustled the woman's long skirt above her knee. On her calf, Buddy spotted a crude black shape tattooed on her skin.

A raven.

He'd found Cora.

24

Safe for now, Stewart iced his shin, cursing himself the entire time. Cora was going to kill him when she and Abe returned. He was pretty sure the old raven dude wasn't going to be too ecstatic either.

His knee sang out in pain. The ice was slow to work. He hoped there wasn't a break or tear inside there. Either way, he wasn't going back to the caves, and that old lady. At least, for now, he had stopped the bleeding, and the ice began to numb the area. Soon he'd have a better idea of the damage.

Klia flew in and hopped around, then sprung over to the balcony. From the guardrail she kept a vigil, peeking back at Stewart to make sure he wasn't doing anything crazy. Satisfied, she returned her attention to the intersection. She watched the policewoman drive by in her blue sedan, checking up and down the street, then out of sight. Then she spied the little black-and-gold dog in a yard off the alley. The dog sniffed the air and looked up at Klia. It barked, then jetted into the alleyway.

Klia clicked her tongue and leaped off the guardrail. Stewart watched in confusion as she disappeared.

Halfway down the alley, she saw the dog cut to the right at the next street, where it vanished behind a wall. She tucked her wings tighter and shot forward, then cut hard at the wall. A flash of the dog's hindquarters slipped into the bushes at the edge of the park. She flapped her wings and followed it into the canyon, then jerked to a halt.

The boy looked at her from the other end of a stick. A butterfly net. She was tangled hopelessly. She screeched and struggled, but the more she flapped her wings, the worse it tangled her. The dog barked. Klia screeched back.

The boy patted the dog on her head, and her tail wagged.

"Good job, Luna."

Klia razzed.

Buddy looked at Klia and said, "Hey, little bird, we need to find Cora."

Klia gave a long sidelong glance to the boy, then clicked her tongue.

It made sense to Buddy, not on a verbal but an emotional scale, like Luna. A sound that told him Klia would take them to the woman.

• • •

"Where, in all that we've talked about, did you think it was okay for you to capture the kid by yourself?" Cora asked.

"I saw an opportunity, and went for it. It seemed like the best moment so far. Why the hell were you guys gone so long, anyway?" Stewart was on the defensive.

"Unexpected hangup," said Abe. "What's done is done, Cora."

"Shit, we may have to move you." She narrowed her eyes.

"What? Fuck that."

"Everyone knows you. You played the solo hero, and now we have to change plans. You're going to have to deal with this."

"Deal with it? What if I 'deal' with kicking you out of my house? It seems like you need me a shitload more than I need you, so why don't you two assholes go make some plans together in your fucking house?"

"While they take you to jail? God damn you're pigheaded." Cora straightened herself up. "Stewart, so help me, if you don't calm down I'm gonna have to get drastic. This is your fault."

"Give it your best fucking shot." He stuck his chin out. Just as she was about to oblige, Abe spoke.

"Stop." The sound came from everywhere, like five echoes at once. Black wires drifted like smoke from his skin. Tendrils void of light swayed into spirals, then became a massive thing that had characteristics of both raven and man, thick and black.

Manic onyx orbs stared at Cora and Stewart. The thing that had been Abe opened its black beak to reveal a toothed mouth inside. Viscous fluid dripped, gurgling and bubbling. Stewart could see both hands and wings stretch, filling the room. Terror brimmed in Stewart's mind.

Stewart and Cora had lost interest in arguing. Abe made a low growl, and the tendrils unraveled, revealing Abe in his rags.

"All that has happened is in the past. We start with a plan. For now. We have asked an awful lot of Stewart, and he deserves our respect."

Cora looked to Abe in utter confusion, but did nothing.

Stewart hadn't heard anything like that from Abe. There was even more to him than meets the eye, Stewart thought. Or it's another trick. The old bastard loves those. Makes me distrust my own thoughts.

"What about Cora's?" said Abe "It's right next door, so we could still get things for you, and you would be safe."

Stewart nodded, bewildered.

As they stacked his things by the door, Stewart asked if they had seen Klia, worried about confusing her. They said no. He picked up a bag, and felt a pinch on his elbow. When he turned around, Abe was shrugging. Stewart shook his head and turned away. A moment later, that patch of skin grew hot.

When they were about to leave, someone knocked on the door. Abe and Stewart retreated to the bedroom and out of sight. Cora looked out the peephole, but saw nothing. She slowly opened the door.

Staring back at her was the kid, black bag draped off his shoulder, his little dog sitting next to him. Klia chirped from her perch on the kid's shoulder.

Cora's eyes were wide as she scooted them in.

Stewart and Abe came back into the room. When Luna caught sight of Stewart, she growled and crouched down, ready to attack. She walked toward Stewart snarling furiously.

Buddy didn't expect the guy to be here. He got lost in indecision, and Cora snagged his shirt. Her grip was firm, and she reeled him in, then locked eyes. Once in her gaze he could not look away. She mouthed a word that sounded like 'boosh,' sending a wave over him. He dropped one hand down, letting Luna know not to attack. Yet. She sniffed the proffered hand, and stopped growling.

Max said to trust Cora. If Cora trusted the bug eater then at least they'd try. For now. Oddly, Buddy didn't feel threatened by the scraggly guy. On the contrary, he thought he could take him.

The other guy was the bundle-of-rags man he had seen with Cora. He didn't pay the boy, dog, or anything else too much attention, just sat on the couch and chuckled softly. Buddy could sense power coming from the man. With one eye the old man peeked at the bag in Buddy's hand, then shut it and began snoring.

Cora was crouched, balancing herself on her heels. "How's it going, my friend? What's your name?"

"It's going weird," he said.

"Sorry. How 'bout the name?"

"Max and Helen call me Buddy. So, for now, that's it."

"Okay, Buddy. Who are Max and Helen?"

"My teachers." Buddy said. His stomach growled. "Can I get something to eat?"

"Of course. But before we get too comfortable, though, let's move to my place next door. That's what we were about to do. My food's better anyway."

As she spoke, she had gone to Stewart's cupboards, opening them until she found some granola bars, and gave Buddy one of them. He devoured it almost instantly.

When they had transferred the things and themselves, Cora was shutting the door to her apartment. She heard footsteps ascending the stairs, and looked through the keyhole as a sandy blonde head of hair walked by, followed by a taller man in blue. A loud and authoritative knock came from Stewart's apartment.

Everyone froze.

A woman's voice sounded from down the hall, "Stewart Zanderson! Open up! San Diego Police!"

25

"Figgins." Clementine answered, shutting the door to her office.

"Clem. It's Amy. I got the results of that jerky DNA back. It's the big pervert in lockup, like you said. Only he's not in lockup anymore."

"What? That's impossible. He had a pending psyche evaluation."

"Apparently a rush was put on it, and he passed."

Clementine couldn't decide which of these things was harder to believe. "Who ordered the rush, and what are we dealing with here?"

"They said it's a result of 'department-wide streamlining,' and something brutal. They pick right now to increase efficiency. Fishy at best. But concerning the big perv, his last known address is a warehouse down at the end of C Street. Guess which ones?"

"I'm guessing not something along the harbor."

"No. The east end. Juniper Street Canyon. Owned by Stillwater, just like Craig James' office. Speaking of whom, I ran the swab from his wound. There's high concentrations of metal, mainly a type of silver. Just like the blood from your biter."

"Rory hinted at that. That means the 'murder investigation that wasn't' is connected to the 'abduction that wasn't'?"

"That's what I'm saying. Rory, eh?"

"We had a feeling."

"Exactly," said Amy. "There's more, though. This warehouse area is a weird holding for Stillwater Enterprises. They almost exclusively do buildings downtown, where the money is, and has been forever. The warehouses are in a very remote location, considering. And the business doesn't fit with his model. It's like a drink distributor or something. Placid Pools Distribution."

"Okay," said Clementine, "check out any other holdings that fit that description. Maybe someone is diversifying. Let's see where else that leads."

"I already did that, there's none. But there are some residences. One was buried in the files. I almost missed it. A small house down inside one of the canyons. It's on Gregory Street. Only the title got transferred a couple years ago, to someone named Jebediah Rawls."

"Wait a minute. I know that name," Clementine said.

Years before she had become pregnant with Rupert, Clementine had been introduced to an awkward and tall fellow named Jeb Rawls. She liked him. He was smart and funny and had sweet manners. It was only an introduction, not a date, but it worked well, and they had decided to go out on one. He was in a band, though, and that weekend they were playing Friday and Saturday in different areas, so a date would have to be the following week. She had said she would just go see his band, and that would be their date. The Saturday gig was near her house, at Auntie Frieda's.

On the way to see the Beneathers, however, she had gotten a flat tire, and a kindly older man, hopelessly pale, had helped her change it. It took a while. She never made it to Jeb's gig, and after that day her life had gone on. She hadn't heard his name again until now.

"Amy, I gotta call you back." She hung up the phone and started searching on the computer for Jeb's band, the Beneathers, and Jeb himself.

After sifting through a quagmire of useless information, she finally hit upon something: a document with the signatures of Stillwater, Jeb Rawls, Frank Rawls, and Nuala McCafferty. The paper was unlike anything she had ever seen. It looked like a contract, but written in the hard-to-pronounce symbols she'd seen in the black book at the park. She took a picture with her phone.

Frank. She remembered Jeb saying he played music with his brother, and Nuala could have been in the band as well. Stillwater probably not. But something linked them all.

She searched bar listings from the past for lineups of bands. The most complete one, Auntie Frieda's, had archived schedules, but didn't have anything on the computer from that far back. The Beneathers were impossible to locate on the Internet, one of countless bands lost to history. At last she found something by searching the other three names simultaneously, on a fansite for incredibly strange music.

The Beneathers was made up of Jeb Rawls on bass, Frank Rawls on guitar. Nuala McCafferty sang, played guitar, and was known as the real talent. Well, truthfully, the fansite said, the talent lay in Nuala and the drummer, Stewart Zanderson.

She did a search on Stewart Zanderson, finding his address in the database connected to his taxes. He lived close to the park where the attempted abduction had happened. On a social media site, she found several old pictures of bands he had been in, and clicked through them.

There were two albums, for two different bands. One, called The Skeez, had seemingly just broken up. There were copies of posters from just under a year ago.

The other was The Beneathers. They were so young. She clicked through a couple of group shots and some live ones. The live ones of the female guitarist usually had her face hidden in her black hair.

The final picture was taken later, and the kids had started growing up. It read, "Last picture of Jeb, me, Frank, and Nuala."

Clem was in awe. The photo was clear and professional, and three of the four people shown were Jeb, the bass player she had met so long ago. Next to him was the hooknose man who shot the webs out of his hands, and the nanny that had stolen her child. The world began to spin.

The final person, though young, matched the suspect description of the would-be kidnapper from the park. The missing piece of her puzzle.

Stewart Zanderson.

Her breath knotted in her chest. She put both hands on her desk and forced herself to breathe deeply. Once she was steady, she called Amy.

"I got that other hit back, the one from the abduction site. What's going on?" Amy said once Clem's door was closed.

"I acted on a hunch, and I think I came up with the other players in this. I know that guy Jeb from my youth," said Clementine, "So I searched how, and found his former bandmates, who, I believe, are all involved. His brother Frank and a woman named Nuala McCafferty are on the Stillwater payroll, or something. And the last guy looks like the would-be kidnapper from the park." She showed Amy the picture on her screen.

"Wow," said Amy, squinting. "It's old, but that's the DNA hit. He's in the database from an arrest years ago. Stewart Zanderson. There's something with his blood, also. The same silver. But separated, The other samples had silver as part of the blood."

"What does that mean?" asked Clementine.

"Not sure yet. Maybe we'll find something out at Stewart's, or those warehouses. So, which one first?"

"Let's see what we're dealing with at the warehouse. That seems like the source."

"How do you want to do it?"

"You and I go to the warehouses, and Gray can check out the Gregory Street cabin."

"Don't you think we'd be better off all together?"

"I'm getting the feeling that time is running out, Amy. I'm sorry. Gray can take care of himself."

• • •

Gray parked the squad car on Gregory Street, outside the tangled greenery passing itself off as a hedge. A golden ball shone from deep within. He put his hand on it, and it unlocked from its housing. A mockingbird and a hummingbird flew off, squawking and chittering in their own tongues. Gray maneuvered over and down the sandy cliffs, a red dust wafting in his wake, illuminated by the sun. At the bottom of the hill, high branches of live oaks formed a cool lattice of shadow that fell on his face. The little cabin lay in front of him, doors open and curtains swaying in the light breeze.

He was going to have to tell Amy about his heritage eventually.

He had meant to, when they were entwined together at her house, before Clementine had radioed them. After that things happened so fast.

He'd tell her the next moment they had together. She deserved that. Plus she was an insane catch, and he didn't want to screw it up. They were harmless, his talents, and if she liked him she'd understand. Maybe even dig it.

He looked in the trees. Another orb, shining green, hung between two branches.

The revealer. One of Jeb's creations.

He kicked dust beneath it, and a plume swirled and folded upon itself, forming lattices of living web. The tendrils felt out toward Gray. Just as they were about to touch him, he hummed, sonorous and robust. The webbing sank back, wafting into the orb. When it had recessed, Gray crouched down, then jumped up, snagging the ball in his fist at the apex.

Jeb knew what he was doing, that was sure. The little orb had all the markings of Gray's people, stretching back for millennia. His mother had been right. The lost art had been reborn with this gangly man. Gray couldn't wait to meet him. He knew why Jeb had come here, to hide his discoveries from the alchemist.

Opening the glass door, he peeled back the curtain and stopped short. The cottage was a wreck, everything strewn all over. A glint shone off the dining table, and Gray saw it was covered in blood. The iron-rich scent filled his nostrils.

He shoved the orb in his pocket and drew his gun. After clearing the house, he stepped outside and circled it. Amidst the piles of rubble was a mound of freshly turned earth seven-feet long. If the mound was what he thought it was, he wouldn't be meeting Jeb.

The man in the grey suit stepped from behind a tree, his silver hair in a slicked-back ponytail. Gray holstered his gun.

"Hello, Gray," said Myron Fox. "How's my son?"

"Hello, Dad," he said, smirking. "That's Jeb, I assume. What happened here? Who did this?"

"It is Jeb. Who buried the poor boy? I did. What a waste."

"It's a crime scene. We're going to have to dig him up anyway," said Gray. "I meant who killed him, of course."

"I don't know that, my boy. But I have commended his spirit

back into the Earth. Whatever happens now, he will be at rest."
Myron motioned to the sage and willow bark scattered upon the
mound, a bowl of water beside it.

"I figured as much. You really don't know?"

"As little as one and as many as four. Five if you count apathy,"
said Mr. Fox.

"Come on, I don't have time for this. Things are heating up."

Myron sighed, lost in thought for the briefest of seconds.
"They're using puppets. They made this fellow create them little
puppet sticks, pinpricks of forgetfulness. The alchemist is the real
driver, letting the sharpest of tooth believe scraps are dreams. They
had a puppet kill Jeb. The puppet they made in the brick building."
Myron looked sadly at the mound, "But I can't tell who gave the
order."

"How do you mean?"

"Somehow they have rediscovered the ancient snare-making
methods. They now possess at least three from different parts of
the world as models, including one of the stone twins. They used
that knowledge to make their own.

"I have no idea how many they've created, or what the new
ones are capable of. Now I come to find they've unearthed the
control words from the oldest of languages, bred from the chaos of
the dawn of man. And, darker still, learned to pronounce them.

"Added to that, Jeb had begun working on his own, creating
these new orbs, with different properties. He even figured out the
one ingredient absolutely necessary for their success. When forging
the alloyed metals, he added drops of his own blood."

Gray had heard of these methods before, in tales from Myron
and his mother when he was a child; the Blood Silver. It flows both
ways, they had said, in and out.

● ● ●

Amy drove down C Street, the setting sun lighting the sky on fire
in her rearview mirror. Clementine held a computer in her lap, looking at maps. On a separate window she had graphs from Found-

Nation of abductions within the last ten years. She switched to the abduction map to compare. Of all the attempts in the city, she noticed a curious amount were centered on Home Avenue, and across the freeway near the police firing range, where Clementine and Amy had both taken their marksmanship tests.

A total of fifteen young girls over the years had gone missing from these areas. They seemed unconnected because they were in four different neighborhoods, and four different ZIP codes, divided by the freeways. She showed the screen to Amy.

"What's over here?" Clementine asked, pointing to a long drainage ditch beside the freeways.

"Storm drains," said Amy. "Tunnels for the rainy season."

Clementine zoomed out, looking at the structures. A chill ran over her skin as she thought of the people in the warehouse creeping through tunnels, spying in the windows of children in the surrounding apartment complexes. She shut down the computer and stashed it under the seat as Amy rounded the final corner. Grifter gave a low growl from the back seat.

Clementine put on a baseball cap and some horn-rimmed glasses without lenses, "How do I look?"

Amy looked over and chuckled. "Like a completely different person."

"Shut up," said Clementine playfully, and hit Amy in the arm.

Amy slowed down as they came parallel to the gate. They didn't see any people, and the few lights didn't illuminate much in the gloaming.

They parked at the end of the street. The only car on the whole strip. The sound of a truck rumbled by on the freeway, hidden by the trees that grew from the wash.

They tucked behind a fence separating the canyon area from the street and warehouse. As they rounded it, they saw one exterior scrolling door had been left open. Grifter growled. Clementine shushed him, then drew her gun and flashlight near the entrance.

Another growl. Deeper. She shined the light on the doorway and saw a massive pit bull, snarling and running at Grifter. The beast let out a ferocious bark, and Clementine felt her trigger finger lock up, like the night in the park. She couldn't fire.

Grifter stood on his hind legs, and Clementine's eyes widened.

She must have chosen the world's stupidest dog for her first pet. The other dog, a killing machine, was charging, and Grifter decides to make the easiest target?

Good Christ, I'm an idiot, she thought.

In full stride, the dog leapt at Grifter from a yard away, mouth open wide

At the last moment, Grifter crouched down. With the pit bull above him, he clamped his jaws down on its rear foot and pulled back hard with his legs anchored. The pit bull landed on its face with a loud crunch. It righted itself instantly, but stood on wobbly legs, dazed.

Clementine's muscles lost their stiffness when the dog's face hit the ground. Inside the yard, people began to slowly shuffle toward the open door.

"Let's go!" she screamed.

Both women immediately sprinted back in the direction of the car. Grifter caught up to them quickly, then turned around. Clementine looked back to see him about to face off with the pit bull, charging again. Behind them, the people with glazed eyes lined up at the open door, none walking beyond the threshold to the world outside. One of them was a thin black man with glasses. This was no time for an interview.

At the car, Clementine called to Grifter. He obeyed, the big dog hot on his heels. Amy opened the door and started the car. Grifter was bolting for them, just a stride in front of the gnashing jaws of the raging pit bull. The dogs ran so fast they were blurry as they rounded the car. In a fit of luck, the big dog skidded out as it tried to corner. Grifter's footing was sure, and he leapt through the open passenger door into Clementine's lap.

She slammed her door as the pit bull righted itself.

The dog's jaws were huge and brutal as Clementine watched it snarl and bark outside the window. It chased the car, attacking the bumper as Amy pulled a tight U-turn and accelerated back up the street. As they sped off, a shrill whistle sounded, piercing the night. Amy looked in her mirror and saw the dog give up the chase and trot back to the warehouse obediently.

After they had caught their breath, Amy said, "That did not go so well."

"No," Clementine agreed, "it did not."

Clementine answered Amy's phone.

"Hey, Gray," she said. "Amy's driving. Our recon was a disaster. How 'bout you?"

"Hi, Clem," he answered, the timbre in his voice high. "Disaster? Is Amy alright?"

"Yes, she's fine. What happened at the cottage? Did you see Jeb?"

"Yes, and no. Jeb's been murdered and buried behind his house," said Gray, bluntly. "I got some blood from the scene. I'm pretty sure it's going to be Jeb's. Cops and techs are on their way now."

Clementine felt a huge hole rip in the case. Jeb was the key, she felt, the lynchpin. "Shit, what happened?" She heard voices in the background.

"I don't know yet. Sorry, I just met the crime techs up here. They're starting the processing. It's that new guy Rory and your partner Jimbo."

"Jesus. I'm glad you already got a sample. Who knows what Jim's gonna cook up with this. Can you meet us down at the station?"

"Sure," he said, "be there in fifteen."

Gray hung up, and looked at his father, Mr. Fox, at the entrance of the property once the small army of police affiliates had arrived.

"Gray," he said, "be careful, son. This is bigger than anything I've seen, and I've been around a long time."

"Thanks, Dad. But do you have at least a guess who did this? Where do we start?"

"I'm not actually sure. The physical killing was done by a puppet, like I said, created with the Oaken Snare. The scent I pick up is that of the fellow Craig James," said Mr. Fox, his nose wrinkling as he sniffed the air.

"As for who was controlling him, I'm not sure. Someone who would have liked to see the research halted. I can't think of anyone inside their organization who fits that description. Certainly not the alchemist. And not Frank.

"Anyone can control a puppet if they know the proper words. Jeb had rediscovered those words, before his demise, and could have shared them with anyone."

"Shit," said Gray. He looked at Jeb's grave, and felt a sense of pity for the man who had simply wanted knowledge. Coupled with others' expectations, that knowledge had killed him. "I'm going to tell Amy everything. I have to go."

"I know, my son," Myron said, then he surprised Gray by walking up to him and pulling him into an embrace. He said to his boy, "Gray, protect those around you. They are incredibly important people. As are you."

"Thanks, Dad." He watched his father turn and walk away. After a few steps he shimmered and became translucent. Smoke spilled, braided together, and the giant fox trotted next to him, into the trees and away.

• • •

The ladies were in the lab when Gray returned to the station. He handed Amy the swab. She prepped it and placed it in the machine, leaning up and kissing Gray.

"I'm so glad you're okay!" she said.

"Me too, about you."

Clementine, knowing they had a few minutes to wait, exited the room to give them some privacy. When she had gone, Gray looked into Amy's eyes and said, "There's a few things I need to talk to you about."

"Fuck," Amy said. "You're married? Got a girlfriend? I knew this was too good to be true."

"It's nothing like that," he said. "It's more like, um, well, you know how this case has some things that don't add up, like the only explanation is something that sounds too fantastic to be true?"

"Yes."

"Well, uh . . . I'm kind of a part of that whole world. My parents, you see . . . "

Amy put her slim brown finger over her lover's lips.

"Gray, sweetie. If you think I didn't figure that out already then you're crazy. When we were at Benito's I was shocked, I admit. But

I know people, and you're good people. Whatever you have going on I can handle, because I trust you, baby," she said. "Apparently you trust me, too."

She removed her finger, and kissed him.

He'd thought of a lot of different scenarios unfolding in his head, but this was not one of them, her beating him to the punch like that. Amy truly was someone special.

Clementine broke the moment when she came back into the room. "Sorry, Amy, but while you work on that, we've gotta go check out Stewart Zanderson's apartment. Gray, can you come with me, please?"

Before Gray broke his gaze, he quietly said, "You'll know everything soon."

He embraced her tightly, kissed her, and followed Clementine out of the lab, feeling Amy's eyes on his back.

26

No one dared breathe following the police officer's command. The silence lasted only a moment before it was broken by the landlady, Mrs. Myers, in the hallway.

"He works nights, usually. He should be around here somewhere," the kind old lady said.

The knock came again. "Stewart Zanderson! Open your door or we'll be forced to break it down!" said the male.

The landlady was shocked. "Why would you do that, when I have the key right here?"

"It's just something I say to make people panic," he said.

"Is it helpful when people panic? I would think that would make things more dangerous."

"Yeah, me too," the female officer responded, sounding put-off, "Can we be quiet please? Now, ma'am, can you please put the key in the lock and step back into the hallway there? Thank you."

Cora glanced back at the ragtag group, shooing them into the bedroom. Then she opened the door and stepped out. "Can I be of any service?"

The tall, well-built male put his hand on his holstered gun, blocking Cora with the other. "Whoa. That's far enough, lady. Who the hell are you?"

"That's Cora. She's harmless. Jeez, buddy," the landlady said.

"I'll be the judge of that, lady, if you don't mind."

"You are a snotty young fellow, aren't you? I don't think I'll let you in there, anyway."

He took the papers from his back pocket. "We already showed

you the warrant! I really will break the door down if you don't fork over those keys."

"Gray!" the female detective yelled. "Stand down right now! What are you doing?" She moved around until she was right in the young man's face. "Now, apologize to this sweet lady so we can get on with this."

Gray looked like he was going to argue, but upon seeing the fire in Clementine's eyes, muttered an apology.

The lady officer turned to Cora, and with forced sweetness said, "Hello, Cora. Did you have something you wanted to talk to us about?"

"Yes, uh . . . so yesterday, Stewart–who I gathered you're looking for–got into a blue sedan, the kind undercover cops use, with a guy that looked an awful lot like police or something." It was the first thing she thought to say.

The officers looked to each other, then back to Cora. "What did this guy look like?" asked Clem.

"White guy. Six-two, two-hundred pounds. Dark brown hair, moustache, pretty buff. Late-thirties, early-forties. Polo shirt and jeans."

"Sounds like Jim," said Gray.

Clementine looked at Cora suspiciously. "Yes," she said, slowly, "yes it does." She held Cora's gaze for a second, then added, "And almost every other male cop in town. Mrs. Myers, give me the key."

"Why? You just heard her say he's not there, didn't you? So what could you—"

"Give. Me. The. Key." Each word hung ominously while Clementine glared at the old woman. "Something's going on with Stewart Zanderson, and we have to search his house. Hence the warrant." She put her hand behind her, silently beckoning to Gray.

Gray wasn't looking at the hand. His eyes had traced across the door. The hinges didn't match the ones on the wall. The halves screwed into the door were covered in rust, while their mates had only spots, and the pins that held them together were bright steel. Upon further inspection, he noticed recent chips and cracks that lined the door.

"Somebody repaired or replaced this door, and not too long ago," he looked at the ladies who lived there. "But you two wouldn't know anything about that, would you?"

"My goodness!" exclaimed Mrs. Myers. "Are you accusing me of covering up some sort of crime?" As she spoke she reluctantly put the key into the palm of Clementine.

Clementine said, "Gray, please do not talk to Mrs. Myers anymore if you cannot be polite." She put the key in the lock and swung the door open.

The house smelled of sweat and stale smoke. "Get back," she said to the two ladies, then into the room yelled, "Police!"

Gray flanked her, and they stepped in, weapons drawn. They flowed from room to room quickly, and had the place secured in no time. Clementine told Gray to call Amy to process the room while she stepped back into the hall. Mrs. Myers and Cora were still waiting.

"It seems that someone was very recently in that apartment. Like maybe within about fifteen minutes or so." She nodded to Mrs. Myers, then looked back to Cora and said, "Did you hear anything? Right before you heard us out here? Or did some generic cop-looking person come out of here?"

"Sorry, no," replied Cora. She thought her lip may have twitched.

"Hmm." said Clementine, looking Cora slowly up and down, her eyes drinking up characteristics and committing them to memory. Five-nine, one-oh-five, athletic build, Hispanic female, mid-length black hair, brown eyes, round facial features. "Do you mind if I have a look inside your apartment, while we're here?"

"I'm not sure. Is my house covered in the warrant? Maybe you should get it from the 'bad cop' guy so I can check." She looked at her fingernails.

"If that's the way you want to go, that's fine," said Clementine. "We'll just wait till a uniformed officer gets here, then we'll go get a warrant that covers your apartment, and you'll be under siege until we get back." She gave a smug look to counter Cora's attitude, secure in her move in the chess game.

"No," Cora answered, "you'll leave a uniformed officer here until he gets called back after you can't find a judge to sign a preposterous warrant to enter the next door neighbor's house of someone wanted for questioning. I'm thinking a black-and-white would be out there for maybe forty-five minutes before your captain reamed your ass." Cora positioned herself so she could look past her captivating fingernails at the female officer.

Clementine got very close to Cora's face, and whispered so only she could hear, "I'm going to find out what's going on."

"I hope you do," whispered Cora.

"We'll see you later," Clementine said. She turned to Mrs. Myers and added, "Sorry for all the disturbance, ma'am, but we do have someone coming out to process the house."

"Are you sure you can't tell me what you want him for?" the old lady asked, her voice breaking.

"We're not supposed to discuss it, ma'am, but we will let you know when we can. I'm terribly sorry. We'll return the key on our way out," she said, and shut the two ladies out of Stewart's apartment.

When the door had closed, Clementine said, "Well, Gray, that probably could have gone a little better with the old lady. It became fairly obvious that Cora was the person of interest here." She shrugged. "What happened?"

The young officer's face flushed. "I don't know. It was weird. I knew where you were going, but it was like someone was pulling my strings, and I couldn't overcome this fixation with the old woman."

His explanation did little to relax Clementine's mind.

● ● ●

Amy arrived wearing her crime scene official blue jumpsuit and carrying her two kit bags. As she walked into the apartment, Gray thought to himself that she would look good even in a paper sack. So delicious.

"How's it going?" she asked.

"Pretty shitty," Clem answered. "I think the guy we want is hiding out next door. His neighbor first lied to me, I think, then she basically told me to piss off."

"We've just got a warrant for here, I'm assuming."

"That would be correct."

"Well," Amy said, "I'll process the shit out of this place, and at the very least we'll have an idea who was in here."

"Thanks, Amy," said Clementine.

"No problem." She set her bags down and said, "Hey, baby," to Gray.

"Hi." He picked her up and kissed her softly on the mouth.

Clementine looked away, embarrassed. Her eyes swept the floor, and came to a stop. She could see through the living room into the kitchen. Beneath the stove was a sharp long . . . something. She walked toward it, squinting, and saw it was another shard of clay. One end of it was a rusty red.

"I've got blood," she said, "on another piece of pottery."

Amy tapped Gray's arm, and he let her down. She put on gloves and brought her bags into the kitchen, where she picked up the shard and observed it before placing it in a paper bag.

Amy was exceptional at her job. That was the first thing that had drawn Clementine to her; the young lady's strong work ethic, and sharp eyes. So many people in various forms of law enforcement seemed to simply skate by or worse. It had been refreshing to meet someone of Amy's caliber.

Amy roared through the house, fast but incredibly thorough, concentrating mainly on the kitchen, where the shard had been, and the bathroom, always a hotbed of DNA.

She knew with certain items, even in a house, it could be difficult to ascertain exactly whose genetic signature was on what. Who used this fork? Did someone borrow the razor? One thing that almost always has the signature of the owner is the trusty toothbrush. Amy bagged the one in Stewart's bathroom, and his comb as well. Satisfied with her work, she placed her bags on the living room floor.

"I found a rock on the back porch with blood on it, and a couple sets of prints off the sliding glass door that leads out there. Also, there are shapes in the dust where things were, and the things in their places don't match up. I don't know what that means, yet."

Clementine shook her head. "Well, I don't either. But I do know we need to run this stuff ASAP. Let's get going. Amy, you run the evidence while I bug a judge for a warrant for those warehouses. Then we'll go see what the hell is going on down there."

"Gotcha," said Amy. "Should Gray go with you?"

"No. I'll just be waiting. You guys both hit the lab," she said.
"Right on," said Gray.

He scooped up Amy's bags and put his arm around her, walking down the hall. Clementine followed, pausing at Cora's peephole and whispering, then descending the stairs.

• • •

Back at the crime lab, Amy pulled the shard from the paper bag, only now it was two pieces, having broken somewhere along the way. She sighed.

The dried blood flaked off of the smaller shard as she dislodged it with a thin scalpel. She processed it and waited for a signature.

At the lab table, she placed the two shards next to each other, trying to see where they lined up so she could repair it. She turned on a small flashlight, focused to a thin beam. As she shined it over the larger splinter of clay, a tinny voice came from it. A whisper, indecipherable. She called to Gray, asking again about the light and sound experiments he had read about.

"Burrs," it said, or "birds." They weren't sure. Amy fanned the beam across it slower, through a steel guard they had fashioned to pinpoint the light, and the voice deepened. In the lower tone, she could tell there was no 'D' sound. Burrs.

Curious. She changed her speed, the refraction of the light, any variable she could find, but the voice said the same syllable. Gray had been right: The voices in the room when the pottery had been made were trapped in the clay, the hands acting as a stylus for the recording process. She never in a million years thought that it would work, but after the other shards had shocked Gray earlier, here she was.

She ran the light over the other shard.

"Irk," it said, the end of the voice distorting from the coating of blood. Having a sample already, she gently cleaned the shard, then tried again.

"Irker," it said.

She lined them up end to end, "Irker burrs."

Amy was at a loss. She entered the phonetic phrase into her

universal translator on her phone. No matches came up. She realigned the pieces again, using a magnifier that fit snugly in her eye socket, the kind a jeweler would wear.

Where she thought they lined up the first time was off, she could now see. The rough clay edges almost snapped together when put the proper way. She ran the beam of light over it, and the clay spoke to her.

She remembered the word from a history book she had read in school. It described warriors who fought with the red rage of fury centuries ago in Scandinavia, crazed men overcome with bloodlust.

It haunted her when she had read it then, but that was nothing compared to the feeling of terror she had now. The word had the effect of jolting her with electricity, and she dropped her flashlight. It clattered noisily to the ground, beam slashing around the room. Gray's mouth hung open as he stared at the shard.

Berserker.

A match was found on the DNA searches. Amy and Gray walked over to the pinging machines and looked at their respective screens. The blood on the shard also belonged to Stewart Zanderson, although the sample had no silver content.

The blood on the stone from the Zanderson deck was from two sources, one being a John Doe. The other was Markuz Vassily Banikoff. She compared the John Doe blood from the stone to the anonymous sample from the brick offices. They matched. The stone had been in the office when the blood event occurred.

Amy called Clementine. "You got that warrant? Blood on the clay is Zanderson, so that may be nothing, being his house. But, the stone from his balcony has the same blood signatures as the office: The same John Doe, and that Banikoff monster. Stewart must have beaten those men with the rock.

"Everything's pointing back to those warehouses," she said.

Clementine was sitting outside the judge's chambers, as patiently as possible. "I'm still waiting on the warrant. I'll let you know the second it's ready."

"Alright. We'll be ready."

When she hung up, Gray asked, "What's going on?"

"Waiting for a judge to issue a warrant, who is mysteriously occupied," she answered. "The timing is questionable, eh?"

"No accidents," answered Gray. "And no coincidences."

27

"What's going on, Cora?" asked Mrs. Myers, "Are you in trouble?"

"Of course not, Alberta."

"What about Stewart? What's he done?"

"Nothing. This whole thing is a misunderstanding. You'll see." Cora put her hand on Mrs. Myers' forearm. "Alberta, Stewart would appreciate it if you wouldn't tell his mom about this."

Stewart's mother, Catherine, lunched with Mrs. Myers a few times a month. They'd known each other for so many years neither woman liked to say the exact amount.

The old lady's face curled into a warm smile."No problem," she said. "And I won't say anything to the pigs, either."

Cora couldn't help but chuckle as Alberta walked away. A few seconds later a female voice asked Mrs. Myers where Stewart Zanderson's apartment was.

Cora slipped back into her apartment.

The curtains were drawn. The room was cloaked in darkness and silence. One by one the others came out of hiding. Everyone but Abe, who had sat on the couch the entire time. Cora looked out the peephole, but saw nothing as footsteps padded by.

"It's Amy," the voice said from the hall.

Cora put her finger to her lips, and they listened to the muted conversation next door. After saying hello, the voices dropped. Tones could be heard through the walls, but no actual words.

They waited for the cops to leave. Buddy pulled on Cora's skirt every so often, but she motioned him to stop, and continued her futile attempt to listen to any progress next door. After an excruciating hour, the officers and the crime tech departed together. Cora watched through the peephole as they walked by.

Clementine stopped, looked in the peephole and said, "See you very soon, Cora. You too, Stewart."

After hearing the cops' vehicles depart, they finally were able to breathe.

Abraham looked up. "Things are starting to happen quickly now, huh?"

Buddy wasn't sure if the old man was addressing him, but answered anyway. "Things have been happening pretty fast ever since I ran away from the warehouse. Now we gotta get back there. C'mon." The boy made for the leash.

The old man stood up, blocking Buddy's path. Luna quietly crept between the boy and the wrinkled man, and growled softly.

"Don't worry about me, little doggy," Abe said.

She responded by laying down, although still between them. Abraham crouched down and balanced, perching. Only the balls of his feet and his toes touched the ground, yet he stood stable as a house.

"Let's talk about this warehouse, and the people who kept you there," he said to Buddy, "If you're ready." He put his hand out, and Luna sniffed it suspiciously before letting the big man scratch behind her ear. When he scratched, she lost the suspicion and pressed her head into his fingers to maximize the satisfaction.

"Can we do it on the way?" Buddy asked. "Helen and Max are in serious trouble."

Cora said, "It will be better if you fill us in while we wait for darkness. We need to hear it free of the distractions outside. Trust us on this. We are going to help you, and you're going to help us. We need to know some things first, or else it could be very bad for all of us, your friends included. Okay, Buddy?"

He could see what Cora was talking about. "Okay. What do you want to know? Where should I start?"

Abe answered, "It has been my finding that it is best to begin at the beginning."

Stewart rolled his eyes. "God, you're a dick."

Buddy started laughing. Abe smiled back at Stewart humorlessly.

After Buddy wiped his eyes, he began his tale. He was the boy with no name, and patchy memories. One of several kept locked in the warehouse mazes. He told them of the knives, and started to finally produce the oaken box that held the snare he'd been carrying, but Cora bade him to continue the story. Abe clicked his tongue in disappointment.

Ysenia. She helped him get outside. The escape. The canyons. Luna. Max. Markuz. Oliver. The pig Garth. Helen.

At the story of the rabbit, their interest was piqued. Cora and Abe were surprised, but Stewart was absolutely transfixed.

"So this little guy turned himself into one of you people?" he asked. "What the fuck? Why haven't you done that with me? Or, could I do that to myself?"

Cora answered, "It's not that simple, Stewart. Abraham's gift is split between Frank and Nuala. The only one with the power to transform more than one life in this area is the Bear Mother. If you wanted something like the boy has, you should have stayed in her cave a few minutes longer. That's what she was doing when you ran away from her."

Stewart clenched his fists in frustration. "No one tells me shit," he said.

"Please, Stewart," said Cora without looking at him. "Buddy, have you met a thin but very strong woman with long silver hair since you've been out of the warehouse?"

"No. Not that I remember. I did have trouble remembering stuff before, but it's starting to come back to me. Ever since I got out. I don't think I saw someone like that, though."

"What the fuck?!" Stewart was fixated. "So I was going to get something from the bear lady when she did that chant thing? And I was too chickenshit to stick around for it?"

Abraham said, "Hey, if the shoe fits." He smiled at Stewart. "Cluck, cluck."

"Chickens don't fucking wear shoes." Stewart gritted his teeth, temples pounding, ready to rush the old man.

Before he could move, Cora placed her hands on his arms and said, "Stewart, listen to me. There's virtually no way you could have known about the Bear Mother. It was Klia's job to get you to stay with the woman, and if she hadn't been injured by Mr. Fox, she

BEN JOHNSON

would have. Anyway, you have her, and that's worth a lot."

Klia chirped, fluffed her wings.

"Yeah. Sorry, girl."

"The world does not always follow a clear cut path. It's up to you to maneuver through as best you can with what you've been given. Considering everything, you're doing alright."

He was calmed by her touch, but still felt needles of disappointment.

"Yeah, I'm doing okay considering two attempts to bring me into your world have failed, and I'm powerless while everyone else, including this kid and even the bird, have some crazy talent. I can't help but feel I'm being set up to take the fall for everyone. And now I can't even go home." He put his head in his hands.

"Hey, asshole," said Buddy.

Stewart raised his eyes. "What'd you say to me?"

"I said, 'Hey. Asshole.'" Buddy repeated, slowly, "I came from a prison that I'd been in my whole life to live in canyons eating plants and stealing food. I don't even know my real name or where I came from. Do you see me crying?"

He waited for a reply. When Stewart shrugged, Buddy said, "We've talked enough. I have to go get Max and Helen. The sun's going down, and you said we would wait till dark. Let's get going. I know the way." He whistled to Luna, and grabbed the leash. "Where's the fucking fire escape?"

Abe laughed out loud. "And the boy becomes a man."

• • •

"Hello, new friends," said Frank, standing in front of Helen and Max. They were seated in wooden chairs, unbound. In Frank's opinion they were quite harmless now. "And welcome."

When Helen had been delivered, Frank knew that Max and the young child who had escaped him would try to break her out. He was not expecting them to come separately.

"Where is my young friend, hmm?" he asked. They said nothing.

"Aash Xashuol!" He shouted. Nothing happened.

He said it again, changing the pronunciation slightly. Perhaps, in his excitement, he had spoken it incorrectly. The words had to be just so, of course, that much he'd learned over the years.

Still, nothing by way of a response registered in his captive's eyes.

Pulsing with anger, he repeated the words, ready to strike, when he felt a sharp pain in his neck. Swatting it, he looked in his hand afterward and saw a dead wasp. He felt another sting on his bicep. The insect venom reacted quickly, puffing up his skin. At the far corner of the room he saw a trail of wasps streaming toward him. Reacting in a flash, he jumped from the room and swung the door shut, yelping in pain when he touched the red-hot handle.

• • •

Beneath the ground, locked in her room, Ysenia Trujillo smiled as she sang droning notes on top of one another. The air around the young girl crackled with energy. Her mind stretched into the web. The hive mind. We. Selfless.

The girl tweaked the bugs through her humming song. Filled the hive spirit with the images of those who would kill their queen.

The walls of her darkened cell rumbled, and wisps of dust spilled from the cracks.

28

On a desert cliff above the warehouses, they sat beneath a willow bush and watched for movement. Cora put her hand on Buddy's shoulder. "Which one had the puppet people?" she asked.

He pointed to the largest building, in the center of the property. "That one."

"Okay. Klia, could you please check it out?" The bird clicked her tongue and flew off down the hill.

Klia's body showed black against the glowing lights of Tijuana, far in the distance. They saw her land on a tree, scanning back and forth, before taking wing again. When she finished, she returned to Stewart's finger. He moved his hand close to his face, and Klia pecked lightly between his eyes, awakening the birdsight.

With her eyes, he saw that the building had no windows and three doors. One was a large scroll that coiled at the top when it opened. The other two were standard security doors. Thick, solid, and secure.

Buddy had remembered being in a building with windows at some point, but they would've changed their system after he'd escaped. The birdsight couldn't tell him where the girl was, or, for that matter, Max and Helen.

There were cameras, and some dead areas where they couldn't see.

Stewart relayed the recon information.

"Alright, let's talk for a second." said Cora. "We don't have any idea what we're getting into, here. If things go south, get out of there and return to my house immediately. Especially you, Buddy."

She looked to the boy, then Luna.

Klia hopped to Stewart's shoulder and made clicks in his ear.

"Nickel is down there also," said Stewart.

The path of the snare had shifted. Buddy took the black bag from his shoulder, held it out to Stewart and said, "You'll probably be wanting this, then."

"Guess so," he replied.

Cora watched the switch. "Be careful, Stewart."

"I'll do my best."

She addressed the group again. "When we're in, the first thing we do is open up the big building and flush the shell-people out of it, for a diversion. Luna, that's your job."

"Abe and Stewart, you're looking for Max and Helen. Hopefully Frank hasn't begun experimenting on them yet. If you see Nickel, well, you can decide what to do with him. But Max and Helen are the priority."

Stewart didn't know Max and Helen, and hoped he didn't lose Klia, who did.

"Luna, after you flush the shufflers out, meet me there." She pointed with a stick. "We'll go look for the girl. Okay?"

The little dog barked back to her.

"Good. You look out for Buddy. This is dangerous stuff."

Luna nuzzled her face into Buddy's pant leg. He reached down and scratched her head.

Klia flew into a bush behind the group and whistled a series of bending notes. Two mockingbirds erupted from a distant tree, flew in and joined her.

"Shouldn't Luna look for Helen? A dog looking for a lady that she knows? She'd find her instantly," Stewart said.

"There are reasons, but no time," said Cora.

"I'm getting sick of being out of the loop." Stewart's skin felt hot.

Cora leaned forward. "Stewart, my dear, you are about to know everything. After tonight I'll answer any question you may have, I swear to you. But I can't right now. I will not now, nor will I ever, betray your trust. Now, feel my truth through this, and remember it. You'll need it."

She pulled his face closer, and planted a kiss on his rough lips.

Rosy thoughts of valiantly protecting Cora to the grave, and beyond, crept into his head. He strapped the spirit snare to his calf, then pulled his pant leg down over it.

Cora eyed the group. "Klia and her friends will pop the front gate, open the door, and wait in the trees while Luna herds the people into the lot. If you happen to get hold of anyone we're here for, get them out of there. Avoid confrontation if you can, and don't wait around. They already know we are coming, so stealth is not an option. Chaos will be our cover." Stewart and Buddy nodded. Abe looked at the buildings, seeming not to have heard. She was used to it.

"If for some reason you do have to fight, do it ruthlessly. Do not, under any circumstances, get caught. Don't underestimate anyone, and listen for signals. There is no one left to save us if we fail."

Buddy was shaking. Luna nuzzled the boy's arm, and he stopped.

"These people that we are trying to rescue are the future, as are you two. This is a new day. The ways of Abe, and of myself, are closing, and the new era will feature you, and them. People chosen from the Web itself, rather than passed down through humans using their own choice. There will be great resistance, and this will be the first of many challenges to overcome. A war may follow.

"But this is what must be done. Our world is corrupt, and your new blood will revive it. The worst example of the corruption lies at the bottom of this hill. Now the world changes, or else we get thrust further into darkness. Right now. In this moment.

"So let's get to it," she said, turning and walking toward the dark buildings.

Her words resonated within them as they snaked down the hill, obscured by shadow, ready for battle.

The river wash was dry. A breeze swept over them, blowing their scents past the gated property. Not one car travelled on the knot of overpasses behind them, leaving an eerie silence. One-by-one they stuck their heads up beneath the sprawling willow across the street from the warehouses.

Abraham's hand rested on Stewart's shoulder. He smiled as he pinched a muscle in Stewart's neck.

"Ouch! The fuck?"

Cora looked at him. "Really feeling it, eh Stewart?"

He grunted, unsure what happened.

"Let's do this," Cora said.

The birds shot from the willow bush, screeching and clicking. A great noise ripped the night apart as the gate creaked open. Flying through it, the birds made a variety of sounds in the effort to pop the huge scrolling door. Nothing was working.

Stewart brought up the rear. Just as the group was entering the gate at the front, he caught two human shapes to his left, closing quickly.

Fucking ambush. He monitored from his periphery as his mind ran wild. Fuck these dicks. I'm done fucking around.

He planted his foot and cut hard.

Markuz's eyes widened as Stewart dodged his swinging fist and thrust his forearm deep into Markuz's Adam's apple. The giant started hacking uncontrollably, doubled over, trying to secure a breath.

Pivoting from the impact, Stewart twirled around and drove his elbow into Oliver's nose, sending his spidery body cartwheeling through the air. He landed limply in the street and lay still.

Markuz coughed. Stewart whipped his leg back and kicked him in the face. The giant shook it off and stood up.

Stewart turned to run, but Markuz palmed his skull and jerked him backward, driving a blow into Stewart's ribs. Stewart felt fractures creak along the bone, a taste of marrow flooding his mouth. The giant smashed his fist into Stewart's face.

A high ringing sound enveloped everything. Stewart was trapped in the peal of a massive bell. A trickle of blood rolled slowly over the stubble on his upper lip. It crested on the division between his skin and the pink of his lips before gravity broke the surface tension and it dripped into his mouth.

The instant the blood hit his tongue, insane fury overtook his mind. Despite being prone to anger, he'd never felt anything like this. The rage inside of him bubbled over. A thin red mist covered his vision. Not obscuring. On the contrary, his sight seemed incredibly clear and vivid, but overlaid in shades of ruby. The night slowed. He looked at Markuz, and could see through the bloodsight the systems at work within the man. Nerves around muscles around bones, all neatly held together with the arteries and veins. Ruby trails brightly ran around his body; blood pumping through. Stewart focused his fury on the underside of the giant's arm, where a thick tube supplied the massive trunk with blood.

He shot his hand up, hitting the huge man's wrist. The shock forced Markuz to slack his grip, and Stewart fell from his grasp.

The pain from his ribs was easy to ignore from within the rage, like it came from far away, through clouds. Endorphins flooded him as he ducked beneath Markuz's next swing. In its wake Stewart pulled the giant's body downward at the collar, using his momentum against him. He shaped his hand into a cone, all the fingertips held together, and thrust it up near the armpit. The blow mashed the thick vein and nerves flat against the bone, and Markuz's arm spasmed. All its feeling drained as it hung limply at his side. He attempted to rub life into it, and momentarily lost sight of Stewart, concentrating on reviving the useless appendage.

Stewart leapt feet first into Markuz's chest, where the knot of blood roared in and out of his heart, and hit the breastplate with a crack. Markuz groaned and fell to the ground writhing.

Stewart left them in the street and followed the group into the parking lot, his mind filled with the red rage.

"Nice of you to join us," said Abe when Stewart had caught up. The rest of the group surrounded the birds at the door further on.

Stewart thought about ripping Abe's head from his shoulders.

"Rrrgh. It's a trap. They know we are here," Stewart said. His hands clenched and he gnashed his teeth.

"I know," said Abe, "it doesn't matter now. The fury. Let it come. We're gonna need it."

He knows, Stewart thought, he did this.

The realization was cut from his mind with a massive clanging. The birds had sprung the great scrolling door.

The sounds of the birds had drawn the shell people to the door, their curious instincts pulling them like moths. As the steel shutters lifted, they saw Max, Helen, and the girl were not there.

One woman shuffled off, laughing, back into the darkened confines of the warehouse, away from the opening door.

Many of the people walked in place, shifting from foot to foot as if awaiting something. This was not the chaotic cover they were hoping for. Only the laughing lady had turned around. Cora peered into the dark after the woman, her scraggly head of hair barely visible as she shuffled into the blackness.

"C'mon, Buddy," she said, and they cut through the listless throng after the woman.

Luna barked. The shuffling horde gave her a wide berth. She herded them out into the parking lot, where they ambled around beneath the dim lights.

The woman with the grey hair drifted past a giant box truck in the dark, and through a door deep inside the large building. Her echoing laughter pinged off the high ceiling and steel walls. Luna caught up, and they followed the laughing lady.

Beyond the doorway was a hall with several doors. The woman was gone. Cora tried one door, Buddy another. Locked. Cora whistled a single blast, high and short, and a few seconds later one of the mockingbirds joined them, appearing from the dark with a flash of its white-banded wings.

The bird clicked on the first door. Cora opened it to find a washroom, unoccupied. The second door was a small room. Inside, a chain hung from the wall. At the end was an open shackle, sitting on a mattress in the corner. Next to it was a small, bare desk. The room smelled musty and oppressive. Cora wrinkled her nose. Buddy turned away as she shut the door.

The third door revealed a staircase descending into darkness. She squinted, able to see three stairs before the black void swallowed them.

From the hallway, blocked by the open door, a bell sounded, its pitch a ridiculously high register. Buddy was unable to move. Cora swung the door open the rest of the way.

Nuala was in the hallway. She wore a wolfish smile and rhythmically chimed a silver bell with little carved leaves upon it.

Luna bounced up and stood next to Buddy, snarling at the blonde woman.

"You want to knock that bell shit off, lady?" Cora said.

Nuala expelled a combination whistle and hum. The sound formed waves upon the chiming of the bell, which began to build pressure inside of Cora's head. Her hands shot to her ears. Plugging them had little effect in staving off the pain. The crest of each wave hit like a tiny hammer inside of her brain.

Cora struggled against the pressure, and eventually regained a measure of composure. She concentrated upon slowly drawing in a breath that ballooned into the tiniest corners of her lungs until they were filled to bursting, ignoring all other muscles in her body. Upon her exhale, she formed a strong, clear note of her own. Waves spilled from her mouth and collided upon those from Nuala's bell and mouth. The assaulting tones turned back at Nuala, and their pressure racked the blonde woman's brain, making her drop the stick. With the bell silenced, Cora altered her pitch, moving her lips into a small "o" and focusing her note like a beam. Nuala was shocked at the strength of Cora's note as it smacked her in the face, effectively stopping her breathy voice.

Buddy snapped out of it.

"Fuck you, lady!" he yelled, flipping off Nuala, and fled down the black staircase in a blur, followed by Luna and the mockingbird. Cora slammed the door after them, leaving herself and Nuala in the hallway.

"Alright bitch, let's fucking rock," she said.

"Yes," said Nuala, "let's." She reached behind her back and pulled out a long thin cone. In a mockery, she bugged her eyes,. "Congratulations on finding the true bearer of the mantle, you sad sack of shit. Too late though. Poor you. Always so underprepared."

Cora shook her head with a wry smile, pulling a curved stone knife from her waistband. The Green Twin: an ancient and hand-hewn piece of savagery

"I'm not stupid." Cora said. The green blade was so finely polished it picked up the scant light in the hallway and magnified it.

Nuala got serious, recognizing the blade. She lunged at Cora, stabbing downward. Her attack narrowly missed as Cora contorted herself just enough for it to swish past her body. The cone smashed into the ground, then popped from Nuala's grip and bounced down the hallway.

Cora had countered the strike by slicing upward, which also missed its target, ripping into Nuala's shirt and snagging. Cora's knife jerked from her hand and flew through the air. The women ended up in a pile, punching and kicking.

Cora landed an elbow solidly to Nuala's cheek. With the jolt,

Nuala freed her hands and got them both around Cora's neck.

Her milky-white hands turned bright red as she choked Cora, who thrashed for a long time, gouging a thumb into Nuala's eye. Nuala choked harder, sheer hatred driving her, until she swore she felt the hyoid bone snap in her adversary's neck.

Cora's body went limp. Nuala held her grip, then slowly released, staring down at the woman who had so fascinated her long ago, now lying still beneath her, vanquished. She waited for the ensuing rush to envelop her, the addictive power to flood her veins with the delicious light of a fallen foe.

And waited.

Something was wrong. There was no power transference. There should be something. She had just snuffed out a Keeper. She cautiously leaned her head over Cora's face.

By the time Nuala realized she had been taken, Cora had snapped forward at the waist and head-butted the bridge of Nuala's nose, shattering the cartilage. Blood erupted as Nuala's body pivoted back. Cora righted herself and pinned her to the ground.

Cora tried to say something, but coughed violently, realizing her little trick had very nearly cost her her own life. She was still in danger. Holding Nuala's bleeding head down, she punched her in the ear twice as she located her knife.

It had slid farther than she thought. A green glint shone twenty feet down the hall. Nuala's cone was only about ten feet the other way. The problem with the nearer weapon, however, was that she had no clue what would happen when she used it. Her knife, The Green Twin, was a killing tool. Taking a life would change her own forever, but sometimes that is the price you have to pay.

Sacrifice.

She leapt up and sprinted for her knife. When her fingers were about to wrap around its handle, a shoe stepped down. She grabbed the shoe instead. Her eyes followed the seam of a polyblend track suit up to the smiling face of Peik.

"Hello, Cora. Thanks for bringing the boy back here," he said. "There's nowhere to go down there but back up, of course." He flashed his blue eyes to the door Buddy had gone through. "Which is to say, the child is trapped. Yet again."

Cora swallowed, repositioning the delicate bones inside her

neck. From behind her, she heard the gurgling coughs of Nuala as she rose to retrieve the black cone. "That fucking bitch is mine," she said.

Cora grabbed Peik's other leg and lifted. His full weight was on the smooth blade, and its frictionless surface sent it shooting forward and past Cora's body. Peik fell on the back of his neck with a hollow thud.

Behind her, Nuala charged. Cora bolted through the door, barely able to swing it shut before Nuala reached the other side. With all her strength, she held it shut, frantically whistling for the bird.

It shot up the stairs from the blackness. Cora held the handle steady while the bird twitted a complicated stream of clicks and whistles. When it was finished, Cora lifted her hands from the handle. She watched it shake, but hold firm.

The doors they had searched so hard to acquire, made of impregnable steel, now held Nuala and Peik out of their own prison cell. Even Markuz and a battering ram would take the better part of an hour to break through.

The little bird flew back into the darkness, and Cora followed it down the flight of stairs to a landing with four doors. All of them were wide open. Each room held a mattress and a table with a dish set up. Two had light but strong looking chains connected to the wall, with shackles large enough to be neck restraints. One room had a vast excess of stained ropes in the corner and several cardboard boxes.

The final room was completely empty. Stone dust hung in the air around a large opening in the far wall. She peered into it, and in the cold darkness could make out small, crude steps chopped into the earthen tunnel.

Cora's nose wrinkled as an ancient wind blew its crackled breath up from deep beneath the Earth.

29

Stewart's mind was on fire, pulsing with the ruby rage of the berzerker. Drool seeped from the corner of his mouth as his body spasmed.

Twenty shell people spilled from the scrolled door, ambling over toward Abe and himself. One of them, a man, broke ranks and charged full-speed, shouting and milky-eyed.

Stewart waited until the man was almost upon him before ducking beneath the man's arms and pushing him in the back, kicking his legs as he passed. The trip sent him spinning to the ground with a smack. His hands shot to his skull as he lay writhing on the ground. Two more people shot from the group. Stewart unloaded a brutal uppercut to the guts of one, doubling the thick woman over. He put his foot on her head and with one shove sent her careening into the heavyset man behind her, taking out his knees and sending him airborne. He landed on top of the woman, where they lay in a tangled knot of limbs and clothing.

"Who wants to get their fucking ass kicked?" Stewart yelled.

A brief silence followed, then they charged screaming as one. Stewart balled his fists up, ready to take the entire throng, but Abraham wrapped him in his rag cloak and ran toward the office building next to the lot's entrance on the street.

One of the mockingbirds flew down from a rooftop and clicked open the lock on the door with Abe nearing. He swung the door open, then slammed it. Fists of the horde pounded on the steel door.

When Abe let go, Stewart thrashed, yelling gibberish. He picked up a chair from the middle of the room and threw it into the wall, then ripped a flat screen TV out of the wall and threw it at the chair.

"Stewart! Stop!" Abe commanded.

Stewart walked toward him, glaring and hostile. He slapped Abraham hard in the face, then jumped backward, swung open another door, and disappeared into the darkness of the next room over, shrieking and destroying.

Abraham laughed at the chaos and followed Stewart into the next room, but he was already gone. A door on the far side of the room hung open. Abe could see the hallway beyond it. Filing cabinets had been kicked over, and papers covered everything. Stewart made quick work. He followed the trail out into the hallway, and walked through another door.

A yellow circle of light illuminated the asphalt around the entrance. Stewart was nowhere to be seen.

Abe gave a whistle to the birds. No answer, and no birds came to him.

The shell people, so animated minutes ago, were gone. Rumbling filled the air, and a huge truck departed from the building that Cora and Buddy had gone into.

Abe chuckled. "Good luck everybody," he said, then sat on the ground, crossing his legs, and began to sing. His notes were old and crackled, like the crust of the earth itself. He sang of mountains growing and rivers cutting, rain and wind wearing down the landscape as it's pushed skyward by the tectonic plates. Magnetic sinews through the city. Ley lines of the desert. He sang of men and animals, birds, trees, amphibians, reptiles, and rocks. He sang to the world a song of itself.

He sang of Keepers, of Makers.

He sang of the Bear Mother, and she heard his voice from beneath the Earth.

A small tremor ran through the ground beneath him as he croaked, undisturbed. His skin sent forth hairs of smoke that swirled around his skin and rippled with his breath. Like the surface of water broken by a stone, the smoke shimmered along the black asphalt. The sky, reddened from the city lights bouncing off the atmosphere, revealed small shapes gathering. Avian silhouettes soon amassed upon wires and rooftops, as well as on the plantlife outside the gated perimeter. Hundreds, then thousands of birds gathered. The dark sky was now rife with birds of all kinds landing and observing the smoky man.

Still Abe chanted.

• • •

Klia looked down from the rooftop, now crowded with birds, as Stewart ran to the rear of the building closest to the canyon. She tweeted a note through the din, but he didn't hear it, or at least made no motion to signify one way or another.

Stewart saw things in the depths of the ruby vision. A pattern of weaknesses, strengths. Tactical advantages of both animate and inanimate objects. All this information processed itself through his genetic structure. You have always been this. It said. Awaken.

The door to the building shone at the hinges when he looked at it. Before the mockingbird could swoop down to help him, he picked up a rock near the door and began furiously beating on the lowest hinge until it was a decimated twist of steel. When he had kicked it loose from the wall, he crammed his fingers beneath the door and pulled up from the freed corner. It creaked, just a little, but when Stewart reached down into the berserker spirit flooding him, the rage bubbled up and his veins stood fat on his skin. A horrendous creak grated the air as he ripped the security door clear off the building.

He ran growling into the large room. It smelled of old cardboard. After a few yards he slowed down. Beneath a lamp that hung from an impossibly long cord sat Nickel, eyes glazed, looking nowhere. The rage subsided, and Stewart felt his emotions mellow as he looked at his old friend.

"Hello, Stewart," came a voice from behind him.

Stewart recognized Frank's voice, even after all these years. He turned around.

"Hey Frank," he said. "Nice life you got here." Stewart fanned his hand around the warehouse with its stacks of boxes.

"I like it."

"You would."

Frank chuckled, "So, you finally figured it out, eh?"

"Are we really going to talk about shit, you pompous fucking windbag? Your shit got your brother killed, and you're not too far off from that."

"You wish," said Frank. "I've got tangible power, something real. What do you have?"

"Come find out, you fucking ass."

Frank said, "Craig, rise."

Stewart watched as Nickel rose silently from his seat. In his hand was a short tantō. The Japanese sword had maple leaves adorning it, inlaid into the silver hilt. The blade burned bright.

A snarl echoed through the warehouse, bouncing off the steel walls. Stewart saw a white dog whose head was the size of a buffalo's. Muscles rippled beneath its short fur. It eyeballed Stewart and growled low.

"You run out of cop dogs, now you're getting dog-fight dogs?" he said. "Nice work, ass."

Frank smiled, looked to the dog and spoke words the likes of which Stewart had never heard.

The dog attacked, running fast from behind.

At the same moment Nickel's body came alive and charged Stewart from the front, holding the tantō high, his eyes a distant milky fire.

Stewart took off running in the only direction not blocked. He thought it must be by design that they were pushing him this way, but he was helpless to resist. Trying desperately to channel the rage and slip back into the berzerker mind, he found it didn't work that way.

Inside the rage, he had forgotten that the spirit snare was still strapped to his leg. He reached down, and tried to lift his pant-leg while still running, almost tripping himself with each step before he finally freed it. About to be sandwiched between Nickel and the charging dog, he chose Nickel. He took two steps and curled into a ball, rolling beneath the swish of the sword. He hoped there was not a special spot for returning a spirit as he jabbed the knife into Nickel's leg on the way by.

The snare shook uncontrollably in Stewart's hand. Nickel stopped running, the milk draining from his eyes. The action confused the dog. It turned on Nickel and knocked him to the ground.

Nickel threw up his arms to fend off the attack. Stewart lunged toward the dog with the snare. Sensing Stewart behind him, the dog twisted, and the knife ripped the air just beside it as he rolled on the ground. It turned its head and charged Stewart, who lifted his knee to his chest and loosed a walloping stomp into the dog's nose. Blood trickled from the beast's nostrils.

Stewart ran, not looking back, toward a metal tube running up the wall to the ceiling, held on with metal braces.

The dog was almost upon him. He ran, lowering his body before he hit the wall, then jumped hard and continued churning his legs, using the tube as a ladder. As he lost momentum, he grabbed on to the tube, barely thicker than his wrist, and stopped. The dog snarled from two stories below.

Nickel sat dazed on the ground, holding his head as Frank picked up the tantō.

"Nickel!" yelled Stewart. "Look out!"

Nickel turned his head. Frank was walking toward him, sword raised.

"What's going on, Frank? I thought I could go home now," Nickel said, confused.

"You thought wrong, Craig," said the hooknosed man, staring with his piercing blue eyes as he walked up to Nickel and stopped in front of him, then slowly fanned the tantō through the air. "Sorry."

As he said the word, Frank sliced, severing Nickel's head from his body in one swift and savage motion. The blade was so thin, so sharp, the neck offered almost no resistance. Blood flew in a wide arc off of it. Nickel's head bounced like a wet ball, then rolled along the floor before coming to a stop with his dead eyes wide open, staring at the ceiling.

Stewart's jaw hung open in disbelief. He felt sick. Nickel had lain with the wolves, for whatever reason, and it had been his demise. The puddle of blood grew as it ran from Nickel's neck.

The dog paid no attention to the violence. It bit the bottom of the metal tube Stewart was perched on and shook its huge head. The braces held. Stewart breathed easy. The dog kept at it, snarling and tugging. Eventually the brace nearest the bottom popped off, then the next one up, then the third clattered across the floor.

Frank walked across the length of the warehouse, watching the dog work.

The only thing that high up besides the fleeting security of the pipe was an air duct that hung from a bracket in the ceiling and disappeared into the wall. Stretching out as far as he could on the shaking perch, Stewart got the tips of his fingers on the circular vent opening. He leaned out until he was teetering, snaking his fingers around the interior lip of the grate that covered the duct, and jerked hard. It dislodged with a puff of dust. He threw it down, meaning to hit Frank, but halfway through the motion thought to try the dog instead, and in his hesitation sent the thing clattering harmlessly to the ground between the two.

The only option at this point was a literal leap of faith. The fourth and fifth braces popped off the wall simultaneously. The remaining three were going to find very little resistance.

Stewart crouched down tight into a ball before exploding into the air. As he thrust his hand up into the vent, the electrical lines were torn from the wall where he had been sitting. The entire pole swayed once before falling like a long thin tree onto the floor of the warehouse with a deafening crash.

One hand slipped off on the dust inside the tubes, and he hung precariously, far above the concrete floor. He shot his left hand back up above him. It grazed on a dusty something, and Stewart reacted quickly, wrapping his hand around a support joist deep inside the tube. Straining hard, he pulled himself up into the safety of the ductwork, shimmying over to the most stable point where it met the wall. At that juncture he sat still and caught his breath, which was ripping at his chest.

He looked out and down at Frank when his breathing evened out. The man and dog looked up at him silently from next to Nickel's headless body on the floor below, waiting to see what Stewart was going to do.

"There's no way to escape me, Stewart," he said. "You idiots played right into my hands. When I kill you there's no next plan for the Raven Man. You're it. Which means I'm it. Forever."

Stewart, not giving Frank the satisfaction of a response, scurried back into the tube. After several more dark yards, it bent upward. Enough to stand up. When he did, his hair brushed another vent. He popped it off, and the stars of the night sky twinkled above him. The birds on the rooftop flapped their wings and squawked nervously before landing again and quieting. Klia flew to him, landing on his shoulder and nipping at his ear.

He stroked her head and peered over the side. A hum sounded from somewhere, and a cloud of smoke floated ten feet off the ground, in the center of the buildings. It flowed out in tendrils, creating the shape of massive wings. Birds were everywhere, following the smoke with their eyes. A door opened on the building beneath him, and Frank stepped out, stopping short when he saw the writhing cloud.

The thick dog charged around him, running full bore, before leaping straight up and trying to bite the smoke. The churning blackness parted around the animal, making it sail past and tumble headlong onto the asphalt.

Frank walked slowly beneath the cloud and stood still, looking into it. Nickel's blood was splattered on his shirt.

With a wave of his hand Frank quieted the battle dog and winked to the cloud.

"Hello, Abraham Blackwing," he said.

The cloud said nothing. The low hum continued.

30

Buddy followed the girl down the stairs, and into the tunnel, which brought a loamy air from deep inside the Earth. He didn't question her direction, she knew her way.

"Come on!" she said, as they passed a spout of water on the wall, trickling down along exposed rocks.

Buddy stuck his hand into the wetness and put it to his mouth as he walked. The water was delicious, pure. Luna drank from it while watching the two walk further, then hopped after Buddy as he redoubled his pace to catch up.

The girl faded into the darkness ahead as the tunnel curved, and he lost her from view for a moment. When he caught up, they headed out of the tunnel's end. It opened into a giant, well-lit cave room. The ceiling was low in the corners and arched twenty-five feet above them, forming a dome. Openings dotted the walls along the base, and streams of light pulsed from the rock, casting an eerie glow.

The cave smelled of dried herbs and old dirt. In the center of the room stood a lone figure. A very thin old woman with long grey hair and brown skin studied them. She wore a ragged poncho, which hung loosely from her body.

Buddy was startled, but the girl seemed calm. Luna growled.

"Come here, dog," said the woman. Luna's ears perked. "Luna. The Moon. Like the Moon, you affect people's feelings, their inner tides. What an aptly named little girl. Who made you what you are, hmm?"

Luna crept toward the woman, almost involuntarily at first.

Then a change occurred. The little dog straightened herself out, trotted over and stood up on her hind legs. She put her forepaws on the woman's thighs and whined.

"I mean your friends no harm, little Luna." She lightly touched the dog between the eyes. Luna returned to all fours and walked back to Buddy wagging her tail.

The power of the woman was obvious. The very air seemed to crackle around her.

"Come here, child," she said to the girl.

Ysenia, who just as Buddy had returned to rescue her had already escaped. He wondered why the girl would do what she had for him, as he had so many times.

"What are you going to do?" he asked.

The woman gave him a stern look. "The same thing Helen has done to you. Open up her spirit to be ready to accept the gifts of the Web."

"Helen? The rabbit gave my skills to me," he said, "I hadn't even met Helen, just fell asleep in her tent."

"And that was enough." replied the woman, "The Rabbit guided it, true, but Helen opened your reception. It could have happened with anything, your bonding. If you were someone else. But you are you, and it was a Rabbit."

Ysenia smirked.

"So you could do that to me, as well?" Buddy asked. Part of his mind remained on Helen. If she was one of these Makers, what is she doing right now?

"Not now," said the woman. "A spirit can only have one Awakener, and Helen is yours. Multiple awakenings lead to madness, death, or worse. Besides, you have always been the Rabbit. You will see."

Buddy didn't want to think about what was worse than madness and death. He looked at Ysenia. "Is this what you want?"

"It is what I am," she said, "and what I want."

"Okay. What should I do?"

"Stay. Watch," the old woman said. "There are stories you will both now learn. The tales and memories that have begun to come back to you will now be made fully known. Buddy, I won't be awakening your spirit, I will be awakening your memories. Stay strong, and keep one hand on Luna. Sit down, now."

He did as he was told, folding his legs and keeping his back straight. Luna curled herself up into his lap, her head propped up on his knee. He put one hand on her head as the woman had instructed. Two wasps hovered along the cave ceiling.

"Now, Ysenia, come to me." The name spilled from the old woman's lips like flower petals.

Ysenia knelt in front of her.

The woman began to chant. Her voice was like a mountain spring quenching the thirst of a desert land. The cave trembled as a massive shadow shook on the far side of the cave. Buddy and Luna beheld the great bear, glowing silver and ghostly in the distance.

The bear sent a low growl reverberating along the walls. The sound crawled, like a slowly rolling wave. Buddy felt the note deep in his stomach, almost to his bowels. Inside he felt a flash of panic, a combination of the sight and sound of such a massive creature. He concentrated on reducing the emotion into a little ball before it could gain momentum, and from there dissipated it completely.

When he had conquered the fear, he looked again to the bear, which had walked across the cave. Upon reaching the old woman and young girl, it stood upright on its thick hind legs, its head almost touching the roof of the cave, and chanted a low harmony to the woman's high voice.

Slowly at first, tendrils came from the woman's hands, from the bear's paws and mouth, from their skin, all over. Gaining momentum, they wrapped around Ysenia's open arms, running over her head and body and down her legs until they covered her completely, save for small openings over her nose and mouth. The tendrils reared back, then burrowed into her pores. Her body sent off tics as they pierced her, then she relaxed into the embrace of the Bear Mother, the Bear, the Web and the Earth.

From within the cocoon, a solitary strand emerged. One each also drifted from the Bear and from the old woman. The three tendrils touched each other and braided themselves together with the ends forming one fine point. It hovered over Buddy like a charmed cobra before coming to land on the center of his forehead.

From within the embrace, their stories were told.

The potter had seen the bowl for the first time as it was to be unloaded into the museum. He always walked this way through the park, and knew the loading area well. He'd never felt the need to take anything before. Such a thought would very simply never have occurred to him. But that day it had. Like never before. No one was around the truck. Very few people who weren't park or museum employees even knew where this loading zone was, so it was not guarded very closely.

The bowl, with its intricate zig-zagging black-and-white patterns, mesmerized the man. It spoke to him. He felt it. As he neared the truck, he looked around, trying to be nonchalant. When he was satisfied no one was watching, he stuffed the bowl beneath his shirt and sprinted off.

The vision shifted.

The bowl is on the mantle. The potter's wife is pregnant. She sits in a chair and cries. He hands her a tissue, and she dabs her joyous tears from her eyes. The woman rises after a few seconds, tissue in hand. The potter takes it from her hand and she departs. He gently rips the wet area away and places the tear-soaked bits in the bowl, then takes the rest and throws it away in front of his wife in the kitchen.

Another shift.

A girl is born to the potter and his wife. She is overjoyed. He takes a job teaching ceramics. The potter has a small class. He takes his wedding ring off when he goes, but he couldn't possibly explain why. In the class, a woman is among six people listening.

When he comes home, the potter picks up his girl and his hands burn. He hands the child to his wife, who feels nothing. When he enters his car to go teach his class the next day, he finds it crawling with bugs. He painstakingly removes them, and arrives to class late.

Staying after class, the woman asks for help. The man never says he is married, and the woman has no reason to think otherwise. His wife wonders where he has been, and his answers do not satisfy her.

The woman in his class wants a child, though she doesn't tell her teacher. She is over thirty, and has no mate, and is unsure she needs one, but perhaps the potter. He seems intelligent, attractive in a certain sort of way, and mannerly. The woman courts her teacher until her fertile time comes, then drops her robe after class to reveal her tight and willing body.

The scene again changes.

The teacher is home. His wife wonders why he smells of soap. As he tells a story of a spill of filthy muck at work, his foot feels as if it's on fire. He removes his shoe, and his wife wonders why his sock is spotless if such a spill occurred. Her slowly roiling suspicions confirmed, she tells him to leave.

Next, the man is at the female student's house. Her eyes grow panicked, demanding to know why he has come here. He tells of his wife, omitting the information about the child. She tells him to go back to his wife, shocked at the information.

She never returns to his class. When he goes back to her house she no longer lives there.

The potter goes home to apologize to his wife. She opens the door and hurls the ceramic bowl at him. The man manages to raise his palms and deflect it in the air, follow it with his eyes, and catch it cradled into his stomach while falling backward across the lawn. She picks up an already packed suitcase and throws that at him as well. Protecting the bowl, he turns around and lets the suitcase bash into his back.

"Your girlfriend stopped by!" she screamed, neglecting the news his student had delivered.

The potter's ex-wife grows to loathe her child. She is constantly reminded of her husband by the girl, and punishes her often for nothing. They have a terrible relationship. The girl dreams of leaving, though she is very young.

A boy is born to the female student. The potter never meets him. When the child is barely a year old, he is left with a nanny and vanishes without a trace, like a shadow into a cloud of dust.

Buddy heard the voice.

We are one, it said to him as he looked into the eyes of his half-sister, *Ysenia*.

Buddy pulled himself from the tale. Tears streamed down his face. He felt a presence behind him, and looked up to see Cora. She silently knelt down so Buddy's body was between her knees, and twined her arms around his shoulders. His tears stopped rolling. Cora was not surprised to see this thing happening, Buddy noted.

"It's alright, Buddy," she said. And it was.

The woman, child and Bear made no acknowledging movement. The webs, also, stayed in position, as if Cora had been expected.

Comfortably snug between Cora and Luna, Buddy re-entered the tale.

The girl learned quickly. She could talk earlier than the children of her mother's friends, and most other things besides. One woman had commented that it was "kind of freaky."

When the same woman had picked up her bag, she found the cloth was scorching to the touch, and dropped it. She looked quizzically at it for a time before picking it up once more and putting it beneath her stroller, then had to throw it down again when a wide assortment of bugs began to crawl out of it. The mother looked aghast at Ysenia.

After they had cleaned off the stroller and the woman had gone, her mother slapped her across the face and sent her to her room.

Eventually the little girl's mother did not have too many friends.

They moved one neighborhood over, toward the canyons. The girl liked solitude and the outdoors, and her mother could keep an eye on her for a great distance from their apartment on the canyon ridge. If she chose, which she did not. She hoped coyotes would get the girl.

The girl began to hear a voice. A boy, only barely younger than she. She said it was her little brother, and that he was in jail. Her mother paid no attention.

This happened for years. The woman had tried to lock her daughter up in a mental facility, hiring counselors and psychiatrists to pass judgment. The little girl told them exactly what she thought they wanted to hear, however, and they all pronounced her perfectly healthy in mind and spirit. The mother was angry, her nefarious plan thwarted.

The girl never spoke to her mother after that.

One day, the girl finally heeded what she believed was her brother's voice, and found her way to exploring the canyons in the night while her mother slept. They were scary in the dark, but the girl reached deep down and found the courage. After several nights, she found herself at the gated entrance to a group of warehouses, and knew her brother was inside. She had to figure out a way to get him out, even if she had to switch places with him.

She had practiced her heat control and insect mind games. She was prepared to suffer for her brother until he could come back. The first thing was to get him out.

She kept going back for several nights. People came and went, usually in trucks. One man came on foot once a week. He was tall and extremely skinny, and wore a scraggly red beard, usually with an old flannel. One time she saw a man with brilliant blue eyes driving a car with a girl next to him barely older than she was. He was looking at the girl the same way that boys at her school looked at her sometimes. Middle school boys were nasty, that's one reason she stopped going. She understood something in that moment that made her shudder; the blue-eyed hooknose liked girls almost her age.

After the car had passed, a whine sounded from behind her. She turned to find a black-and-gold dog approaching her with its tail between its legs. She smiled as the dog wagged its tail and sat in her lap. It licked her cheek, and a warm wave enveloped the girl. The dog was like her. A freak. The only other one she had met so far. The rest of them were in that warehouse, and probably not this nice.

She would go in. She could take it. The dog would help her brother escape once she had got him out.

"Thank you," she said to the dog, scratching its head.

Luna wagged her tail in response, then led the girl to a circle of trees where a thin man and a large woman sat upon a log, smiling. They introduced themselves as Max and Helen.

• • •

At the conclusion of the vision, the tendrils uniting the woman and Bear to Ysenia glowed with a silver fire, and the cave was blanketed in light. It was so bright Buddy couldn't make out any shapes. All was lost in a silver haze.

When the light faded, Buddy watched the tendrils extract themselves and retract back into the woman and the bear. The girl was revealed. She looked much the same, except her eyes, which sparkled like emeralds.

Now when Buddy looked into them he saw not just his half-sister looking back, but also an old soul holding the wisdom of the ancients. She had been rebirthed into the cave of the Bear Mother, with all that that entailed. She would not go back to live on the surface. Her final awakening would be coming soon.

Ysenia approached Buddy with her arms out. She wrapped him into an embrace and said, "You must return and help your friends, then find your mother. This will be my home now."

It was hard for him to accept. His sister, come and gone. "Can't you come find my mother with me?"

"No," she replied, "this is me. This will be my life."

"Will I see you again?" he asked.

"Yes, a lot."

The webs retreated into the cracks of the cave as Cora and the Bear Mother locked eyes and nodded. Cora stood and put her hand on Buddy's shoulder.

"C'mon Buddy, we gotta go find Helen and Max and finish this thing."

"Okay." He walked over to Ysenia and embraced her. "I'll see you."

Ysenia smiled warmly, a solitary tear breaking down her cheek.

He was filled with a feeling of invincibility, warm and true. Then, with Luna by his side, he followed Cora back up the rough steps to the warehouse.

31

Frank's cold eyes peered up into the free-floating column of smoke that Abe had become. The pit bull sat beside him, growling menacingly.

"This has been fun, really," he said, smiling, before letting loose two oily-looking filaments of web from his hands. The tendrils oozed out, searching, until they honed in on the smoke, then plunged themselves inside.

The hum turned to a wail. The smoke shook uncontrollably, locked inside a sinister vibration. Stewart beheld the scene from the roof. He could see Abe's face, then the huge black wing of a raven, each disappearing as quickly as they had come.

Frank had trapped the old Raven Master between two forms. Stewart's most powerful ally, or perhaps adversary, had been neutralized by the madman he had helped create. If Abe couldn't fight Frank, how could he?

A sharp pain shot from his temple. Stewart turned his head, and Klia hovered next to his face. She had pecked a small hole in his head between the ear and the eye.

"What the fuck?" he said, putting his hand to it. He looked at his bloody fingers afterward. Understanding, he put them into his mouth.

Iron flooded his senses as the cold fire of the berserker overtook his mind. Amidst the ruby sheen of blood, he condensed all his power into a ball. He took two steps back as he pulled out the spirit snare, then sprinted hard toward the edge of the building and launched himself off the roof.

Only a couple birds took wing from his path. He didn't give any battle cry, nothing to give himself away, and his trajectory looked perfect as he fell toward Frank's back. His breath hitched. It was going to work.

Just as Stewart let himself slide into the joyous feeling of revenge from a well-thought-out plan, Frank spun around and whipped a tendril right into Stewart's gut. In the berserker trance, the feeling was muted, but its physical force knocked Stewart backward, sending him tumbling along the asphalt. Frank instantly returned his focus to Abe, seeing Stewart as a bothersome gnat to be swatted away at will.

When Stewart righted himself, he saw the pit bull charging for him. Slobber flew in an arc from its mouth as it neared. Stewart lay helpless in its path.

The dog whipped its head as a bird shot just under its chin, then a roar of wings filled the night.

In an instant, the space between Stewart and the dog had been filled with a flying wall. The birds swooshed and dove, confusing it. Thousands of birds swirled, hundreds of different kinds. In the eye of the feathery hurricane stood the snarling dog, Frank, and the living smoke.

On the outside stood Stewart with the spirit snare.

He held the knife firmly, made a faint whistle, and lunged with the knife. The wall of birds parted exactly around his arm as he sank the knife next to the dog's shoulder blade. It yelped, then stood silently with milky eyes.

"Attack," Stewart said, pointing to Frank. Nothing happened.

Frank smiled sideways and said, "Aash kzashiil," then laughed.

To Frank's surprise, instead of charging at Stewart, the dog growled and turned toward himself, its puppet mind full of rage. When it rushed him, he easily brushed the dog to the side, as he had done to Stewart.

The animal shot back up and tried again. This time Frank pulled out the stops and with almost full-power sent the dog careening across the asphalt far away from him. Undaunted, the animal righted itself and charged. He readied to kill the beast as the smoky column around Abraham begin to dissipate, reforming itself.

The birds silenced, and in the vacuum of sound came

realization. Frank turned just in time to meet Abraham's swinging fist. Frank was rocked. Blood and stars filled his vision as he fell to the ground.

"Stop," Stewart said to the mutant dog. It sat and stared at Stewart, who was as shocked as anyone when the command worked.

Frank stood up quickly and wiped his face with the back of his hand. "Old man," he said, "I am going to kill you for that."

Abraham smiled, patronizing. "Won't that be fun?"

The following laugh pushed a trigger within Frank, and his hands began to glow. His fiery blue eyes were manic.

From behind Frank, a door creaked open, and Nuala stepped into the parking lot, followed by Peik. They walked slowly, in no hurry.

Stewart looked toward the gate. In the distance, the huge figure of Markuz carried the limp body of Oliver toward them as well. The giant stared at Stewart with menacing purpose as his great feet shook the ground.

The tide was turning, and not for the better.

32

A warm breeze found its way down to the caves, far beneath the surface. Luna guided Cora and Buddy up through the ancient tunnel until it connected to the staircase. As they raced by the trickle of water, Buddy slipped. Cora picked him up and he rocketed up the stairs. When they came through the wall and into the dimly lit room, they heard it.

A loud hum morphed into a wail somewhere outside. Cora gave a look to the mockingbird, who sat sentry by the door, keeping the lock fastened. The bird screeched, and the lock popped open. Cora held Buddy behind her as she darted her head out into the hallway and back in again. The coast was clear, and the door at the end of the hall was open. Dim light trickled from outside.

After a few cautious steps, Luna sprinted through the door and into the pale lights of the parking lot. Buddy and Cora followed, then stopped just outside the door at the scene before them.

Abe and Frank stood in the center. Thousands of birds flew around them, circling and screeching. Wisps of smoke drifted from the old man's rag cloak, tendrils of black light from Frank. Abe smiled. Frank did not look entertained.

Nuala and Peik were between the two groups, and Stewart was farthest away, shaking with rage and looking at a white pit bull.

To the side, the lumbering figure of Markuz approached, cradling Oliver in his arms.

Luna tore through, keeping a wide berth from Peik in particular, and stopped between Stewart and the prone white dog. She brushed her wet nose against Stewart's leg and whined, and the rage again drained from him.

"Goddamn it, Luna," he said.

She barked, looking in his eyes, then at the snare in his hand. Then she turned and barked at the white dog.

"Really?" Stewart asked.

Luna repeated the process step-by-step.

Stewart pricked the dog, then stood back. Its eyes lost the milk, and it snarled anew, tensing its muscles. Luna darted in front of it and the pit bull gave chase.

She led the beast all the way around one of the smaller buildings, ending up where only Buddy and Cora could see. Luna whipped her body around, barking. The muscular white dog stopped short, as if someone had jerked an invisible chain, and a change occurred. Its growling ceased and it yelped, then sat quietly, waiting for Luna. She walked over and touched noses with it. It licked Luna's face and stood beside her, then both of them trotted over to Cora and Buddy.

"Something happened to you," Buddy said to Luna

They rounded into view, getting the attention of the others.

Stewart stood with his finger poised near his mouth, more of his blood on the tip, ready to sink again into the rage.

Peik looked very interested as the animals growled at him. A wry smile curled upon his lips. "What is up with this little dog?"

Nuala looked past the dogs, far more interested in Cora. She had no smile at all. "This bitch? I have no fucking idea. Boy!" She glared at Buddy. "Get over here right now!" She pointed at him, then to her feet. "Aash Xasuol."

At the sound of the words, Frank cocked his head from across the lot, intrigued.

Nuala didn't look pleased when the words had no effect.

Nuala, his fake mother during his ten-year captivity, had not fully appreciated his new talents yet, Buddy thought.

"Okay," he said, then charged full speed at her, deep in the Rabbit spirit. He closed the distance in quite literally the blink of an eye, jamming his heel just above Nuala's kneecap with all the force he could muster.

Her screams tore through the lot as her knee snapped straight backwards with three pops. She wailed, sonic pressure shooting from her mouth. Waves of deafening noise rang inside every skull, and several birds dropped from the rooftop perches. Everyone had to cover their ears before their eardrums burst.

Buddy was frozen in the sonic blast, his hands doing nothing to alleviate the insane screech that pounded his mind. Using the advantage, Nuala reached out and grabbed onto his ankle. When she touched him he bucked and tried to run, but her grip was iron. His fingers burrowed into his ears to silence the deafening scream. Blood began to seep from his leg as her fingernails cut his flesh. He was going nowhere, having seriously underestimated her in his hubris.

The dogs howled in pain. Cora couldn't take her hands from her ears to help them. She tried to sandwich Luna's ears between her knees, which worked for an instant. She couldn't help the pit bull, or whatever this thing was.

Nuala was running out of breath, and the horrible sound ebbed. Cora slapped each dog on the ass, rushing behind them at Nuala and Peik.

Nuala, from the ground, held Buddy upside-down from his bleeding leg. He pistoned his legs, dangling.

"I'll kill him," Nuala said, matter-of-factly. She brought four rigid fingers near the side of his neck. Her blonde hair whipped around her head in the rising wind.

Cora and Luna pulled up immediately, but the big pit bull rushed forward with a vengeance, remembering Nuala. Cora yelled to stop it, but her command fell on deaf ears as the rampaging dog leapt. Before Nuala could respond, it chomped down on the arm that held Buddy.

He dropped to the ground, running to Cora, who latched onto him and backed away.

The dog pulled Nuala's arm toward the ground, shaking its giant head back and forth and ripping a gaping hole in her skin. Her blood poured down the dog's neck. Nuala's look of confusion and pain turned to anger, and she screamed point blank into the dog's face. A high, piercing shriek stabbed into the dog's mind, and it thrashed violently in its attempt to escape the horrible noise. The concentration of sound ate slowly through its eardrums and into its brain. When it realized it was dying, it struggled with renewed vigor before the life drained from its body with a final twitch.

"Fucking stupid animal," Nuala said as she hurled its limp body to the side. When she turned back, a rock hit her in the face.

After throwing the rock, Cora followed in its path. Nuala recovered instantly, however, and when Cora was almost upon her she was ready. Cora was in the air, preparing to kick her in the face before Nuala knew what hit her, but Nuala punched Cora between her leg and torso. Cora's groin muscle spasmed from the blow and she fell, landing on her ear. Nuala was quickly upon her, wrapping her hands around Cora's neck and choking her.

"This time you better die!" screamed Nuala, her voice breaking in her fury.

Through bulging eyes Cora watched Nuala try to extinguish her life. Realizing that playing possum would not save her a second time, she punched twice into Nuala's kidney. The blonde woman grimaced from the blows, but still choked her.

One of the mockingbirds flew at Nuala's face. She turned her head up and made a horrible sound at the bird and it fell from the sky.

"Klia!" Stewart yelled. His arm shot toward his mouth. The blood would bring the answer. Before he could, his hand was enveloped by a much larger one, which whipped Stewart around until he looked into the scarred face of Markuz.

The giant drove his fist into Stewart's already shattered ribcage, knowing exactly where to hit. The sound and feel of broken glass ripped his insides. He couldn't speak, couldn't breathe. Every movement brought more pain. Markuz buried his fist in the same spot. Bile seeped up into Stewart's mouth as Markuz dropped him to the ground and stomped upon his ankle. Stewart howled.

The screams woke up Oliver. The spidery youth saw Buddy's attention focused on Nuala and Cora. He pulled up behind Buddy while Luna crept closer to the women fighting, then wrapped his thin arms around Buddy's neck before Buddy could react.

Luna noticed, and charged a couple feet before she realized Buddy was incapacitated. Oliver would hurt her boy if she attacked. The little dog changed course and rocketed back into the warehouse.

Buddy looked after her in horror.

In the center of the lot, Abe and Frank stood, faced off. Abe was no longer smiling. Frank saw the moment had shifted. He shot a tendril that hit Abe, reverting him to smoke. The great Raven appeared, its ancient eyes filled with an agonizing madness.

Peik smiled as he looked around, taking in the moment of triumph. Frank glared at him, cursing his apparent laziness. He'd have a talk with Peik later. The guy was starting to take far too many liberties.

Stewart, from his crumpled heap, saw his group neutralized. *All this crap for nothing, we're all gonna get killed now anyway. These fucking bastards just killed Klia.*

A shift overtook his spirit. Righteous indignation and the will to honor the memory of a fallen comrade took his mind into the berserker's rage, without needing blood. Stewart's pupils shrunk to pinholes as the red fury sank into his core, and he erupted into Markuz with a blinding volley of fists, feet, elbows, and knees, landing blow after blow. Markuz was quick, but not enough, and soon was overwhelmed.

Stewart jammed his thumb into the giant's eye and sank his teeth into his ear. When he bit down, Markuz's blood sent Stewart's mind deeper into frenzy.

The tasting of the enemies' flesh and blood.

An uncontrollable fire consumed his spirit. He screamed and spit blood into Markuz's face and headbutted him on the bridge of the nose while pounding the heels of his hands against the huge man's temples. The three-prong concussive attack worked its violent magic. Markuz fell and stayed there.

Blood ran down Stewart's face as he let a scream of triumph rip through the air.

Peik's smile faded.

Stewart rushed instinctively to help Cora escape from Nuala. The thing that stood in his way was Peik. Well, if he had just felled Markuz, how hard was this going to be? He ran and readied himself to dismantle the sardonic pale asshole.

Peik didn't move. Rather, his body disappeared and reappeared a few feet closer to Stewart, landing a haymaker to his face before shifting to the left. His easy smile returned.

Stewart lunged for him again, but the same formula repeated itself. The ghostly shift. Stewart's nose streamed blood down his face. He was trapped in the rage, but his opponent was so surprisingly skilled that it made no difference.

The pale man phased behind Stewart and said, "Hey, berserker. I used to create armies of you."

Stewart swung his fist, but Peik was already gone. He tried to turn, but Peik shifted, and kicked Stewart's legs out from under him, sending him sprawling along the asphalt.

The tracksuit swished behind his ear, and Peik said, "I used to destroy them when I was finished, as well." He kicked Stewart in the back of his head with his heel, and his forehead bounced on the blacktop.

Peik laughed a deep and uproarious belly laugh, surveying the carnage unfolding. A smug satisfaction overtook him. A warmth.

It took him a few seconds to realize that the warmth wasn't coming from him. It was from underneath. The ground steamed as the temperature shot up. A deep rumble sounded from far beneath the Earth.

Then the bugs came, like rain.

They arose from the south, a huge humming tornado of insects sweeping between the buildings, filling the night sky. The birds instantly shot after the cloud of living food. Chaos reigned with the veiny wings of the insects and the feathery wings of the birds.

A huge, ripping roar came from the warehouse, followed by the sounds of walls buckling. The whole building shook as tremors from within rocked it. Something terrible and large smashed on the interior wall. It creaked and swayed, then the wall fell down, the resulting wind sending the insect and birds sprawling through the air.

When the dust had settled, Ysenia rode high atop the giant ghostly Bear into the lot. The old woman walked behind, long staff in her hand. From the Bear Mother's side, Luna ran toward Buddy. She barked at Oliver, whose hands drifted from Buddy's neck while he stood and backed away, eyes darting between the dog and the bear.

Luna jumped up and kissed her boy.

A light grey mockingbird landed in front of Stewart, who lay on the asphalt, and the rage drained. Klia rubbed her beak on his face tenderly. Tears broke from his eyes and streamed down his cheek. His greatest friend still lived. Such relief.

The Bear Mother looked at the suddenly humorless Peik, and

said, "This ends right now."

Peik glared long and hard.

"I think not, Ursula," he said, crouching over Stewart, who lay on his chest on the blacktop. The pale man's hands reached down for Stewart's neck. All the while his cold stare monitored the old woman. Klia flew at his face.

Ursula nodded silently to Ysenia. The young woman brought her hands up from the bear's fur, humming and whistling. The tone infected the insectoid minds flying and crawling everywhere, making them concentrate their mass back into the swarm.

Klia flew out of the way as the dark cloud of bugs condensed into a thin stream and shot like a living spear into Peik's face. He was battered by thousands, then millions of insects. They flew into his mouth, up his nose, into any opening they could find. Their force drove him off of Stewart's body, who rolled to safety, but the bugs did not relent.

Beetles. Moths. Wasps. Termites. Innumerable insects united by the girl's voice. Peik pulled his jacket over his head and curled into a ball on the hot asphalt, trying desperately to shield himself. The bugs crawled and landed on him by the millions, piling up and creating a writhing dome over him, incapacitating him with their sheer volume.

Frank assayed the scene and grew impatient, not wishing to be next with the bugs. He couldn't figure out why Peik was warranting so much attention from everyone, but he was going to level the playing field. He focused his hateful energy into his hands and let fly what he assumed would be a death blow to Abraham Blackwing. Once he had snuffed out his own Awakener he would get everyone's focus back.

He was Frank, the spirit thief.

He plunged his hand into the black smoke surrounding Abe, who now had his back to Frank. His palm prickled. It felt odd. From within his core, Frank let loose a death blow.

Nothing came from his hand.

The trickster spirit of the Raven had shot a tendril of shimmering smoke up Frank's arm through a solitary pore on his palm, which wound through his body and into his mind. There it planted a seed. Of knowledge and understanding. Of doubt about

BEN JOHNSON

what he was, and what he had been used for.

"You're the real experiment," it said, "and the real failure."

The thought hit him in an instant, and would not leave. The cloud separated itself, and Abe stood in front of him. The ragged man made a whooshing sound, and a small puff of smoke hung in the air in front of his mouth, impervious to the breeze. Abraham blew, and the cloud shot into Frank's nose. Frank fought to move, to no avail.

In a state of forced paralysis, Frank watched as Ursula approached. She reached into her cloak and pulled out a vial, dropped a solitary drop of amber liquid onto the end of her index finger, and rubbed it onto Frank's forehead.

From within the liquid came visions. A story told long before. Ancient spirits passed to human hosts, commingling. A man from the east. Far away, a thousand years before. He learned how to pass his spirit like the ancients. The alchemist. Used a knife he'd made, or helped make. The Keepers and Awakeners distrusted the man. And the knife.

One that reached beyond his distrust was the Raven. The Raven liked the knife, so shiny. He said he'd help the man.

The Raven played a trick on the Council in an attempt to secure the knife for himself. When a position became open, it was the right of one of the inner sanctum to appoint a successor. It was the Raven's turn. There was always a pool of acceptable candidates, children who showed promise, or those particularly adept at certain things. Although it was acceptable for a Keeper to choose whoever they deemed appropriate. That was the way.

Many of the current Council had never even known of the Web and its permutations prior to their awakenings, and all were considered quite capable. The Raven shocked them all, however, when he appointed the pale man from the East as the new Water Spirit. More exactly, the spirit of water left sitting. Puddles, lakes, pooled water in crags and cracks.

Still water.

The Raven gets the shiny knife. The Council gets a foreigner to sit among them, to their dismay.

Hundreds of years later, the Water Spirit and the Raven Spirit make pottery high inside red cliff walls. The men look different, but unmistakable. The pale alchemist tells the black-haired Raven man of a formula his adopted people had used to make warriors of men. Warriors with an insatiable bloodlust.

The men speak in caves, spinning bowls of clay. They also make wagers.

Generations later, it is time again for the Raven to choose one to hold a spirit. Over the ages his trickery had dimmed, and the Council had, mainly begrudgingly, given him another opportunity. As a failsafe, he would make the choice three years prior to the transformation. That way, if he opts for a bad apple, the Council could work on correcting the person before the inaugural moment.

He opts for an adolescent many had their eye on, and is championed for his choice. He is someone they all agree is suited well for the job. Before the transformation, however, the Raven Spirit and Water Spirit make the wager that another will be awakened, instead of this candidate, and also on whether or not the original boy chosen will make his way back to his rightful place on his own, and eventually depose the imposter.

A replacement is found. The Water Spirit is not to tell the replacement before the moment of truth, but behind the Raven's back does so anyway. For three years the youthful mind of the replacement is corrupted with the impatience and greed created with the suggestion he would have magic powers. Magic. If he tells no one.

Just before the transformation, the pale Water Spirit wipes from the mind of the boy any memories of himself. He uses a cone he has made, a crude experiment modeled on the silver one from across the sea. Through his old language, it has been modified. He would only remember the Raven, never the Water. Frank recognizes his younger self in the vision.

There is a ripple in the plan. A girl is with him. The intrigued Raven is delighted with the concept of a duality. He bestows his Making upon the boy and girl. The Water Spirit is furious when he finds out about the improvisation. The Raven and Water spirits quarrel mightily. When the Raven leaves, he feels for the first time in his long life that he has been tricked. He has made for the pale man a puppet prince.

After the transformation of Frank, the Water Spirit puts

himself in a position to be hired by Frank and Nuala, along with a companion he has picked up; the giant Markuz. The timing is such that Frank believes the choice to be his own, and one circle is completed.

The alchemist that had travelled so far, his spirit spanning the ages, had his first disciples, and his best pet project thought he was in control. He is exhilarated.

The Bear Mother again put her finger to Frank's forehead, and he snapped back into the world, where everything came crashing down upon him.

"These are lies!" he shouted, and tried to shoot his filaments out at Abe, at the bug-covered figure of Peik, anywhere. Nothing happened. His glorious powers had vanished, and, for the first time in twenty years, Frank felt the hot energy of a blind panic. In a state of disbelief, he stared at his hands and flexed his fingers.

"Nuala, help me!" he pleaded.

Nuala sifted back through her memories since she and Frank had been awakened so many ages past. What should have been a time of discovery of marvels turned to a dark nightmare of Frank's imaginings. From the kidnappings, starting with this little kid, and all the girls, younger and younger. Then whomever. So long ago she became an iron shell, impervious to the evils. She would never be the same, but she would never be with Frank. And when she'd stolen the knowledge of his control words, she'd gained the pawn she had needed to ensure Frank would have no more experiments.

Poor Nickel. And Jeb.

"No," she simply said, almost pitying her childhood friend, now a broken psychopath. She turned her back to him and walked toward Peik, still beneath the pile of bugs.

Abraham, free of his mutually distasteful bond with Frank, morphed back into the smoke, which took the form of the huge black bird. The Raven wrapped its vast wings around Frank, completely enshrouding him in a deep and terrible embrace.

Frank screamed in agony, a sound muffled by the shadows, as his memories were pulled violently from his head.

Abraham had a fire in his eye as he turned to Stewart. "Now you must finish this, Stewart Zanderson."

A wave of darkness overcame Stewart, and he saw two

pathways merging along the great web, and only one continuing. He was the one. The One. It would all be his, and rightfully so.

The voice of Abraham croaked on, guiding him. "Only with his killing will you assume the mantle of his power. It stands here. Before you."

Stewart looked at Frank, tendrils of the rage propelling his muscles. Tension within him built as he stood, about to strike, the silver snare held high, then he stopped short. He glared at Peik, then Nuala.

Wheezing ragged breaths, his gaze circled around the group, into the concerned eyes of the Bear Mother, Cora, Buddy, the bird, and dog. Then back to Abe.

"Fuck that," said Stewart. "I'll pass." He dropped the blade to the ground.

"Then you're a fool," said the Raven Man, clicking his tongue, "big surprise."

Abraham chuckled before making the whooshing sound with his lips. Smoke curled around his body in heavy wisps, like fog. As he began to dissipate, he sent a long tendril of smoke shooting out to the silver snare, which lay on the ground near Stewart. It was now empty of anyone's spirit. The smoke wrapped around it, and, before anyone knew what was happening, snapped back to the rapidly transforming old man. His body morphed into a dense ball of smoke, and hung briefly in the air before trailing off into the night sky with a crackling laugh.

The Raven had his shiny prize, and was gone.

The bugs began to trail off of Peik and fly or crawl into the darkness.

Frank stood, a look of utter bewilderment on his face. He recognized nothing.

"Where's my brother?" he asked Peik. Peik stared coldly, then turned to the Bear Mother. Frank began to wander in a small circle, mumbling about Jeb.

The Bear Mother spoke to Peik.

"Your time has come to an end. You are to give up the Water Spirit here and now, and this woman and boy are to have their memories modified with your horrible weapons, which I will then destroy," she said, signaling to Nuala and Oliver. "Whatever deals you had with the Raven are now forfeit, as he may well be when I see him next."

She looked from Peik to Frank, then at the others. "Your police are coming, and if you do not agree to this I will do it by force and give you to them."

"I am not some child, you arrogant bitch," replied Peik. "You'll need help if you want to tear out what I have, and anyone who could help you is gone."

Stewart stood next to Markuz. Both men were bloody and exhausted. Stewart gurgled through a mouth of blood. "What about this guy?"

To Stewart's shock, Ursula said, "He's coming with me."

"What the hell? He's an animal," protested Stewart.

"As are we all," said Ursula, turning to Markuz. "You have been misused, my friend. I see beneath your shell. Come beneath with me, and we will reshape you. I need you to be this child's protector." She motioned to Ysenia.

Markuz looked to Oliver. The boy said nothing, and did not move.

Peik had an expression that continued to darken, but still a smirk spread across his pale face. "There's something else you're forgetting as well," he said, "aside from the fact that Markuz will most surely be coming with me."

Oliver scrambled over to Peik's side. Nuala, sensing no resistance, followed suit. Both were monitored, but allowed to join him. They posed no threat to the Bear Mother, really. Markuz did not follow.

"Markuz, we must be going," said Peik.

Markuz, the giant man of few words, said, "I believe our time is at an end, Mr. Stillwater."

"You're not supposed to call me that."

"I know," said Markuz, "but things have changed."

The fucking Raven. What did he tell Markuz? They hadn't flown under his or the Bear Mother's radar nearly as much as they thought. For the millionth time, Peik cursed himself for his deals with the trickster. All the Raven did was play forces against each other. That's what they do.

"What about Max and Helen?" said Buddy, pointing to the

empty warehouse missing a wall.

"That's what you're forgetting," said Peik, "when and if you carry out your new plan, the boy's new adoptive parents will never be seen or heard from again. Or any of the other people that were here."

"So it shall be," Ursula growled. The Bear roared, trembling the ground. Birds took wing by the hundreds. Undaunted, Ursula readied to follow through.

"Please," Buddy said. "Please don't. They're my family."

"Heartbreaking, no?" Peik said. "Perhaps we can negotiate? Their freedom for ours?"

"Where are they?" Ursula stayed her hand. "How do we know you'll let them go?"

"They are being transported. I will allow the birds to locate the truck and let his friends out when the birds catch up," he answered. "Stewart can monitor the events in the birdsight. When the birds reach the van, you will be shown Max and Helen. We will then be permitted to leave, and Max and Helen will be released fifteen minutes later."

"No," said Cora, "release everyone."

Ursula agreed, as did Peik, begrudgingly.

"What happens to him?" asked Cora, pointing to Frank. She was still grappling with Abe's departure. What was really happening? There was something beneath the surface of Abe's relations with the ancient alchemist that she couldn't put her finger on. And she was unwilling to admit that Abe had very simply betrayed everyone for the knife, even as attractive and powerful as it was.

Stewart spoke. "Frank sent Craig to kill Jeb, then killed Craig himself. To the police it will look like a revenge killing. When the cops come, it will be pretty cut-and-dry what to do with him. He'll go to prison. Are you okay?" he asked Cora.

"No, Stewart, I'm not. And that's not what happened, but that is what the cops will be led to believe. Isn't that right, Nuala?" Cora turned to the blonde woman.

"Why are you asking me, if you're so clever?" asked Nuala.

"Alright. I'll tell you what I think. Feel free to butt in anytime," said Cora. "Jeb left, and took his brains with him, and what he was making using them. He was on the verge of breaking through to a whole new level concerning all his tools.

"You'd already lost Frank. The lust for more power and the corruption of children had pushed him over the edge, and you trembled to think of what would happen if he ever did get hold of Jeb's new technology. Somehow, you learned the control words he had discovered, and when you realized that you could control Nickel's body, you sent him to kill Jeb. Unfortunately for Nickel, he didn't know that that same cabin had the snare, which held his spirit inside it.

"Close?" she asked.

Nuala looked steely daggers at Cora.

• • •

The truck rumbled west on C Street, away from the warehouses. The security guard thought this was getting a little excessive, driving the junkies around in the back, but what was he going to do? As he came over the cusp of the hill, a giant white wolf stood snarling in the middle of the street. Having been up all night, he overreacted, and cut the turn too sharp, driving up a dirt embankment and bottoming out. One tire bounced over the berm, and the truck came down hard on the axle, snapping it, and immobilizing the vehicle.

The guard cursed. His boss was going to be pissed. He got out and ran down the street, leaving the junkies in the locked truck. The wolf didn't pursue him.

• • •

Klia pecked Stewart's forehead and awakened the birdsight. She flew after the truck, and Stewart, in his mind, flew with her. After a mile she caught up to it. The truck was bottomed out, and the guard who drove it was at the rear of the truck, opening the door. Helen and Max were there with several others, who began to crawl out.

When Stewart reported the events, Peik smiled at him, not the reaction Stewart expected. Stewart had suspicions, and tried to speak, but couldn't. Something had locked his tongue.

The vision is a lie.

The pale man motioned to Oliver and Nuala, and the three quickly walked to the gate, where they looked back at the group.

Peik stared icily at Stewart as he wrapped the woman and the youth in his arms. Their forms lost definition, and they vanished into the night.

"Something's wrong," said Stewart, able to speak only after they had disappeared.

33

While they had been locked in the warehouse with the rest of the shuffling horde, Max and Helen hadn't understood fully where they were. Or who they were, for that matter. Helen's talents had gone to work immediately, however, in much the same way they had done with Buddy. Her scents provoked memories, parts of people's spirits that should have been locked inside the strange black cones.

One by one, pieces of spirit floated from the snares. The black cones were bunched in a tote bag behind the passenger seat of the truck, drifting back into the minds of the captives.

To Juan Escamillo, a baker, the smell of bread brought him to his mother's oven as a boy. From there, more memories came. The effect was like pulling a thread that is connected to a chain. By the time the truck left the warehouses, he had almost a complete picture of who he was.

A big bump, then a loud snap rocked the truck.

When it stopped, he was Juan, and the last thing he remembered was the hot blonde cougar lady talking to him behind the bakery. Now he was in the darkened rear of a truck with a bunch of people he didn't recognize.

It happened to the others as well. Subtle smells gave way to memories, which led to fog being lifted. Some slowly, some quickly. They rubbed their eyes and looked around in a state of bewilderment.

Along with the baker, Helen and Max were the first to snap out of it. Their last memories were amidst battles, so they came out ready to fight. Max kicked at the van's locked door. He jammed his fingers into the rusty corner of the roof and pulled down hard, ripping a hole into it. After a few seconds it was big enough for his thin body. He shimmied out and dropped down. At the rear, Klia sat frustrated by the lock. She had popped it, naturally, but someone had strung a rope through the latch.

One hundred yards up the street Tia Louisa, Peik's cleaner, had put on her white cleaning suit, the kind reserved for toxic spills, and filled her spray tank with the acid that she had perfected herself, the stuff that ate through flesh like a knife through butter. She looped the tank onto her back and walked toward the stalled truck. She could see the thin black man that Peik had warned her about working on the rope through the lock, and doubled her pace, pumping the handle on the tank. As she crossed the street, the white wolf attacked. She was surprised as the creature leaped up and knocked her back between the parked cars with its paws. Before she could stop it, the animal had grabbed her spraying hand and shook hard. The spray nozzle ripped a small opening between the headpiece and body of the hazard suit and got stuck in the torn fabric. Trying to free it, her hand accidentally gripped the trigger, and the acid shot into her neck where it began to eat through her skin and muscle.

Tia Louisa panicked, ripping the headpiece off. She felt her neck muscles separate, and her final realization was that she had pulled her own head off.

Its work done, the white wolf looked at Max, then disappeared.

Max, nodding thanks, undid the knot and threw the doors open. The people rubbed their eyes and spilled out beneath the streetlight. Helen made sure everyone was okay, then stepped out herself and pulled Max into an embrace. Sirens sounded as a man crawled out of the truck, then helped an older lady down. Klia flew to Helen and chirped happily when she saw she was alright.

• • •

The police cars sped by the people in the street. Clementine made a mental note of it as she turned the corner and floored it toward the warehouses owned by Mr. Stillwater. When they arrived, they found the gate wide open.

Frank Rawls, Jeb's brother, stood alone in the center of the parking lot. Blood covered him in streaks. He held a Japanese tantō in his hand, crimson dripping from the blade onto the blacktop. He did not look at them, or really anything else, appearing in some sort of deep trance.

"Frank Rawls!" shouted Clementine. "Put the sword down!"

Frank looked at her with a bewildered expression. The fringes of memories taunted him from within. His name had given him something. He was someone. Someone the police couldn't touch. He was invincible. Someone made him that way. This was a test. Yes.

"Drop the fucking weapon! Now!" shouted Gray, his pistol leveled at Frank's torso from across the lot. "I'm not going to ask you again."

"No, you're not," said Frank as he bent over with the blade held horizontally in front of him, close to the blacktop. Gray walked toward him, gun ready.

Frank flicked his wrist, a subtle yet powerful movement, and the blade shot straight and true as an arrow. It was faster than even one with Gray's speed could avoid. The sword sliced through his ribs and sunk deep into his chest.

Gray's eyes bugged out in disbelief. They had just wrapped up his biggest case. He was going to be a hero. To many different people. A fallen hero. And he was in love. Yes. His body collapsed to the asphalt in a heap, and a pool of blood grew quickly beneath him.

Amy screamed, running. She pulled out her pistol and, above the rising protests of Clementine, emptied the full clip into Frank. Chunks of flesh flew as the bullets tore him up.

Frank's eyes were filled with confusion as the life left his body. He was invincible, wasn't he?

Before he could fall, Amy kicked him full blast in the face. He pivoted backwards, and lay on the asphalt, dead.

Without pause, Amy turned back and ran to Gray, cradling his head in her lap.

"Call an ambulance!" she pleaded to Clementine, who was already on the radio.

"Officer down! Repeat. Officer down!" Clementine screamed into the mic, knowing that Gray wouldn't be coming back from being run through with a sword, but needing to do it just as much as Amy needed to hear it.

Amy cried as she held him. His eyes, barely alive, had tears streaming as well.

"Shh," he said, "we did it, baby. I love you. Just hold me."

His body spasmed. She held him tighter. "I love you, too," she said. She'd never said it to a man before. She thought she never would again.

"No," he groaned, losing steam, "there's so much I didn't tell you." Then he said, "You were my only love, Amy. Kiss me goodbye."

She did, and after the last kiss, felt the life go from his body into the ethers. Her technical mind could not help but notice the blood pool. It was smaller, by quite a bit. The Japanese sword had a glow to it she hadn't noticed before.

From up the hill, they heard the volley of gunshots. Buddy turned to take a look and report back, followed by Luna. When he got to a proper vantage point, he saw Frank's body on the ground, looking dead. A small woman cried and held a male police officer in her lap. The guy did not look good.

In the center of the asphalt stood Detective Clementine Figgins.

Luna whined and trotted behind her boy while he walked to the fence. If he broke eye contact, he might never see her again, Buddy thought.

The birds were gone, the bugs also. The Bear Mother and her new companions had sunk back beneath the surface. All that remained were Stewart, Cora, two dead men, two living women, himself, the bird, and his Luna.

Stewart and Cora could feel the importance of what was happening, and gave no protest as Buddy walked through the gate.

Amy saw them first as they entered. The disheveled boy and the little dog. She couldn't make words through her tears, so she cleared her throat and looked to Clementine, then nodded her head toward the boy.

Clementine slowly turned around, still in shock herself from losing Gray. She wiped her tears, leaving her vision blurry, and couldn't make out the features of the dog and boy. She rubbed her eyes once more, and her heart began to melt.

"Mom?" said Buddy, walking faster toward her.

She could scarcely believe it. "Rupert?" she answered, then, "Oh, Rupert! Oh! My god!" A tingling sensation put her hairs on end as she ran toward the child she had not seen in ten long years. Her child, who she thought a thousand times she would never see again. She wrapped him in her arms tightly, never wanting to put him down. The weight of the years spilled from her as she was racked with sobs.

"Oh, my precious baby boy! I've looked so long for you!" she said through tears.

Buddy sank into the embrace. A true and pure love wrapped itself around the mother and child, frozen in time. Forgotten was all the chaos and terror that had precluded this one shining moment. Only the blessed reunion existed.

Luna barked and stood on her hind legs, propping her forepaws on their thighs. Buddy's hand slid down and scratched her head. She licked his hand.

"Who's this little one?" asked Clementine.

"Luna. Basically the reason I'm still alive. My dog, I guess," he said. It was easier than he had anticipated, speaking to his long lost mother.

Clementine looked with love and pride from her son to Luna. She crouched down and cradled the dog's face in her hands, looking Luna in the eyes, then kissed her forehead.

"Thank you, little Luna," she said.

The dog's tongue lashed out and kissed her lips only slightly. She chuckled. Though a friend had fallen, Clementine was full of relief and joy. She stood up and held her Rupert close, hearing the sirens in the distance.

Amy was not full of those feelings. The sirens from the cops and ambulance grew louder as they rounded the corner down to the cul-de-sac that the warehouses occupied. She held the lifeless body of Gray in her lap and cried as the din surrounded her. Through her tears, she witnessed the reunion, but in her crushed heart she could find little consolation to offset the pain. Killing her first person had not quenched her desire for revenge. The petite woman swore to her ancestors that she would find the rest of this psycho's group and bring them to justice, or to their graves, no matter who they were.

The ambulance charged the open gate and came screeching to a halt. The EMT's burst from the rear, ready for anything. They didn't have to work on Gray very long before he was indeed pronounced dead. They loaded him into the rear of the ambulance. Amy insisted on riding with him, though she knew he wouldn't be coming back. It had all happened so suddenly, and she wasn't quite willing to let go. At the hospital, maybe, but not now. There's so much he had wanted to show her, he had said, and now he never would.

An EMT pulled the tantō from his body and gave it to Amy, who quickly bagged it and put it in her car before someone else ended up with it. She would be processing this. He asked if the body had been moved, as there was so little blood for a man whose chest was pierced.

"What? Of course not," she had said, so abruptly he had broken off any inquiry.

"You're the tech," he said, before loading up Gray's body into the ambulance with his partner.

Amy asked the same question in her mind: Why was there so little blood? She thought there was much more at first. Maybe her own shock distorted her memory.

A separate morgue truck was called for Frank.

When the ambulance had departed, the officers and techs began to process the scene. Frank's corpse was tagged and bagged and driven off to the morgue, blood collected from various pools, and fingerprints and trace evidence collected.

Clementine's partner, Jim, was on the scene, and suggested that Rupert be checked out at the hospital, maybe held for observation.

Clementine looked at Jim like he had been lobotomized.

"If you think I'm letting my son, who was kidnapped ten years ago and imprisoned in these buildings since then, out of my sight for one second, you are far, far, stupider than even I have ever thought."

Actually, Jim's stock, according to Clementine, was rising from plain dumb to corrupt or evil. Not wanting to get caught in some red tape, she herded Buddy and Luna into her unmarked sedan and pulled out of the parking lot while Jim got on the radio, eyeing her the entire time.

Up the hill, they shot by the box truck, now empty, with no one around it.

If things hadn't gone the way they had from his escape until now, Buddy would have almost been surprised when he got out of the car at the same blue cottage where they'd stopped on the day of his escape.

Grifter's tail wagged so hard when he came running up that he lost his balance and half tumbled into an aloe vera plant before righting himself and charging for the fence.

When Clementine opened the wooden gate, Luna leaped into the yard and jumped up on her hind legs. Grifter did as well, and they began to wrestle and run around all the plants of Clementine's urban oasis. She marvelled at the dogs, so alike they looked related. They seemed like it in personality as well, she thought, as the two canine friends eventually snuggled together in a ball. Then they, with her son, followed her in the house.

She locked all the doors, and got Rupert and the dogs some water, then moved the group into the living room. Once they had gotten comfortable on the couch, Clementine let Buddy relax, and soon everyone was silent. The new family fell asleep in a pile, dreaming intertwined dreams of their lives apart and the glorious new beginnings together.

• • •

Clementine awoke to Luna whining at the door. It was far from a warning sound. She probably needs to go to the bathroom, Clem thought as she opened the latch on the dog door. Luna ran out and around to the front of the house. Grifter followed her, giving a slight growl as he crossed the porch. Clementine felt a hand on hers, and looked down to see Buddy rubbing his eyes. Holding hands, they opened the front door.

When she looked up, she was shocked to see Stewart

Zanderson.

"Freeze! Police!" she said, pushing Rupert behind her. She hoped her tone of voice worked, as she had no weapon in her hand. Now she could see other people behind the gangly man. She did have a giant maglite near the door, one of several objects of defense strategically placed around her house. She turned it on and swept the beam over the faces staring back at her.

"Mom?" Rupert was pulling on her shirt urgently. "Um, these are my friends. Even that guy," he said, pointing at Stewart.

Clementine looked down to her beloved son, her miracle twice over, who gazed out into the yard upon the lit faces of Stewart, Cora, Max, and Helen. The large woman had tears pouring down her face while smiling back at the boy.

"Hello, Rupert," said Helen, "and hello, Clementine."

"Hello. Wow. Let's get you all into the house," she said, ushering them inside. A little mockingbird stood on the gate, looking back at her.

"I guess you're part of the tribe, too, eh? Well, get in here," said Clementine to the bird.

Klia tweeted and glided past her into the warm house. Clementine shut the door, then introduced herself to the unlikely group of people and animals who had saved her son and somehow, against all odds, returned him to her life.

ABOUT THE AUTHOR

Ben Johnson has been a drummer, a delivery driver, a fisherman in Alaska, a night porter for the haunted El Tovar Hotel in the Grand Canyon, a singer, a bartender, a rapper, a busboy, a cook, a percussionist, an actor, a director, a river rafter, an outdoor enthusiast, a teacher, a barback, a student at the infamous St. Anthony's Seminary in Santa Barbara, a beatsmith, and an artist. But never an author.

Until now.

He lives in San Diego, California with his wife Monique and dog Rooners.

ALSO FROM GRAND MAL PRESS

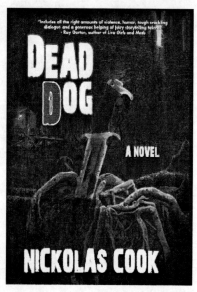

"Includes all the right amounts of violence, humor, tough crackling dialogue and a generous helping of juicy storytelling talent!"
—Ray Garton, author of Live Girls and Meds

DEAD DOG
BY NICKOLAS COOK

It's the late 70s and Max and Little Billy are back from Vietnam trying to mind their own business when they stumble onto the murder of a local boy. With organized crime and local thugs on their trail, it's up to these two heroes to solve the murder.

ISBN: 978-1937727246

WALKING SHADOW
by Clifford Royal Johns

Benny tries to ignore the payment-overdue messages he keeps getting from "Forget What?," a memory removal company. Benny's a slacker, after all, and couldn't pay them even if he wanted to. Then people start trying to kill him, and his life suddenly depends on finding out what memories he has forgotten. Benny relies on his wits, latent skills, and new friends as he investigates his own past; delving deeper and deeper into the underworld of criminals, bad cops, and shady news organizations, all with their own reasons for wanting him to remain ignorant or die.

ISBN: 9781937727253

HAFTMANN'S RULES
BY ROBERT WHITE

The first full-length novel to feature White's recurring private investigator, Thomas Haftmann! Out of jail and back on the streets, Haftmann is hired to find a missing young girl in Boston. But what he uncovers goes beyond just murder, into a world of secret societies, bloodshed, and betrayal beyond anything he has experienced before. HAFTMANN'S RULES is an exhilarating read into one man's maddening journey for truth, justice, and self destruction.

ISBN: 9780982945971

DEAD WRANGLER
by Justin Coke

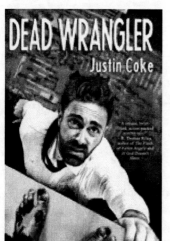

The Airborne killed a lot of people. The dead killed most of the rest. Something lies behind the mass of hungry dead, something that makes them more dangerous than the survivors can imagine. Ordinary people must become extraordinary to survive. They must become heroes to unravel the mystery of the Airborne.

ASIN: B0168QB06M

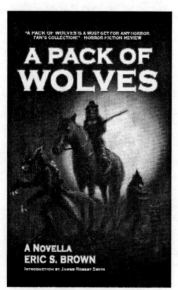

For more Grand Mal Press titles
please visit us online at
www.grandmalpress.com